The Works of Robert E. Howard

The Riot at Bucksnort and
Other Western Tales

The Riot at Bucksnort and Other Western Tales

Robert E. Howard

Edited and
with an introduction by
David Gentzel

University of Nebraska Press
Lincoln

© 2005 by REH Properties, Inc.
Introduction © 2005 by the Board of Regents
of the University of Nebraska.
All rights reserved. Manufactured in the United
States of America.
Set in Fred Smeijers' Quadraat by Kim Essman.
Designed by Richard Eckersley.
Printed and bound by Edwards Brothers, Inc.
⊚
Library of Congress Cataloging-in-Publication Data
Howard, Robert Ervin, 1906–1936.
The riot at Bucksnort and other Texas tales /
Robert E. Howard ; edited and with an
introduction by David Gentzel.
p. cm. – (The works of Robert E. Howard)
ISBN 0-8032-2425-7 (cloth : alk. paper) –
ISBN 0-8032-7354-1 (pbk. : alk. paper)
1. Texas – Social life and customs – Fiction.
2. Western stories.   I. Gentzel, David.   II. Title.
PS3515.O842A6 2005D
813'.52–dc22   2004028624

CONTENTS

DAVID GENTZEL

Introduction

Mayhem, Mirth, and Myth: Robert E. Howard's Humorous Westerns

There is no denying that Robert E. Howard's heroic fantasy tales are his most popular, but some who have been inspired to dig deeper (or have been lucky enough to encounter the random fugitive paperback) have discovered the wealth and depth of the author's range and versatility. Conan, Kull, and their breed have been adapted into comics, served as the basis for several movies, and inspired seemingly countless pastiches and continuations. Howard's historical adventures, westerns, and boxing tales all have strong followings, and his horror stories have also received modest attention and have been included in numerous anthologies. But many of those familiar with Howard's writings and characters would probably be surprised to learn that humor was a dominant theme in his published works. In fact, there are fewer completed stories featuring Conan of Cimmeria (twenty-one stories), easily Howard's best-known character, than there are of either of his most successful humor characters: Sailor Steve Costigan (twenty-five stories) and Breckinridge Elkins (twenty-two stories).

I have a special affection for Howard's humorous westerns. These larger-than-life tales have an amazing vitality and power. The combination of intense action and broad slapstick carries the stories like a runaway freight train toward the inevitable conflagration. Howard created three unique characters for these tales: Breckinridge Elkins of Bear Creek, Nevada; Buckner J. Grimes of Knife River, Texas; and Pike Bearfield of Wolf Mountain, Texas. "Breck" was the original creation – Pike and Buckner were primarily created to sell to different markets, although they certainly have discriminating features (both in character and in story structure). There can be little doubt that this is due, at least partially, to practical rather than artistic considerations. As a writer working in the Great Depression, Howard saw many magazines (and hence markets for his writing) come and go. It was very important for him to sell to a variety of publishers so that his livelihood would not be jeopardized by the financial problems of a single market. Conan, for example, was published solely by the magazine *Weird Tales*. There was no guarantee that a Conan tale would be accepted by that magazine, and once a story was accepted and published, payment was notoriously tardy. With Sailor Steve Costigan and, later, Breckinridge Elkins, both sold to Fiction House publications, Howard managed to develop an important secondary market.

Still, there is more to these works than just tackling a market. From his earliest days of writing, Howard showed an active and sharp sense of humor. The letters to friends from his teen years are full of wit, including bawdy poetry, parodies of popular songs and poetry, and political commentary. It was natural, therefore, for Howard to combine this sense of humor with his love of tall tales and his knowledge of the Southwest. And this combination developed into Breckinridge Elkins, the central character in most of the stories included in this volume.

But before diving more deeply into Howard's humorous westerns, let's step back a few years. One cannot understand the genesis of the westerns that make up this volume without some knowledge of the humorous boxing stories that were their direct precursors. From July 1929 until March 1932, eighteen Sailor Steve Costigan stories were published in *Fight Stories* and its sister publication *Action Stories*. These stories built on Howard's well-documented following of the sweet science and showed the rapid development of a very broad, slapstick style. Unfortunately both *Fight Stories* and *Action Stories* suspended publication in 1932. As the Costigan stories formed a significant percentage of Howard's sales during the preceding two years, this was a serious blow to his finances. Howard did manage to sell a few yarns to other boxing periodicals but with nowhere near the reliability and regularity he had previously enjoyed. So it was doubtless excellent news when Howard learned that *Action Stories* was resuming publication in late 1933. As he wrote to August Derleth around December 1933:

Recently – or rather a few months ago – an old stand-by of mine, *Action Stories*, returned to the wars on a bi-monthly basis, but I've been so busy trying to learn to hammer out detectives that I haven't given it the consideration I intend to. So far, since coming back into circulations, I've landed only one yarn with them, but I hope to work out a series, as I used to in the past with Steve Costigan, the fighting sailor. (Whom, if you read the latest Magic Carpet, you encountered under the cognomen of Dennis Dorgan.) My new character is one Breckinridge Elkins, a giant of the Humbolt mountains whose exploits are of the Pecos Bill style.

Howard's concentration on detective stories turned out to be fairly short-lived, and the suspension of his best detective markets coincided nicely with the resurrection of *Action Stories*. As a result, the Breckinridge Elkins series soon became Howard's most reliably saleable character.

From his debut in "Mountain Man" in the March–April 1934 issue until Howard's death in June 1936, a Breckinridge Elkins story appeared in every issue of *Action Stories*. In fact, Breckenridge continued to appear for several months after Howard's death as the stories already sold were published.

Breckinridge is larger than life, a veritable man in a world of boys. Just about the only folks he meets who come close to his sheer physical stature are other members of his own family. He is, as Howard noted in the letter to Derleth, a direct literary descendent of Pecos Bill, the mythical prototypical cowboy. Breckinridge first strode onto the scene in "Mountain Man," and from the very first page, he showed the seeming invulnerability that would become his trademark:

He come up, and said: "Breckinridge, ain't that a bee settin' on yore ear?"

I reached up, and sure enough, it was. Come to think about it, I had felt kind of like something was stinging me somewhere.

In the first story alone, Breckenridge encounters bee stings, cactus needles, clubs, fists, knees, bullets, and buckshot. These things are shaken off like you or I might deal with a splinter or a pebble in our shoe. And yet Breck's legend is not yet fully formed. His steed is a most unflattering, if physically impressive, mule named Alexander – hardly a suitable mount for one such as Breck. This deficiency is quickly addressed in the very next Elkins story, "Guns of the Mountains." Here we catch our first glimpses of a character who was to appear in every subsequent story in the series: Breck's horse, Cap'n Kidd. Though to call Cap'n Kidd merely "Breck's horse" is to underestimate greatly his contribution to the series. In some stories, Cap'n Kidd has a presence almost as dominating as Breck himself. And only Breck has the strength to keep Cap'n Kidd's temper in some semblance of check. But what happened to Alexander? Therein lies a tale, but we have to jump ahead a bit.

The success of the Breckinridge Elkins series eventually led to Howard's first book publication, *A Gent from Bear Creek*, published in England in 1937. Howard had been trying to break into the British markets since at least 1933, as a potentially lucrative source for second sales. He tried a fantasy short story collection first but was told that there was a prejudice against such in Britain at the time and that he should try a novel. He tried again in 1934 with the Conan novel *The Hour of the Dragon*, written specifically for this purpose, and was again rebuffed. Finally, he reworked several of the previously published Elkins stories and wrote several new stories to create the episodic novel *A Gent from Bear Creek*.

I call *Gent* an "episodic novel" because it shows its short story origin rather clearly. Most of the original stories have received only minor editing, primarily the inclusion of references to a running romantic thread that serves to tie the stories together. New stories were written to begin and end the volume (and to introduce and tie up the romantic thread). In addition, one more new story was written that covers the previously unexplained transition in the Elkins stories: the advent of Cap'n Kidd in the story "Meet Cap'n Kidd." Chris Gruber notes in his introduction to the Bison Books edition of *Boxing Stories* that Howard did not introduce "the final missing piece to the Costigan formula," his bulldog Mike, until the second story. In an interesting parallel, Howard introduced the key series component of Cap'n Kidd in the second published Breckinridge Elkins story. And unlike the other new *Gent* stories, "Meet Cap'n Kidd" actually works quite well as a stand-alone story outside of the novel.

Although immensely successful, the Elkins stories were not a guaranteed sale for Howard. One example is the story "The Peaceful Pilgrim," which was rejected by John Byrne, editor of *Action Stories*, in a letter to a representative of Howard's agent dated March 1, 1935. The letter begins:

> I didn't think that Breckinridge Elkins was up to snuff in "The Peaceful Pilgrim." It seemed to me that the plot was rather lightweight, and I didn't like the arsenic business – I thought it too slap-stick.
>
> I think, however, that Howard can take the same set-up and build a better yarn around it, saving a great deal of the present action. I am jotting down a few ideas which I have in this connection. Howard may get some suggestions from them.

He proceeds to describe an entire story plot, based only vaguely on "The Peaceful Pilgrim." Howard did indeed write this new story – as "Cupid from Bear Creek," which appeared in the April 1935 *Action Stories*, but only about the first 15 percent of it was actually reworked from the originally rejected story. The original version of "The Peaceful Pilgrim" would not see publication until 1968. Is "Cupid" really a better story? Obviously this is a matter of taste, but I find "The Peaceful Pilgrim" all the better for having some elements that are different from most of the Elkins tales; hence its inclusion in this volume.

"War on Bear Creek" begins with what is possibly my favorite opening among these stories:

> Pap dug the nineteenth buckshot out of my shoulder and said, "Pigs is more disturbin' to the peace of a community than scandal, divorce, and corn-licker put together. And," says pap, pausing to strop his bowie on my scalp where the hair was all burnt off, "when the pig is a razorback hawg, and is mixed up with a lady school-teacher, a English tenderfoot, and a passle of bloodthirsty relatives, the result is appallin' for a peaceable man to behold. Hold still till John gits yore ear sewed back on."

The image of Breck's pap using his bare scalp to sharpen his bowie knife is sheer magic and a perfect embodiment of the casual acceptance of the extraordinary that forms the heart of these tales. This story has several other aspects that help make it something of a prototype for much of what follows. It has its mayhem enhanced by the presence of several of Breck's kin, in particular his uncle Jeppard Grimes (a name Howard was to make further use of, as we will see later). It has Breck falling for a pretty "Eastern gal" who has no idea what to make of his advances. And it has a complete outsider in the form of an Englishman who serves to draw an even greater contrast between the denizens of Bear Creek and the mere mortals who inhabit the normal world.

Although the Breckinridge Elkins stories make up the bulk of Howard's output in this genre, he was alert for other opportunities to make sales in the same vein. The Breckinridge Elkins series was so successful that Howard ultimately developed two more series to allow him to branch into other publications. When John Byrne moved from *Action Stories* to *Argosy*, Howard approached him with the idea of a series for that magazine. This represented a major coup, since *Argosy* was both a more prestigious and better paying publication than either the Fiction House's *Action Stories* and *Fight Stories* and than his other most steady market of *Weird Tales*. It was also a weekly and hence had the potential for even greater sales. This was the origin of Pike Bearfield, who appeared in three issues of *Argosy* published in October 1936.

While superficially similar to the Elkins stories, there is a very specific style to the Bearfield stories that sets them apart. For example, Howard decided to use a consistent story device: every story will be told, to one degree or another, through correspondence written from one character to another. The exact approach did vary from story to story, but the basic device is always present. In "A Gent from the Pecos," we have a short letter that serves to set up the remainder of the story. By contrast, the entire body of "Gents on the Lynch" consists of a single letter. "The Riot at Bucksnort" is told entirely through a dizzying sequence of newspaper articles, letters, and telegrams. The unfinished "The Diablos Trail" also keeps with this structure.

The final character we will meet in this collection is Buckner J. Grimes of Knife River, Texas. Grimes first saw the light of day in "A Man-Eating Jeopard" in the June 1936 issue of *Cowboy Stories* and appeared again in July of the following year in "Knife-River Prodigal." The Grimes stories do not have an obvious story device like the one used in the Pike Bearfield stories to set them apart; nonetheless, they do have a different feel from the Elkins stories. Buckner is a bit less thick-headed than Breck. He's certainly as naive, but he actually manages to outthink his enemies on occasion rather than just outmuscle or outgun them.

Although Howard had a steady market in *Action Stories*, he still did get the occasional rejection. Never one to waste a story, Howard did a very slight rework of the tale "A Elkins Never Surrenders," mainly to change place and character names, and it saw print as "The Curly Wolf of Sawtooth" in the September 1936 issue of *Star Western*. The star of this odd one-shot was Bearfield Elston. The original Breckinridge Elkins version would not see print for more than forty years.

It is interesting to speculate what the future of Howard's humorous westerns would have been had he not taken his own life in June 1936. At the time, he had three active characters, at least two of which were running as regular series. This at a time when he had already begun transitioning away from fantasy and beginning to work more on serious westerns as well. As Howard wrote to H. P. Lovecraft in May 1936, "If I can get a series running in *Argosy*, keep the Elkins series running in *Action Stories*, now a monthly, and the Buckner J. Grimes yarns in *Cowboy Stories*, I'll feel justified in devoting practically all my time to the writing of western stories." While it is clear that Howard's most lasting literary legacy has been in the fantasy genre, and in particular in the area of heroic fantasy, he had the potential to have as significant an impact in the field of the western. And count me among those who feel that a Howard leaving fantasy to devote himself to the western would have been as much a gift as a loss.

But this is not the time to dwell on what might have been. Grab yourself a drink, prop up your feet, and prepare yourself for a headlong dive into some of the finest tall tales ever to see print. Just make sure that you won't wake anyone with your belly laughs. And I'll let Pike Bearfield sign off for me in his own inimitable way:

> I am going to kick the seat of yore britches up around yore neck and sweep the streets with you till you don't know whether yo're setting or standing. Hoping this finds you in good health and spirits, I am,
> Yore affectionate brother,
> P. BEARFIELD ESQUIRE.

The Riot at Bucksnort and
Other Western Tales

Mountain Man

I was robbing a bee tree, when I heard my old man calling, "Breckinridge! Oh, Breckinridge! Where air you? I see you now. You don't need to climb that tree. I ain't goin' to larrup you."

He come up, and said, "Breckinridge, ain't that a bee settin' on yore ear?"

I reached up, and sure enough, it was. Come to think about it, I had felt kind of like something was stinging me somewhere.

"I swan, Breckinridge," said Pap, "I never seen a hide like your'n. Listen to me: old Buffalo Rogers is back from Tomahawk, and the postmaster there said they was a letter for me, from Mississippi. He wouldn't give it to nobody but me or some of my folks. I dunno who'd be writin' me from Mississippi; last time I was there was when I was fightin' the Yankees. But anyway, that letter is got to be got. Me and yore maw has decided you're to go git it. Yuh hear me, Breckinridge?"

"Clean to Tomahawk?" I said. "Gee whiz, Pap!"

"Well," he said, combing his beard with his fingers, "yo're growed in size, if not in years. It's time you seen somethin' of the world. You ain't never been more'n thirty miles away from the cabin you was born in. Yore brother John ain't able to go on account of that b'ar he tangled with, and Bill is busy skinnin' the b'ar. You been to whar the trail passes, goin' to Tomahawk. All you got to do is foller it and turn to the right where it forks. The left goes on to Perdition."

Well, I was all eager to see the world and the next morning I was off, dressed in new buckskins and riding my mule, Alexander. Pap rode with me a few miles and give me advice.

"Be keerful how you spend that dollar I give you," he said. "Don't gamble. Drink in reason; half a gallon of corn juice is enough for any man. Don't be techy – but don't forgit that yore pap was once the rough-and-tumble champeen of Gonzales County, Texas. And whilst yo're feelin' for the other feller's eye, don't be keerless and let him chaw yore ear off. And don't resist no officer."

"What's them, Pap?" I inquired.

"Down in the settlements," he explained, "they has men which their job is to keep the peace. I don't take no stock in law myself, but them city folks is different from us. You do what they says, and if they says give up yore gun, why, you up and do it!"

I was shocked, and meditated a while, and then says: "How can I tell which is them?"

"They'll have a silver star on their shirt," he says, so I said I'd do like he told me. He reined around and went back up the mountains, and I rode on down the path.

Well, I camped that night where the path come out on to the main trail, and the next morning I rode on down the trail, feeling like I was a long way from home. I hadn't went far till I passed a stream, and decided I'd take a bath. So I tied Alexander to a tree and hung my buckskins near by, but I took my gun belt with my old cap-and-ball .44 and hung it on a limb reaching out over the water. There was thick bushes all around the hole.

Well, I div deep, and as I come up, I had a feeling like somebody had hit me over the head with a club. I looked up, and there was a feller holding on to a limb with one hand and leaning out over the water with a club in the other hand.

He yelled and swung at me again, but I div, and he missed, and I come up right under the limb where my gun hung. I reached up and grabbed it and let bam at him just as he dived into the bushes, and he let out a squall and grabbed the seat of his pants. Next minute I heard a horse running, and glimpsed him tearing away through the brush on a pinto mustang, setting his horse like it was a red-hot stove, and dern him, he had my clothes in one hand! I was so upsot by this that I missed him clean, and jumping out, I charged through the bushes and saplings, but he was already out of sight. I knowed it was one of them derned renegades which hid up in the hills and snuck down to steal, and I wasn't afraid none. But what a fix I was in! He'd even stole my moccasins.

I couldn't go home, in that shape, without the letter, and admit I missed a robber twice. Pap would larrup the tar out of me. And if I went on, what if

I met some women in the valley settlements? I don't reckon they was ever a youngster half as bashful as what I was in them days. Cold sweat bust out all over me. At last, in desperation, I buckled my belt on and started down the trail toward Tomahawk. I was desperate enough to commit murder to get me some pants.

I was glad the Indian didn't steal Alexander, but the going was so rough I had to walk and lead him, because I kept to the brush alongside the trail. He had a tough time getting through the bushes, and the thorns scratched him so he hollered, and ever' now and then I had to lift him over jagged rocks. It was tough on Alexander, but I was too bashful to travel in the open trail without no clothes on.

After I'd gone maybe a mile I heard somebody in the trail ahead of me, and peeking through the bushes, I seen a most peculiar sight. It was a man on foot, going the same direction as me, and he had on what I instinctively guessed was city clothes. They wasn't buckskin, and was very beautiful, with big checks and stripes all over them. He had on a round hat with a narrow brim, and shoes like I hadn't never seen before, being neither boots nor moccasins. He was dusty, and he cussed as he limped along. Ahead of him I seen the trail made a horseshoe bend, so I cut straight across and got ahead of him, and as he come along, I stepped out of the brush and threw down on him with my cap-and-ball.

He throwed up his hands and hollered, "Don't shoot!"

"I don't want to, mister," I said, "but I got to have clothes!"

He shook his head like he couldn't believe I was so, and he said, "You ain't the color of a Injun, but – what kind of people live in these hills, anyway?"

"Most of 'em's Democrats," I said, "but I got no time to talk politics. You climb out of them clothes."

"My God!" he wailed. "My horse threw me off and ran away, and I've been walkin' for hours, expecting to get scalped by Injuns any minute, and now a naked lunatic on a mule demands my clothes! It's too much!"

"I can't argy, mister," I said; "somebody may come up the trail any minute. Hustle!" So saying I shot his hat off to encourage him.

He give a howl and shucked his duds in a hurry.

"My underclothes, too?" he demanded, shivering though it was very hot.

"Is that what them things is?" I demanded, shocked. "I never heard of a man wearin' such womanish things. The country is goin' to the dogs, just like Pap says. You better get goin'. Take my mule. When I get to where I can get some regular clothes, we'll swap back."

He clumb on to Alexander kind of dubious, and says to me, despairful, "Will you tell me one thing – how do I get to Tomahawk?"

"Take the next turn to the right," I said, "and – "

Just then Alexander turned his head and seen them underclothes on his back, and he give a loud and ringing bray and sot sail down the trail at full speed, with the stranger hanging on with both hands. Before they was out of sight they come to where the trail forked, and Alexander took the left instead of the right and vanished amongst the ridges.

I put on the clothes, and they scratched my hide something fierce. I hadn't never wore nothing but buckskin. The coat split down the back, and the pants was too short, but the shoes was the worst; they pinched all over. I throwed away the socks, having never wore none, but put on what was left of the hat.

I went on down the trail, and took the right-hand fork, and in a mile or so I come out on a flat and heard horses running. The next thing a mob of horsemen bust into view. One of 'em yelled, "There he is!" and they all come for me, full tilt. Instantly I decided that the stranger had got to Tomahawk, after all, and set a posse on to me for stealing his clothes.

So I left the trail and took out across the sage grass and they all charged after me, yelling for me to stop. Well, them dern shoes pinched my feet so bad I couldn't hardly run, so after I had run five or six hundred yards, I perceived that the horses were beginning to gain on me. So I wheeled with my cap-and-ball in my hand, but I was going so fast, when I turned, them dern shoes slipped and I went over backward into some cactus just as I pulled the trigger. So I only knocked the hat off of the first horseman. He yelled and pulled up his horse, right over me nearly, and as I drawed another bead on him, I seen he had a bright shiny star on his shirt. I dropped my gun and stuck up my hands.

They swarmed around me – cowboys, from their looks. The man with the star dismounted and picked up my gun and cussed.

"What did you lead us this chase through this heat and shoot at me for?" he demanded.

"I didn't know you was a officer," I said.

"Hell, McVey," said one of 'em, "you know how jumpy tenderfeet is. Likely he thought we was Santry's outlaws. Where's yore horse?"

"I ain't got none," I said.

"Got away from you, hey?" said McVey. "Well, climb up behind Kirby here, and let's get goin'."

To my astonishment, the sheriff stuck my gun back in the scabbard, and I clumb up behind Kirby, and away we went. Kirby kept telling me not to fall off, and it made me mad, but I said nothing. After a hour or so we come to a bunch of houses they said was Tomahawk. I got panicky when I seen all them houses, and would have jumped down and run for the mountains, only I knowed they'd catch me, with them dern pinchy shoes on.

I hadn't never seen such houses before. They was made out of boards, mostly, and some was two stories high. To the northwest and west the hills riz up a few hundred yards from the backs of the houses, and on the other sides there was plains, with brush and timber on them.

"You boys ride into town and tell the folks that the shebangs starts soon," said McVey. "Me and Kirby and Richards will take him to the ring."

I could see people milling around in the streets, and I never had no idee there was that many folks in the world. The sheriff and the other two fellows rode around the north end of the town and stopped at a old barn and told me to get off. So I did, and we went in and they had a kind of room fixed up in there with benches and a lot of towels and water buckets, and the sheriff said, "This ain't much of a dressin' room, but it'll have to do. Us boys don't know much about this game, but we'll second as good as we can. One thing – the other fellow ain't got no manager or seconds neither. How do you feel?"

"Fine," I said, "but I'm kind of hungry."

"Go get him somethin', Richards," said the sheriff.

"I didn't think they ate just before a bout," said Richards.

"Aw, I reckon he knows what he's doin'," said McVey. "Gwan."

So Richards left, and the sheriff and Kirby walked around me like I was a prize bull and felt my muscles, and the sheriff said, "By golly, if size means anything, our dough is as good as in our britches right now!"

My dollar was in my belt. I said I would pay for my keep, and they haw-hawed and slapped me on the back and said I was a great joker. Then Richards come back with a platter of grub, with a lot of men wearing boots and guns, and they stomped in and gawped at me, and McVey said, "Look him over, boys! Tomahawk stands or falls with him today!"

They started walking around me like him and Kirby done, and I was embarrassed and et three or four pounds of beef and a quart of mashed potaters and a big hunk of white bread, and drunk about a gallon of water, because I was pretty thirsty. Then they all gaped like they was surprised about something, and one of 'em said, "How come he didn't arrive on the stagecoach yesterday?"

"Well," the sheriff said, "the driver told me he was so drunk they left him at Bisney, and come on with his luggage, which is over there in the corner. They got a horse and left it there with instructions for him to ride to Tomahawk as soon as he sobered up. Me and the boys got nervous today when he didn't show up, so we went out lookin' for him, and met him hoofin' it down the trail."

"I bet them Perdition hombres starts somethin'," said Kirby. "Ain't a one of 'em showed up yet. They're settin' over at Perdition soakin' up bad licker and broodin' on their wrongs. They shore wanted this show staged over there. They claimed that since Tomahawk was furnishin' one-half of the attraction, and Gunstock the other half, the razee ought to be throwed at Perdition."

"Nothin' to it," said McVey. "It laid between Tomahawk and Gunstock, and we throwed a coin and won it. If Perdition wants trouble, she can get it. Is the boys rarin' to go?"

"Is they!" said Richards. "Every bar in Tomahawk is crowded with hombres full of licker and civic pride. They're bettin' their shirts, and they has been nine fights already. Everybody in Gunstock's here."

"Well, let's get goin'," said McVey, getting nervous. "The quicker it's over, the less blood there's likely to be spilt."

The first thing I knowed, they had laid hold of me and was pulling my clothes off, so it dawned on me that I must be under arrest for stealing the stranger's clothes. Kirby dug into the baggage which was in one corner of the stall, and dragged out a funny looking pair of pants; I know now they was white silk. I put 'em on because I hadn't nothing else to put on, and they fit me like my skin. Richards tied a American flag around my waist, and they put some spiked shoes on my feet.

I let 'em do like they wanted to, remembering what Pap said about not resisting an officer. Whilst so employed, I began to hear a noise outside, like a lot of people whooping and cheering. Pretty soon in come a skinny old gink with whiskers and two guns on, and he hollered, "Listen, Mac, dern it, a big shipment of gold is down there waitin' to be took off by the evenin' stage, and the whole blame town is deserted on account of this foolishness. Suppose Comanche Santry and his gang gets wind of it?"

"Well," said McVey, "I'll send Kirby here to help you guard it."

"You will like hell," said Kirby; "I'll resign as deputy first. I got every cent of my dough on this scrap, and I aim to see it."

"Well, send somebody!" said the old codger. "I got enough to do runnin' my store, and the stage stand, and the post office, without – "

He left, mumbling in his whiskers, and I said, "Who's that?"

"Aw," said Kirby, "that's Old Man Braxton that runs that store down at the other end of town, on the east side of the street. The post office is in there, too."

"I got to see him," I said, "there's a letter – "

Just then another man come surging in and hollered, "Hey, is your man ready? Everybody's gettin' impatient."

"All right," said McVey, throwing over me a thing he called a bathrobe. Him and Kirby and Richards picked up towels and buckets and we went out the opposite door from what we come in, and there was a big crowd of people there, and they whooped and shot off their pistols. I would have bolted back into the barn, only they grabbed me and said it was all right. We went through the crowd and I never seen so many boots and pistols in my life, and we come to a square pen made out of four posts set in the ground, and ropes stretched between. They called this a ring, and told me to get in it. I done so, and they had turf packed down so the ground was level as a floor and hard and solid. They told me to set down on a stool in one corner, and I did, and wrapped my robe around me like a Injun.

Then everybody yelled, and some men, from Gunstock, they said, clumb through the ropes on the other side. One of them was dressed like I was, and I never seen such a human. His ears looked like cabbages, his nose was flat, and his head was shaved. He set down in a opposite corner.

Then a fellow got up and waved his arms, and hollered, "Gents, you all know the occasion of this here suspicious event. Mr. Bat O'Tool, happenin' to pass through Gunstock, consented to fight anybody which would meet him. Tomahawk 'lowed to furnish that opposition, by sendin' all the way to Denver to procure the services of Mr. Bruiser McGoorty, formerly of San Francisco."

He pointed at me. Everybody cheered and shot off their pistols and I was embarrassed and bust out in a cold sweat.

"This fight," said the fellow, "will be fit accordin' to London Prize Ring Rules, same as in a champeenship go. Bare fists, round ends when one of 'em's knocked down or throwed down. Fight lasts till one or t'other ain't able to come up to the scratch at the call of time. I, Yucca Blaine, have been selected referee because, bein' from Chawed Ear, I got no prejudices either way. Are you all ready? Time!"

McVey hauled me off my stool and pulled off my bathrobe and pushed me out into the ring. I nearly died with embarrassment, but I seen the fellow they called O'Tool didn't have on more clothes than me. He approached and held out his hand, so I held out mine. We shook hands and then without no warning, he hit me an awful lick on the jaw with his left. It was like being kicked by a mule. The first part of me which hit the turf was the back of my head. O'Tool stalked back to his corner, and the Gunstock boys was dancing and hugging each other, and the Tomahawk fellows was growling in their whiskers and fumbling for guns and bowie knives.

McVey and his men rushed into the ring before I could get up and dragged me to my corner and began pouring water on me.

"Are you hurt much?" yelled McVey.

"How can a man's fist hurt anybody?" I asked. "I wouldn't have fell down, only it was so unexpected. I didn't know he was goin' to hit me. I never played no game like this before."

McVey dropped the towel he was beating me in the face with, and turned pale. "Ain't you Bruiser McGoorty of San Francisco?" he hollered.

"Naw," I said; "I'm Breckinridge Elkins, from up in the Humbolt mountains. I come here to get a letter for Pap."

"But the stage driver described them clothes – " he begun wildly.

"A feller stole my clothes," I explained, "so I took some off'n a stranger. Maybe he was Mr. McGoorty."

"What's the matter?" asked Kirby, coming up with another bucket of water. "Time's about ready to be called."

"We're sunk!" bawled McVey. "This ain't McGoorty! This is a derned hillbilly which murdered McGoorty and stole his clothes."

"We're rooint!" exclaimed Richards, aghast. "Everybody's bet their dough without even seein' our man, they was that full of trust and civic pride. We can't call it off now. Tomahawk is rooint! What'll we do?"

"He's goin' to get in there and fight his derndest," said McVey, pulling his gun and jamming it into my back. "We'll hang him after the fight."

"But he can't box!" wailed Richards.

"No matter," said McVey; "the fair name of our town is at stake; Tomahawk promised to furnish a fighter to fight this fellow O'Tool, and – "

"Oh," I said, suddenly seeing light. "This here is a fight, ain't it?" McVey give a low moan, and Kirby reached for his gun, but just then the referee hollered time, and I jumped up and run at O'Tool. If a fight was all they wanted, I was satisfied. All that talk about rules, and the yelling of the crowd had had me so confused I hadn't knowed what it was all about. I hit at O'Tool, and he ducked and hit me in the belly and on the nose and in the eye and on the ear. The blood spurted, and the crowd yelled, and he looked dumbfounded and gritted between his teeth, "Are you human? Why don't you fall?"

I spit out a mouthful of blood and got my hands on him and started chewing his ear, and he squalled like a catamount. Yucca run in and tried to pull me loose, and I give him a slap under the ear and he turned a somersault into the ropes.

"Your man's fightin' foul!" he squalled, and Kirby said, "You're crazy! Do you see this gun? You holler 'foul' once more, and it'll go off!"

Meanwhile O'Tool had broke loose from me, and caved in his knuckles on my jaw, and I come for him again, because I was mad by this time. He gasped, "If you want to make an alley fight out of it, all right! I wasn't raised in Five Points for nothing!" He then rammed his knee into my groin, and groped for my eye, but I got his thumb in my teeth and begun masticating it, and the way he howled was a caution.

By this time the crowd was crazy, and I throwed O'Tool and begun to stomp him, when somebody let bang at me from the crowd, and the bullet cut my silk belt and my pants started to fall down.

I grabbed 'em with both hands, and O'Tool riz and rushed at me, bloody and bellering, and I didn't dare let go my pants to defend myself. So I whirled and bent over and lashed out backward with my right heel like a mule, and I caught him under the chin. He done a cartwheel in the air, his head hit the turf, and he bounced on over and landed on his back with his knees hooked over the lower rope. There wasn't no question about him being out. The only question was, was he dead?

A great roar of "Foul" went up from the Gunstock men, and guns bristled all around the ring.

The Tomahawk men was cheering and yelling that I had won fair and square, and the Gunstock men was cussing and threatening me, when somebody hollered, "Leave it to the referee!"

"Sure," said Kirby. "He knows our man won fair, and if he don't say so, I'll blow his head off!"

"That's a lie!" bellered a man from Gunstock. "He knows it was a foul, and if he says it wasn't, I'll carve his liver with this here bowie knife!"

At these words Yucca keeled over in a dead faint, and then a clatter of hoofs sounded above the din, and out of the timber that hid the trail from the east, a gang of horsemen rode at a run. Everybody whirled and yelled, "Look out, here comes them Perdition illegitimates!"

Instantly a hundred guns covered them, and McVey demanded, "Come ye in peace or in war?"

"We come to unmask a fraud!" roared a big man with a red bandanner around his neck. "McGoorty, come forth!"

A familiar figger, now dressed in cowboy togs, pushed forward on my mule. "There he is!" this figger yelled, pointing at me. "That's the desperado which robbed me! Them's my tights he's got on!"

"What's this?" roared the crowd.

"A dern fake!" bellered the man with the red bandanner. "This here is Bruiser McGoorty!"

"Then who's he?" somebody bawled, pointing at me.

"My name's Breckinridge Elkins and I can lick any man here!" I roared, getting mad. I brandished my fists in defiance, but my britches started sliding down again, so I had to shut up and grab 'em.

"Aha!" the man with the red bandanner howled like a hyener. "He admits it! I dunno what the idee is, but these Tomahawk polecats has double-crossed somebody! I trusts that you jackasses from Gunstock realizes the blackness and hellishness of their hearts! This man McGoorty rode into Perdition a few hours ago in his unmentionables, astraddle of that there mule, and told us how he'd been held up and robbed and put on the wrong road. You skunks was too proud to stage this fight in Perdition, but we ain't the men to see justice scorned with impunity! We brought McGoorty here to show you you was bein' gypped by Tomahawk! That man ain't no prize fighter; he's a highway robber!"

"These Tomahawk coyotes has framed us!" squalled a Gunstock man, going for his gun.

"You're a liar!" roared Richards, bending a .45 barrel over his head.

The next instant guns was crashing, knives was gleaming, and men was yelling blue murder. The Gunstock braves turned frothing on the Tomahawk warriors, and the men from Perdition, yelping with glee, pulled their guns and begun fanning the crowd indiscriminately, which give back their fire. McGoorty give a howl and fell down on Alexander's neck, gripping around it with both arms, and Alexander departed in a cloud of dust and smoke.

I grabbed my gunbelt, which McVey had hung over the post in my corner, and I headed for cover, holding on to my britches whilst the bullets hummed around me as thick as bees. I wanted to take to the brush, but I remembered that blamed letter, so I headed for town. Behind me there rose a roar of banging guns and yelling men. Just as I got to the backs of the row of buildings which lined the street, I run into something soft head on. It was McGoorty, trying to escape on Alexander. He had hold of only one rein, and Alexander, evidently having circled one end of the town, was traveling in a circle and heading back where he started from.

I was going so fast I couldn't stop, and I run right over Alexander and all three of us went down in a heap. I jumped up, afraid Alexander was killed, but he scrambled up snorting and trembling, and then McGoorty weaved up, making funny noises. I poked my cap-and-ball into his belly.

"Off with them pants!" I yelped.

"My God!" he screamed. "*Again?* This is getting to be a habit!"

"Hustle!" I bellered. "You can have these scandals I got on now."

He shucked his britches, grabbed them tights and run like he was afeard I'd want his underwear too. I jerked on the pants, forked Alexander and headed for the south end of town. I kept behind the buildings, though the town seemed to be deserted, and purty soon I come to the store where Kirby had told me Old Man Braxton kept the post office. Guns was barking there, and across the street I seen men ducking in and out behind a old shack, and shooting.

I tied Alexander to a corner of the store and went in the back door. Up in the front part I seen Old Man Braxton kneeling behind some barrels with a .45–90, and he was shooting at the fellows in the shack across the street. Every now and then a slug would hum through the door and comb his whiskers, and he would cuss worse'n Pap did that time he sot down in a bear trap.

I went up to him and tapped him on the shoulder and he give a squall and flopped over and let go *bam!* right in my face and singed off my eyebrows. And the fellows across the street hollered and started shooting at both of us.

I'd grabbed the barrel of his Winchester, and he was cussing and jerking at it with one hand and feeling in his boot for a knife with the other'n, and I said, "Mr. Braxton, if you ain't too busy, I wish you'd gimme that there letter which come for Pap."

"Don't never come up behind me that way again!" he squalled. "I thought you was one of them dern outlaws! Look out! Duck, you fool!"

I let go his gun, and he took a shot at a head which was aiming around the shack, and the head let out a squall and disappeared.

"Who are them fellows?" I asked.

"Comanche Santry and his bunch, from up in the hills," snarled Old

Man Braxton, jerking the lever of his Winchester. "They come after that gold. A hell of a sheriff McVey is; never sent me nobody. And them fools over at the ring are makin' so much noise, they'll never hear the shootin' over here. Look out, here they come!"

Six or seven men rushed out from behind the shack and ran across the street, shooting as they come. I seen I'd never get my letter as long as all this fighting was going on, so I unslung my old cap-and-ball and let *bam!* at them three times, and three of them outlaws fell across each other in the street, and the rest turned around and run back behind the shack.

"Good work, boy!" yelled Old Man Braxton. "If I ever – oh, Judas Iscariot, we're blowed up now!"

Something was pushed around the corner of the shack and come rolling down toward us, the shack being on higher ground than the store was. It was a keg, with a burning fuse which whirled as the keg revolved and looked like a wheel of fire.

"What's in that keg?" I asked.

"Blastin' powder!" screamed Old Man Braxton, scrambling up. "Run, you dern fool! It's comin' right into the door!"

He was so scared he forgot all about the fellows across the street, and one of 'em caught him in the thigh with a buffalo rifle, and he plunked down again, howling blue murder. I stepped over him to the door – that's when I got that slug in my hip – and the keg hit my legs and stopped, so I picked it up and heaved it back across the street. It hadn't no more'n hit the shack when *bam!* it exploded, and the shack went up in smoke. When it stopped raining pieces of wood and metal, they wasn't any sign to show any outlaws had ever hid behind where that shack had been.

"I wouldn't believe it if I hadn't saw it," Old Man Braxton moaned faintly.

"Are you hurt bad, Mr. Braxton?" I asked.

"I'm dyin'," he groaned. "Plumb dyin'!"

"Well, before you die, Mr. Braxton," I said, "would you mind givin' me that there letter for Pap?"

"What's yore pap's name?" he asked.

"Roarin' Bill Elkins," I said.

He wasn't hurt as bad as he thought. He reached up and got hold of a leather bag and fumbled in it and pulled out a envelope. "I remember tellin' old Buffalo Rogers I had a letter for Bill Elkins," he said, fingering it over. Then he said, "Hey, wait! This ain't for yore pap. My sight is gettin' bad. I read it wrong the first time. This is for Bill Elston that lives between here and Perdition."

I want to spike a rumor which says I tried to murder Old Man Braxton and tore his store down for spite. I've done told how he got his leg broke, and the rest was accidental. When I realized that I had went through all that embarrassment for nothing, I was so mad and disgusted I turned and run out of the back door, and I forgot to open the door and that's how it got tore off the hinges.

I then jumped on to Alexander and forgot to untie him from the store. I kicked him in the ribs, and he bolted and tore loose that corner of the building, and that's how come the roof to fall in. Old Man Braxton inside was scared and started yelling bloody murder, and about that time a lot of men come up to investigate the explosion which had stopped the three-cornered battle between Perdition, Tomahawk, and Gunstock, and they thought I was the cause of everything, and they all started shooting at me as I rode off.

Then was when I got that charge of buckshot in my back.

I went out of Tomahawk and up the hill trail so fast I bet me and Alexander looked like a streak. And I says to myself the next time Pap gets a letter in the post office, he can come after it hisself, because it's evident that civilization ain't no place for a boy which ain't reached his full growth and strength.

Meet Cap'n Kidd

I didn't pull up Alexander till I was plumb out of sight of Tomahawk. Then I slowed down and taken stock of myself, and my spirits was right down in my spiked shoes which still had some of Mister O'Tool's hide stuck onto the spikes. Here I'd started forth into the world to show Glory McGraw what a he-bearcat I was, and now look at me. Here I was without even no clothes but them derned spiked shoes which pinched my feet, and a pair of britches some cowpuncher had wore the seat out of and patched with buckskin. I still had my gunbelt and the dollar Pap gimme, but no place to spend it. I likewise had a goodly amount of lead under my hide.

"By golly!" I says, shaking my fists at the universe at large. "I ain't goin' to go back to Bear Creek like this and have Glory McGraw laughin' at me! I'll head for the Wild River settlements and git me a job punchin' cows till I got money enough to buy me store-bought boots and a hoss!"

I then pulled out my bowie knife which was in a scabbard on my gunbelt, and started digging the slug out of my hip and the buckshot out of my back. Them buckshot was kinda hard to get to, but I done it. I hadn't never held a job of punching cows, but I'd had plenty experience roping wild bulls up in the Humbolts. Them bulls wanders off the lower ranges into the mountains and grows most amazing big and mean. Me and Alexander had had plenty experience with them, and I had me a lariat which would hold any steer that ever bellered. It was still tied to my saddle, and I was glad none of them cowpunchers hadn't stole it. Maybe they didn't know it was a lariat. I'd made it myself, especial, and used it to rope them bulls and also cougars and grizzlies which infests the Humbolts. It was made out of buffalo hide, ninety foot long and half again as thick and heavy as the average lariat, and the honda was a half-pound chunk of iron beat into shape with a sledge hammer. I reckoned I was qualified for a *vaquero* even if I didn't have no cowboy clothes and was riding a mule.

So I headed across the mountains for the cow country. They warn't no trail the way I taken, but I knowed the direction Wild River lay in, and that was enough for me. I knowed if I kept going that way I'd hit it after a while. Meanwhile, they was plenty of grass in the draws and along the creeks to keep Alexander fat and sleek, and plenty of squirrels and rabbits for me to knock over with rocks. I camped that night away up in the high ranges and cooked me nine or ten squirrels over a fire and et 'em, and while that warn't much of a supper for a appertite like mine, still I figgered next day I'd stumble on to a b'ar or maybe a steer which had wandered offa the ranges.

Next morning before sunup I was on Alexander and moving on, without no breakfast, because it looked like they warn't no rabbits nor nothing near abouts, and I rode all morning without sighting nothing. It was a high range, and nothing alive there but a buzzard I seen onst, but late in the afternoon I crossed a backbone and come down into a whopping big plateau about the size of a county, with springs and streams and grass growing stirrup-high along 'em, and clumps of cottonwood, and spruce, and pine thick up on the hillsides. They was canyons and cliffs, and mountains along the rim, and altogether it was as fine a country as I ever seen, but it didn't look like nobody lived there, and for all I know I was the first white man that ever come into it. But they was more soon, as I'll relate.

Well, I noticed something funny as I come down the ridge that separated the bare hills from the plateau. First I met a wildcat. He come lipping along at a right smart clip, and he didn't stop. He just gimme a wicked look sidewise and kept right on up the slope. Next thing I met a lobo wolf, and after that I counted nine more wolves, and they was all heading west, up the slopes. Then Alexander give a snort and started trembling, and a cougar slid out of a blackjack thicket and snarled at us over his shoulder as he went past at a long lope. All them varmints was heading for the dry bare country I'd just left, and I wondered why they was leaving a good range like this one to go into that dern no-account country.

It worried Alexander too, because he smelt of the air and brayed kind of plaintively. I pulled him up and smelt the air too, because critters run like that before a forest fire, but I couldn't smell no smoke, nor see none. So I rode on down the slopes and started across the flats, and as I went I seen more bobcats, and wolves, and painters, and they was all heading west, and they warn't lingering none, neither. They warn't no doubt that them critters was pulling their freight because they was scairt of something, and it warn't humans, because they didn't 'pear to be scairt of me a mite. They just swerved around me and kept trailing. After I'd gone a few miles I met a herd of wild hosses, with the stallion herding 'em. He was a big mean-looking cuss, but he looked scairt as bad as any of the critters I'd saw.

The sun was getting low, and I was getting awful hungry as I come into a open spot with a creek on one side running through clumps of willers and cottonwoods, and on the other side I could see some big cliffs looming up over the tops of the trees. And whilst I was hesitating, wondering if I ought to keep looking for eatable critters, or try to worry along on a wildcat or a wolf, a big grizzly come lumbering out of a clump of spruces and headed west. When he seen me and Alexander he stopped and snarled like he was mad about something, and then the first thing I knowed he was charging us. So I pulled my .44 and shot him through the head, and got off and onsaddled Alexander and turnt him loose in grass stirrup-high, and skun the b'ar. Then I cut me off some steaks and started a fire and begun reducing my appertite. That warn't no small job, because I hadn't had nothing to eat since the night before.

Well, while I was eating I heard hosses and looked up and seen six men riding toward me from the east. One was as big as me, but the other ones warn't but about six foot tall apiece. They was cowpunchers, by their look, and the biggest man was dressed plumb as elegant as Mister Wilkinson was, only his shirt was jest only one color. But he had on fancy boots and a white Stetson and a ivory-butted Colt, and what looked like the butt of a sawed-off shotgun jutted out of his saddle scabbard. He was dark and had awful mean eyes, and a jaw which it looked like he could bite the spokes out of a wagon wheel if he wanted to.

He started talking to me in Piute, but before I could say anything, one of the others said: "Aw, that ain't no Injun, Donovan, his eyes ain't the right color."

"I see that, now," says Donovan. "But I shore thought he was a Injun when I first rode up and seen them old ragged britches and his sunburnt hide. Who the devil air you?"

"I'm Breckinridge Elkins, from Bear Creek," I says, awed by his magnificence.

"Well," says he, "I'm Wild Bill Donovan, which name is heard with fear and tremblin' from Powder River to the Rio Grande. Just now I'm lookin' for a wild stallion. Have you seen sech?"

"I seen a bay stallion headin' west with his herd," I said.

"'Twarn't him," says Donovan. "This here one's a pinto, the biggest, meanest hoss in the world. He come down from the Humbolts when he was a colt, but he's roamed the West from Border to Border. He's so mean he ain't never got him a herd of his own. He takes mares away from other stallions, and then drifts on alone just for pure cussedness. When he comes into a country all other varmints takes to the tall timber."

"You mean the wolves and painters and b'ars I seen headin' for the high ridges was runnin' away from this here stallion?" I says.

"Exactly," says Donovan. "He crossed the eastern ridge sometime durin' the night, and the critters that was wise hightailed it. We warn't far behind him; we come over the ridge a few hours ago, but we lost his trail somewhere on this side."

"You chasin' him?" I ast.

"Ha!" snarled Donovan with a kind of vicious laugh. "The man don't live what can chase Cap'n Kidd! We're just follerin' him. We been follerin' him for five hundred miles, keepin' outa sight, and hopin' to catch him off guard or somethin'. We got to have some kind of a big advantage before we closes in, or even shows ourselves. We're right fond of life! That devil has kilt more men than any other ten hosses on this continent."

"What you call him?" I says.

"Cap'n Kidd," says Donovan. "Cap'n Kidd was a big pirate long time ago. This here hoss is like him in lots of ways, particularly in regard to morals. But I'll git him, if I have to foller him to the Gulf and back. Wild Bill Donovan always gits what he wants, be it money, woman, or hoss! Now lissen here, you range-country hobo: we're a-siftin' north from here, to see if we cain't pick up Cap'n Kidd's sign. If you see a pinto stallion bigger'n you ever dreamed a hoss could be, or come onto his tracks, you drop whatever yo're doin' and pull out and look for us, and tell me about it. You keep lookin' till you find us, too. If you don't, you'll regret it, you hear me?"

"Yessir," I said. "Did you gents come through the Wild River country?"

"Maybe we did and maybe we didn't," he says with haughty grandeur. "What business is that of yore'n, I'd like to know?"

"Not any," I says. "But I was aimin' to go there and see if I could git me a job punchin' cows."

At that he throwed back his head and laughed long and loud, and all the other fellers laughed too, and I was embarrassed.

"You git a job punchin' cows?" roared Donovan. "With them britches and shoes, and not even no shirt, and that there ignorant-lookin' mule I see gobblin' grass over by the creek? Haw! haw! haw! haw! You better stay up here in the mountains whar you belong and live on roots and nuts and jackrabbits like the other Piutes, red or white! Any self-respectin' rancher would take a shotgun to you if you was to ast him for a job. Haw! haw! haw!" he says, and rode off still laughing.

I was that embarrassed I bust out into a sweat. Alexander was a good mule, but he did look kind of funny in the face. But he was the only critter I'd ever found which could carry my weight very many miles without giving plumb out. He was awful strong and tough, even if he was kind of dumb and potbellied. I begun to get kind of mad, but Donovan and his men was already gone, and the stars was beginning to blink out. So I cooked me some more b'ar steaks and et 'em, and the land sounded awful still, not a wolf howling nor a cougar squalling. They was all west of the ridge. This critter Cap'n Kidd sure had the country to hisself, as far as the meat-eating critters was consarned.

I hobbled Alexander close by and fixed me a bed with some boughs and his saddle blanket, and went to sleep. I was woke up shortly after midnight by Alexander trying to get in bed with me.

I sot up in irritation and prepared to bust him in the snoot, when I heard what had scairt him. I never heard such a noise. My hair stood straight up. It was a stallion neighing, but I never heard no hoss critter neigh like that. I bet you could of heard it for fifteen miles. It sounded like a combination of a wild hoss neighing, a rip saw going through a oak log full of knots, and a hungry cougar screeching. I thought it come from somewhere within a mile of the camp, but I warn't sure. Alexander was shivering and whimpering he was that scairt, and stepping all over me as he tried to huddle down amongst the branches and hide his head under my shoulder. I shoved him away, but he insisted on staying as close to me as he could, and when I woke up again next morning he was sleeping with his head on my belly.

But he must of forgot about the neigh he heard, or thought it was jest a bad dream or something, because as soon as I taken the hobbles off of him he started cropping grass and wandered off amongst the thickets in his pudding-head way.

I cooked me some more b'ar steaks, and wondered if I ought to go and try to find Mister Donovan and tell him about hearing the stallion neigh, but I figgered he'd heard it. Anybody that was within a day's ride ought to of heard it. Anyway, I seen no reason why I should run errands for Donovan.

I hadn't got through eating when I heard Alexander give a horrified bray, and he come lickety-split out of a grove of trees and made for the camp, and behind him come the biggest hoss I ever seen in my life. Alexander looked like a potbellied bull pup beside of him. He was painted – black and white – and he r'ared up with his long mane flying agen the sunrise, and give a scornful neigh that nigh busted my eardrums, and turned around and sa'ntered back toward the grove, cropping grass as he went, like he thunk so little of Alexander he wouldn't even bother to chase him.

Alexander come blundering into camp, blubbering and hollering, and run over the fire and scattered it every which a way, and then tripped hisself over the saddle which was laying near by, and fell on his neck braying like he figgered his life was in danger.

I catched him and throwed the saddle and bridle on to him, and by that time Cap'n Kidd was out of sight on the other side of the thicket. I onwound my lariat and headed in that direction. I figgered not even Cap'n Kidd could break that lariat. Alexander didn't want to go; he sot back on his haunches and brayed fit to deefen you, but I spoke to him sternly, and it seemed to convince him that he better face the stallion than me, so he moved out, kind of reluctantly.

We went past the grove and seen Cap'n Kid cropping grass in the patch of rolling prairie just beyond, so I rode toward him, swinging my lariat. He looked up and snorted kinda threateningly, and he had the meanest eye I ever seen in man or beast; but he didn't move, just stood there looking contemptuous, so I throwed my rope and piled the loop right around his neck, and Alexander sot back on his haunches.

Well, it was about like roping a roaring hurricane. The instant he felt that rope Cap'n Kidd give a convulsive start, and made one mighty lunge for freedom. The lariat held, but the girths didn't. They held jest long enough for Alexander to get jerked head over heels, and naturally I went along with him. But right in the middle of the somesault we taken, both girths snapped.

Me and the saddle and Alexander landed all in a tangle, but Cap'n Kidd jerked the saddle from amongst us, because I had my rope tied fast to the horn, Texas-style, and Alexander got loose from me by the simple process of kicking me vi'lently in the ear. He also stepped on my face when he jumped up, and the next instant he was hightailing it through the bresh in the general direction of Bear Creek. As I learned later he didn't stop till he run into Pap's cabin and tried to hide under my brother John's bunk.

Meanwhile Cap'n Kidd had throwed the loop offa his head and come for me with his mouth wide open, his ears laid back and his teeth and eyes flashing. I didn't want to shoot him, so I riz up and run for the trees. But he was coming like a tornado, and I seen he was going to run me down before I could get to a tree big enough to climb, so I grabbed me a sapling about as thick as my laig and tore it up by the roots, and turned around and busted him over the head with it, just as he started to r'ar up to come down on me with his front hoofs.

Pieces of roots and bark and wood flew every which a way, and Cap'n Kidd grunted and batted his eyes and went back on to his haunches. It was a right smart lick. If I'd ever hit Alexander that hard it would have busted his skull like a egg – and Alexander had a awful thick skull, even for a mule.

Whilst Cap'n Kidd was shaking the bark and stars out of his eyes, I run to a big oak and clumb it. He come after me instantly, and chawed chunks out of the tree as big as washtubs, and kicked most of the bark off as high up as he could rech, but it was a good substantial tree, and it held. He then tried to climb it, which amazed me most remarkable, but he didn't do much good at that. So he give up with a snort of disgust and trotted off.

I waited till he was out of sight, and then I clumb down and got my rope and saddle, and started follering him. I knowed there warn't no use trying to catch Alexander with the lead he had. I figgered he'd get back to Bear Creek safe. And Cap'n Kidd was the critter I wanted now. The minute I lammed him with that tree and he didn't fall, I knowed he was the hoss for me – a hoss which could carry my weight all day without giving out, and likewise full of spirit. I says to myself I rides him or the buzzards picks my bones.

I snuck from tree to tree, and presently seen Cap'n Kidd swaggering along and eating grass, and biting the tops off of young sapling, and occasionally tearing down a good sized tree to get the leaves off. Sometimes he'd neigh like a steamboat whistle, and let his heels fly in all directions just out of pure cussedness. When he done this the air was full of flying bark and dirt and rocks till it looked like he was in the middle of a twisting cyclone. I never seen such a critter in my life. He was as full of pizen and rambunctiousness as a drunk Apache on the warpath.

I thought at first I'd rope him and tie the other end of the rope to a big tree, but I was a-feared he'd chawed the lariat apart. Then I seen something that changed my mind. We was close to the rocky cliffs which jutted up above the trees, and Cap'n Kidd was passing a canyon mouth that looked like a big knife cut. He looked in and snorted, like he hoped they was a mountain lion hiding in there, but they warn't, so he went on. The wind was blowing from him towards me and he didn't smell me.

After he was out of sight amongst the trees I come out of cover and looked into the cleft. It was kinda like a short blind canyon. It warn't but about thirty foot wide at the mouth, but it widened quick till it made a kind of bowl a hundred yards acrost, and then narrowed to a crack again. Rock walls five hundred foot high was on all sides except at the mouth.

"And here," says I to myself, "is a readymade corral!"

Then I lay to and started to build a wall to close the mouth of the canyon. Later on I heard that a scientific expedition (whatever the hell that might be) was all excited over finding evidences of a ancient race up in the mountains. They said they found a wall that could of been built only by giants. They was crazy; that there was the wall I built for Cap'n Kidd.

I knowed it would have to be high and solid if I didn't want Cap'n Kidd to jump it or knock it down. They was plenty of boulders laying at the foot of the cliffs which had weathered off, and I didn't use a single rock which weighed less'n three hundred pounds, and most of 'em was a lot heavier than that. It taken me most all morning, but when I quit I had me a wall higher'n the average man could reach, and so thick and heavy I knowed it would hold even Cap'n Kidd.

I left a narrer gap in it, and piled some boulders close to it on the outside, ready to shove 'em into the gap. Then I stood outside the wall and squalled like a cougar. They ain't even a cougar hisself can tell the difference when I squalls like one. Purty soon I heard Cap'n Kidd give his war-neigh off yonder, and then they was a thunder of hoofs and a snapping and crackling of bresh, and he come busting into the open with his ears laid back and his teeth bare and his eyes as red as a Comanche's war-paint. He sure hated cougars. But he didn't seem to like me much neither. When he seen me he give a roar of rage, and come for me lickety-split. I run through the gap and hugged the wall inside, and he come thundering after me going so fast he run clean across the bowl before he checked hisself. Before he could get back to the gap I'd run outside and was piling rocks in it. I had a good big one about the size of a fat hawg and I jammed it in the gap first and piled t'others on top of it.

Cap'n Kidd arriv at the gap all hoofs and teeth and fury, but it was already filled too high for him to jump and too solid for him to tear down. He done his best, but all he done was to knock some chunks offa the rocks with his heels. He sure was mad. He was the maddest hoss I ever seen, and when I got up on the wall and he seen me, he nearly busted with rage.

He went tearing around the bowl, kicking up dust and neighing like a steamboat on the rampage, and then he come back and tried to kick the wall down again. When he turned to gallop off I jumped offa the wall and landed square on his back, but before I could so much as grab his mane he throwed me clean over the wall and I landed in a cluster of boulders and cactus and skun my shin. This made me mad so I got the lariat and the saddle and clumb back on the wall and roped him, but he jerked the rope out of my hand before I could get any kind of a purchase, and went bucking and pitching around all over the bowl trying to get shet of the rope. So purty soon he pitched right into the cliff wall and he lammed it so hard with his hind hoofs that a whole section of overhanging rock was jolted loose and hit him right between the ears. That was too much even for Cap'n Kidd.

It knocked him down and stunned him, and I jumped down into the bowl and before he could come to I had my saddle on to him, and a hackamore I'd fixed out of a piece of my lariat. I'd also mended the girths with pieces of the lariat, too, before I built the wall.

Well, when Cap'n Kidd recovered his senses and riz up, snorting and war-like, I was on his back. He stood still for a instant like he was trying to figger out jest what the hell was the matter, and then he turned his head and seen me on his back. The next instant I felt like I was astraddle of a ringtailed cyclone.

I dunno what all he done. He done so many things all at onst I couldn't keep track. I clawed leather. The man which could have stayed onto him without clawing leather ain't born yet, or else he's a cussed liar. Sometimes my feet was in the stirrups and sometimes they warn't, and sometimes they was in the wrong stirrups. I cain't figger out how that could be, but it was so. Part of the time I was in the saddle and part of the time I was behind it on his rump, or on his neck in front of it. He kept reching back trying to snap my laig and onst he got my thigh between his teeth and would ondoubtedly of tore the muscle out if I hadn't shook him loose by beating him over the head with my fist.

One instant he'd have his head betwixt his feet and I'd be setting on a hump so high in the air I'd get dizzy, and the next thing he'd come down stiff-laiged and I could feel my spine telescoping. He changed ends so fast I got sick at my stummick and he nigh unjointed my neck with his sunfishing. I calls it sunfishing because it was more like that than anything. He occasionally rolled over and over on the ground, too, which was very uncomfortable for me, but I hung on, because I was afeared if I let go I'd never get on him again. I also knowed that if he ever shaken me loose I'd had to shoot him to keep him from stomping my guts out. So I stuck, though I'll admit that they is few sensations more onpleasant than having a hoss as big as Cap'n Kidd roll on you nine or ten times.

He tried to scrape me off agen the walls, too, but all he done was scrape off some hide and most of my pants, though it was when he lurched agen that outjut of rock that I got them ribs cracked, I reckon.

He looked like he was able to go on forever, and aimed to, but I hadn't never met nothing which could outlast me, and I stayed with him, even after I started bleeding at the nose and mouth and ears, and got blind, and then all to onst he was standing stock still in the middle of the bowl, with his tongue hanging out about three foot, and his sweat-soaked sides heaving, and the sun was just setting over the mountains. He'd bucked nearly all afternoon!

But he was licked. I knowed it and he knowed it. I shaken the stars and sweat and blood out of my eyes and dismounted by the simple process of pulling my feet out of stirrups and falling off. I laid there for maybe a hour, and was most amazing sick, but so was Cap'n Kidd. When I was able to stand on my feet I taken the saddle and the hackamore off and he didn't kick me nor nothing. He jest made a half-hearted attempt to bite me but all he done was to bite the buckle offa my gunbelt. They was a little spring back in the cleft where the bowl narrered in the cliff, and plenty of grass, so I figgered he'd be all right when he was able to stop blowing and panting long enough to eat and drink.

I made a fire outside the bowl and cooked me what was left of the b'ar meat, and then I lay down on the ground and slept till sunup.

When I riz up and seen how late it was, I jumped up and run and looked over the wall, and there was Cap'n Kidd mowing the grass down as ca'm as you please. He give me a mean look, but didn't say nothing. I was so eager to see if he was going to let me ride him without no more foolishness that I didn't stop for breakfast, nor to fix the buckle onto my gunbelt. I left it hanging on a spruce limb, and clumb into the bowl. Cap'n Kidd laid back his ears but didn't do nothing as I approached outside of making a swipe at me with his left hoof. I dodged and give him a good hearty kick in the belly and he grunted and doubled up, and I clapped the saddle on him. He showed his teeth at that, but he let me cinch it up, and put on the hackamore, and when I got on him he didn't pitch but about ten jumps and make but one snap at my laig. Well, I was plumb tickled as you can imagine. I clumb down and opened the gap in the wall and led him out, and when he found he was outside the bowl he bolted and dragged me for a hundred yards before I managed to get the rope around a tree. After I tied him up though, he didn't try to bust loose. I started back towards the tree where I left my gunbelt when I heard hosses running, and the next thing I knowed Donovan and his five men busted into the open and pulled up with their mouths wide open. Cap'n Kidd snorted war-like when he seen 'em, but didn't cut up no other way.

"Blast my soul!" says Donovan. "Can I believe my eyes? If there ain't Cap'n Kidd hisself, saddled and tied to that tree! Did *you* do that?"

"Yeah," I said.

He looked me over and said, "I believes it. You looked like you been through a sausage grinder. Air you still alive?"

"My ribs is kind of sore," I said.

" – !" says Donovan. "To think that a blame half-naked hillbilly should do what the best hossmen of the West has attempted in vain! I don't aim to stand for it! I knows my rights! That there is my hoss by rights! I've trailed him nigh a thousand miles, and combed this cussed plateau in a circle. He's my hoss!"

"He ain't, nuther," I says. "He come from the Humbolts original, jest like me. You said so yoreself. Anyway, I caught him and broke him, and he's mine."

"He's right, Bill," one of the men says to Donovan.

"You shet up!" roared Donovan. "What Wild Bill Donovan wants, he gits!"

I reched for my gun and then remembered in despair that it was hanging on a limb a hundred yards away. Donovan covered me with the sawed-off shotgun he jerked out of his saddle holster as he swung down.

"Stand where you be," he advised me. "I ought to shoot you for not comin' and tellin' me when you seen the hoss, but after all you've saved me the trouble of breakin' him in."

"So yo're a hoss thief!" I said wrathfully.

"You be keerful what you calls me!" he roared. "I ain't no hoss thief. We gambles for that hoss. Set down!"

I sot and he sot on his heels in front of me, with his sawed-off still covering me. If it'd been a pistol I would of took it away from him and shoved the barrel down his throat. But I was quite young in them days and bashful about shotguns. The others squatted around us, and Donovan says: "Smoky, haul out yore deck – the special one. Smoky deals, hillbilly, and the high hand wins the hoss."

"I'm puttin' up my hoss, it looks like," I says fiercely. "What *you* puttin' up?"

"My Stetson hat!" says he. "Haw! haw! haw!"

"Haw! haw! haw!" chortles the other hoss thieves.

26

Smoky started dealing and I said, "Hey! Yo're dealin' Donovan's hand offa the bottom of the deck!"

"Shet up!" roared Donovan, poking me in the belly with his shotgun. "You be keerful how you slings them insults around! This here is a fair and square game, and I just happen to be lucky. Can you beat four aces?"

"How you know you got four aces?" I says fiercely. "You ain't looked at yore hand yet."

"Oh," says he, and picked it up and spread it out on the grass, and they was four aces and a king. "By golly!" says he. "I shore called that shot right!"

"Remarkable foresight!" I said bitterly, throwing down my hand which was a three, five, and seven of hearts, a ten of clubs, and a jack of diamonds.

"Then I wins!" gloated Donovan, jumping up. I riz too, quick and sudden, but Donovan had me covered with that cussed shotgun.

"Git on that hoss and ride him over to our camp, Red," says Donovan, to a big redheaded hombre which was shorter than him but jest about as big. "See if he's properly broke. I wants to keep my eye on this hillbilly myself."

So Red went over to Cap'n Kidd which stood there saying nothing, and my heart sunk right down to the tops of my spiked shoes. Red ontied him and clumb on him and Cap'n Kidd didn't so much as snap at him. Red says: "Git goin', cuss you!" Cap'n Kidd turnt his head and looked at Red and then he opened his mouth like a alligator and started laughing. I never seen a hoss laugh before, but now I know what they mean by a hoss laugh. Cap'n Kidd didn't neigh nor nicker. He jest laughed. He laughed till the acorns come rattling down outa the trees and the echoes rolled through the cliffs like thunder. And then he reched his head around and grabbed Red's laig and dragged him out of the saddle, and held him upside down with guns and things spilling out of his scabbards and pockets, and Red yelling blue murder. Cap'n Kidd shaken him till he looked like a rag and swung him around his head three or four times, and then let go and throwed him clean through a alder thicket.

Them fellers all stood gaping, and Donovan had forgot about me, so I grabbed the shotgun away from him and hit him under the ear with my left fist and he bit the dust. I then swung the gun on the others and roared, "Onbuckle them gunbelts, cuss ye!" They was bashfuller about buckshot at close range than I was. They didn't argy. Them four gunbelts was on the grass before I stopped yelling.

"All right," I said. "Now go catch Cap'n Kidd."

Because he had gone over to where their hosses was tied and was chawing and kicking the tar out of them and they was hollering something fierce.

"He'll kill us!" squalled the men.

"Well, what of it?" I snarled. "Gwan!"

So they made a desperate foray onto Cap'n Kidd and the way he kicked 'em in the belly and bit the seat out of their britches was beautiful to behold. But whilst he was stomping them I come up and grabbed his hackamore and when he seen who it was he stopped fighting, so I tied him to a tree away from the other hosses. Then I throwed Donovan's shotgun onto the men and made 'em get up and come over to where Donovan was laying, and they was a bruised and battered gang. The way they taken on you'd of thought somebody had mistreated 'em.

I made 'em take Donovan's gunbelt offa him and about that time he come to and sot up, muttering something about a tree falling on him.

"Don't you remember me?" I says. "I'm Breckinridge Elkins."

"It all comes back," he muttered. "We gambled for Cap'n Kidd."

"Yeah," I says, "and you won, so now we gambles for him again. You sot the stakes before. This time I sets 'em. I matches these here britches I got on agen Cap'n Kidd, and yore saddle, bridle, gunbelt, pistol, pants, shirt, boots, spurs, and Stetson."

"Robbery!" he bellered. "Yo're a cussed bandit!"

"Shet up," I says, poking him in the midriff with his shotgun. "Squat! The rest of you, too."

"Ain't you goin' to let us do somethin' for Red?" they said. Red was laying on the other side of the thicket Cap'n Kidd had throwed him through, groaning loud and fervent.

"Let him lay for a spell," I says. "If he's dyin' they ain't nothin' we can do for him, and if he ain't, he'll keep till this game's over. Deal, Smoky, and deal from the top of the deck this time."

So Smoky dealt in fear and trembling, and I says to Donovan, "What you got?"

"A royal flush of diamonds, by God!" he says. "You cain't beat that!"

"A royal flush of hearts'll beat it, won't it, Smoky?" I says, and Smoky says: "Yuh-yuh-yeah! Yeah! Oh, yeah!"

"Well," I said, "I ain't looked at my hand yet, but I bet that's jest what I got. What you think?" I says, p'inting the shotgun at Donovan's upper teeth. "Don't you reckon I've got a royal flush in hearts?"

"It wouldn't surprise me a bit," says Donovan, turning pale.

"Then everybody's satisfied and they ain't no use in me showin' my hand," I says, throwing the cards back into the pack. "Shed them duds!"

He shed 'em without a word, and I let 'em take up Red, which had seven busted ribs, a dislocated arm and a busted laig, and they kinda folded him acrost his saddle and tied him in place. Then they pulled out without saying a word or looking back. They all looked purty wilted, and Donovan particularly looked very pecooliar in the blanket he had wropped around his middle. If he'd had a feather in his hair he'd of made a lovely Piute, as I told him. But he didn't seem to appreciate the remark. Some men just naturally ain't got no sense of humor.

They headed east, and as soon as they was out of sight, I put the saddle and bridle I'd won onto Cap'n Kidd and getting the bit in his mouth was about like rassling a mountain tornado. But I done it, and then I put on the riggins I'd won. The boots was too small and the shirt fit a mite too snug in the shoulders, but I sure felt elegant, nevertheless, and stalked up and down admiring myself and wishing Glory McGraw could see me then.

I cached my old saddle, belt and pistol in a holler tree, aiming to send my younger brother Bill back after 'em. He could have 'em, along with Alexander. I was going back to Bear Creek in style, by golly!

With a joyful whoop I swung onto Cap'n Kidd, headed him west and tickled his flanks with my spurs – them trappers in the mountains which later reported having seen a blue streak traveling westwardly so fast they didn't have time to tell what it was, and was laughed at and accused of being drunk, was did a injustice. What they seen was me and Cap'n Kidd going to Bear Creek. He run fifty miles before he even pulled up for breath.

I ain't going to tell how long it took Cap'n Kidd to cover the distance to Bear Creek. Nobody wouldn't believe me. But as I come up the trail a few miles from my home cabin, I heard a hoss galloping and Glory McGraw bust into view. She looked pale and scairt, and when she seen me she give a kind of a holler and pulled up her hoss so quick it went back onto its haunches.

"Breckinridge!" she gasped. "I jest heard from yore folks that yore mule come home without you, and I was just startin' out to look for – oh!" says she, noticing my hoss and elegant riggings for the first time. She kind of froze up, and said stiffly, "Well, Mister Elkins, I see yo're back home again."

"And you sees me rigged up in store-bought clothes and ridin' the best hoss in the Humbolts, too, I reckon," I said. "I hope you'll excuse me, Miss McGraw. I'm callin' on Ellen Reynolds as soon as I've let my folks know I'm home safe. Good day!"

"Don't let me detain you!" she flared, but after I'd rode on past she hollered, "Breckinridge Elkins, I hate you!"

"I know that," I said bitterly; "they warn't no use in tellin' me again – "

But she was gone, riding lickety-split off through the woods toward her home cabin and I rode on for mine, thinking to myself what curious critters gals was anyway.

Guns of the Mountains

This business begun with Uncle Garfield Elkins coming up from Texas to visit us. Between Grizzly Run and Chawed Ear the stage got held up by some masked bandits, and Uncle Garfield, never being able to forget that he was a gunfighting fool thirty or forty years ago, pulled his old cap-and-ball instead of putting up his hands like he was advised to. For some reason, instead of blowing out his light, they merely busted him over the head with a .45 barrel, and when he come to he was rattling on his way toward Chawed Ear with the other passengers, minus his money and watch.

It was his watch what caused the trouble. That there timepiece had been his grandpap's, and Uncle Garfield sot more store by it than he did all his kin folks.

When he arriv up in the Humbolt mountains where our cabin was, he imejitly let into howling his woes to the stars like a wolf with the bellyache. And from then on we heered nothing but that watch. I'd saw it and thunk very little of it. It was big as my fist, and wound up with a key which Uncle Garfield was always losing and looking for. But it was solid gold, and he called it a hairloom, whatever them things is. And he nigh driv the family crazy.

"A passle of big hulks like you-all settin' around and lettin' a old man get robbed of all his property," he would say bitterly. "When I was a young buck, if'n my uncle had been abused that way, I'd of took the trail and never slept nor et till I brung back his watch and the scalp of the skunk which stole it. Men now days – " And so on and so on, till I felt like drownding the old jassack in a barrel of corn licker.

Finally Pap says to me, combing his beard with his fingers; "Breckinridge," says he, "I've endured Uncle Garfield's bellyachin' all I aim to. I want you to go look for his cussed watch, and don't come back without it."

"How'm I goin' to know where to look?" I protested, aghast. "The feller which got it may be in Californy or Mexico by now."

"I realizes the difficulties," says Pap. "But if Uncle Garfield knows somebody is out lookin' for his dern timepiece, maybe he'll give the rest of us some peace. You git goin', and if you can't find that watch, don't come back till after Uncle Garfield has went home."

"How long is he goin' to stay?" I demanded.

"Well," said Pap, "Uncle Garfield's visits allus lasts a year, at least."

At this I bust into profanity.

I said, "I got to stay away from home a year? Dang it, Pap, Jim Braxton'll steal Ellen Reynolds away from me whilst I'm gone. I been courtin' that girl till I'm ready to fall dead. I done licked her old man three times, and now, just when I got her lookin' my way, you tells me I got to up and leave her for a year for that dern Jim Braxton to have no competition with."

"You got to choose between Ellen Reynolds, and yore own flesh and blood," said Pap. "I'm darned if I'll listen to Uncle Garfield's squawks any longer. You make yore own choice – but if you don't choose to do what I asks you to, I'll fill yore hide with buckshot every time I see you from now on."

Well, the result was that I was presently riding morosely away from home and Ellen Reynolds, and in the general direction of where Uncle Garfield's blasted watch might possibly be.

I passed by the Braxton cabin with the intention of dropping Jim a warning about his actions whilst I was gone, but he wasn't there. So I issued a general defiance to the family by slinging a .45 slug through the winder which knocked a cob pipe outa Old Man Braxton's mouth. That soothed me a little, but I knowed very well that Jim would make a beeline for the Reynolds' cabin the second I was out of sight. I could just see him gorging on Ellen's bear meat and honey, and bragging on hisself. I hoped Ellen would notice the difference between a loudmouthed boaster like him, and a quiet, modest young man like me, which never bragged, though admittedly the biggest man and the best fighter in the Humbolts.

I hoped to meet Jim somewhere in the woods as I rode down the trail, for I was intending to do something to kinda impede his courting while I was gone, like breaking his leg, or something, but luck wasn't with me.

I headed in the general direction of Chawed Ear, and the next day seen me riding in gloomy grandeur through a country quite some distance from Ellen Reynolds.

Pap always said my curiosity would be the ruination of me some day, but I never could listen to guns popping up in the mountains without wanting to find out who was killing who. So that morning, when I heard the rifles talking off amongst the trees, I turned Cap'n Kidd aside and left the trail and rode in the direction of the noise.

A dim path wound up through the big boulders and bushes, and the shooting kept getting louder. Purty soon I come out into a glade, and just as I did, *bam!* somebody let go at me from the bushes and a .45–70 slug cut both my bridle reins nearly in half. I instantly returned the shot with my .45, getting just a glimpse of something in the brush, and a man let out a squall and jumped out into the open, wringing his hands. My bullet had hit the lock of his Winchester and mighty nigh jarred his hands off him.

"Cease that ungodly noise," I said sternly, p'inting my .45 at his bay winder, "and tell me how come you waylays innercent travelers."

He quit working his fingers and moaning, and he said, "I thought you was Joel Cairn, the outlaw. You're about his size."

"Well, I ain't," I said. "I'm Breckinridge Elkins, from the Humbolts. I was just ridin' over to learn what all the shootin' was about."

The guns was firing in the trees behind the fellow, and somebody yelled what was the matter.

"Ain't nothin' the matter," he hollered back. "Just a misunderstandin'." And he said to me, "I'm glad to see you, Elkins. We need a man like you. I'm Sheriff Dick Hopkins, from Grizzly Run."

"Where at's your star?" I inquired.

"I lost it in the bresh," he said. "Me and my deputies have been chasin' Tarantula Bixby and his gang for a day and a night, and we got 'em cornered over there in a old deserted cabin in a holler. The boys is shootin' at 'em now. I heard you comin' up the trail and snuck over to see who it is. Just as I said, I thought you was Cairn. Come on with me. You can help us."

"I ain't no deputy," I said. "I got nothin' against Tranchler Bixby."

"Well, you want to uphold the law, don't you?" he said.

"Naw," I said.

"Well, gee whiz!" he wailed. "If you ain't a hell of a citizen! The country's goin' to the dogs. What chance has a honest man got?"

"Aw, shut up," I said. "I'll go over and see the fun, anyhow."

So he picked up his gun, and I tied Cap'n Kidd, and follered the sheriff through the trees till we come to some rocks, and there was four men laying behind them rocks and shooting down into a hollow. The hill sloped away mighty steep into a small basin that was just like a bowl, with a rim of slopes all around. In the middle of this bowl there was a cabin and puffs of smoke was coming from the cracks between the logs.

The men behind the rocks looked at me in surprise, and one of them said, "What the hell – ?"

But the sheriff scowled at them and said, "Boys, this here is Breck Elkins. I done told him already about us bein' a posse from Grizzly Run, and about how we got Tarantula Bixby and two of his cutthroats trapped in that there cabin."

One of the deputies bust into a guffaw and Hopkins glared at him and said: "What you laughin' about, you spotted hyener?"

"I swallered my tobaccer and that allus gives me the hystericals," mumbled the deputy, looking the other way.

"Hold up your right hand, Elkins," requested Hopkins, so I done so, wondering what for, and he said, "Does you swear to tell the truth, the whole truth and nothing but the truth, e pluribus unum, anno dominecker, to wit in status quo?"

"What the hell are you talkin' about?" I demanded.

"Them which God has j'ined asunder let no man put together," said Hopkins. "Whatever you say will be used against you and the Lord have mercy on yore soul. That means you're a deputy. I just swore you in."

"Go set on a tack," I snorted disgustedly. "Go catch your own thieves. And don't look at me like that. I might bend a gun over your skull."

"But Elkins," pleaded Hopkins, "with yore help we can catch them rats easy. All you got to do is lay up here behind this big rock and shoot at the cabin and keep 'em occupied till we can sneak around and rush 'em from the rear. See, the bresh comes down purty close to the foot of the slope on the other side, and gives us cover. We can do it easy, with somebody keepin' their attention over here. I'll give you part of the reward."

"I don't want no derned blood money," I said, backing away. "And besides – *ow!*"

I'd absent-mindedly backed out from behind the big rock where I'd been standing, and a .30–30 slug burned its way acrost the seat of my britches.

"Dern them murderers!" I bellered, seeing red. "Gimme a rifle! I'll learn 'em to shoot a man behind his back. Gwan, take 'em in the rear. I'll keep 'em busy."

"Good boy!" said Hopkins. "You'll get plenty for this!"

It sounded like somebody was snickering to theirselves as they snuck away, but I give no heed. I squinted cautiously around the big boulder, and begun sniping at the cabin. All I could see to shoot at was the puffs of smoke which marked the cracks they was shooting through, but from the cussing and yelling which begun to float up from the shack, I must have throwed some lead mighty close to them.

They kept shooting back, and the bullets splashed and buzzed on the rocks, and I kept looking at the further slope for some sign of Sheriff Hopkins and the posse. But all I heard was a sound of horses galloping away toward the west. I wondered who it could be, and I kept expecting the posse to rush down the opposite slope and take them desperadoes in the rear, and whilst I was craning my neck around a corner of the boulder – *whang!* A bullet smashed into the rock a few inches from my face and a sliver of stone took a notch out of my ear. I don't know of nothing that makes me madder'n to get shot in the ear.

I seen red and didn't even shoot back. A mere rifle was too paltry to satisfy me. Suddenly I realized that the big boulder in front of me was just poised on the slope, its underside partly embedded in the earth. I throwed down my rifle and bent my knees and spread my arms and gripped it.

I shook the sweat and blood outa my eyes, and bellered so them in the hollow could hear me, "I'm givin' you-all a chance to surrender! Come out, your hands up!"

They give loud and sarcastic jeers, and I yelled, "All right, you ringtailed jackasses! If you gets squashed like a pancake, it's your own fault. *Here she comes!*"

And I heaved with all I had. The veins stood out on my temples, my feet sunk into the ground, but the earth bulged and cracked all around the big rock, rivulets of dirt begun to trickle down, and the big boulder groaned, give way and lurched over.

A dumfounded yell riz from the cabin. I leaped behind a bush, but the outlaws was too surprised to shoot at me. That enormous boulder was tumbling down the hill, crushing bushes flat and gathering speed as it rolled. And the cabin was right in its path.

Wild yells bust the air, the door was throwed violently open, and a man hove into view. Just as he started out of the door I let *bam* at him and he howled and ducked back just like anybody will when a .45–90 slug knocks their hat off. The next instant that thundering boulder hit the cabin. Smash! It knocked it sidewise like a ten pin and caved in the wall, and the whole structure collapsed in a cloud of dust and bark and splinters.

I run down the slope, and from the yells which issued from under the ruins, I knowed they hadn't all been killed.

"Does you-all surrender?" I roared.

"Yes, dern it!" they squalled. "Get us out from under this landslide!"

"Throw out yore guns," I ordered.

"How in hell can we throw anything?" they hollered wrathfully. "We're pinned down by a ton of rocks and boards and we're bein' squoze to death. Help, murder!"

"Aw, shut up," I said. "You don't hear *me* carryin' on in no such hysterical way, does you?"

Well, they moaned and complained, and I sot to work dragging the ruins off them, which wasn't no great task. Purty soon I seen a booted leg and I laid hold of it and dragged out the critter it was fastened to, and he looked more done up than what my brother Bill did that time he rassled a mountain lion for a bet. I took his pistol out of his belt, and laid him down on the ground and got the others out. There was three, altogether, and I disarm 'em and laid 'em out in a row.

Their clothes was nearly tore off, and they was bruised and scratched, and had splinters in their hair, but they wasn't hurt permanent. They sot up and felt of theirselves, and one of 'em said, "This here is the first earthquake I ever seen in this country."

"T'warn't no earthquake," said another'n. "It was a avalanche."

"Listen here, Joe Partland," said the first'n, grinding his teeth, "I says it was a earthquake, and I ain't the man to be called a liar – "

"Oh, you ain't?" said the other'n, bristling up. "Well, lemme tell you somethin', Frank Jackson – "

"This ain't no time for such argyments," I admonished 'em sternly. "As for that there rock, I rolled that at you myself."

They gaped at me. "Who are you?" said one of 'em, mopping the blood offa his ear.

"Never mind," I said. "You see this here Winchester? Well, you all set still and rest yourselves. Soon as the sheriff gets here, I'm goin' to hand you over to him."

His mouth fell open. "Sheriff?" he said, dumb-like. "What sheriff?"

"Dick Hopkins, from Grizzly Run," I said.

"Why, you derned fool!" he screamed, scrambling up.

"Set down!" I roared, shoving my rifle barrel at him, and he sank back, all white and shaking. He could hardly talk.

"Listen to me!" he gasped. "I'm Dick Hopkins! I'm sheriff of Grizzly Run! These men are my deputies."

"Yeah?" I said sarcastically. "And who was the fellows shootin' at you from the brush?"

"Tarantula Bixby and his gang," he said. "We was follerin' 'em when they jumped us, and bein' outnumbered and surprised, we took cover in that old hut. They robbed the Grizzly Run bank day before yesterday. And now they'll be gettin' further away every minute! Oh, Judas J. Iscariot! Of all the dumb, boneheaded jackasses – "

"Heh! heh! heh!" I said cynically. "You must think I ain't got no sense. If you're the sheriff, where at's your star?"

"It was on my suspenders," he said despairingly. "When you hauled me out by the laig my suspenders caught on somethin' and tore off. If you'll lemme look amongst them ruins – "

"You set still," I commanded. "You can't fool me. You're Tranchler Bixby yourself. Sheriff Hopkins told me so. Him and the posse will be here in a little while. Set still and shut up."

We stayed there, and the fellow which claimed to be the sheriff moaned and pulled his hair and shed a few tears, and the other fellows tried to convince me they was deputies till I got tired of their gab and told 'em to shut up or I'd bend my Winchester over their heads. I wondered why Hopkins and them didn't come, and I begun to get nervous, and all to once the fellow which said he was the sheriff give a yell that startled me so I jumped and nearly shot him. He had something in his hand and was waving it around.

"See here?" His voice cracked he hollered so loud. "I found it! It must have fell down into my shirt when my suspenders busted! Look at it, you dern mountain grizzly!"

I looked and my flesh crawled. It was a shiny silver star.

"Hopkins said he lost his'n," I said weakly. "Maybe you found it in the brush."

"You know better!" he bellered. "You're one of Bixby's men. You was sent to hold us here while Tarantula and the rest made their getaway. You'll get ninety years for this!"

I turned cold all over as I remembered them horses I heard galloping. I'd been fooled! This *was* the sheriff! That potbellied thug which shot at me had been Bixby hisself! And whilst I held up the real sheriff and his posse, them outlaws was riding out of the country.

Now wasn't that a caution?

"You better gimme that gun and surrender," opined Hopkins. "Maybe if you do they won't hang you."

"Set still!" I snarled. "I'm the biggest sap that ever straddled a mustang, but even saps has their feelin's. You ain't goin' to put me behind no bars. I'm goin' up this slope, but I'll be watchin' you. I've throwed your guns over there in the brush. If any of you makes a move toward 'em, I'll put a harp in his hand."

Nobody craved a harp.

They set up a chant of hate as I backed away, but they sot still. I went up the slope backward till I hit the rim, and then I turned and ducked into the brush and run. I heard 'em cussing somethin' awful down in the hollow, but I didn't pause. I come to where I'd left Cap'n Kidd, and a forked him and rode, thankful them outlaws had been in too big a hurry to steal him. I throwed away the rifle they give me, and headed west.

I aimed to cross Wild River at Ghost Canyon, and head into the uninhabited mountain region beyond there. I figgered I could dodge a posse indefinite once I got there. I pushed Cap'n Kidd hard, cussing my reins which had been notched by Bixby's bullet. I didn't have time to fix 'em, and Cap'n Kidd was a iron-jawed outlaw.

He was sweating plenty when I finally hove in sight of the place I was heading for. As I topped the canyon's crest before I dipped down to the crossing, I glanced back. They was a high notch in the hills a mile or so behind me. And as I looked three horsemen was etched in that notch, against the sky behind 'em. I cussed fervently. Why hadn't I had sense enough to know Hopkins and his men was bound to have horses tied somewheres near? They'd got their mounts and follered me, figgering I'd aim for the country beyond Wild River. It was about the only place I could go.

Not wanting no running fight with no sheriff's posse, I raced recklessly down the sloping canyon wall, busted out of the bushes – and stopped short. Wild River was on the rampage – bank full in the narrow channel and boiling and foaming. Been a big rain somewhere away up on the head, and the horse wasn't never foaled which could swum it.

They wasn't but one thing to do, and I done it. I wheeled Cap'n Kidd and headed up the canyon. Five miles up the river there was another crossing, with a bridge – if it hadn't been washed away.

Cap'n Kidd had his second wind and we was going lickety-split, when suddenly I heard a noise ahead of us, above the roar of the river and the thunder of his hoofs on the rocky canyon floor. We was approaching a bend in the gorge where a low ridge run out from the canyon wall, and beyond that ridge I heard guns banging. I heaved back on the reins – and both of 'em snapped in two!

Cap'n Kidd instantly clamped his teeth on the bit and bolted, like he always done when anything out of the ordinary happened. He headed straight for the bushes at the end of the ridge, and I leaned forward and tried to get hold of the bit rings with my fingers. But all I done was swerve him from his course. Instead of following the canyon bed on around the end of the ridge, he went right over the rise, which sloped on that side. It didn't slope on t'other side; it fell away abrupt. I had a fleeting glimpse of five men crouching amongst the bushes on the canyon floor with guns in their hands. They looked up – and Cap'n Kidd braced his legs and slid to a halt at the lip of the low bluff and simultaneously bogged his head and throwed me heels over head down amongst 'em.

My boot heel landed on somebody's head, and the spur knocked him cold and blame near scalped him. That partly bust my fall, and it was further cushioned by another fellow which I landed on in a sitting position, and which took no further interest in the proceedings. The other three fell on me with loud brutal yells, and I reached for my .45 and found to my humiliation that it had fell out of my scabbard when I was throwed.

So I riz with a rock in my hand and bounced it off a the head of a fellow which was fixing to shoot me, and he dropped his pistol and fell on top of it. At this juncture one of the survivors put a buffalo gun to his shoulder and sighted, then evidently fearing he would hit his companion which was carving at me on the other side with a bowie knife, he reversed it and run in swinging it like a club.

The man with the knife got in a slash across my ribs and I then hit him on the chin which was how his jawbone got broke in four places. Meanwhile the other'n swung at me with his rifle, but missed my head and broke the stock off across my shoulder. Irritated at his persistency in trying to brain me with the barrel, I laid hands on him and throwed him head-on against the bluff, which is when he got his fractured skull and concussion of the brain, I reckon.

I then shook the sweat from my eyes, and glaring down, rekernized the remains as Bixby and his gang. I might have knew they'd head for the wild country across the river, same as me. Only place they could go.

Just then, however, a clump of bushes parted, near the river bank, and a big black-bearded man riz up from behind a dead horse. He had a six-shooter in his hand and he approached me cautiously.

"Who're you?" he demanded. "Where'd you come from?"

"I'm Breckinridge Elkins," I answered, mopping the blood offa my shirt. "What is this here business, anyway?"

"I was settin' here peaceable waitin' for the river to go down so I could cross," he said, "when up rode these yeggs and started shootin'. I'm a honest citizen – "

"You're a liar," I said with my usual diplomacy. "You're Joel Cairn, the wust outlaw in the hills. I seen your pitcher in the post office at Chawed Ear."

With that he p'inted his .45 at me, and his beard bristled like the whiskers of a old timber wolf.

"So you know me, hey?" he said. "Well, what you goin' to do about it, hey? Want to colleck the reward money, hey?"

"Naw, I don't," I said. "I'm a outlaw myself, now. I just run foul of the law account of these skunks. They's a posse right behind me."

"They is?" he snarled. "Why'ntyousayso? Here, le's catch these fellers' horses and light out. Cheap skates! They claims I double-crossed 'em in the matter of a stagecoach holdup we pulled together recently. I been avoidin' 'em 'cause I'm a peaceful man by nater, but they rode onto me onexpected today. They shot my horse first crack; we been tradin' lead for more'n a hour without doin' much damage, but they'd got me eventually, I reckon. Come on. We'll pull out together."

"No, we won't," I said. "I'm a outlaw by force of circumstances, but I ain't no murderin' bandit."

"Purty particular of yore comperny, ain'tcha?" he sneered. "Well, anyways, help me catch me a horse. Yore's is still up there on that bluff. The day's still young – "

He pulled out a big gold watch and looked at it; it was one which wound with a key.

I jumped like I was shot. "Where'd you get that watch?" I hollered.

He jerked up his head kinda startled, and said, "My grandpap gimme it. Why?"

"You're a liar!" I bellered. "You took that off'n my Uncle Garfield. *Gimme that watch!*"

"Are you crazy?" he yelled, going white under his whiskers. I plunged for him, seeing red, and he let *bang!* and I got it in the left thigh. Before he could shoot again I was on top of him, and knocked the gun up. It banged but the bullet went singing up over the bluff and Cap'n Kidd squealed and started changing ends. The pistol flew outa Cairn's hand and he hit me vi'lently on the nose which made me see stars. So I hit him in the belly and he grunted and doubled up; and come up with a knife out of his boot which he cut me across the boozum with, also in the arm and shoulder and kicked me in the groin. So I swung him clear of the ground and throwed him headfirst and jumped on him with both feet. And that settled him.

I picked up the watch where it had fell, and staggered over to the cliff, spurting blood at every step like a stuck hawg.

"At last my search is at a end!" I panted. "I can go back to Ellen Reynolds who patiently awaits the return of her hero – "

It was at this instant that Cap'n Kidd, which had been stung by Cairn's wild shot and was trying to buck off his saddle, bucked hisself off the bluff. He fell on me. . . .

The first thing I heard was bells ringing, and then they turned to horses galloping. I set up and wiped off the blood which was running into my eyes from where Cap'n Kidd's left hind hoof had split my scalp. And I seen Sheriff Hopkins, Jackson and Partland come tearing around the ridge. I tried to get up and run, but my right leg wouldn't work. I reached for my gun and it still wasn't there. I was trapped.

"Look there!" yelled Hopkins, wild-eyed. "That's Bixby on the ground – and all his gang. And ye gods, there's Joel Cairn! What is this, anyhow? It looks like a battlefield! What's that settin' there? He's so bloody I can't recognize him!"

"It's the hillbilly!" yelped Jackson. "Don't move or I'll shoot 'cha!"

"I already been shot," I snarled. "Gwan – do yore wust. Fate is against me."

They dismounted and stared in awe.

"Count the dead, boys," said Hopkins in a still, small voice.

"Aw," said Partland, "ain't none of 'em dead, but they'll never be the same men again. Look! Bixby's comin' to! Who done this, Bixby?"

Bixby cast a wabbly eye about till he spied me, and then he moaned and shriveled up.

"He done it!" he waited. "He trailed us down like a bloodhound and jumped on us from behind! He tried to scalp me! He ain't human!" And he bust into tears.

They looked at me, and all took off their hats.

"Elkins," said Hopkins in a tone of reverence, "I see it all now. They fooled you into thinkin' they was the posse and us the outlaws, didn't they? And when you realized the truth, you hunted 'em down, didn't you? And cleaned 'em out single handed, and Joel Cairn, too, didn't you?"

"Well," I said groggily, "the truth is – "

"We understand," Hopkins soothed. "You mountain men is all modest. Hey, boys, tie up them outlaws whilst I look at Elkins' wounds."

"If you'll catch my horse," I said, "I got to be ridin' back – "

"Gee whiz, man!" he said, "you ain't in no shape to ride a horse! Do you know you got four busted ribs and a broke arm, and one leg broke and a bullet in the other'n, to say nothin' of bein' slashed to ribbons? We'll rig up a litter for you. What's that you got in your good hand?"

I suddenly remembered Uncle Garfield's watch which I'd kept clutched in a death grip. I stared at what I held in my hand; and I fell back with a low moan. All I had in my hand was a bunch of busted metal and broken wheels and springs, bent and smashed plumb beyond recognition.

"Grab him!" yelled Hopkins. "He's fainted!"

"Plant me under a pine tree, boys," I murmured weakly; "just carve on my tombstone: 'He fit a good fight but Fate dealt him the joker.' "

A few days later a melancholy procession wound its way up the trail into the Humbolts. I was packed on a litter. I told 'em I wanted to see Ellen Reynolds before I died, and to show Uncle Garfield the rooins of the watch, so he'd know I done my duty as I seen it.

As we approached the locality where my home cabin stood, who should meet us but Jim Braxton, which tried to conceal his pleasure when I told him in a weak voice that I was a dying man. He was all dressed up in new buckskins and his exuberance was plumb disgustful to a man in my condition.

"Too bad," he said. "Too bad, Breckinridge. I hoped to meet you, but not like this, of course. Yore pap told me to tell you if I seen you about yore Uncle Garfield's watch. He thought I might run into you on your way to Chawed Ear to git a license – "

"Hey?" I said, pricking up my ears.

"Yeah, me and Ellen Reynolds is goin' to git married. Well, as I started to say, seems like one of them bandits which robbed the stage was a fellow whose dad was a friend of yore Uncle Garfield's back in Texas. He reckernized the name in the watch and sent it back, and it got here the day after you left – "

They say it was jealousy which made me rise up on my litter and fracture Jim Braxton's jawbone. I denies that. I stoops to no such petty practices. What impelled me was family conventions. I couldn't hit Uncle Garfield – I had to hit somebody – and Jim Braxton just happened to be the nearest one to me.

The Peaceful Pilgrim

Gettin' shot at by strangers and relatives is too plumb common to bother about, and I don't generally pay no attention to it. But it's kind of irritating to git shot at by yore best friend, even when yo're as mild and gentle-natured as what I am. But I reckon I better explain. I'd been way up nigh the Oregon line, and was headin' home when I happened to pass through the mining camp of Moose Jaw, which was sot right in the middle of a passle of mountains nigh as wild and big as the Humbolts. I was takin' me a drink at the bar of the Lazy Elk Saloon and Hotel, when the barkeep says, after studying me a spell, he says, "You must be Breckinridge Elkins, of Bear Creek."

I give the matter due consideration, and 'lowed as how I was.

"How come you knowed me?" I inquired suspiciously, because I hadn't never been in Moose Jaw before, and he says, "Well, I've often heard tell of Breckinridge Elkins, and when I seen you, I figgered you must be him, because I don't see how they can be two men in the world that big. By the way, they's a friend of yore'n upstairs – Blaze Carson. He come up here from the southern part of the state, and I've often heered him brag about knowin' you personal. He's upstairs now, fourth door from the stair – head, on the right."

Well, I remembered Blaze. He warn't a Bear Creek man; he was from War Paint, but I didn't hold that agen him. He was kind of addle-headed, but I don't expeck everybody to be smart like me.

So I went upstairs and knocked on the door, and bam! went a gun inside and a .45 slug ripped through the door and taken a nick out of my ear. As I remarked before, it irritates me to be shot at by a man which has no reason to shoot at me, and my patience is quickly exhausted. So, without waiting for any more exhibitions of hospitality, I give a exasperated beller and knocked the door off its hinges and busted into the room over its rooins.

45

For a second I didn't see nobody, but then I heard a kind of gurgle going on, and happened to remember that the door seemed kind of squshy when I tromped over it, so I knowed that whichever was in the room had got pinned under the door when I knocked it down.

So I reched under it with one hand and got him by the collar and hauled him out, and shore enough it was Blaze Carson. He was limp as a rag and glassy-eyed, and pale, and wild-looking, and was still vaguely trying to shoot me with his six-shooter when I taken it away from him.

"What the hell is the matter with you?" I demanded sternly, dangling him by the collar with one hand, whilst shaking him till his teeth rattled. "Air you got deliritus trimmins, or what, shootin' at yore friends through the door?"

"Lemme down, Breck," he gasped. "I didn't know it was you. I thought it was Lobo Ferguson comin' after my gold."

So I sot him down and he grabbed a jug of licker and poured hisself a dram and his hand shaken so he spilled half of it down his neck when he tried to drink.

"Well?" I demanded. "Ain't you goin' to offer me a snort, dern it?"

"Excuse me, Breckinridge," he apolergized. "I'm so dern jumpy I dunno what I'm doin'. I been livin' in this here room for a week, too scairt to stick my head out. You see them buckskin pokes?" says he, p'inting at some bags on the bed. "Them is bustin' full of nuggets. I been minin' up the Gulch for over a year now, and I got myself a neat fortune in them bags. But it ain't doin' me no good."

"What you mean?" I demanded.

"These mountains is full of outlaws," says he. "They robs and murders every man which tries to take his gold out. The stagecoach has been stuck up so often nobody sends their dust out onto it no more. When a man makes his pile, he watches his chance and sneaks out through the mountains at night, with his gold on pack-mules. Sometimes he makes it and sometimes he don't. That's what I aimed to do. But them outlaws has got spies all over the camp. I know they got me spotted. I been afeared to make my break, and afeared if I didn't, they'd git impatient and come right into camp and cut my throat. That's what I thought when I heard you knock. Lobo Ferguson's the big chief of 'em. I been squattin' over this here gold with my pistol night and day, makin' the barkeep bring my licker and grub up to me. I'm dern near loco!"

And he shaken like he had the aggers, and shivered and cussed kind of whimpery, and taken another dram, and cocked his pistol and sot there shakin' like he'd saw a ghost or two.

"How'd you go if you snuck out?" I demanded.

"Up the ravine south of the camp and hit the old Injun path that winds up through Scalplock Pass," says he. "Then I'd circle wide down to Wahpeton and grab the stagecoach there. I'm safe, onst I git to Wahpeton."

"I'll take yore gold out for you," I says.

"But them outlaws'll kill you!" says he.

"Naw, they won't," I says. "First place, they won't know I got the gold. Second place, I'll bust their heads if they start anything with me in the first place. Is this all the gold they is?" I ast.

"Ain't it enough?" says he. "My hoss and pack-mule is in the stables behind the saloon – "

"I don't need no pack-mule," I says. "Cap'n Kidd can pack that easy."

"And you, too?" he ast.

"You ought to know Cap'n Kidd well enough not to have to ast no sech dern fool question as that there," I said irritably. "Wait till I git my saddlebags."

Cap'n Kidd was getting fed out in the corral next to the hotel. I went out there and got my saddlebags, which is a lot bigger'n most, because my plunder has to be made to fit my size. They're made outa three-ply elkskin, stitched with rawhide thongs, and a wildcat couldn't claw his way out of 'em.

Well, I noticed quite a bunch of men standing around the corral looking at Cap'n Kidd, but thought nothing of it, because he is a hoss which naturally attracts attention.

But whilst I was getting my saddlebags, a long lanky cuss with long yaller whiskers come up and said, "Is that yore hoss in the corral?"

"If he ain't he ain't nobody's," I said.

"Well, he looks a lot like a hoss that was stole off my ranch six months ago," he said, and I seen ten or fifteen hard-looking hombres gatherin' around us. I laid down my saddlebags sudden-like and started to pull my guns, when it occurred to me that if I had a fight there, I might git arrested and it would interfere with me taking out Blaze's gold.

If that there is yore hoss," I said, "you ought to be able to lead him out of that there corral."

"Shore I can," he says with a oath. "And what's more, I aim to."

"That's the stuff, Bill," somebody says. "Don't let the big hillbilly tromple on yore rights!"

But I noticed some men in the crowd looked like they didn't like it, but was scairt to say anything.

"All right," I says to Bill, "here's a lariat. Climb over that fence and go and put it on that hoss, and he's yore'n."

He looked at me suspiciously, but he taken the rope and clumb the fence and started towards Cap'n Kidd which was chawing on a block of hay in the middle of the corral, and Cap'n Kidd threw up his head and laid back his ears and showed his teeth. Bill stopped sudden and turned pale, and said, "I – I don't believe that there is my hoss, after all!"

"Put that lariat on him!" I roared, pulling my right-hand gun. "You say he's yore'n; I say he's mine. One of us is a liar and a hoss thief, and I aim to prove which'n it is! Gwan, before I ventilates yore yaller system with hot lead!"

He looked at me and he looked at Cap'n Kidd, and he turned bright green all over. He looked agen at my .45 which I now had cocked and p'inted at his long neck, which his Adam's apple was going up and down like a monkey on a pole, and he begun to aidge towards Cap'n Kidd again, holding the rope behind him and sticking out one hand.

"Whoa, boy," he says kind of shudderingly. "Whoa – good old feller – whoa, boy – ow!"

He let out a awful howl as Cap'n Kidd made a snap and bit a chunk out of his hide. He turned to run but Cap'n Kidd wheeled and let fly both heels which caught Bill in the seat of the britches, and his shriek of despair was horrible to hear as he went headfirst through the corral fence into a hoss trough on the other side. From this he ariz dripping water, blood and profanity. He shook a quivering fist at me and croaked, "You derned murderer! I'll have yore life for this."

"I don't hold no conversation with hoss thieves," I snorted, and picked up my saddlebags and stalked through the crowd which give back in a hurry on each side to let me through. And I noticed when I tromped on some fellers' toes, they done their cussing under their breath, and pertended to be choking on their terbaccer when I glared back at 'em. Folks oughta keep their derned hoofs out of the way if they don't want to be stepped on.

I taken the saddlebags up to Blaze's room, and told him about Bill, thinking he'd be amoosed, but he got a case of aggers agen, and said, "That was one of Ferguson's men! He meant to take yore hoss. It's a old trick, and honest folks don't dare interfere. Now they got you spotted! You better wait till night, at least."

"Time, tide and a Elkins waits for no man!" I snorted, dumping the gold into the saddlebags. "If that yaller-whiskered coyote wants any trouble, he can git a bellyful. Tomorrer you git on the stagecoach and hit for Wahpeton. If I ain't there, wait for me. I ought to pull in a day or so after you git there, anyway. And don't worry about yore gold. It'll be plumb safe in my saddlebags."

"Don't yell so loud," begged Blaze. "The derned camp's full of spies, and some of 'em may be downstairs."

"I warn't speakin' above a whisper," I said indignantly.

"That bull's beller may pass for a whisper on Bear Creek," says he, wiping off the perspiration, "but I bet they can hear it from one end of the Gulch to the other, at least."

It's a pitable sight to see a man with a case of the scairts; I shaken hands with him and left him pouring red licker down his gullet like so much water, and I swung the saddlebags over my shoulder and went downstairs, and the barkeep leaned over the bar and whispered to me, "Look out for Bill Price! He was in here a minute ago, lookin' for trouble. He pulled out just before you come down, but he won't be forgettin' what yore hoss done to him!"

"Not when he tries to sit down, he won't!" I agreed, and went on out to the corral, and they was a crowd of men watching Cap'n Kidd eat his hay, and one of 'em seen me and hollered, "Hey, boys, here comes the giant! He's goin' to saddle that man-eatin' monster! Hey, Tom! Tell the boys at the bar!"

And here come a whole passel of fellers running out of all the saloons, and they lined the corral fence solid, and started laying bets whether I'd git the saddle on Cap'n Kidd, or git my brains kicked out. I thought miners must all be crazy; they ought to knowed I rode into camp on him and was able to saddle my own hoss.

Well, I saddled him, and throwed on the saddlebags, and clumb aboard, and he pitched about ten jumps like he always does when I first fork him – t'war't nothing, but them miners hollered like wild Injuns. And when he accidentally bucked hisself and me through the fence and knocked down a section of it along with about fifteen men which was setting on the toprail, the way they howled you'd of thought something terrible had happened. Me and Cap'n Kidd don't generally bother about gates. We usually makes our own through whatever happens to be in front of us. But them miners is a weakly breed, because as I rode out of the town I seen the crowd dipping four or five of 'em into a hoss trough to bring 'em to, on account of Cap'n Kidd having accidentally stepped on 'em.

This trivial occurrence seemed to excite everybody so much nobody noticed me as I rode off, which suited me fine, because I am a modest man, shy and retiring by nature, which don't crave no publicity. I didn't see no sign of the feller they called Bill Price.

Well, I rode out of the Gulch and up the ravine to the south, and come out into the high-timbered country, and was casting around for the old Injun trail Blaze had told me about, when somebody said, "Hey!" I wheeled with both guns in my hands, and a long, lean, black-whiskered old cuss rode out of the bresh toward me.

"Who are you and what the hell you mean by hollerin' 'Hey!' at me?" I demanded. A Elkins is always perlite.

"Air you the man with the man-eatin' stallion?" he ast, and I says, "I dunno what yo're talkin' about. This here hoss is Cap'n Kidd, which I catched down in the Humbolt country, and a milder mannered critter never kicked the brains out of a mountain lion."

"He's the biggest hoss I ever see," he said. "Looks fast, though."

"Fast?" says I, with the pride a Elkins always takes in his hoss flesh. "Cap'n Kidd can outrun anything in this State, and carry me, and you, and all this here gold in these saddlebags whilst doing it." Then I shaken my head in disgust, because I hadn't meant to mention the gold, but I couldn't see no harm it would do.

"Well," he said, "you've made a enemy of Bill Price, one of Lobo

Ferguson's gunmen, and as pizenous a critter as ever wore boot leather. He come by here a few minutes ago, frothin' at the mouth, and swearin' to have yore heart's blood. He's headin' up into the mountains to round up forty or fifty of his gang and take yore sculp."

"Well, what about it?" I inquired, not impressed. Somebody is always wanting my life, and forty or fifty outlaws ain't no odds to a Elkins.

"They'll waylay you," he predicted. "Yo're a fine, upstandin' young man, which deserves a better fate'n to git dry-gulched by a passle of lowdown bandit varmints. I'm jest headin' for my cabin up in the hills. It's a right smart piece off the trail. Whyn't you come along with me and lay low till they've give up the search? They won't find you there."

"I ain't in the habit of hidin' from my enemies," I begun, when suddenly I remembered that there gold in my saddlebags. It was my duty to git it to Wahpeton. If I was to tangle with Ferguson's gang, they was just a slim chance that they might down me, shooting from the bresh, and run off with pore Blaze's hard-earned dough. It was hard to do, but I decided I'd avoid a battle till after I'd give Blaze his gold safe and sound. Then, I was determined, I'd come back and frail the daylights outa Lobo Ferguson for forcing me into this here humiliating position.

"Lead on!" I says. "Lead me to yore hermitage in the wildwood, out of the reach of the maddenin' crowd and Lobo Ferguson's bullets. But I imposes a sacred trust of secrecy onto you. Let the world never know that Breckinridge Elkins, the pride of Bear Creek, took to kiver to dodge a mangy passle of minin' country road-agents."

"My lips is sealed," says he. "Yore fatal secret is safe with Polecat Rixby. Foller me."

He led me through the bresh till we hit the old Injun trail, which warn't more'n a trace through the hills, and we pushed hard all the rest of the day, not seeing anybody coming or going.

"They'll be lookin' for you in Moose jaw," said the Polecat. "When they don't find you, they'll comb the hills. But they'll never find my cabin, even if they knowed you was hidin' there, which they don't."

Close to sundown we turned off the trail onto a still dimmer trace that led east, and wound amongst crags and boulders till a snake would of broke his back tryin' to foller it, and just before it got good and dark we come to a log bridge acrost a deep, narrer canyon. They was a river at the bottom of that there canyon, which was awful swift, and went roaring and foaming along betwixt rock walls a hundred feet high. But at one place the canyon wasn't only about seventy foot wide, and they'd felled a whopping big pine tree on one side so it fell acrost and made a bridge, and the top side was trimmed down flat so a hoss could walk acrost, though the average hoss wouldn't like it very much. Polecat's hoss was used to it, but he was scairt jest the same. But they ain't nothin' between Kingdom Come and Powder River that Cap'n Kidd's scairt of, except maybe me, and he walzed acrost that there tree like he was on a quartertrack.

The path wound through a lot of bresh on the other side, and so did we, and after awhile we come to a cabin built nigh the foot of a big cliff. It was on a kind of thick-timbered shelf, and the land fell away in a gradual slope to a breshy run, and they was a clear spring nigh the aidge of the bresh. It was a good place for a cabin.

They was a stone corral built up agen the foot of the cliff, and it looked to be a dern sight bigger'n Polecat oughta need for his one saddle hoss and the three pack hosses which was in there, but I have done learnt that there ain't no accounting for the way folks builds things. Polecat told me to turn Cap'n Kidd loose in the corral, but I knowed if I done that they would be one dead saddle hoss and three dead pack hosses in there before midnight, so I turned him loose to graze, knowing he wouldn't go far. Cap'n Kidd likes me too much to run off and leave me, regardless of the fact that he frequently tries to kill me.

By this time it was night, and Polecat said come in and he'd fix up a snack of supper. So we went in and he lit a candle and made coffee and fried bacon and sot out some beans and corn pone, and he taken a good look at me settin' there at the table all ready to fall to, and he fried up a lot more bacon and sot out more beans. He hadn't talked much all day, and now he was about as talkative as a clam with the lockjaw. He was jumpy, too, and nervous, and I decided he was scairt Lobo Ferguson might find him after all, and do vi'lence to him for hiding me. It's a dreary sight to see a grown man scairt of something. Being scairt must be some kind of a disease; I cain't figger it out no other way.

I was watching Polecat, even if I didn't seem to, because that's a habit us Bear Creek folks gits into; if we didn't watch each other awful close, we'd never live to git grown. So when he poured a lot of white-looking powder into my coffee out of a box on the shelf, he didn't think I seen him, but I did, and I noticed he didn't put none in his'n. But I didn't say nothing, because it ain't perlite to criticize a man's cooking when yo're his guest; if Polecat had some new-fangled way of making coffee t'warn't for me to object.

He sot the grub on the table and sot down opposite me, with his head down, and looking at me kinda furtive-like from under his brows, and I laid into the grub and et hearty.

"Yore coffee'll git cold," he said presently, and I remembered it, and emptied the cup at one gulp, and it was the best coffee I ever drunk.

"Ha!" says I, smacking my lips. "You ain't much shakes of a man to look at, Polecat, but you shore can b'ile coffee! Gimme another cup! What's the matter; you ain't eatin' hardly anything?"

"I ain't a very hearty eater," he mumbled. "You – you want some more coffee?"

So I drunk six more cups, but they didn't taste near as good as the first, and I knowed it was because he didn't put none of that white stuff in 'em, but I didn't say nothing because it wouldn't have been perlite.

After I'd cleaned up everything in sight, I said I'd help him wash the pans and things, but he said, kind of funny-like, "Let 'em go. I – we can do that – tomorrer. How – how do you feel?"

"I feel fine," I said. "You can make coffee nigh as good as I can. Le's sit down out on the stoop. I hate to be inside walls any more'n I have to."

He follered me out and we sot down and I got to telling him about the Bear Creek country, because I was kind of homesick; but he didn't talk at all, just sot there staring at me in a most pecooliar manner. Finally I got sleep and said I believed I'd go to bed, so he got a candle and showed me where I was to sleep. The cabin had two rooms, and my bunk was in the back room. They wasn't any outside door to that room, just the door in the partition, but they was a winder in the back wall.

I throwed my saddlebags under the bunk, and leaned my Winchester agen the wall, and sot down on the bunk and started pulling off my boots, and Polecat stood in the door looking at me, with the candle in his hand, and a very strange expression on his face.

"You feel good?" he says. "You – you ain't got no bellyache nor nothin'?"

"Hell, no!" I says heartily. "What I want to have a bellyache for? I never had one of them things in my life, only onst when my brother Buckner shot me in the belly with a buffalo gun. Us Elkinses is healthy."

He shaken his head and muttered something in his beard, and backed out of the room, closing the door behind him. But the light didn't go out in the next room. I could see it shining through the crack of the door. It struck me that Polecat was acting kind of queer, and I begun to wonder if he was crazy or something. So I riz up in my bare feet and snuck over to the door, and looked through the crack.

Polecat was standing by the table with his back to me, and he had that box he'd got the white stuff out of, and he was turning it around in his hand, and shaking his head and muttering to hisself.

"I didn't make no mistake," he mumbled. "This is the right stuff, all right. I put dern near a handful in his coffee. That oughta been enough for a elephant. I don't understand it. I wouldn't believe it if I hadn't saw it myself."

Well, I couldn't make no sense out of it, and purty soon he sot the box back on the shelf behind some pans and things, and snuck out the door. But he didn't take his rifle, and he left his pistol belt hanging on a peg nigh the door. What he took with him was the fire-tongs off of the hearth. I decided he must be a little locoed from living by hisself, and I went back to bed and went to sleep.

It was some hours later when I woke up and sot up with my guns in my hands, and demanded, "Who's that? Speak up before I drills you."

"Don't shoot," says the voice of Polecat Rixby, emanating from the shadowy figger hovering nigh my bunk. "It's just me. I just wanted to see if you wanted a blanket. It gits cold up here in these mountains before mornin'."

"When it gits colder'n fifteen below zero," I says, "I generally throws a saddle blanket over me. This here's summertime. Gwan back to bed and lemme git some sleep."

I could of swore he had one of my boots in his hand when I first woke up, but he didn't have it when he went out. I went back to sleep and I slept so sound it seemed like I hadn't more'n laid back till daylight was oozing through the winder.

I got up and pulled on my boots and went into the other room, and coffee was b'iling, and bacon was frying onto a skillet, but Polecat warn't in there. I laughed when I seen he'd just sot one place on the table. He'd lived by hisself so much he'd plump forgot he had company for breakfast. I went over to the shelf where he'd got the white stuff he put in my coffee, and retched back and pulled out the box. It had some letters onto it, and while I couldn't read very good then, I knowed the alphabet, and was considered a highly educated man on Bear Creek. I spelled them letters out and they went "A-r-s-e-n-i-c." It didn't mean nothing to me, so I decided it was some foreign word for a new-fangled coffee flavor. I decided the reason Polecat didn't put none in his coffee was because he didn't have enough for both of us, and wanted to be perlite to his guest. But they was quite a bit of stuff left in the box. I heard him coming back just then, so I put it back on the shelf and went over by the table.

He come through the door with a armload of wood, and when he seen me he turned pale under his whiskers and let go the wood and it fell onto the floor. Some good-sized chunks bounced off of his feet but he didn't seem to notice it.

"What the heck's the matter with you?" I demanded. "Yo're as jumpy as Blaze Carson."

He stood there licking his lips for a minute, and then he says faintly, "It's my nerves. I've lived up here so long by myself I kind of forgot I had company. I apolergizes."

"Aw, hell, don't apolergize," I said. "Just fry some more bacon."

So he done it, and pretty soon we sot down and et, and the coffee was purty sorry that morning.

"How long you reckon I ought to hide out here?" I ast, and he said, "You better stay here today and tomorrer. Then you can pull out, travelin' southwest, and hit the old Injun trail again just this side of Scalplock Pass. Did – did you shake out yore boots this mornin'?"

"Naw," I said. "Why?"

"Well," he says, "they's a awful lot of varmints around here, and sometimes they crawls into the cabin. I've found Santa Fes and stingin' lizards in my boots some mornins."

"I didn't look," I says, drinking my fifth cup of coffee, "but now you mention it, I believe they must be a flea in my left boot. I been feelin' a kind of ticklin'."

So I pulled the boot off, and retched in my hand and pulled it out, and it warn't a flea at all, but a tarantula as big as your fist. I squshed it betwixt my thumb and forefinger and throwed it out the door, and Polecat looked at me kind of wild-like and said, "Did – did it bite you?"

"It's been nibblin' on my toe for the past half hour or so," I said, "but I thought it was just a flea."

"But my God!" he wailed. "Them things is pizen! I've seen men die from bein' bit by 'em!"

"You mean to tell me men in these parts is so puny they suffers when a tranchler bites 'em?" I says. "I never heard of nothin' so derned effeminate! Pass the bacon."

He done so in a kind of pale silence, and after I had mopped up all the grease out of my plate with the last of the corn pone, I ast, "What does a-r-s-e-n-i-c spell?"

He was jest taking a swig of coffee and he strangled and sprayed it all over the table and fell backwards off his stool and would probably have choked to death if I hadn't pounded him in the back.

"Don't you know what arsenic is?" he gurgled when he could talk, and he was shaking like he had the aggers.

"Never heard of it," I said, and he hove a shuddering sigh and said, "It's a Egyptian word which means sugar."

"Oh," I said, and he went over and sot down and held his head in his hands like he was sick at the stummick. He shore was a queer-acting old codger.

Well, I seen the fire needed some wood, so I went out and got a armload and started back into the cabin, and jest as I sot a foot on the stoop bam! went a Winchester inside the cabin, and a .45–70 slug hit me a glancing lick on the side of the head and ricocheted off down towards the run.

"What the hell you doin'?" I roared angrily, and Polecat's pale face appeared at the door, and he said, "Excuse me, Elkins! I war just cleanin' my rifle-gun and it went off accidental!"

"Well, be careful," I advised, shaking the blood off. "Glancin' bullets is dangerous. It might of hit Cap'n Kidd."

"Don't you want to give yore hoss some corn?" he says. "They's plenty out there in that shed nigh the corral."

I thought that was a good idee, so I got a sack and dumped in about a bushel, because Cap'n Kidd is as hearty a eater as what I am, and I went down the run looking for him, and found him mowing down the high grass like a reaping machine, and he neighed with joy at the sight of the corn. Whilst he was gorging I went down the trail a ways to see if they was any outlaws sneaking up it, but I didn't see no signs of none.

It was about noon when I got back to the cabin, and Polecat warn't nowheres in sight, so I decided I'd cook dinner. I fried up a lot of bacon and fixed some bread and beans and potaters, and b'iled a whopping big pot of coffee, and whilst it was b'iling I emptied all the Gypshun sugar they was in the box into it, and taken a good swig, and it was fine. I thought foreigners ain't got much sense, but they shore know how to make sugar.

I was putting the things on the table when Polecat came in looking kind of pale and wayworn, but he perked up when he seen the grub, and sot down and started to eat with a better apperite than he'd been showing. I was jest finishing my first cup of coffee when he taken a swig of his'n, and he spit it out on the floor and said, "What in hell's the matter with this here coffee?"

Now, despite the fact that I am timid and gentle as a lamb by nature, they is one thing I will not endure, and that is for anybody to criticize my cooking. I am the best coffee-maker in Nevada, and I've crippled more'n one man for disagreeing with me. So I said sternly, "There ain't nothin' the matter with that there coffee."

"Well," he said, "I cain't drink it." And he started to pour it out.

At that I was overcome by culinary pride.

"Stop that!" I roared, jerking out one of my .45's. "They is a limit to every man's patience, and this here's mine! Even if I am yore guest, you cain't sneer at my coffee! Sech is a deadly insult, and not to be put up with by any man of spirit and self-respect! You drink that there coffee and display a proper amount of admiration for it, by golly!

"Yore lack of good taste cuts me to the marrer of my soul," I continued bitterly, as he lifted the cup to his lips in fear and trembling. "After I'd done gone to all the trouble of makin' that coffee specially good, and even flavorin' it with all the white stuff they was in that box on the shelf!"

At that he screeched, "Murder!" and fell offa his stool backwards, spitting coffee in every direction. He jumped up and bolted for the door, but I grabbed him, and he pulled a bowie out of his boot and tried to stab me, all the time yowling like a catamount. Irritated at this display of bad manners, I taken the knife away from him and slammed him back down on the stool so hard it broke off all three of the laigs, and he rolled on the floor again, letting out ear-splitting screams.

By this time I was beginning to lose my temper, so I pulled him up and sot him down on the bench I'd been sitting on, and shoved the coffee pot under his nose with one hand and my .45 with the other.

"This is the wust insult I ever had offered to me," I growled blood-thirstily. "So you'd do murder before you'd drink my coffee, hey? Well, you empty that there pot before you put her down, and you smack yore lips over it, too, or I'll – "

"It's murder!" he howled, twisting his head away from the pot. "I ain't ready to die! I got too many sins a-stainin' my soul! I'll confess! I'll tell everything! I'm one of Ferguson's men! This here is the hideout where they keeps the hosses they steals, only they ain't none here now. Bill Price was in the Lazy Elk Bar and heard you talkin' to Blaze Carson about totin' out his gold for him. Bill figgered it would take the whole gang to down you, so he lit out for 'em, and told me to try to git you up to my cabin if I could work it, and send up a smoke signal when I did, so the gang would come and murder you and take the gold.

"But when I got you up here, I decided to kill you myself and skip out with the gold, whilst the gang was waitin' for my signal. You was too big for me to tackle with a knife or a gun, so I put pizen in yore coffee, and when that didn't work I catched a tranchler last night with the tongs and dropped it into yore boot. This mornin' I got desperate and tried to shoot you. Don't make me drink that pizen coffee. I'm a broken man. I don't believe mortal weppins can kill you. Yo're a jedgment sent onto me because of my evil ways. If you'll spare my life, I swear I'll go straight from now on!"

"What I care how you go, you back-whiskered old sarpent?" I snarled. "My faith in humanity has been give a awful lick. You mean to tell me that there arsenic stuff is pizen?"

"It's considered shore death to ordinary human beings," says he.

"Well, I'll be derned!" I says. "I never tasted nothin' I liked better. Say!" I says, hit by another thought, "when you was out of the cabin awhile ago, did you by any chance build that there signal smoke?"

"I done so," he admitted. "Up on top of the cliff. Ferguson and his gang is undoubtedly on their way here now."

"Which way will they come?" I ast.

"Along the trail from the west," says he. "Like we come."

"All right," I says, snatching up my Winchester, and the saddlebags in the other hand. "I'll ambush 'em on this side of the gorge. I'm takin' the gold along with me in case yore natural instincts overcomes you to the extent of lightin' a shuck with it whilst I'm massacreein' them idjits."

I run out and whistled for Cap'n Kidd and jumped onto him bareback and went lickety-split through the bresh till I come to the canyon. And by golly, just as I jumped off of Cap'n Kidd and run through the bushes to the edge of the gorge, out of the bresh on the other side come ten men on horses, with Winchesters in their hands, riding hard. I reckoned the tall, lean, black-whiskered devil leading was Ferguson; I recognized Bill Price right behind him.

They couldn't see me for the bushes, and I drawed a bead on Ferguson and pulled the trigger. And the hammer just clicked. Three times I worked the lever and jerked the trigger, and every time the derned gun snapped. By that time them outlaws had reached the bridge and strung out on it single-file, Ferguson in the lead. In another minute they'd be acrost, and my chance of ambushing 'em would be plumb sp'iled.

I throwed down my Winchester and busted out of the bresh and they seen me and started yelling, and Ferguson started shooting at me, but the others didn't dare shoot for fear of hitting him, and some of the hosses started rearing, and the men was fighting to keep 'em from falling offa the bridge, but the whole passle come surging on. But I got to the end of the bridge in about three jumps, paying no attention to the three slugs Ferguson throwed into various parts of my anatomy. I bent my knees and got hold of the end of the tree and heaved up with it. It was such a big tree and had so many hosses and men on it even I couldn't lift it very high, but that was enough. I braced my laigs and swung the end around clear of the rim and let go and it went end over end a hundred feet down into the canyon, taking all them outlaws and their hosses along with it, them a-yelling and squalling like the devil. A regular geyer of water splashed up when they hit, and the last I seen of 'em they was all swirling down the river together in a thrashing tangle of arms and laigs and heads and manes.

Whilst I stood looking after 'em, Polecat Rixby bust out of the bresh behind me, and he give a wild look, and shaken his head weakly, and then he said, "I forgot to tell you – I taken the powder out of the ca'tridges in yore Winchester this mornin' whilst you was gone."

"This is a hell of a time to be tellin' me about it," I says. "But it don't make no difference now."

"I suppose it's too trivial to mention," says he, "but it looks to me like you been shot in the hind laig and the hip and the shoulder."

"It's quite likely," I agreed. "And if you really want to make yoreself useful, you might take this bowie and help me dig the lead out. Then I'm headin' for Wahpeton. Blaze'll be waitin' for his gold, and I want to git me some of that there arsenic stuff. It makes coffee taste better'n skunk ile or rattlesnake pizen."

War on Bear Creek

Pap dug the nineteenth buckshot out of my shoulder and said, "Pigs is more disturbin' to the peace of a community than scandal, divorce, and corn-licker put together. And," says Pap, pausing to strop his bowie on my scalp where the hair was all burnt off, "when the pig is a razorback hawg, and is mixed up with a lady school teacher, a English tenderfoot, and a passle of bloodthirsty relatives, the result is appallin' for a peaceable man to behold. Hold still till John gits yore ear sewed back on."

Pap was right. I warn't to blame for what happened. Breaking Joel Gordon's laig was a mistake, and Erath Elkins is a liar when he says I caved in them five ribs of his'n plumb on purpose. If Uncle Jeppard Grimes had been tending to his own business he wouldn't have got the seat of his britches filled with bird-shot, and I don't figger it was my fault that cousin Bill Kirby's cabin got burned down. And I don't take no blame for Jim Gordon's ear which Jack Grimes shot off, neither. I figger everybody was more to blame than I was, and I stand ready to wipe up the earth with anybody which disagrees with me.

But it was that derned razorback hawg of Uncle Jeppard Grimes which started the whole mess.

It begun when that there tenderfoot come riding up the trail with Tunk Willoughby, from War Paint. Tunk ain't got no more sense than the law allows, but he shore showed good jedgement that time, because having delivered his charge to his destination, he didn't tarry. He merely handed me a note, and p'inted dumbly at the tenderfoot, whilst holding his hat reverently in his hand meanwhile.

"What you mean by that there gesture?" I ast him rather irritably, and he said, "I doffs my sombrero in respect to the departed. Bringin' a specimen like that onto Bear Creek is just like heavin' a jackrabbit to a pack of starvin' loboes."

He hove a sigh and shook his head, and put his hat back on. "Rassle a cat in pieces," he says, gathering up the reins.

"What the hell are you talkin' about?" I demanded.

"That's Latin," he said. "It means rest in peace."

And with that he dusted it down the trail and left me alone with the tenderfoot which all the time was setting his cayuse and looking at me like I was a curiosity or something.

I called my sister Ouachita to come read that there note for me, which she did and it run as follows:

Dere Breckinridge: This will interjuice Mr. J. Pembroke Pemberton a English sportsman which I met in Frisco recent. He was disapinted because he hadn't found no adventures in America and was fixin to go to Aferker to shoot liuns and elerfants but I perswaded him to come with me because I knowed he would find more hell on Bear Creek in a week than he would find in a yere in Aferker or any other place. But the very day we hit War Paint I run into a old ackwaintance from Texas I will not speak no harm of the ded but I wish the son of a buzzard had shot me somewheres besides in my left laig which already had three slugs in it which I never could get cut out. Anyway I am lade up and not able to come on to Bear Creek with J. Pembroke Pemberton. I am dependin on you to show him some good bear huntin and other excitement and pertect him from yore relatives I know what a awful responsibility I am puttin on you but I am askin' this as yore frend, William Harrison Glanton, Esqy.

I looked J. Pembroke over. He was a medium sized young feller and looked kinda soft in spots. He had yaller hair and very pink cheeks like a gal; and he had on whip-cord britches and tan riding boots which was the first I ever seen. And he had on a funny kinda coat with pockets and a belt which he called a shooting jacket, and a big hat like a mushroom made outa cork with a red ribbon around it. And he had a pack-horse loaded with all kinds of plunder, and four or five different kinds of shotguns and rifles.

"So yo're J. Pembroke," I says, and he says, "Oh, rahther! And you, no doubt, are the person Mr. Glanton described to me, Breckinridge Elkins?"

"Yeah," I said. "Light and come in. We got b'ar meat and honey for supper."

"I say," he said, climbing down. "Pardon me for being a bit personal, old chap, but may I ask if your – ah – magnitude of bodily stature is not a bit unique?"

"I dunno," I says, not having the slightest idee what he was talking about. "I always votes a straight Democratic ticket, myself."

He started to say something else, but just then Pap and my brothers John and Bill and Jim and Buckner and Garfield come to the door to see what the noise was about, and he turned pale and said faintly, "I beg your pardon; giants seem to be the rule in these parts."

"Pap says men ain't what they was when he was in his prime," I said, "but we manage to git by."

Well, J. Pembroke laid into them b'ar steaks with a hearty will, and when I told him we'd go after b'ar next day, he ast me how many days travel it'd take till we got to the b'ar country.

"Heck!" I said. "You don't have to travel to git b'ar in these parts. If you forgit to bolt yore door at night yo're liable to find a grizzly sharin' yore bunk before mornin'. This here'n we're eatin' was ketched by my sister Ellen there whilst tryin' to rob the pigpen out behind the cabin last night."

"My word!" he says, looking at her peculiarly. "And may I ask, Miss Elkins, what caliber of firearm you used?"

"I knocked him in the head with a wagon tongue," she said, and he shook his head to hisself and muttered, "Extraordinary!"

J. Pembroke slept in my bunk and I took the floor that night; and we was up at daylight and ready to start after the b'ar. Whilst J. Pembroke was fussing over his guns, Pap come out and pulled his whiskers and shook his head and said, "That there is a perlite young man, but I'm afeared he ain't as hale as he oughta be. I just give him a pull at my jug, and he didn't gulp but one good snort and like to choked to death."

"Well," I said, buckling the cinches on Cap'n Kidd, "I've done learnt not to jedge outsiders by the way they takes their licker on Bear Creek. It takes a Bear Creek man to swig Bear Creek corn juice."

"I hopes for the best," sighed Pap. "But it's a dismal sight to see a young man which cain't stand up to his licker. Whar you takin' him?"

"Over toward Apache Mountain," I said. "Erath seen a exter big grizzly over there day before yesterday."

"Hmmmm!" says Pap. "By a pecooliar coincidence the schoolhouse is over on the side of Apache Mountain, ain't it, Breckinridge?"

"Maybe it is and maybe it ain't," I replied with dignerty, and rode off with J. Pembroke ignoring Pap's sourcastic comment which he hollered after me, "Maybe they is a connection between book larnin' and b'ar huntin', but who am I to say?"

J. Pembroke was a purty good rider, but he used a funny looking saddle without no horn nor cantle, and he had the derndest gun I ever seen. It was a double-barrel rifle, and he said it was a elerfant-gun. It was big enough to knock a hill down. He was surprised I didn't tote no rifle and ast me what would I do if we met a b'ar. I told him I was depending on him to shoot it, but I said if it was necessary for me to go into action, my six-shooter was plenty.

"My word!" says he. "You mean to say you can bring down a grizzly with a shot from a pistol?"

"Not always," I said. "Sometimes I have to bust him over the head with the butt to finish him."

He didn't say nothing for a long time after that.

Well, we rode over on the lower slopes of Apache Mountain, and tied the horses in a holler and went through the bresh on foot. That was a good place for b'ars, because they come there very frequently looking for Uncle Jeppard Grimes' pigs which runs loose all over the lower slopes of the mountain.

But just like it always is when yo're looking for something, we didn't see a cussed b'ar.

The middle of the evening found us around on the south side of the mountain where they is a settlement of Kirbys and Grimeses and Gordons. Half a dozen families has their cabins within a mile of each other, and I dunno what in hell they want crowd up together that way for, it would plumb smother me, but Pap says they was always peculiar that way.

We warn't in sight of the settlement, but the schoolhouse warn't far off, and I said to J. Pembroke, "You wait here a while and maybe a b'ar will come by. Miss Margaret Ashley is teachin' me how to read and write, and it's time for my lesson."

I left J. Pembroke setting on a log hugging his elerfant-gun, and I strode through the bresh and come out at the upper end of the run which the settlement was at the other'n, and school had just turned out and the chillern was going home, and Miss Ashley was waiting for me in the log schoolhouse.

That was the first school that was ever taught on Bear Creek, and she was the first teacher. Some of the folks was awful sot agen it at first, and said no good would come of book larning, but after I licked six or seven of them they allowed it might be a good thing after all, and agreed to let her take a whack at it.

Miss Margaret was a awful purty gal and come from somewhere away back East. She was setting at her handmade desk as I come in, ducking my head so as not to bump it agen the top of the door and perlitely taking off my coonskin cap. She looked kinda tired and discouraged, and I said, "Has the young'uns been rasin' any hell today, Miss Margaret?"

"Oh, no," she said. "They're very polite – in fact I've noticed that Bear Creek people are always polite except when they're killing each other. I've finally gotten used to the boys wearing their bowie knives and pistols to school. But somehow it seems so futile. This is all so terribly different from everything to which I've always been accustomed. I get discouraged and feel like giving up."

"You'll git used to it," I consoled her. "It'll be a lot different once yo're married to some honest reliable young man."

She give me a startled look and said, "Married to some one here on Bear Creek?"

"Shore," I said, involuntarily expanding my chest under my buckskin shirt. "Everybody is just wonderin' when you'll set the date. But le's git at the lesson. I done learnt the words you writ out for me yesterday."

But she warn't listening, and she said, "Do you have any idea of why Mr. Joel Grimes and Mr. Esau Gordon quit calling on me? Until a few days ago one or the other was at Mr. Kirby's cabin where I board almost every night."

"Now don't you worry none about them," I soothed her. "Joel'll be about on crutches before the week's out, and Esau can already walk without bein' helped. I always handles my relatives as easy as possible."

"You fought with them?" she exclaimed.

"I just convinced 'em you didn't want to be bothered with 'em," I reassured her. "I'm easygoin', but I don't like competition." "Competition!"

Her eyes flared wide open and she looked at me like she never seen me before. "Do you mean, that you – that I – that – "

"Well," I said modestly, "everybody on Bear Creek is just wonderin' when you're goin' to set the day for us to git hitched. You see gals don't stay single very long in these parts, and – hey, what's the matter?"

Because she was getting paler and paler like she'd et something which didn't agree with her.

"Nothing," she said faintly. "You – you mean people are expecting me to marry you?"

"Shore," I said.

She muttered something that sounded like "My God!" and licked her lips with her tongue and looked at me like she was about ready to faint. Well, it ain't every gal which has a chance to get hitched to Breckinridge Elkins, so I didn't blame her for being excited.

"You've been very kind to me, Breckinridge," she said feebly. "But I – this is so sudden – so unexpected – I never thought – I never *dreamed* – "

"I don't want to rush you," I said. "Take yore time. Next week will be soon enough. Anyway, I got to build us a cabin, and – "

Bang! went a gun, too loud for a Winchester.

"Elkins!" It was J. Pembroke yelling for me up the slope. "Elkins! Hurry!"

"Who's that?" she exclaimed, jumping to her feet like she was working on a spring.

"Aw," I said in disgust, "it's a fool tenderfoot Bill Glanton wished on me. I reckon a b'ar is got him by the neck. I'll go see."

"I'll go with you!" she said, but from the way J. Pembroke was yelling I figgered I better not waste no time getting to him, so I couldn't wait for her, and she was some piece behind me when I mounted the lap of the slope and met him running out from amongst the trees. He was gibbering with excitement.

"I winged it!" he squawked. "I'm sure I winged the blighter! But it ran in among the underbrush and I dared not follow it, for the beast is most vicious when wounded. A friend of mine once wounded one in South Africa, and – "

"A b'ar?" I ast.

"No, no!" he said. "A wild boar! The most vicious brute I have ever seen! It ran into that brush there!"

"Aw, they ain't no wild boars in the Humbolts," I snorted. "You wait here. I'll go see just what you did shoot."

I seen some splashes of blood on the grass, so I knowed he'd shot something. Well, I hadn't gone more'n a few hunderd feet and was just out of sight of J. Pembroke when I run into Uncle Jeppard Grimes.

Uncle Jeppard was one of the first white men to come into the Humbolts. He's as lean and hard as a pine-knot, and wears fringed buckskins and moccasins just like he done fifty years ago. He had a bowie knife in one hand and he waved something in the other'n like a flag of revolt, and he was frothing at the mouth.

"The derned murderer!" he howled. "You see this? That's the tail of Daniel Webster, the finest derned razorback boar which ever trod the Humbolts! That danged tenderfoot of your'n tried to kill him! Shot his tail off, right spang up to the hilt! He cain't muterlate my animals like this! I'll have his heart's blood!"

And he done a war-dance waving that pigtail and his bowie and cussing in English and Spanish and Apache Injun all at once.

"You ca'm down, Uncle Jeppard," I said sternly. "He ain't got no sense, and he thought Daniel Webster was a wild boar like they have in Aferker and England and them foreign places. He didn't mean no harm."

"No harm!" said Uncle Jeppard fiercely. "And Daniel Webster with no more tail onto him than a jackrabbit!"

"Well," I said, "here's a five dollar gold piece to pay for the dern hawg's tail, and you let J. Pembroke alone."

"Gold cain't satisfy honor," he said bitterly, but nevertheless grabbing the coin like a starving man grabbing a beefsteak. "I'll let this outrage pass for the time. But I'll be watchin' that maneyack to see that he don't muterlate no more of my prize razorbacks."

And so saying he went off muttering in his beard.

I went back to where I left J. Pembroke, and there he was talking to Miss Margaret which had just come up. She had more color in her face than I'd saw recent.

"Fancy meeting a girl like you here!" Pembroke was saying.

"No more surprising than meeting a man like you!" says she with a kind of fluttery laugh.

"Oh, a sportsman wanders into all sorts of out-of-the-way places," says he, and seeing they hadn't noticed me coming up, I says, "Well, J. Pembroke, I didn't find yore wild boar, but I met the owner."

He looked at me kinda blank, and said vaguely, "Wild boar? *What* wild boar?"

"That-un you shot the tail off of with that there fool elerfant gun," I said. "Listen: next time you see a hawg-critter you remember there ain't no wild boars in the Humbolts. They is critters called haverleeners in South Texas, but they ain't even none of them in Nevada. So next time you see a hawg, just reflect that it's merely one of Uncle Jeppard Grimes' razorbacks and refrain from shootin' at it."

"Oh, quite!" he agreed absently, and started talking to Miss Margaret again.

So I picked up the elerfant gun which he'd absent-mindedly laid down, and said, "Well, it's gittin' late. Let's go. We won't go back to Pap's cabin tonight, J. Pembroke. We'll stay at Uncle Saul Garfield's cabin on t'other side of the Apache Mountain settlement."

As I said, them cabins was awful close together. Uncle Saul's cabin was below the settlement, but it warn't much over three hundred yards from cousin Bill Kirby's cabin where Miss Margaret boarded. The other cabins was on t'other side of Bill's, mostly, strung out up the run, and up and down the slopes.

I told J. Pembroke and Miss Margaret to walk on down to the settlement whilst I went back and got the horses.

They'd got to the settlement time I catched up with 'em, and Miss Margaret had gone into the Kirby cabin, and I seen a light spring up in her room. She had one of them new-fangled ile lamps she brung with her, the only one on Bear Creek. Candles and pine chunks was good enough for us folks. And she'd hanged rag things over the winders which she called curtains. You never seen nothing like it. I tell you she was that elegant you wouldn't believe it.

We walked on toward Uncle Saul's, me leading the horses, and after a while J. Pembroke says, "A wonderful creature!"

"You mean Daniel Webster?" I ast.

"No!" he said. "No, no. I mean Miss Ashley."

"She shore is," I said. "She'll make me a fine wife."

He whirled like I'd stabbed him and his face looked pale in the dusk.

"You?" he said. "*You* a wife?"

"Well," I said bashfully, "she ain't sot the day yet, but I've shore sot my heart on that gal."

"Oh!" he says. "Oh!" says he, like he had the toothache. Then he said kinda hesitatingly, "Suppose – er, just suppose, you know! Suppose a rival for her affections should appear? What would you do?"

"You mean if some dirty, lowdown son of a mangy skunk was to try to steal my gal?" I said, whirling so sudden he staggered backwards.

"*Steal my gal?*" I roared, seeing red at the mere thought. "Why, I'd – I'd – "

Words failing me I wheeled and grabbed a good-sized sapling and tore it up by the roots and broke it acrost my knee and throwed the pieces clean through a rail fence on the other side of the road.

"That there is a faint idee!" I said, panting with passion.

"That gives me a very good conception," he said faintly, and he said nothing more till we reached the cabin and seen Uncle Saul Garfield standing in the light of the door combing his black beard with his fingers.

Next morning J. Pembroke seemed like he'd kinda lost interest in b'ars. He said all that walking he done over the slopes of Apache Mountain had made his laig muscles sore. I never heard of such a thing, but nothing that gets the matter with these tenderfeet surprises me much, they is such a effemernate race, so I ast him would he like to go fishing down the run and he said all right.

But we hadn't been fishing more'n a hour when he said he believed he'd go back to Uncle Saul's cabin and take him a nap, and he insisted on going alone, so I stayed where I was and ketched me a nice string of trout.

I went back to the cabin about noon, and ast Uncle Saul if J. Pembroke had got his nap out.

"Why, heck," said Uncle Saul. "I ain't seen him since you and him started down the run this mornin'. Wait a minute – yonder he comes from the other direction."

Well, J. Pembroke didn't say where he'd been all morning, and I didn't ast him, because a tenderfoot don't generally have no reason for anything he does.

We et the trout I ketched, and after dinner he perked up a right smart and got his shotgun and said he'd like to hunt some wild turkeys. I never heard of anybody hunting anything as big as a turkey with a shotgun, but I didn't say nothing, because tenderfeet is like that.

So we headed up the slopes of Apache Mountain, and I stopped by the schoolhouse to tell Miss Margaret I probably wouldn't get back in time to take my reading and writing lesson, and she said, "You know, until I met your friend, Mr. Pembroke, I didn't realize what a difference there was between men like him, and – well, like the men on Bear Creek."

"I know," I said. "But don't hold it agen him. He means well. He just ain't got no sense. Everybody cain't be smart like me. As a special favor to me, Miss Margaret, I'd like for you to be exter nice to the poor sap, because he's a friend of my friend Bill Glanton down to War Paint."

"I will, Breckinridge," she replied heartily, and I thanked her and went away with my big manly heart pounding in my gigantic bosom.

Me and J. Pembroke headed into the heavy timber, and we hadn't went far till I was convinced that somebody was follering us. I kept hearing twigs snapping, and oncet I thought I seen a shadowy figger duck behind a bush. But when I run back there, it was gone, and no track to show in the pine needles. That sort of thing would of made me nervous, anywhere else, because they is a awful lot of people which would like to get a clean shot at my back from the bresh, but I knowed none of them dast come after me in my own territory. If anybody was trailing us it was bound to be one of my relatives and to save my neck I couldn't think of no reason why any one of 'em would be gunning for me.

But I got tired of it, and left J. Pembroke in a small glade while I snuck back to do some shaddering of my own. I aimed to cast a big circle around the opening and see could I find out who it was, but I'd hardly got out of sight of J. Pembroke when I heard a gun bang.

I turned to run back and here come J. Pembroke yelling, "I got him! I got him! I winged the bally aborigine!"

He had his head down as he busted through the bresh and he run into me in his excitement and hit me in the belly with his head so hard he bounced back like a rubber ball and landed in a bush with his riding boots brandishing wildly in the air.

"Assist me, Breckinridge!" he shrieked. "Extricate me! They will be hot on our trail!"

"Who?" I demanded, hauling him out by the hind laig and setting him on his feet.

"The Indians!" he hollered, jumping up and down and waving his smoking shotgun frantically. "The bally redskins! I shot one of them! I saw him sneaking through the bushes! I saw his legs! I know it was an Indian because he had on moccasins instead of boots! Listen! That's him now!"

"A Injun couldn't cuss like that," I said. "You've shot Uncle Jeppard Grimes!"

Telling him to stay there, I run through the bresh, guided by the maddened howls which riz horribly on the air, and busting through some bushes I seen Uncle Jeppard rolling on the ground with both hands clasped to the rear bosom of his buckskin britches which was smoking freely. His langwidge was awful to hear.

"Air you in misery, Uncle Jeppard?" I inquired solicitously. This evoked another ear-splitting squall.

"I'm writhin' in my death throes," he says in horrible accents, "and you stands there and mocks my mortal agony! My own blood kin!" he says. "#$%&*?@¢!" says Uncle Jeppard with passion.

"Aw," I says, "that there bird-shot wouldn't hurt a flea. It cain't be very deep under yore thick old hide. Lie on yore belly, Uncle Jeppard," I said, stropping my bowie on my boot, "and I'll dig out them shot for you."

"Don't tech me!" he said fiercely, painfully climbing onto his feet. "Where's my rifle-gun? Gimme it! Now then, I demands that you bring that English murderer here where I can git a clean lam at him! The Grimes honor is besmirched and my new britches is rooint. Nothin' but blood can wipe out the stain on the family honor!"

"Well," I said, "you hadn't no business sneakin' around after us thataway – "

Here Uncle Jeppard give tongue to loud and painful shrieks.

"Why shouldn't I?" he howled. "Ain't a man got no right to pertect his own property? I was follerin' him to see that he didn't shoot no more tails offa my hawgs. And now he shoots me in the same place! He's a fiend in human form – a monster which stalks ravelin' through these hills bustin' for the blood of the innercent!"

"Aw, J. Pembroke thought you was a Injun," I said.

"He thought Daniel Webster was a wild wart hawg," gibbered Uncle Jeppard. "He thought I was Geronimo. I reckon he'll massacre the entire population of Bear Creek under a misapprehension, and you'll uphold and defend him! When the cabins of yore kinfolks is smolderin' ashes, smothered in the blood of yore own relatives, I hope you'll be satisfied – bringin' a foreign assassin into a peaceful community!"

Here Uncle Jeppard's emotions choked him, and he chawed his whiskers and then yanked out the five-dollar gold piece I give him for Daniel Webster's tail, and throwed it at me.

"Take back yore filthy lucre," he said bitterly. "The day of retribution is close onto hand, Breckinridge Elkins, and the Lord of battles shall jedge between them which turns agen their kinfolks in their extremerties!"

"In their which?" I says, but he merely snarled and went limping off through the trees, calling back over his shoulder, "They is still men on Bear Creek which will see justice did for the aged and helpless. I'll git that English murderer if it's the last thing I do, and you'll be sorry you stood up for him, you big lunkhead!"

I went back to where J. Pembroke was waiting bewilderedly, and evidently still expecting a tribe of Injuns to bust out of the bresh and sculp him, and I said in disgust, "Let's go home. Tomorrer I'll take you so far away from Bear Creek you can shoot in any direction without hittin' a prize razorback or a antiquated gunman with a ingrown disposition. When Uncle Jeppard Grimes gits mad enough to throw away money, it's time to ile the Winchesters and strap your scabbard-ends to yore laigs."

"Legs?" he said mistily. "But what about the Indian?"

"There warn't no Injun, gol-dern it!" I howled. "They ain't been any on Bear Creek for four or five year. They – aw, hell! What's the use? Come on. It's gittin' late. Next time you see somethin' you don't understand, ast me before you shoot it. And remember, the more ferocious and woolly it looks, the more likely it is to be a leadin' citizen of Bear Creek."

It was dark when we approached Uncle Saul's cabin, and J. Pembroke glanced back up the road, toward the settlement, and said, "My word, is it a political rally? Look! A torchlight parade!"

I looked, and I said, "Quick! Git into the cabin and stay there!"

He turned pale, but said, "If there is danger, I insist on – "

"Insist all you dern please," I said. "But git in that house and stay there. I'll handle this. Uncle Saul, see he gits in there."

Uncle Saul is a man of few words. He taken a firm grip on his pipe stem and grabbed J. Pembroke by the neck and the seat of the britches and throwed him bodily into the cabin, and shet the door, and sot down on the stoop.

"They ain't no use in you gittin' mixed up in this, Uncle Saul," I said.

"You got yore faults, Breckinridge," he grunted. "You ain't got much sense, but yere my favorite sister's son – and I ain't forgot that lame mule Jeppard traded me for a sound animal back in '69. Let 'em come!"

They come all right, and surged up in front of the cabin – Jeppard's boys Jack and Buck and Esau and Joash and Polk County. And Erath Elkins, and a mob of Gordons and Buckners and Polks, all more or less kin to me, except Joe Braxton who wasn't kin to any of us, but didn't like me because he was sweet on Miss Margaret. But Uncle Jeppard warn't with 'em. Some had torches and Polk County Grimes had a rope with a noose in it.

"Where-at air you all goin' with that there lariat?" I ast them sternly, planting my enormous bulk in their path.

"Perjuice the scoundrel!" said Polk County, waving his rope around his head. "Bring out the foreign invader which shoots hawgs and defenseless old men from the bresh!"

"What you aim to do?" I inquired.

"We aim to hang him!" they replied with hearty enthusiasm.

Uncle Saul knocked the ashes out of his pipe and stood up and stretched his arms which looked like knotted oak limbs, and he grinned in his black beard like a old timber wolf, and he says, "Whar is dear cousin Jeppard to speak for hisself?"

"Uncle Jeppard was havin' the shot picked outa his hide when we left," says Joel Gordon. "He'll be along directly. Breckinridge, we don't want no trouble with you, but we aims to have that Englishman."

"Well," I snorted, "you all cain't. Bill Glanton is trustin' me to return him whole of body and limb, and – "

"What you want to waste time in argyment for, Breckinridge?" Uncle Saul reproved mildly. "Don't you know it's a plumb waste of time to try to reason with the offspring of a lame-mule trader?"

"What would you suggest, old man?" sneeringly remarked Polk County.

Uncle Saul beamed on him benevolently, and said gently, "I'd try moral suasion – like this!" And he hit Polk County under the jaw and knocked him clean acrost the yard into a rain barrel amongst the ruins of which he reposed until he was rescued and revived some hours later.

But they was no stopping Uncle Saul oncet he took the warpath. No sooner had he disposed of Polk County than he jumped seven foot into the air, cracked his heels together three times, give the rebel yell and come down with his arms around the necks of Esau Grimes and Joe Braxton, which he went to the earth with and starting mopping up the cabin yard with 'em.

That started the fight, and they is no scrap in the world where mayhem is committed as free and fervent as in one of these here family rukuses.

Polk County had hardly crashed into the rain barrel when Jack Grimes stuck a pistol in my face. I slapped it aside just as he fired and the bullet missed me and taken a ear offa Jim Gordon. I was scared Jack would hurt somebody if he kept on shooting reckless that way, so I kinda rapped him with my left fist and how was I to know it would dislocate his jaw. But Jim Gordon seemed to think I was to blame about his ear because he give a maddened howl and jerked up his shotgun and let *bam* with both barrels. I ducked just in time to keep from getting my head blowed off, and catched most of the double charge in my shoulder, whilst the rest hived in the seat of Steve Kirby's britches. Being shot that way by a relative was irritating, but I controlled my temper and merely taken the gun away from Jim and splintered the stock over his head.

In the meantime Joel Gordon and Buck Grimes had grabbed one of my laigs apiece and was trying to rassle me to the earth, and Joash Grimes was trying to hold down my right arm, and cousin Pecos Buckner was beating me over the head from behind with a ax handle, and Erath Elkins was coming at me from the front with a bowie knife. I reached down and got Buck Grimes by the neck with my left hand, and I swung my right and hit Erath with it, but I had to lift Joash clean off his feet and swing him around with the lick, because he wouldn't let go, so I only knocked Erath through the rail fence which was around Uncle Saul's garden.

About this time I found my left laig was free and discovered that Buck Grimes was unconscious, so I let go of his neck and begun to kick around with my left laig and it ain't my fault if the spur got tangled up in Uncle Jonathan Polk's whiskers and jerked most of 'em out by the roots. I shaken Joash off and taken the ax handle away from Pecos because I seen he was going to hurt somebody if he kept on swinging it around so reckless, and I dunno why he blames me because his skull got fractured when he hit that tree. He oughta look where he falls when he gets throwed across a cabin yard. And if Joel Gordon hadn't been so stubborn trying to gouge me he wouldn't of got his laig broke neither.

I was handicapped by not wanting to kill any of my kinfolks, but they was so mad they all wanted to kill me, so in spite of my carefulness the casualties was increasing at a rate which would of discouraged anybody but Bear Creek folks. But they are the stubbornnest people in the world. Three or four had got me around the laigs again, refusing to be convinced that I couldn't be throwed that way, and Erath Elkins, having pulled hisself out of the ruins of the fence, come charging back with his bowie.

By this time I seen I'd have to use violence in spite of myself, so I grabbed Erath and squoze him with a grizzly hug and that was when he got them five ribs caved in, and he ain't spoke to me since. I never seen such a cuss for taking offense over trifles.

For a matter of fact, if he hadn't been so bodaciously riled up – if he had of kept his head like I did – be would seen how kindly I felt toward him, even in the fever of that there battle. If I had dropped him underfoot he might have been tromped on fatally for I was kicking folks right and left without caring where they fell. So I carefully flung Erath out of the range of that ruckus – and if he thinks I aimed him at Ozark Grimes and his pitchfork – well, I just never done it. It was Ozark's fault more than mine for toting that pitchfork, and it ought to be Ozark that Erath cusses when he starts to sit down these days.

It was at this moment that somebody swung at me with a ax and ripped my ear nigh offa my head, and I begun to lose my temper. Four or five other relatives was kicking and hitting and biting at me all at oncet, and they is a limit even to my timid manners and mild nature. I voiced my displeasure with a beller of wrath, and lashed out with both fists, and my misguided relatives fell all over the yard like persimmons after a frost. I grabbed Joash Grimes by the ankles and begun to knock them ill-advised idjits in the head with him, and the way he hollered you'd of thought somebody was manhandling him. The yard was beginning to look like a battlefield when the cabin door opened and a deluge of b'iling water descended on us.

I got about a gallon down my neck, but paid very little attention to it, however the others ceased hostilities and started rolling on the ground and hollering and cussing, and Uncle Saul riz up from amongst the ruins of Esau Grimes and Joe Braxton, and bellered, "Woman! What air you at?"

Aunt Zavalla Garfield was standing in the doorway with a kettle in her hand, and she said, "Will you idjits stop fightin'? The Englishman's gone. He run out the back door when the fightin' started, saddled his nag and pulled out. Now will you born fools stop, or will I give you another deluge? Land save us! What's that light?"

Somebody was yelling toward the settlement, and I was aware of a peculiar glow which didn't come from such torches as was still burning. And here come Medina Kirby, one of Bill's gals, yelping like a Comanche.

"Our cabin's burnin'!" she squalled. "A stray bullet went through the winder and busted Miss Margaret's ile lamp!"

With a yell of dismay I abandoned the fray and headed for Bill's cabin, follered by everybody which was able to foller me. They had been several wild shots fired during the melee and one of 'em must have hived in Miss Margaret's winder. The Kirbys had dragged most of their belongings into the yard and some was bringing water from the creek, but the whole cabin was in a blaze by now.

"Whar's Miss Margaret?" I roared.

"She must be still in there!" shrilled Miss Kirby. "A beam fell and wedged her door so we couldn't open it, and – "

I grabbed a blanket one of the gals had rescued and plunged it into the rain barrel and run for Miss Margaret's room. They wasn't but one door in it, which led into the main part of the cabin, and was jammed like they said, and I knowed I couldn't never get my shoulders through either winder, so I just put down my head and rammed the wall full force and knocked four or five logs outa place and made a hole big enough to go through.

The room was so full of smoke I was nigh blinded but I made out a figger fumbling at the winder on the other side. A flaming beam fell outa the roof and broke acrost my head with a loud report and about a bucketful of coals rolled down the back of my neck, but I paid no heed.

I charged through the smoke, nearly fracturing my shin on a bedstead or something, and enveloped the figger in the wet blanket and swept it up in my arms. It kicked wildly and fought and though its voice was muffled in the blanket I ketched some words I never would of thought Miss Margaret would use, but I figgered she was hysterical. She seemed to be wearing spurs, too, because I felt 'em every time she kicked.

By this time the room was a perfect blaze and the roof was falling in and we'd both been roasted if I'd tried to get back to the hole I knocked in the oppersite wall. So I lowered my head and butted my way through the near wall, getting all my eyebrows and hair burnt off in the process, and come staggering through the ruins with my precious burden and fell into the arms of my relatives which was thronged outside.

"I've saved her!" I panted. "Pull off the blanket! Yo're safe, Miss Margaret!"

"#$%&*?@¢!" said Miss Margaret, and Uncle Saul groped under the blanket and said, "By golly, if this is the teacher she's growed a remarkable set of whiskers since I seen her last!"

He yanked off the blanket – to reveal the bewhiskered countenance of Uncle Jeppard Grimes!

"Hell's fire!" I bellered. "What you doin' here?"

"I was comin' to jine the lynchin', you blame fool!" he snarled. "I seen Bill's cabin was afire so I clumb in through the back winder to save Miss Margaret. She was gone, but they was a note she'd left. I was fixin' to climb out the winder when this maneyack grabbed me."

"Gimme that note!" I bellered, grabbing it. "Medina! Come here and read it for me."

That note run:

Dear Breckinridge: I am sorry, but I can't stay on Bear Creek any longer. It was tough enough anyway, but being expected to marry you was the last straw. You've been very

*kind to me, but it would be too much like marrying a grizzly bear. Please forgive me.
I am eloping with J. Pembroke Pemberton. We're going out the back window to avoid
any trouble, and ride away on his horse. Give my love to the children. We are going
to Europe on our honeymoon.*

With love,

Margaret Ashley.

"Now what you got to say?" sneered Uncle Jeppard.

"I'm a victim of foreign entanglements," I said dazedly. "I'm goin' to
chaw Bill Glanton's ears off for saddlin' that critter on me. And then I'm
goin' to lick me a Englishman if I have to go all the way to Californy to
find one."

Which same is now my aim, object and ambition. This Englishman
took my girl and ruined my education, and filled my neck and spine with
burns and bruises. A Elkins never forgets – and the next one that pokes
his nose into the Bear Creek country had better be a fighting fool or a
powerful fast runner.

The Haunted Mountain

The reason I despises tarantulas, stinging lizards, and hydrophobia skunks is because they reminds me so much of Aunt Lavaca, which my Uncle Jacob Grimes married in a absent-minded moment, when he was old enough to know better.

That there woman's voice plumb puts my teeth on aidge, and it has the same effect on my horse, Cap'n Kidd, which don't generally shy at nothing less'n a rattlesnake. So when she stuck her head out of her cabin as I was riding by and yelled "Breckinri-i-idge," Cap'n Kidd jumped straight up in the air, and then tried to buck me off.

"Stop tormentin' that pore animal and come here," Aunt Lavaca commanded, whilst I was fighting for my life against Cap'n Kidd's spine-twisting sun-fishing. "I never see such a cruel, worthless, no-good – "

She kept right on yapping away until I finally wore him down and reined up alongside the cabin stoop and said, "What you want, Aunt Lavaca?"

She give me a scornful snort, and put her hands onto her hips and glared at me like I was something she didn't like the smell of.

"I want you should go git yore Uncle Jacob and bring him home," she said at last. "He's off on one of his idiotic prospectin' sprees again. He snuck out before daylight with the bay mare and a pack-mule – I wisht I'd woke up and caught him. I'd of fixed him! If you hustle you can catch him this side of Haunted Mountain Gap. You bring him back if you have to lasso him and tie him to his saddle. Old fool! Off huntin' gold when they's work to be did in the alfalfa fields. Says he ain't no farmer. Huh! I 'low I'll make a farmer outa him yet. You git goin'."

"But I ain't got time to go chasin' Uncle Jacob all over Haunted Mountain," I protested. "I'm headin' for the rodeo over to Chawed Ear. I'm goin' to win me a prize bull-doggin' some steers – "

"Bull-doggin'!" she snapped. "A fine ockerpashun! Gwan, you worthless loafer! I ain't goin' to stand here all day argyin' with a big ninny like you be. Of all the good-for-nothin', triflin', lunkheaded – "

When Aunt Lavaca starts in like that you might as well travel. She can talk steady for three days and nights without repeating herself, her voice getting louder and shriller all the time till it nigh splits a body's eardrums. She was still yelling at me as I rode up the trail toward Haunted Mountain Gap, and I could hear her long after I couldn't see her no more.

Pore Uncle Jacob! He never had much luck prospecting, but trailing around through the mountains with a jackass is a lot better'n listening to Aunt Lavaca. A jackass's voice is mild and soothing alongside of hers.

Some hours later I was climbing the long rise that led up to the Gap, and I realized I had overtook the old coot when something went *ping*! up on the slope, and my hat flew off. I quick reined Cap'n Kidd behind a clump of bresh, and looked up toward the Gap, and seen a pack-mule's rear end sticking out of a cluster of boulders.

"You quit that shootin' at me, Uncle Jacob!" I roared.

"You stay whar you be," his voice come back, sharp as a razor. "I know Lavacky sent you after me, but I ain't goin' home. I'm onto somethin' big at last, and I don't aim to be interfered with."

"What you mean?" I demanded.

"Keep back or I'll ventilate you," he promised. "I'm goin' for the Lost Haunted Mine."

"You been huntin' that thing for thirty years," I snorted.

"This time I finds it," he says. "I bought a map off'n a drunk Mex down to Perdition. One of his ancestors was a Injun which helped pile up the rocks to hide the mouth of the cave where it is."

"Why didn't he go find it and git the gold?" I asked.

"He's skeered of ghosts," said Uncle Jacob. "All Mexes is awful superstitious. This-un 'ud ruther set and drink, nohow. They's millions in gold in that there mine. I'll shoot you before I'll go home. Now will you go on back peaceable, or will you throw in with me? I might need you, in case the pack-mule plays out."

"I'll come with you," I said, impressed. "Maybe you have got somethin', at that. Put up yore Winchester. I'm comin'."

He emerged from his rocks, a skinny leathery old cuss, and he said,

"What about Lavacky? If you don't come back with me, she'll foller us herself. She's that strong-minded."

"I'll leave a note for her," I said. "Joe Hopkins always comes down through the Gap onct a week on his way to Chawed Ear. He's due through here today. I'll stick the note on a tree, where he'll see it and take it to her."

I had a pencil stub in my saddlebag, and I tore a piece of wrapping paper off'n a can of tomaters Uncle Jacob had in his pack, and I writ:

Dere Ant Lavaca: I am takin uncle Jacob way up in the mountins dont try to foler us it wont do no good gold is what Im after. Breckinridge.

I folded it and writ on the outside:

Dere Joe: pleeze take this here note to Miz Lavaca Grimes on the Chawed Ear rode.

Then me and Uncle Jacob sot out for the higher ranges, and he started telling me all about the Lost Haunted Mine again, like he'd already did about forty times before. Seems like they was onct a old prospector which stumbled onto a cave about fifty years before then, which the walls was solid gold and nuggets all over the floor till a body couldn't walk, as big as mushmelons. But the Indians jumped him and run him out and he got lost and nearly starved in the desert, and went crazy. When he come to a settlement and finally regained his mind, he tried to lead a party back to it, but never could find it. Uncle Jacob said the Indians had took rocks and bresh and hid the mouth of the cave so nobody could tell it was there. I asked him how he knowed the Indians done that and he said it was common knowledge. Any fool oughta know that's just what they done.

"This here mine," says Uncle Jacob, "is located in a hidden valley which lies away up amongst the high ranges. I ain't never seen it, and I thought I'd explored these mountains plenty. Ain't nobody more familiar with 'em than me except old Joshua Braxton. But it stands to reason that the cave is awful hard to find, or somebody'd already found it. Accordin' to this here map, that lost valley must lie just beyond Apache Canyon. Ain't many whitemen knows whar that is, even. We're headin' there."

We had left the Gap far behind us, and was moving along the slanting side of a sharp-angled crag whilst he was talking. As we passed it, we seen two figgers with horses emerge from the other side, heading in the same direction we was, so our trails converged. Uncle Jacob glared and reached for his Winchester.

"Who's that?" he snarled.

"The big un's Bill Glanton," I said. "I never seen t'other'n."

"And nobody else, outside of a freak museum," growled Uncle Jacob.

This other feller was a funny-looking little maverick, with laced boots and a cork sun helmet and big spectacles. He sot his horse like he thought it was a rockingchair, and held his reins like he was trying to fish with 'em. Glanton hailed us. He was from Texas, original, and was rough in his speech and free with his weapons, but me and him had always got along very well.

"Where you all goin'?" demanded Uncle Jacob.

"I am Professor Van Brock, of New York," said the tenderfoot, whilst Bill was getting rid of his tobaccer wad. "I have employed Mr. Glanton, here, to guide me up into the mountains. I am on the track of a tribe of aborigines, which, according to fairly well substantiated rumor, have inhabited the Haunted Mountains since time immemorial."

"Lissen here, you four-eyed runt," said Uncle Jacob in wrath, "are you givin' me the horse laugh?"

"I assure you that equine levity is the furthest thing from my thoughts," says Van Brock. "Whilst touring the country, in the interests of science, I heard the rumors to which I have referred. In a village possessing the singular appellation of Chawed Ear, I met an aged prospector who told me that he had seen one of the aborigines, clad in the skin of a wild animal and armed with a bludgeon. The wildman, he said, emitted a most peculiar and piercing cry when sighted, and fled into the recesses of the hills. I am confident that it is some survivor of a pre-Indian race, and I am determined to investigate."

"They ain't no such critter in these hills," snorted Uncle Jacob. "I've roamed all over 'em for thirty year, and I ain't seen no wildman."

"Well," says Glanton, "they's somethin' onnatural up there, because I been hearin' some funny yarns myself. I never thought I'd be huntin' wildmen," he says, "but since that hash slinger in Perdition turned me down to elope with a travelin' salesman, I welcomes the chance to lose myself in the mountains and forgit the perfidy of womenkind. What you all doin' up here? Prospectin'?" he said, glancing at the tools on the mule.

82

"Not in earnest," said Uncle Jacob hurriedly. "We're just kinda whilin' away our time. They ain't no gold in these mountains."

"Folks says that Lost Haunted Mine is up here somewhere," said Glanton.

"A pack of lies," snorted Uncle Jacob, busting into a sweat. "Ain't no such mine. Well, Breckinridge, let's be shovin'. Got to make Antelope Peak before sundown."

"I thought we was goin' to Apache Canyon," I says, and he give me a awful glare, and said, "Yes, Breckinridge, that's right, Antelope Peak, just like you said. So long, gents."

"So long," said Glanton.

So we turned off the trail almost at right angles to our course, me follering Uncle Jacob bewilderedly. When we was out of sight of the others, he reined around again.

"When Nature give you the body of a giant, Breckinridge," he said, "she plumb forgot to give you any brains to go along with yore muscles. You want everybody to know what we're lookin' for?"

"Aw," I said, "them fellers is just lookin' for wildmen."

"Wildmen!" he snorted. "They don't have to go no further'n Chawed Ear on payday night to find more wildmen than they could handle. I ain't swallerin' no such stuff. Gold is what they're after, I tell you. I seen Glanton talkin' to that Mex in Perdition the day I bought that map from him. I believe they either got wind of that mine, or know I got that map, or both."

"What you goin' to do?" I asked him.

"Head for Apache Canyon by another trail," he said.

So we done so and arriv there after night, him not willing to stop till we got there. It was deep, with big high cliffs cut with ravines and gulches here and there, and very wild in appearance. We didn't descend into the canyon that night, but camped on a plateau above it. Uncle Jacob 'lowed we'd begin exploring next morning. He said they was lots of caves in the canyon, and he'd been in all of 'em. He said he hadn't never found nothing except b'ars and painters and rattlesnakes; but he believed one of them caves went on through into another, hidden canyon, and there was where the gold was at.

Next morning I was awoke by Uncle Jacob shaking me, and his whiskers was curling with rage.

"What's the matter?" I demanded, setting up and pulling my guns.

"They're here!" he squalled. "Dawgone it, I suspected 'em all the time! Git up, you big lunk. Don't set there gawpin' with a gun in each hand like a idjit! They're here, I tell you!"

"Who's here?" I asked.

"That dern tenderfoot and his cussed Texas gunfighter," snarled Uncle Jacob. "I was up just at daylight, and purty soon I seen a wisp of smoke curlin' up from behind a big rock t'other side of the flat. I snuck over there, and there was Glanton fryin' bacon, and Van Brock was pertendin' to be lookin' at some flowers with a magnifyin' glass – the blame' fake. He ain't no perfessor. I bet he's a derned crook. They're follerin' us. They aim to murder us and rob us of my map."

"Aw, Glanton wouldn't do that," I said. And Uncle Jacob said, "You shet up! A man will do anything whar gold is consarned. Dang it all, git up and do somethin'! Air you goin' to set there, you big lummox, and let us git murdered in our sleep?"

That's the trouble of being the biggest man in yore clan; the rest of the family always dumps all the onpleasant jobs onto yore shoulders. I pulled on my boots and headed across the flat, with Uncle Jacob's war-songs ringing in my ears, and I didn't notice whether he was bringing up the rear with his Winchester or not.

They was a scattering of trees on the flat, and about halfway across a figger emerged from amongst them, headed my direction with fire in his eye. It was Glanton.

"So, you big mountain grizzly," he greeted me rambunctiously, "you was goin' to Antelope Peak, hey? Kinda got off the road, didn't you? Oh, we're on to you, we are!"

"What you mean?" I demanded. He was acting like he was the one which oughta feel righteously indignant, instead of me.

"You know what I mean!" he says, frothing slightly at the mouth. "I didn't believe it when Van Brock first said he suspicioned you, even though you hombres did act funny yesterday when we met you on the trail. But this mornin' when I glimpsed yore fool Uncle Jacob spyin' on our camp, and then seen him sneakin' off through the bresh, I knowed Van Brock was right. Yo're after what we're after, and you all resorts to dirty onderhanded tactics. Does you deny yo're after the same thing we are?"

"Naw, I don't," I said. "Uncle Jacob's got more right to it than you all. And when you says we uses underhanded tricks, yo're a liar."

"That settles it!" gnashed he. "Go for yore gun!"

"I don't want to perforate you," I growled.

"I ain't hankerin' to conclude yore mortal career," he admitted. "But Haunted Mountain ain't big enough for both of us. Take off yore guns and I'll maul the livin' daylights outa you, big as you be."

I unbuckled my gunbelt and hung it on a limb, and he laid off his'n, and hit me in the stummick and on the ear and in the nose, and then he socked me in the jaw and knocked out a tooth. This made me mad, so I taken him by the neck and throwed him against the ground so hard it jolted all the wind outa him. I then sot on him and started banging his head against a convenient boulder, and his cussing was terrible to hear.

"If you all had acted like whitemen," I gritted, "we'd of *give* you a share in that there mine."

"What you talkin' about?" he gurgled, trying to haul his bowie out of his boot which I had my knee on.

"The Lost Haunted Mine, of course," I snarled, getting a fresh grip on his ears.

"Hold on," he protested. "You mean you all are just lookin' for gold? On the level?"

I was so astonished I quit hammering his skull against the rock.

"Why, what else?" I demanded. "Ain't you all follerin' us to steal Uncle Jacob's map which shows where at the mine is hid?"

"Git offa me," he snorted disgustfully, taking advantage of my surprise to push me off. "Hell!" he said, starting to knock the dust offa his britches. "I might of knowed that tenderfoot was wool gatherin'. After we seen you all yesterday, and he heard you mention 'Apache Canyon' he told me he believed you was follerin' us. He said that yarn about prospectin' was just a blind. He said he believed you was workin' for a rival scientific society to git ahead of us and capture that there wildman yoreselves."

"What?" I said. "You mean that wildman yarn is straight?"

"So far as we're consarned," said Bill. "Prospectors is been tellin' some onusual stories about Apache Canyon. Well, I laughed at him at first, but he kept on usin' so many .45-caliber words that he got me to believin' it might be so. 'Cause, after all, here was me guidin' a tenderfoot on the trail of a wildman, and they wasn't no reason to think you and Jacob Grimes was any more sensible than me.

"Then, this mornin' when I seen Jacob peekin' at me from the bresh, I decided Van Brock must be right. You all hadn't never went to Antelope Peak. The more I thought it over, the more sartain I was that you was follerin' us to steal our wildman, so I started over to have a showdown."

"Well," I said, "we've reached a understandin' at last. You don't want our mine, and we shore don't want yore wildman. They's plenty of them amongst my relatives on Bear Creek. Le's git Van Brock and lug him over to our camp and explain things to him and my weak-minded uncle."

"All right," said Glanton, buckling on his guns. "Hey, what's that?"

From down in the canyon come a yell, "Help! Aid! Assistance!"

"It's Van Brock!" yelped Glanton. "He's wandered down into the canyon by hisself! Come on!"

Right near their camp they was a ravine leading down to the floor of the canyon. We pelted down that at full speed, and emerged near the wall of the cliffs. They was the black mouth of a cave showing nearby, in a kind of cleft, and just outside this cleft Van Brock was staggering around, yowling like a hound dawg with his tail caught in the door.

His cork helmet was laying on the ground all bashed outa shape, and his specs was lying near it. He had a knob on his head as big as a turnip and he was doing a kind of ghost dance or something all over the place.

He couldn't see very good without his specs, 'cause when he sighted us he give a shriek and started legging it for the other end of the canyon, seeming to think we was more enemies. Not wanting to indulge in no sprint in that heat, Bill shot a heel offa his boot, and that brung him down squalling blue murder.

"Help!" he shrieked. "Mr. Glanton! Help! I am being attacked! Help!"

"Aw, shet up," snorted Bill. "I'm Glanton. Yo're all right. Give him his specs, Breck. Now what's the matter?"

He put 'em on, gasping for breath, and staggered up, wild-eyed, and p'inted at the cave and hollered, "The wildman! I saw him, as I descended into the canyon on a private exploring expedition! A giant with a panther skin about his waist, and a club in his hand. He dealt me a murderous blow with the bludgeon when I sought to apprehend him, and fled into that cavern. He should be arrested!"

I looked into the cave. It was too dark to see anything except for a hoot-owl.

"He must of saw *somethin'*, Breck," said Glanton, hitching his gun harness. "Somethin' shore cracked him on the conk. I've been hearin' some queer tales about this canyon, myself. Maybe I better sling some lead in there – "

"No, no, no!" broke in Van Brock. "We must capture him alive!"

"What's goin' on here?" said a voice, and we turned to see Uncle Jacob approaching with his Winchester in his hands.

"Everything's all right, Uncle Jacob," I said. "They don't want yore mine. They're after the wildman, like they said, and we got him cornered in that there cave."

"All right, huh?" he snorted. "I reckon you thinks it's all right for you to waste yore time with such dern foolishness when you oughta be helpin' me look for my mine. A big help you be!"

"Where was you whilst I was argyin' with Bill here?" I demanded.

"I knowed you could handle the sityation, so I started explorin' the canyon," he said. "Come on, we got work to do."

"But the wildman!" cried Van Brock. "Your nephew would be invaluable in securing the specimen. Think of science! Think of progress! Think of – "

"Think of a striped skunk!" snorted Uncle Jacob. "Breckinridge, air you comin'?"

"Aw, shet up," I said disgustedly. "You both make me tired. I'm goin' in there and run that wildman out, and Bill, you shoot him in the hind laig as he comes out, so's we can catch him and tie him up."

"But you left yore guns hangin' onto that limb up on the plateau," objected Glanton.

"I don't need 'em," I said. "Didn't you hear Van Brock say we was to catch him alive? If I started shootin' in the dark I might rooin him."

"All right," says Bill, cocking his six-shooters. "Go ahead. I figger yo're a match for any wildman that ever come down the pike."

So I went into the cleft and entered the cave, and it was dark as all get-out. I groped my way along and discovered the main tunnel split into two, so I taken the biggest one. It seemed to get darker the further I went, and purty soon I bumped into something big and hairy and it went "Wump!" and grabbed me.

Thinks I, it's the wildman, and he's on the warpath. We waded into each other and tumbled around on the rocky floor in the dark, biting and mauling and tearing. I'm the biggest and the fightingest man on Bear Creek, which is famed far and wide for its ringtailed scrappers, but this wildman shore give me my hands full. He was the biggest hairiest critter I ever laid hands on, and he had more teeth and talons than I thought a human could possibly have. He chawed me with vigor and enthusiasm, and he waltzed up and down my frame free and hearty, and swept the floor with me till I was groggy.

For a while I thought I was going to give up the ghost, and I thought with despair of how humiliated my relatives on Bear Creek would be to hear their champion battler had been clawed to death by a wildman in a cave.

That made me plumb ashamed for weakening, and the socks I give him ought to of laid out any man, wild or tame, to say nothing of the pile-driver kicks in his belly, and butting him with my head so he gasped. I got what felt like a ear in my mouth and commenced chawing on it, and presently, what with this and other mayhem I committed on him, he give a most inhuman squall and bust away and went lickety-split for the outside world.

I riz up and staggered after him, hearing a wild chorus of yells break forth outside, but no shots. I bust out into the open, bloody all over, and my clothes hanging in tatters.

"Where is he?" I hollered. "Did you let him git away?"

"Who?" said Glanton, coming out from behind a boulder, whilst Van Brock and Uncle Jacob dropped down out of a tree nearby.

"The wildman, damn it!" I roared.

"We ain't seen no wildman," said Glanton.

"Well, what was that thing I just run outa the cave?" I hollered.

"That was a grizzly b'ar," said Glanton.

"Yeah," sneered Uncle Jacob, "and that was Van Brock's 'wildman'! And now, Breckinridge, if yo're through playin', we'll – "

"No, no!" hollered Van Brock, jumping up and down. "It was a human being which smote me and fled into the cavern. Not a bear! It is still in there somewhere, unless there is another exit to the cavern."

"Well, he ain't in there now," said Uncle Jacob, peering into the mouth of the cave. "Not even a wildman would run into a grizzly's cave, or if he did, he wouldn't stay long – *ooomp!*"

A rock come whizzing out of the cave and hit Uncle Jacob in the belly, and he doubled up on the ground.

"Aha!" I roared, knocking up Glanton's ready six-shooter. "I know! They's two tunnels in here. He's in that smaller cave. I went into the wrong one! Stay here, you all, and gimme room! This time I gets him!"

With that I rushed into the cave mouth again, disregarding some more rocks which emerged, and plunged into the smaller opening. It was dark as pitch, but I seemed to be running along a narrer tunnel, and ahead of me I heered bare feet pattering on the rock. I follered 'em at full lope, and presently seen a faint hint of light. The next minute I rounded a turn and come out into a wide place, which was lit by a shaft of light coming in through a cleft in the wall, some yards up. In the light I seen a fantastic figger climbing up on a ledge, trying to reach that cleft.

"Come down offa that!" I thundered, and give a leap and grabbed the ledge by one hand and hung on, and reached for his legs with t'other hand. He give a squall as I grabbed his ankle and splintered his club over my head. The force of the lick broke off the lip of the rock ledge I was holding to, and we crashed to the floor together, because I didn't let loose of him. Fortunately, I hit the rock floor headfirst which broke my fall and kept me from fracturing any of my important limbs, and his head hit my jaw, which rendered him unconscious.

I riz up and picked up my limp captive and carried him out into the daylight where the others was waiting. I dumped him on the ground and they stared at him like they couldn't believe it. He was a ga'nt old cuss with whiskers about a foot long and matted hair, and he had a mountain lion's hide tied around his waist.

"A white man!" enthused Van Brock, dancing up and down. "An unmistakable Caucasian! This is stupendous! A prehistoric survivor of a pre-Indian epoch! What an aid to anthropology! A wildman! A veritable wildman!"

"Wildman, hell!" snorted Uncle Jacob. "That there's old Joshua Braxton, which was tryin' to marry that old maid school teacher down at Chawed Ear all last winter."

"I was tryin' to marry her!" said Joshua bitterly, setting up suddenly and glaring at all of us. "That there is good, that there is! And me all the time fightin' for my life against it. Her and all her relations was tryin' to marry *her* to me. They made my life a curse. They was finally all set to kidnap me and marry me by force. That's why I come away off up here, and put on this rig to scare folks away. All I craves is peace and quiet and no dern women."

Van Brock begun to cry because they wasn't no wildman, and Uncle Jacob said, "Well, now that this dern foolishness is settled, maybe I can git to somethin' important. Joshua, you know these mountains even better'n I do. I want you to help me find the Lost Haunted Mine."

"There ain't no such mine," said Joshua. "That old prospector imagined all that stuff whilst he was wanderin' around over the desert crazy."

"But I got a map I bought from a Mexican in Perdition," hollered Uncle Jacob.

"Lemme see that map," said Glanton. "Why, hell," he said, "that there is a fake. I seen that Mexican drawin' it, and he said he was goin' to try to sell it to some old jassack for the price of a drunk."

Uncle Jacob sot down on a rock and pulled his whiskers. "My dreams is bust," he said weakly. "I'm goin' home to my wife."

"You must be desperate if it's come to that," said old Joshua acidly. "You better stay up here. If they ain't no gold, they ain't no women to torment a body, either."

"Women is a snare and a delusion," agreed Glanton. "Van Brock can go back with these fellers. I'm stayin' with Joshua."

"You all oughta be ashamed talkin' about women that way," I reproached 'em. "What, in this here lousy and troubled world can compare to women's gentle sweetness – "

"There the scoundrel is!" screeched a familiar voice. "Don't let him git away! Shoot him if he tries to run!"

We turned sudden. We'd been argying so loud amongst ourselves we hadn't noticed a gang of folks coming down the ravine. There was Aunt Lavaca and the sheriff of Chawed Ear with ten men, and they all p'inted sawed-off shotguns at me.

"Don't get rough, Elkins," warned the sheriff nervously. "They're all loaded with buckshot and ten-penny nails. I knows yore repertation and I takes no chances. I arrests you for the kidnapin' of Jacob Grimes."

"Are you plumb crazy?" I demanded.

"Kidnapin'!" hollered Aunt Lavaca, waving a piece of paper. "Abductin' yore pore old uncle! Aimin' to hold him for ransom! It's all writ down in yore own handwritin' right here on this here paper! Sayin' yo're takin' Jacob away off into the mountains – warnin' me not to try to foller! Same as threatenin' me! I never heered of such doins! Soon as that good-for-nothin' Joe Hopkins brung me that there insolent letter, I went right after the sheriff . . . Joshua Braxton, what air you doin' in them ondecent togs? My land, I dunno what we're comin' to! Well, sheriff, what you standin' there for like a ninny? Why'n't you put some handcuffs and chains and shackles on him? Air you skeered of the big lunkhead?"

"Aw, heck," I said. "This is all a mistake. I warn't threatenin' nobody in that there letter – "

"Then where's Jacob?" she demanded. "Prejuice him imejitely, or – "

"He ducked into that cave," said Glanton. I stuck my head in and roared, "Uncle Jacob! You come outa there and explain before I come in after you!"

He snuck out looking meek and downtrodden, and I says, "You tell these idjits that I ain't no kidnaper."

"That's right," he said. "I brung him along with me."

"Hell!" said the sheriff, disgustedly. "Have we come all this way on a wild goose chase? I should of knew better'n to listen to a woman – "

"You shet yore fool mouth!" squalled Aunt Lavaca. "A fine sheriff you be. Anyway – what was Breckinridge doin' up here with you, Jacob?"

"He was helpin' me look for a mine, Lavacky," he said.

"Helpin' you?" she screeched. "Why, I sent him to fetch you back! Breckinridge Elkins, I'll tell yore pap about this, you big, lazy, good-for-nothin', lowdown, ornery – "

"Aw, *shet up!*" I roared, exasperated beyond endurance. I seldom lets my voice go its full blast. Echoes rolled through the canyon like thunder, the trees shook and the pine cones fell like hail, and rocks tumbled down the mountainsides. Aunt Lavaca staggered backwards with a outraged squall.

"Jacob!" she hollered. "Air you goin' to 'low that ruffian to use that there tone of voice to me? I demands that you frail the livin' daylights outa the scoundrel right now!"

Uncle Jacob winked at me.

"Now, now, Lavacky," he started soothing her, and she give him a clip under the ear that changed ends with him. The sheriff and his posse and Van Brock took out up the ravine like the devil was after 'em, and Glanton bit off a chaw of tobaccer and says to me, he says, "Well, what was you fixin' to say about women's gentle sweetness?"

"Nothin'," I snarled. "Come on, let's git goin'. I yearns to find a more quiet and secluded spot than this here'n. I'm stayin' with Joshua and you and the grizzly."

The Feud Buster

These here derned lies which is being circulated around is making me sick and tired. If this slander don't stop I'm liable to lose my temper, and anybody in the Humbolts can tell you when I loses my temper the effect on the population is wuss'n fire, earthquake, and cyclone.

First off, it's a lie that I rode a hundred miles to mix into a feud which wasn't none of my business. I never heard of the Hopkins-Barlow war before I come in the Mezquital country. I hear tell the Barlows is talking about suing me for destroying their property. Well, they ought to build their cabins solider if they don't want 'em tore down. And they're all liars when they says the Hopkinses hired me to exterminate 'em at five dollars a sculp. I don't believe even a Hopkins would pay five dollars for one of their mangy sculps. Anyway, I don't fight for hire for nobody. And the Hopkinses needn't bellyache about me turning on 'em and trying to massacre the entire clan. All I wanted to do was kind of disable 'em so they couldn't interfere with my business. And my business, from first to last, was defending the family honor. If I had to wipe up the earth with a couple of feuding clans whilst so doing, I can't help it. Folks which is particular of their hides ought to stay out of the way of tornadoes, wild bulls, devastating torrents, and a insulted Elkins.

But it was Uncle Jeppard Grimes' fault to begin with, like it generally is. Dern near all the calamities which takes places in southern Nevada can be traced back to that old lobo. He's got a ingrown disposition and a natural talent for pestering his feller man. Specially his relatives.

I was setting in a saloon in War Paint, enjoying a friendly game of kyards with a horse thief and three train robbers, when Uncle Jeppard come in and spied me, and he come over and scowled down on me like I was the missing lynx or something. Purty soon he says, just as I was all sot to make a killing, he says, "How can you set there so free and keerless, with four ace kyards into yore hand, when yore family name is bein' besmirched?"

I flang down my hand in annoyance, and said, "Now look what you done! What you mean blattin' out information of sech a private nature? What you talkin' about, anyhow?"

"Well," he says, "durin' the three months you been away from home roisterin' and wastin' yore substance in riotous livin' – "

"I been down on Wild River punchin' cows at thirty a month!" I said fiercely. "I ain't squandered nothin' nowheres. Shut up and tell me whatever yo're a-talkin' about."

"Well," says he, "whilst you been gone young Dick Jackson of Chawed Ear has been courtin' yore sister Ellen, and the family's been expectin' 'em to set the day, any time. But now I hear he's been braggin' all over Chawed Ear about how he done jilted her. Air you goin' to set there and let yore sister become the laughin' stock of the country? When I was a young man – "

"When you was a young man Dan'l Boone warn't whelped yet!" I bellered, so mad I included him and everybody else in my irritation. They ain't nothing upsets me like injustice done to some of my close kin. "Git out of my way! I'm headin' for Chawed Ear – what *you* grinnin' at, you spotted hyener?" This last was addressed to the horse thief in which I seemed to detect signs of amusement.

"I warn't grinnin'," he said.

"So I'm a liar, I reckon!" I said. I felt a impulse to shatter a demi-john over his head, which I done, and he fell under a table hollering bloody murder, and all the fellers drinking at the bar abandoned their licker and stampeded for the street hollering, "Take cover, boys! Breckinridge Elkins is on the rampage!"

So I kicked all the slats out of the bar to relieve my feelings, and stormed out of the saloon and forked Cap'n Kidd. Even he seen it was no time to take liberties with me – he didn't pitch but seven jumps – then he settled down to a dead run, and we headed for Chawed Ear.

Everything kind of floated in a red haze all the way, but them folks which claims I tried to murder 'em in cold blood on the road between War Paint and Chawed Ear is just narrer-minded and super-sensitive. The reason I shot everybody's hats off that I met was just to kind of ca'm my nerves, because I was afraid if I didn't cool off some by the time I hit Chawed Ear I might hurt somebody. I am that mild-mannered and retiring by nature that I wouldn't willing hurt man, beast, nor Injun unless maddened beyond endurance.

That's why I acted with so much self-possession and dignity when I got to Chawed Ear and entered the saloon where Dick Jackson generally hung out.

"Where's Dick Jackson?" I said, and everybody must of been nervous, because when I boomed out they all jumped and looked around, and the bartender dropped a glass and turned pale.

"Well," I hollered, beginning to lose patience. "Where is the coyote?"

"G-gimme time, will ya?" stuttered the barkeep. "I – uh – he – uh – "

"So you evades the question, hey?" I said, kicking the foot rail loose. "Friend of his'n, hey? Tryin' to pertect him, hey?" I was so overcome by this perfidy that I lunged for him and he ducked down behind the bar and I crashed into it bodily with all my lunge and weight, and it collapsed on top of him, and all the customers run out of the saloon hollering, "Help, murder, Elkins is killin' the bartender!"

This feller stuck his head up from amongst the ruins of the bar and begged, "For God's sake, lemme alone! Jackson headed south for the Mezquital Mountains yesterday."

I throwed down the chair I was fixing to bust all the ceiling lamps with, and run out and jumped on Cap'n Kidd and headed south, whilst behind me folks emerged from their cyclone cellars and sent a rider up in the hills to tell the sheriff and his deputies they could come on back now.

I knowed where the Mezquitals was, though I hadn't never been there. I crossed the Californy line about sundown, and shortly after dark I seen Mezquital Peak looming ahead of me. Having ca'med down somewhat, I decided to stop and rest Cap'n Kidd. He warn't tired, because that horse has got alligator blood in his veins, but I knowed I might have to trail Jackson clean to The Angels, and they warn't no use in running Cap'n Kidd's laigs off on the first lap of the chase.

It warn't a very thickly settled country I'd come into, very mountainous and thick timbered, but purty soon I come to a cabin beside the trail and I pulled up and hollered, "Hello!"

The candle inside was instantly blowed out, and somebody pushed a rifle barrel through the winder and bawled, "Who be you?"

"I'm Breckinridge Elkins from Bear Creek, Nevada," I said. "I'd like to stay all night, and git some feed for my horse."

"Stand still," warned the voice. "We can see you agin the stars, and they's four rifle-guns a-kiverin' you."

"Well, make up yore minds," I said, because I could hear 'em discussing me. I reckon they thought they was whispering. One of 'em said, "Aw, he can't be a Barlow. Ain't none of 'em that big." T'other'n said, "Well, maybe he's a derned gunfighter they've sent for to help 'em out. Old Jake's nephew's been up in Nevady."

"Le's let him in," said a third. "We can mighty quick tell what he is."

So one of 'em come out and 'lowed it would be all right for me to stay the night, and he showed me a corral to put Cap'n Kidd in, and hauled out some hay for him.

"We got to be keerful," he said. "We got lots of enemies in these hills."

We went into the cabin, and they lit the candle again, and sot some corn pone and sow belly and beans on the table and a jug of corn licker. They was four men, and they said their names was Hopkins – Jim, Bill, Joe, and Joshua, and they was brothers. I'd always heard tell the Mezquital country was famed for big men, but these fellers wasn't so big – not much over six foot high apiece. On Bear Creek they'd been considered kind of puny and undersized.

They warn't very talkative. Mostly they sot with their rifles acrost their knees and looked at me without no expression onto their faces, but that didn't stop me from eating a hearty supper, and would of et a lot more only the grub give out; and I hoped they had more licker somewheres else because I was purty dry. When I turned up the jug to take a snort it was brim-full, but before I'd more'n dampened my gullet the dern thing was plumb empty.

When I got through I went over and sot down on a rawhide bottomed chair in front of the fireplace where they was a small fire going, though they warn't really no need for it, and they said, "What's yore business, stranger?" "Well," I said, not knowing I was going to get the surprise of my life, "I'm lookin' for a feller named Dick Jackson – "

By golly, the words wasn't clean out of my mouth when they was four men onto my neck like catamounts!

"He's a spy!" they hollered. "He's a cussed Barlow! Shoot him! Stab him! Hit him in the head!"

All of which they was endeavoring to do with such passion they was getting in each other's way, and it was only his overeagerness which caused Jim to miss me with his bowie and sink it into the table instead, but Joshua busted a chair over my head and Bill would of shot me if I hadn't jerked back my head so he just singed my eyebrows. This lack of hospitality so irritated me that I riz up amongst 'em like a b'ar with a pack of wolves hanging onto him, and commenced committing mayhem on my hosts, because I seen right off they was critters which couldn't be persuaded to respect a guest no other way.

Well, the dust of battle hadn't settled, the casualities was groaning all over the place, and I was just relighting the candle when I heard a horse galloping down the trail from the south. I wheeled and drawed my guns as it stopped before the cabin. But I didn't shoot, because the next instant they was a barefooted gal standing in the door. When she seen the rooins she let out a screech like a catamount.

"You've kilt 'em!" she screamed. "You murderer!"

"Aw, I ain't neither," I said. "They ain't hurt much – just a few cracked ribs, and dislocated shoulders and busted laigs and sech – like trifles. Joshua's ear'll grow back on all right, if you take a few stitches into it."

"You cussed Barlow!" she squalled, jumping up and down with the hystericals. "I'll kill you! You damned Barlow!"

"I ain't no Barlow," I said. "I'm Breckinridge Elkins, of Bear Creek. I ain't never even heard of no Barlows."

At that Jim stopped his groaning long enough to snarl, "If you ain't a friend of the Barlows, how come you askin' for Dick Jackson? He's one of 'em."

"He jilted my sister!" I roared. "I aim to drag him back and make him marry her!"

"Well, it was all a mistake," groaned Jim. "But the damage is done now."

"It's wuss'n you think," said the gal fiercely. "The Hopkinses has all forted theirselves over at Pap's cabin, and they sent me to git you all. We got to make a stand. The Barlows is gatherin' over to Jake Barlow's cabin, and they aims to make a foray onto us tonight. We was outnumbered to begin with, and now here's our best fightin' men laid out! Our goose is cooked plumb to hell!"

"Lift me on my horse," moaned Jim. "I can't walk, but I can still shoot." He tried to rise up, and fell back cussing and groaning.

"You got to help us!" said the gal desperately, turning to me. "You done laid out our four best fightin' men, and you owes it to us. It's yore duty! Anyway, you says Dick Jackson's yore enemy – well, he's Jake Barlow's nephew, and he come back here to help 'em clean out us Hopkinses. He's over to Jake's cabin right now. My brother Bill snuck over and spied on 'em, and he says every fightin' man of the clan is gatherin' there. All we can do is hold the fort, and you got to come help us hold it! Yo're nigh as big as all four of these boys put together."

Well, I figgered I owed the Hopkinses something, so, after setting some bones and bandaging some wounds and abrasions of which they was a goodly lot, I saddled Cap'n Kidd and we sot out.

As we rode along she said, "That there is the biggest, wildest, meanest-lookin' critter I ever seen. Where'd you git him?"

"He was a wild horse," I said. "I catched him up in the Humbolts. Nobody ever rode him but me. He's the only horse west of the Pecos big enough to carry my weight, and he's got painter's blood and a shark's disposition. What's this here feud about?"

"I dunno," she said. "It's been goin' on so long everybody's done forgot what started it. Somebody accused somebody else of stealin' a cow, I think. What's the difference?"

"They ain't none," I assured her. "If folks wants to have feuds it's their own business."

We was following a winding path, and purty soon we heard dogs barking and about that time the gal turned aside and got off her horse, and showed me a pen hid in the brush. It was full of horses.

"We keep our mounts here so's the Barlows ain't so likely to find 'em and run 'em off," she said, and she turned her horse into the pen, and I put Cap'n Kidd in, but tied him over in one corner by hisself – otherwise he would of started fighting all the other horses and kicked the fence down.

Then we went on along the path and the dogs barked louder and purty soon we come to a big two-story cabin which had heavy board-shutters over the winders. They was just a dim streak of candle light come through the cracks. It was dark, because the moon hadn't come up. We stopped in the shadder of the trees, and the gal whistled like a whippoorwill three times, and somebody answered from up on the roof. A door opened a crack in the room which didn't have no light at all, and somebody said, "That you, Elizerbeth? Air the boys with you?"

"It's me," says she, starting toward the door. "But the boys ain't with me."

Then all to oncet he throwed open the door and hollered, "Run, gal! They's a grizzly b'ar standin' up on his hind laigs right behind you!"

"Aw, that ain't no b'ar," says she. "That there's Breckinridge Elkins, from up in Nevady. He's goin' to help us fight the Barlows."

We went on into a room where they was a candle on the table, and they was nine or ten men there and thirty-odd women and chillern. They all looked kinda pale and scairt, and the men was loaded down with pistols and Winchesters.

They all looked at me kind of dumb-like, and the old man kept staring like he warn't any too sure he hadn't let a grizzly in the house, after all. He mumbled something about making a natural mistake, in the dark, and turned to the gal.

"Whar's the boys I sent you after?" he demanded, and she says, "This gent mussed 'em up so's they ain't fitten for to fight. Now, don't git rambunctious, Pap. It war just a honest mistake all around. He's our friend, and he's gunnin' for Dick Jackson."

"Ha! Dick Jackson!" snarled one of the men, lifting his Winchester. "Just lemme line my sights on him! I'll cook his goose!"

"You won't, neither," I said. "He's got to go back to Bear Creek and marry my sister Ellen . . . Well," I says, "what's the campaign?"

"I don't figger they'll git here till well after midnight," said Old Man Hopkins. "All we can do is wait for 'em."

"You means you all sets here and waits till they comes and lays siege?" I says.

"What else?" says he. "Lissen here, young man, don't start tellin' me how to conduck a feud. I growed up in this here'n. It war in full swing when I was born, and I done spent my whole life carryin' it on."

"That's just it," I snorted. "You lets these dern wars drag on for generations. Up in the Humbolts we brings such things to a quick conclusion. Mighty near everybody up there come from Texas, original, and we fights our feuds Texas style, which is short and sweet – a feud which lasts ten years in Texas is a humdinger. We winds 'em up quick and in style. Where-at is this here cabin where the Barlows is gatherin'?"

" 'Bout three mile over the ridge," says a young feller they called Bill.

"How many is they?" I ast.

"I counted seventeen," says he.

"Just a fair-sized mouthful for a Elkins," I said. "Bill, you guide me to that there cabin. The rest of you can come or stay, it don't make no difference to me."

Well, they started jawing with each other then. Some was for going and some for staying. Some wanted to go with me, and try to take the Barlows by surprise, but the others said it couldn't be done – they'd git ambushed theirselves, and the only sensible thing to be did was to stay forted and wait for the Barlows to come. They given me no more heed – just sot there and augered.

But that was all right with me. Right in the middle of the dispute, when it looked like maybe the Hopkinses would get to fighting amongst theirselves and finish each other before the Barlows could git there, I lit out with the boy Bill, which seemed to have considerable sense for a Hopkins.

He got him a horse out of the hidden corral, and I got Cap'n Kidd, which was a good thing. He'd somehow got a mule by the neck, and the critter was almost at its last gasp when I rescued it. Then me and Bill lit out.

We follered winding paths over thick-timbered mountainsides till at last we come to a clearing and they was a cabin there, with light and profanity pouring out of the winders. We'd been hearing the last mentioned for half a mile before we sighted the cabin.

We left our horses back in the woods a ways, and snuck up on foot and stopped amongst the trees back of the cabin.

"They're in there tankin' up on corn licker to whet their appetites for Hopkins blood!" whispered Bill, all in a shiver. "Lissen to 'em! Them fellers ain't hardly human! What you goin' to do? They got a man standin' guard out in front of the door at the other end of the cabin. You see they ain't no doors nor winders at the back. They's winders on each side, but if we try to rush it from the front or either side, they'll see us and fill us full of lead before we could git in a shot. Look! The moon's comin' up. They'll be startin' on their raid before long."

I'll admit that cabin looked like it was going to be harder to storm than I'd figgered. I hadn't had no idee in mind when I sot out for the place. All I wanted was to get in amongst them Barlows – I does my best fighting at close quarters. But at the moment I couldn't think of no way that wouldn't get me shot up. Of course I could just rush the cabin, but the thought of seventeen Winchesters blazing away at me from close range was a little stiff even for me, though I was game to try it, if they warn't no other way.

Whilst I was studying over the matter, all to once the horses tied out in front of the cabin snorted, and back up the hills something went *Oooaaaw-w-w!* And a idee hit me.

"Git back in the woods and wait for me," I told Bill, as I headed for the thicket where we'd left the horses.

I mounted and rode up in the hills toward where the howl had come from. Purty soon I lit and throwed Cap'n Kidd's reins over his head, and walked on into the deep bresh, from time to time giving a long squall like a cougar. They ain't a catamount in the world can tell the difference when a Bear Creek man imitates one. After a while one answered, from a ledge just a few hundred feet away.

I went to the ledge and clumb up on it, and there was a small cave behind it, and a big mountain lion in there. He give a grunt of surprise when he seen I was a human, and made a swipe at me, but I give him a bat on the head with my fist, and whilst he was still dizzy I grabbed him by the scruff of the neck and hauled him out of the cave and lugged him down to where I left my horse.

Cap'n Kidd snorted at the sight of the cougar and wanted to kick his brains out, but I give him a good kick in the stummick hisself, which is the only kind of reasoning Cap'n Kidd understands, and got on him and headed for the Barlow hangout.

I can think of a lot more pleasant jobs than toting a full-growed mountain lion down a thick-timbered mountain side on the back of a iron jaw outlaw at midnight. I had the cat by the back of the neck with one hand, so hard he couldn't squall, and I held him out at arm's length as far from the horse as I could, but every now and then he'd twist around so he could claw Cap'n Kidd with his hind laigs, and when this would happen Cap'n Kidd would squall with rage and start bucking all over the place. Sometimes he would buck the derned cougar onto me, and pulling him loose from my hide was wuss'n pulling cockleburrs out of a cow's tail.

But presently I arriv close behind the cabin. I whistled like a whippoor-will for Bill, but he didn't answer and warn't nowheres to be seen, so I decided he'd got scairt and pulled out for home. But that was all right with me. I'd come to fight the Barlows, and I aimed to fight 'em, with or without assistance. Bill would just of been in the way.

I got off in the trees back of the cabin and throwed the reins over Cap'n Kidd's head, and went up to the back of the cabin on foot, walking soft and easy. The moon was well up, by now, and what wind they was, was blowing toward me, which pleased me, because I didn't want the horses tied out in front to scent the cat and start cutting up before I was ready.

The fellers inside was still cussing and talking loud as I approached one of the winders on the side, and one hollered out, "Come on! Let's git started! I craves Hopkins gore!" And about that time I give the cougar a heave and throwed him through the winder.

He let out a awful squall as he hit, and the fellers in the cabin hollered louder'n he did. Instantly a most awful bustle broke loose in there and of all the whooping and bellering and shooting I ever heard, and the lion squalling amongst it all, and clothes and hides tearing so you could hear it all over the clearing, and the horses busting loose and tearing out through the bresh.

As soon as I hove the cat I run around to the door and a man was standing there with his mouth open, too surprised at the racket to do anything. So I takes his rifle away from him and broke the stock off on his head, and stood there at the door with the barrel intending to brain them Barlows as they run out. I was plumb certain they *would* run out, because I have noticed that the average man is funny that way, and hates to be shut up in a cabin with a mad cougar as bad as the cougar would hate to be shut up in a cabin with a infuriated settler of Bear Creek.

But them scoundrels fooled me. 'Pears like they had a secret door in the back wall, and whilst I was waiting for them to storm out through the front door and get their skulls cracked, they knocked the secret door open and went piling out that way.

By the time I realized what was happening and run around to the other end of the cabin, they was all out and streaking for the trees, yelling blue murder, with their clothes all tore to shreds and them bleeding like stuck hawgs.

That there catamount sure improved the shining hours whilst he was corralled with them Barlows. He come out after 'em with his mouth full of the seats of men's britches, and when he seen me he give a kind of despairing yelp and taken out up the mountain with his tail betwixt his laigs like the devil was after him with a red-hot branding iron.

I taken after the Barlows, sot on scuttling at least a few of 'em, and I was on the p'int of letting *bam* at 'em with my six-shooters as they run, when, just as they reached the trees, all the Hopkins men riz out of the bresh and fell on 'em with piercing howls.

That fray was kind of peculiar. I don't remember a single shot being fired. The Barlows had dropped their guns in their flight, and the Hopkinses seemed bent on whipping out their wrongs with their bare hands and gun butts. For a few seconds they was a hell of a scramble – men cussing and howling and bellering, and rifle-stocks cracking over heads, and the bresh crashing underfoot, and then before I could get into it, the Barlows broke every which way and took out through the woods like jack-rabbits squalling Jedgment Day.

Old Man Hopkins come prancing out of the bresh waving his Winchester and his beard flying in the moonlight and he hollered, "The sins of the wicked shall return onto 'em! Elkins, we have hit a powerful lick for righteousness this here night!"

"Where'd you all come from?" I ast. "I thought you was still back in yore cabin chawin' the rag."

"Well," he says, "after you pulled out we decided to trail along and see how you come out with whatever you planned. As we come through the woods expectin' to git ambushed every second, we met Bill here who told us he believed you had a idea of circumventin' them devils, though he didn't know what it was. So we come on and hid ourselves at the aidge of the trees to see what'd happen. I see we been too timid in our dealins with these heathens. We been lettin' them force the fightin' too long. You was right. A good offense is the best defense."

"We didn't kill any of the varmints, wuss luck," he said, "but we give 'em a prime lickin'. Hey, look there! The boys has caught one of the critters! Take him into that cabin, boys!"

They lugged him into the cabin, and by the time me and the old man got there, they had the candles lit, and a rope around the Barlow's neck and one end throwed over a rafter.

That cabin was a sight, all littered with broke guns and splintered chairs and tables, pieces of clothes and strips of hide. It looked just about like a cabin ought to look where they has just been a fight between seventeen polecats and a mountain lion. It was a dirt floor, and some of the poles which helped hold up the roof was splintered, so most of the weight was resting on a big post in the center of the hut.

All the Hopkinses was crowding around their prisoner, and when I looked over their shoulders and seen the feller's pale face in the light of the candle I give a yell, "Dick Jackson!"

"So it is!" said Old Man Hopkins, rubbing his hands with glee. "So it is! Well, young feller, you got any last words to orate?"

"Naw," said Jackson sullenly. "But if it hadn't been for that derned lion spilin' our plans we'd of had you danged Hopkinses like so much pork. I never heard of a cougar jumpin' through a winder before."

"That there cougar didn't jump," I said, shouldering through the mob. "He was hev. I done the heavin'."

His mouth fell open and he looked at me like he'd saw the ghost of Sitting Bull. "Breckinridge Elkins!" says he. "I'm cooked now, for sure!"

"I'll say you air!" gritted the feller who'd spoke of shooting Jackson earlier in the night. "What we waitin' for? Le's swing him up."

The rest started howlin'.

"Hold on," I said. "You all can't hang him. I'm goin' to take him back to Bear Creek."

"You ain't neither," said Old Man Hopkins. "We're much obleeged to you for the help you've give us tonight, but this here is the first chance we've had to hang a Barlow in fifteen year, and we aim to make the most of it. String him, boys!"

"Stop!" I roared, stepping for'ard.

In a second I was covered by seven rifles, whilst three men laid hold of the rope and started to heave Jackson's feet off the floor. Them seven Winchesters didn't stop me. But for one thing I'd of taken them guns away and wiped up the floor with them ungrateful mavericks. But I was afeared Jackson would get hit in the wild shooting that was certain to foller such a plan of action.

What I wanted to do was something which would put 'em all horse-de-combat as the French say, without killing Jackson. So I laid hold on the center post and before they knowed what I was doing, I tore it loose and broke it off, and the roof caved in and the walls fell inwards on the roof.

In a second they wasn't no cabin at all – just a pile of lumber with the Hopkinses all underneath and screaming blue murder. Of course I just braced my laigs and when the roof fell my head busted a hole through it, and the logs of the falling walls hit my shoulders and glanced off, so when the dust settled I was standing waist deep amongst the ruins and nothing but a few scratches to show for it.

The howls that riz from beneath the ruins was blood-curdling, but I knowed nobody was hurt permanent because if they was they wouldn't be able to howl like that. But I expect some of 'em would of been hurt if my head and shoulders hadn't kind of broke the fall of the roof and wall-logs.

I located Jackson by his voice, and pulled pieces of roof board and logs off until I come onto his laig, and I pulled him out by it and laid him on the ground to get his wind back, because a beam had fell acrost his stummick and when he tried to holler he made the funniest noise I ever heard.

I then kind of rooted around amongst the debris and hauled Old Man Hopkins out, and he seemed kind of dazed and kept talking about earthquakes.

"You better git to work extricatin' yore misguided kin from under them logs, you hoary-haired old sarpent," I told him sternly. "After that there display of ingratitude I got no sympathy for you. In fact, if I was a short-tempered man I'd feel inclined to violence. But bein' the soul of kindness and generosity, I controls my emotions and merely remarks that if I *wasn't* mild-mannered as a lamb, I'd hand you a boot in the pants – like this!"

I kicked him gentle,

"Owww!" says he, sailing through the air and sticking his nose to the hilt in the dirt. "I'll have the law on you, you derned murderer!" He wept, shaking his fists at me, and as I departed with my captive I could hear him chanting a hymn of hate as he pulled chunks of logs off of his bellering relatives.

Jackson was trying to say something, but I told him I warn't in no mood for perlite conversation and the less he said the less likely I was to lose my temper and tie his neck into a knot around a black jack.

Cap'n Kidd made the hundred miles from the Mezquital Mountains to Bear Creek by noon the next day, carrying double, and never stopping to eat, sleep, nor drink. Them that don't believe that kindly keep their mouths shet. I have already licked nineteen men for acting like they didn't believe it.

I stalked into the cabin and throwed Dick Jackson down on the floor before Ellen which looked at him and me like she thought I was crazy.

"What you finds attractive about this coyote," I said bitterly, "is beyond the grasp of my dust-coated brain. But here he is, and you can marry him right away."

She said, "Air you drunk or sun-struck? Marry that good-for-nothin', whiskey-swiggin', card-shootin' loafer? Why, ain't been a week since I run him out of the house with a buggy whip."

"Then he didn't jilt you?" I gasped.

"Him jilt me?" she said. "I jilted him!"

I turned to Dick Jackson more in sorrer than in anger.

"Why," said I, "did you boast all over Chawed Ear about jiltin' Ellen Elkins?"

"I didn't want folks to know she turned me down," he said sulkily. "Us Jacksons is proud. The only reason I ever thought about marryin' her was I was ready to settle down, on the farm Pap gave me, and I wanted to marry me a Elkins gal so I wouldn't have to go to the expense of hirin' a couple of hands and buyin' a span of mules, and – "

They ain't no use in Dick Jackson threatening to have the law on me.

He got off light to what's he'd have got if Pap and my brothers hadn't all been off hunting. They've got terrible tempers. But I was always too soft-hearted for my own good. In spite of Dick Jackson's insults I held my temper. I didn't do nothing to him at all, except escort him in sorrow for five or six miles down the Chawed Ear trail, kicking the seat of his britches.

The Riot at Cougar Paw

I was out in the blacksmith shop by the corral beating out some shoes for Cap'n Kidd, when my brother John come sa'ntering in. He'd been away for a few weeks up in the Cougar Paw country, and he'd evidently done well, whatever he'd been doing, because he was in a first class humor with hisself, and plumb spilling over with high spirits and conceit. When he feels prime like that he wants to rawhide everybody he meets, especially me. John thinks he's a wit, but I figger he's just half right.

"Air you slavin' over a hot forge for that mangy, flea-bit hunk of buzzard meat again?" he greeted me. "That broom-tail ain't wuth the iron you wastes on his splayed-out hooves!"

He knows the easiest way to git under my hide is to poke fun at Cap'n Kidd. But I reflected it was just envy on his part, and resisted my natural impulse to bend the tongs over his head. I taken the white-hot iron out of the forge and put it on the anvil and started beating it into shape with the sixteen-pound sledge I always uses. I got no use for the toys which most blacksmiths uses for hammers.

"If you ain't got nothin' better to do than criticize a animal which is a damn sight better hoss than you'll ever be a man," I said with dignerty, between licks, "I calls yore attention to a door right behind you which nobody ain't usin' at the moment."

He bust into loud rude laughter and said, "You call that thing a hossshoe? It's big enough for a snow plow! Here, long as yo're in the business, see can you fit a shoe for that!"

He sot his foot up on the anvil and I give it a good slam with the hammer. John let out a awful holler and begun hopping around over the shop and cussing fit to curl yore hair. I kept on hammering my iron.

Just then Pap stuck his head in the door and beamed on us, and said, "You boys won't never grow up! Always playin' yore childish games, and sportin' in yore innercent frolics!"

"He's busted my toe," said John bloodthirstily, "and I'll have his heart's blood if it's the last thing I do."

"Chips off the old block," beamed Pap. "It takes me back to the time when, in the days of my happy childhood, I emptied a sawed-off shotgun into the seat of brother Joel's britches for tellin' our old man it was me which put that b'ar trap in his bunk."

"He'll rue the day," promised John, and hobbled off to the cabin with moans and profanity. A little later, from his yells, I gathered that he had persuaded maw or one of the gals to rub his toe with hoss liniment. He could make more racket about nothing then any Elkins I ever knowed.

I went on and made the shoes and put 'em on Cap'n Kidd, which is a job about like roping and hawg tying a mountain cyclone, and by the time I got through and went up to the cabin to eat, John seemed to have got over his mad spell. He was laying on his bunk with his foot up on it all bandaged up, and he says, "Breckinridge, they ain't no use in grown men holdin' a grudge. Let's fergit about it."

"Who's holdin' any grudge?" I ast, making sure he didn't have a bowie knife in his left hand. "I dunno why they should be so much racket over a trifle that didn't amount to nothin', nohow."

"Well," he said, "this here busted foot discommodes me a heap. I won't be able to ride for a day or so, and they is business up to Cougar Paw I ought to 'tend to."

"I thought you just come from there," I says.

"I did," he said, "but they is a man up there which has promised me somethin' which is due me, and now I ain't able to go collect. Whyn't you go collect for me, Breckinridge? You ought to, dern it, because it's yore fault I cain't ride. The man's name is Bill Santry, and he lives up in the mountains a few miles from Cougar Paw. You'll likely find him in Cougar Paw any day, though."

"What's this he promised you?" I ast.

"Just ask for Bill Santry," he said. "When you find him say to him: 'I'm John Elkins' brother, and you can give me what you promised him.'"

My family always imposes onto my good nature; generally I'd rather go do what they want me to do than to go to the trouble with arguing with 'em.

"Oh, all right," I said. "I ain't got nothin' to do right now."

"Thanks, Breckinridge," he said. "I knowed I could count on you."

So a couple of days later I was riding through the Cougar Range, which is very thick-timbered mountains, and rapidly approaching Cougar Paw. I hadn't never been there before, but I was follering a winding wagon road which I knowed would eventually fetch me there.

The road wound around the shoulder of a mountain, and ahead of me I seen a narrer path opened into it, and just before I got there I heard a bull beller, and a gal screamed, "Help! Help! Old Man Kirby's bull's loose!"

They came a patter of feet, and behind 'em a smashing and crashing in the underbrush, and a gal run out of the path into the road, and a rampaging bull was right behind her with his head lowered to toss her. I reined Cap'n Kidd between her and him, and knowed Cap'n Kidd would do the rest without no advice from me. He done so by wheeling and lamming his heels into that bull's ribs so hard he kicked the critter clean through a rail fence on the other side of the road. Cap'n Kidd hates bulls, and he's too big and strong for any of 'em. He would of then jumped on the critter and stomped him, but I restrained him, which made him mad, and whilst he was trying to buck me off, the bull ontangled hisself and high-tailed it down the mountain, bawling like a scairt yearling.

When I had got Cap'n Kidd in hand, I looked around and seen the gal looking at me very admiringly. I swept off my Stetson and bowed from my saddle and says, "Can I assist you any father, m'am?"

She blushed purty as a pitcher and said, "I'm much obliged, stranger. That there critter nigh had his hooks into my hide. Whar you headin'? If you ain't in no hurry I'd admire to have you drop by the cabin and have a snack of b'ar meat and honey. We live up the path about a mile."

"They ain't nothin' I'd ruther do," I assured her. "But just at the present I got business in Cougar Paw. How far is it from here?"

" 'Bout five mile down the road," says she. "My name's Joan; what's yore'n?"

"Breckinridge Elkins, of Bear Creek," I said. "Say, I got to push on to Cougar Paw, but I'll be ridin' back this way tomorrer mornin' about sunup. If you could – "

"I'll be waitin' right here for you," she said so promptly it made my head swim. No doubt about it; it was love at first sight. "I – I got store-bought shoes," she added shyly. "I'll be a-wearin' 'em when you come along."

"I'll be here if I have to wade through fire, flood and hostile Injuns," I assured her, and rode on down the wagon trace with my manly heart swelling with pride in my bosom. They ain't many mountin men which can awake the fire of love in a gal's heart at first sight – a gal, likewise, which was as beautiful as that there gal, and rich enough to own store-bought shoes. As I told Cap'n Kidd, they was just something about a Elkins.

It was about noon when I rode into Cougar Paw which was a tolerably small village sot up amongst the mountains, with a few cabins where folks lived, and a few more which was a grocery store and a jail and a saloon. Right behind the saloon was a good-sized cabin with a big sign onto it which said: *Jonathan Middleton, Mayor of Cougar Paw.*

They didn't seem to be nobody in sight, not even on the saloon porch, so I rode on to the corrals which served for a livery stable and wagon yard, and a man come out of the cabin nigh it, and took charge of Cap'n Kidd. He wanted to turn him in with a couple of mules which hadn't never been broke, but I knowed what Cap'n Kidd would do to them mules, so the feller give him a corral to hisself, and bellyached just because Cap'n Kidd playfully bit the seat out of his britches.

He ca'med down when I paid for the britches. I ast him where I could find Bill Santry, and he said likely he was up to the store.

So I went up to the store, and it was about like all them stores you see in them kind of towns – groceries, and dry goods, and grindstones, and harness and such-like stuff, and a wagon tongue somebody had mended recent. They warn't but the one store in the town and it handled a little of everything. They was a sign onto it which said: *General Store; Jonathan Middleton, Prop.*

They was a bunch of fellers setting around on goods boxes and benches eating sody crackers and pickles out of a barrel, and they was a tolerable hard-looking gang. I said, "I'm lookin' for Bill Santry."

The biggest man in the store, which was setting on a bench, says, "You don't have to look no farther. I'm Bill Santry."

"Well," I says, "I'm Breckinridge Elkins, John Elkins' brother. You can give me what you promised him."

"Ha!" he says with a snort like a hungry catamount rising sudden. "They is nothin' which could give me more pleasure! Take it with my blessin'!" And so saying he picked up the wagon tongue and splintered it over my head.

It was so onexpected that I lost my footing and fell on my back, and Santry give a wolfish yell and jumped into my stummick with both feet, and the next thing I knowed nine or ten more fellers was jumping up and down on me with their boots.

Now I can take a joke as well as the next man, but it always did make me mad for a feller to twist a spur into my hair and try to tear the sculp off. Santry having did this, I throwed off them lunatics which was trying to tromp out my innards, and riz up amongst them with a outraged beller. I swept four or five of 'em into my arms and give 'em a grizzly hug and when I let go all they was able to do was fall on the floor and squawk about their busted ribs.

I then turned onto the others which was assaulting me with pistols and bowie knives and the butt ends of quirts and other villainous weppins, and when I laid into 'em you should of heard 'em howl. Santry was trying to dismember my ribs with a butcher knife he'd got out of the pork barrel, so I picked up the pickle barrel and busted it over his head. He went to the floor under a avalanche of splintered staves and pickles and brine, and then I got hold of a grindstone and really started getting destructive. A grindstone is a good comforting implement to have hold of in a melee, but kind of clumsy. For instance when I hove it at a feller which was trying to cock a sawed-off shotgun, it missed him entirely and knocked all the slats out of the counter and nigh squshed four or five men which was trying to shoot me from behind it. I settled the shotgun-feller's hash with a box of canned beef, and then I got hold of a double-bitted axe, and the embattled citizens of Cougar Paw quit the field with blood-curdling howls of fear – them which was able to quit and howl.

I stumbled over the thickly strewn casualties to the door, taking a few casual swipes at the shelves as I went past, and knocking all the cans off of them. Just as I emerged into the street, with my axe lifted to chop down anybody which opposed me, a skinny looking human bobbed up in front of me and hollered, "Halt, in the name of the law!"

Paying no attention to the double-barreled shotgun he shoved in my face, I swung back my axe for a swipe, and accidentally hit the sign over the door and knocked it down on top of him. He let out a squall as he went down and let *bam!* with the shotgun right in my face so close it singed my eyebrows. I pulled the sign board off of him so I could git a good belt at him with my axe, but he hollered, "I'm the sheriff! I demands that you surrenders to properly constupated authority!"

I then noticed that he had a star pinned onto one gallus, so I put down my axe and let him take my guns. I never resists a officer of the law – well, seldom ever, that is.

He p'inted his shotgun at me and says, "I fines you ten dollars for disturbin' the peace!"

About this time a lanky maverick with side whiskers come prancing around the corner of the building, and he started throwing fits like a locoed steer.

"The scoundrel's rooint my store!" he howled. "He's got to pay me for the counters and winders he busted, and the shelves he knocked down, and the sign he rooint, and the pork keg he busted over my clerk's head!"

"What you think he ought to pay, Mr. Middleton?" ast the sheriff.

"Five hundred dollars," said the mayor bloodthirstily.

"Five hundred hell!" I roared, stung to wrath. "This here whole dern town ain't wuth five hundred dollars. Anyway, I ain't got no money but fifty cents I owe to the feller that runs the wagon yard."

"Gimme the fifty cents," ordered the mayor. "I'll credit that onto yore bill."

"I'll credit my fist onto yore skull," I snarled, beginning to lose my temper, because the butcher knife Bill Santry had carved my ribs with had salt on the blade, and the salt got into the cuts and smarted. "I owes this fifty cents and I gives it to the man I owes it to."

"Throw him in jail!" raved Middleton. "We'll keep him there till we figures out a job of work for him to do to pay out his fine."

So the sheriff marched me down the street to the log cabin which they used for a jail, whilst Middleton went moaning around the rooins of his grocery store, paying no heed to the fellers which lay groaning on the floor. But I seen the rest of the citizens packing them out on stretchers to take 'em into the saloon to bring 'em to. The saloon had a sign; *Square Deal Saloon;*

Jonathan Middleton, Prop. And I heard fellers cussing Middleton because he made 'em pay for the licker they poured on the victims' cuts and bruises. But they cussed under their breath. Middleton seemed to pack a lot of power in that there town.

Well, I laid down on the jailhouse bunk as well as I could, because they always build them bunks for ordinary-sized men about six foot tall, and I wondered what in hell Bill Santry had hit me with that wagon tongue for. It didn't seem to make no sense.

I laid there and waited for the sheriff to bring me my supper, but he didn't bring none, and purty soon I went to sleep and dreamed about Joan, with her store-bought shoes.

What woke me up was a awful racket in the direction of the saloon. I got up and looked out of the barred winder. Night had fell, but the cabins and the saloon was well lit up, but too far away for me to tell what was going on. But the noise was so familiar I thought for a minute I must be back on Bear Creek again, because men was yelling and cussing, and guns was banging, and a big voice roaring over the din. Once it sounded like somebody had got knocked through a door, and it made me right homesick, it was so much like a dance on Bear Creek.

I pulled the bars out of the winder trying to see what was going on, but all I could see was what looked like men flying headfirst out of the saloon, and when they hit the ground and stopped rolling, they jumped up and run off in all directions, hollering like the Apaches was on their heels.

Purty soon I seen somebody running toward the jail as hard as he could leg it, and it was the sheriff. Most of his clothes was tore off, and he had blood on his face, and he was gasping and panting.

"We got a job for you, Elkins!" he panted. "A wildman from Texas just hit town, and is terrorizin' the citizens! If you'll perfect us, and lay out this fiend from the prairies, we'll remit yore fine! Listen at that!"

From the noise I jedged the aforesaid wildman had splintered the panels out of the bar.

"What started him on his rampage?" I ast.

"Aw, somebody said they made better chili con carne in Santa Fe than they did in El Paso," says the sheriff. "So this maneyack starts cleanin' up the town – "

"Well, I don't blame him," I said. "That was a dirty lie and a lowdown slander. My folks all come from Texas, and if you Cougar Paw coyotes thinks you can slander the State and git away with it – "

"We don't think nothin'!" wailed the sheriff, wringing his hands and jumping like a startled deer every time a crash resounded up the street. "We admits the Lone Star State is the cream of the West in all ways! Lissen, will you lick this homicidal lunatic for us? You got to, dern it. You got to work out yore fine, and – "

"Aw, all right," I said, kicking the door down before he could unlock it. "I'll do it. I cain't waste much time in this town. I got a engagement down the road tomorrer at sunup."

The street was deserted, but heads was sticking out of every door and winder. The sheriff stayed on my heels till I was a few feet from the saloon, and then he whispered, "Go to it, and make it a good job! If anybody can lick that grizzly in there, it's you!" He then ducked out of sight behind the nearest cabin after handing me my gun belt.

I stalked into the saloon and seen a gigantic figger standing at the bar and just fixing to pour hisself a dram out of a demijohn. He had the place to hisself, but it warn't near as much of a wreck as I'd expected.

As I come in he wheeled with a snarl, as quick as a cat, and flashing out a gun. I drawed one of mine just as quick, and for a second we stood there, glaring at each other over the barrels.

"Breckinridge Elkins!" says he. "My own flesh and blood kin!"

"Cousin Bearfield Buckner!" I says, shoving my gun back in its scabbard. "I didn't even know you was in Nevada."

"I got a ramblin' foot," says he, holstering his shooting iron. "Put 'er there, Cousin Breckinridge!"

"By golly, I'm glad to see you!" I said, shaking with him. Then I recollected. "Hey!" I says. "I got to lick you."

"What you mean?" he demanded.

"Aw," I says, "I got arrested, and ain't got no money to pay my fine, and I got to work it out. And lickin' you was the job they gimme."

"I ain't got no use for law," he said grumpily. "Still and all, if I had any dough, I'd pay yore fine for you."

"A Elkins don't accept no charity," I said slightly nettled. "We works for what we gits. I pays my fine by lickin' the hell out of you, Cousin Bearfield."

At this he lost his temper; he was always hot-headed that way. His black brows come down and his lips curled up away from his teeth and he clenched his fists which was about the size of mallets.

"What kind of kinfolks air you?" he scowled. "I don't mind a friendly fight between relatives, but yore intentions is mercenary and unworthy of a true Elkins. You puts me in mind of the fact that yore old man had to leave Texas account of a hoss gittin' its head tangled in a lariat he was totin' in his absent-minded way."

"That there is a cussed lie," I said with heat. "Pap left Texas because he wouldn't take the Yankee oath after the Civil War, and you know it. Anyway," I added bitingly, "nobody can ever say a Elkins ever stole a chicken and roasted it in a chaparral thicket."

He started violently and turned pale.

"What you hintin' at, you son of Baliol?" he hollered.

"Yore iniquities ain't no family secret," I assured him bitterly. "Aunt Atascosa writ Uncle Jeppard Grimes about you stealin' that there Wyandotte hen off of Old Man Westfall's roost."

"Shet up!" he bellered, jumping up and down in his wrath, and clutching his six-shooters convulsively. "I war just a yearlin' when I lifted that there fowl and et it, and I war plumb famished, because a posse had been chasin' me six days. They was after me account of Joe Richardson happenin' to be in my way when I was emptyin' my buffalo rifle. Blast yore soul, I have shot better men than you for talkin' about chickens around me."

"Nevertheless," I said, "the fact remains that yo're the only one of the clan which ever swiped a chicken. No Elkins never stole no hen."

"No," he sneered, "they prefers hosses."

Just then I noticed that a crowd had gathered timidly outside the doors and winders and was listening eagerly to this exchange of family scandals, so I said, "We've talked enough. The time for action has arriv. When I first seen you, Cousin Bearfield, the thought of committin' mayhem onto you was very distasteful. But after our recent conversation, I feels I can scramble yore homely features with a free and joyful spirit. Le's have a snort and then git down to business."

"Suits me," he agreed, hanging his gunbelt on the bar. "Here's a jug with about a gallon of red licker into it."

So we each taken a medium-sized snort, which of course emptied the jug, and then I hitched my belt and says, "Which does you desire first, Cousin Bearfield – a busted laig or a fractured skull?"

"Wait a minute," he requested as I approached him. "What's that on yore boot?"

I stooped over to see what it was, and he swung his laig and kicked me in the mouth as hard as he could, and imejitately busted into a guffaw of brutal mirth. Whilst he was thus employed I spit his boot out and butted him in the belly with a vi'lence which changed his haw-haw to a agonized grunt, and then we laid hands on each other and rolled back and forth acrost the floor, biting and gouging, and that was how the tables and chairs got busted. Mayor Middleton must of been watching through a winder because I heard him squall, "My Gawd, they're wreckin' my saloon! Sheriff, arrest 'em both."

And the sheriff hollered back, "I've took yore orders all I aim to, Jonathan Middleton! If you want to stop that double-cyclone git in there and do it yoreself!"

Presently we got tired scrambling around on the floor amongst the cuspidors, so we riz simultaneous and I splintered the roulette wheel with his carcass, and he hit me on the jaw so hard he knocked me clean through the bar and all the bottles fell off the shelves and showered around me, and the ceiling lamp come loose and spilled about a gallon of red hot ile down his neck.

Whilst he was employed with the ile I clumb up from among the debris of the bar and started my right fist in a swing from the floor, and after it traveled maybe nine feet it took Cousin Bearfield under the jaw, and he hit the oppersite wall so hard he knocked out a section and went clean through it, and that was when the roof fell in.

I started kicking and throwing the rooins off me, and then I was aware of Cousin Bearfield lifting logs and beams off of me, and in a minute I crawled out from under 'em.

"I could of got out all right," I said. "But just the same I'm much obleeged to you."

"Blood's thicker'n water," he grunted, and hit me under the jaw and knocked me about seventeen feet backwards toward the mayor's cabin. He then rushed forward and started kicking me in the head, but I riz up in spite of his efforts.

"Git away from that cabin!" screamed the mayor, but it was too late. I hit Cousin Bearfield between the eyes and he crashed into the mayor's rock chimney and knocked the whole base loose with his head, and the chimney collapsed and the rocks come tumbling down on him.

But being a Texas Buckner, Bearfield riz out of the rooins. He not only riz, but he had a rock in his hand about the size of a watermelon and he busted it over my head. This infuriated me, because I seen he had no intention of fighting fair, so I tore a log out of the wall of the mayor's cabin and belted him over the ear with it, and Cousin Bearfield bit the dust. He didn't git up that time.

Whilst I was trying to git my breath back and shaking the sweat out of my eyes, all the citizens of Cougar Paw come out of their hiding places and the sheriff yelled, "You done a good job, Elkins! Yo're a free man!"

"He is like hell!" screamed Mayor Middleton, doing a kind of war-dance, whilst weeping and cussing together. "Look at my cabin! I'm a rooint man! Sheriff, arrest that man!"

"Which 'un?" inquired the sheriff.

"The feller from Texas," said Middleton bitterly. "He's unconscious, and it won't be no trouble to drag him to jail. Run the other'n out of town. I don't never want to see him no more."

"Hey!" I said indignantly. "You cain't arrest Cousin Bearfield. I ain't goin' to stand for it."

"Will you resist a officer of the law?" ast the sheriff, sticking his gallus out on his thumb.

"You represents the law whilst you wear yore badge?" I inquired.

"As long as I got that badge on," boasts he, "I am the law!"

"Well," I said, spitting on my hands, "you ain't got it on now. You done lost it somewhere in the shuffle tonight, and you ain't nothin' but a common citizen like me! Git ready, for I'm comin' head-on and wide open!"

I whooped me a whoop.

He glanced down in a stunned sort of way at his empty gallus, and then he give a scream and took out up the street with most of the crowd streaming out behind him.

"Stop, you cowards!" screamed Mayor Middleton. "Come back here and arrest these scoundrels – "

"Aw, shet up," I said disgustedly, and give him a kind of push and how was I to know it would dislocate his shoulder blade. It was just beginning to git light by now, but Cousin Bearfield wasn't showing no signs of consciousness, and I heard them Cougar Paw skunks yelling to each other back and forth from the cabins where they'd forted themselves, and from what they said I knowed they figgered on opening up on us with their Winchesters as soon as it got light enough to shoot good.

Just then I noticed a wagon standing down by the wagon yard, so I picked up Cousin Bearfield and lugged him down there and throwed him into the wagon. Far be it from a Elkins to leave a senseless relative to the mercy of a Cougar Paw mob. I went into the corral where them two wild mules was and started putting harness onto 'em, and it warn't no child's play. They hadn't never been worked before, and they fell onto me with a free and hearty enthusiasm. Onst they had me down stomping on me, and the citizens of Cougar Paw made a kind of half-hearted sally. But I unlimbered my .45s and throwed a few slugs in their direction and they all hollered and run back into their cabins.

I finally had to stun them fool mules with a bat over the ear with my fist, and before they got their senses back, I had 'em harnessed to the wagon, and Cap'n Kidd and Cousin Bearfield's hoss tied to the rear end.

"He's stealin' our mules!" howled somebody, and taken a wild shot at me, as I headed down the street, standing up in the wagon and keeping them crazy critters straight by sheer strength on the lines.

"I ain't stealin' nothin'!" I roared as we thundered past the cabins where spurts of flame was already streaking out of the winders. "I'll send this here wagon and these mules back tomorrer!"

The citizens answered with bloodthirsty yells and a volley of lead, and with their benediction singing past my ears, I left Cougar Paw in a cloud of dust and profanity.

Them mules, after a vain effort to stop and kick loose from the harness, laid their bellies to the ground and went stampeding down that crooking mountain road like scairt jackrabbits. We went around each curve on one wheel, and sometimes we'd hit a stump that would throw the whole wagon several foot into the air, and that must of been what brung Cousin Bearfield to hisself. He was laying sprawled in the bed, and finally we taken a bump that throwed him in a somersault clean to the other end of the wagon. He hit on his neck and riz up on his hands and knees and looked around dazedly at the trees and stumps which was flashing past, and bellered, "What the hell's happenin'? Where-at am I, anyway?"

"Yo're on yore way to Bear Creek, Cousin Bearfield!" I yelled, cracking my whip over them fool mules' backs. "Yippee ki-yi! This here is fun, ain't it, Cousin Bearfield?"

I was thinking of Joan waiting with her store-bought shoes for me down the road, and in spite of my cuts and bruises, I was rolling high and handsome.

"Slow up!" roared Cousin Bearfield, trying to stand up. But just then we went crashing down a steep bank, and the wagon tilted, throwing Cousin Bearfield to the other end of the wagon where he rammed his head with great force against the front gate. "#$%&*?@¢!" says Cousin Bearfield. "Glug!" Because he had hit the creek bed going full speed and knocked all the water out of the channel, and about a hundred gallons splashed over into the wagon and nearly washed Cousin Bearfield out.

"If I ever git out of this alive," promised Cousin Bearfield, "I'll kill you if it's the last thing I do – "

But at that moment the mules stampeded up the bank on the other side and Cousin Bearfield was catapulted to the rear end of the wagon so hard he knocked out the end gate with his head and nearly went out after it, only he just managed to grab hisself.

We went plunging along the road and the wagon hopped from stump to stump and sometimes it crashed through a thicket of bresh. Cap'n Kidd and the other hoss was thundering after us, and the mules was braying and I was whooping and Cousin Bearfield was cussing, and purty soon I looked back at him and hollered, "Hold on, Cousin Bearfield! I'm goin' to stop these critters. We're close to the place where my gal will be waitin' for me – "

"Look out, you blame fool!" screamed Cousin Bearfield, and then the mules left the road and went one on each side of a white oak tree, and the tongue splintered, and they run right out of the harness and kept high-tailing it, but the wagon piled up on that tree with a jolt that throwed me and Cousin Bearfield headfirst into a blackjack thicket.

Cousin Bearfield vowed and swore, when he got back home, that I picked this thicket special on account of the hornets' nest that was there, and drove into it plumb deliberate. Which same is a lie which I'll stuff down his gizzard next time I cut his sign. He claimed they was trained hornets which I educated not to sting me, but the fact was I had sense enough to lay there plumb quiet. Cousin Bearfield was fool enough to run.

Well, he knows by this time, I reckon, that the fastest man afoot can't noways match speed with a hornet. He taken out through the bresh and thickets, yelpin' and hollerin' and hoppin' most bodacious. He run in a circle, too, for in three minutes he come bellerin' back, gave one last hop and dove back into the thicket. By this time I figgered he'd wore the hornets out, so I came alive again.

I extricated myself first and locating Cousin Bearfield by his profanity, I laid hold onto his hind laig and pulled him out. He lost most of his clothes in the process, and his temper wasn't no better. He seemed to blame me for his misfortunes.

"Don't tech me," he said fiercely. "Leave me be. I'm as close to Bear Creek right now as I want to be. Whar's my hoss?"

The hosses had broke lose when the wagon piled up, but they hadn't gone far, because they was fighting with each other in the middle of the road. Bearfield's hoss was about as big and mean as Cap'n Kidd. We separated 'em and Bearfield clumb aboard without a word.

"Where you goin', Cousin Bearfield?" I ast.

"As far away from you as I can," he said bitterly. "I've saw all the Elkinses I can stand for awhile. Doubtless yore intentions is good, but a man better git chawed by lions than rescued by a Elkins!"

And with a few more observations which highly shocked me, and which I won't repeat, he rode off at full speed, looking very pecooliar, because his pants was about all that hadn't been tore off of him, and he had scratches and bruises all over him.

I was sorry Cousin Bearfield was so sensitive, but I didn't waste no time brooding over his ingratitude. The sun was up and I knowed Joan would be waiting for me where the path come down into the road from the mountain.

Sure enough, when I come to the mouth of the trail, there she was, but she didn't have on her store-bought shoes, and she looked flustered and scairt.

"Breckinridge!" she hollered, running up to me before I could say a word. "Somethin' terrible's happened! My brother was in Cougar Paw last night, and a big bully beat him up somethin' awful! Some men are bringin' him home on a stretcher! One of 'em rode ahead to tell me!"

"How come I didn't pass 'em on the road?" I said, and she said, "They walked and taken a short cut through the hills. There they come now."

I seen some men come into the road a few hundred yards away and come toward us, lugging somebody on a stretcher like she said.

"Come on!" she says, tugging at my sleeve. "Git down off yore hoss and come with me. I want him to tell you who done it, so you can whup the scoundrel!"

"I got a idee, I know who done it," I said, climbing down. "But I'll make sure." I figgered it was one of Cousin Bearfield's victims.

"Why, look!" said Joan. "How funny the men are actin' since you started toward 'em! They've sot down the litter and they're runnin' off into the woods! Bill!" she shrilled as we drawed nigh. "Bill, air you hurt bad?"

"A busted laig and some broke ribs," groaned the victim on the litter, which also had his head so bandaged I didn't recognize him. Then he sot up with a howl. "What's that ruffian doin' with you?" he roared, and to my amazement I recognized Bill Santry.

"Why, he's a friend of our'n, Bill – " Joan begun, but he interrupted her loudly and profanely, "Friend, hell! He's John Elkins' brother, and furthermore he's the one which is responsible for the crippled and mutilated condition in which you now sees me!"

Joan said nothing. She turned and looked at me in a very pecooliar manner, and then dropped her eyes shyly to the ground.

"Now, Joan," I begun, when all at once I saw what she was looking for. One of the men had dropped a Winchester before he run off. Her first bullet knocked off my hat as I forked Cap'n Kidd, and her second, third and fourth missed me so close I felt their hot wind. Then Cap'n Kidd rounded a curve with his belly to the ground, and my busted romance was left far behind me . . .

A couple of days later a mass of heartaches and bruises which might of been recognized as Breckinridge Elkins, the pride of Bear Creek, rode slowly down the trail that led to the settlements on the aforesaid creek. And as I rode, it was my fortune to meet my brother John coming up the trail on foot.

"Where you been?" he greeted me hypocritically. "You look like you been rasslin' a pack of mountain lions."

I eased myself down from the saddle and said without heat, "John, just what was it that Bill Santry promised you?"

"Oh," says John with a laugh, "I skinned him in a hoss trade before I left Cougar Paw, and he promised if he ever met me, he'd give me the lickin' of my life. I'm glad you don't hold no hard feelins, Breck. It war just a joke, me sendin' you up there. You can take a joke, cain't you?"

"Sure," I said. "By the way, John, how's yore toe?"

"It's all right," says he.

"Lemme see," I insisted. "Set yore foot on that stump."

He done so and I give it a awful belt with the butt of my Winchester.

"That there is a receipt for yore joke," I grunted, as he danced around on one foot and wept and swore. And so saying I mounted and rode on in gloomy grandeur. A Elkins always pays his debts.

Pistol Politics

Politics and book learning is bad enough took separate; together they're a blight and a curse. Take Yeller Dog for a instance, a mining camp over in the Apache River country, where I was rash enough to take up my abode in onst.

Yeller Dog was a decent camp till politics reared its head in our midst and education come slithering after. The whiskey was good and middling cheap. The poker and faro games was honest if you watched the dealers clost. Three or four piddlin' fights a night was the usual run, and a man hadn't been shot dead in more than a week by my reckoning. Then, like my Aunt Tascosa Polk would say, come the deluge.

It all begun when Forty-Rod Harrigan moved his gambling outfit over to Alderville and left our one frame building vacant, and Gooseneck Wilkerson got the idee of turning it into a city hall. Then he said we ought to have a mayor to go with it, and announced hisself as candidate. Naturally Bull Hawkins, our other leading citizen, come out agen him. The election was sot for April 11. Gooseneck established his campaign headquarters in the Silver Saddle saloon, and Bull taken up his'n in the Red Tomahawk on t'other side of the street. First thing we knowed, Yeller Dog was in the grip of politics.

The campaign got under way, and the casualties was mounting daily as public interest become more and more fatally aroused, and on the afternoon of the 9th Gooseneck come into his headquarters, and says, "We got to make a sweepin' offensive, boys. Bull Hawkins is outgeneralin' us. That shootin' match he put on for a prime beef steer yesterday made a big hit with the common herd. He's tryin' to convince Yeller Dog that if elected he'd pervide the camp with more high-class amusement than I could. Breck Elkins, will you pause in yore guzzlin' and lissen here a minute? As chief of this here political organization I demand yore attention!"

"I hear you," I says. "I was to the match, and they barred me on a tecknicality, otherwise I would of won the whole steer. It warn't so excitin', far as I could see. Only one man got shot."

"And he was one of my voters," scowled Gooseneck. "But we got to outshine Bull's efforts to seduce the mob. He's resortin' to low, onderhanded tactics by buyin' votes outright. I scorns sech measures – anyway, I've bought all I'm able to pay for. We got to put on a show which outdazzles his dern' shootin' match."

"A rodeo, maybe," suggested Mule McGrath. "Or a good dogfight."

"Naw, naw," says Gooseneck. "My show will be a symbol of progress and culture. We stages a spellin' match tomorrow night in the city hall. Next mornin' when the polls opens the voters'll still be so dazzled by the grandeur of our entertainment they'll eleck me by a vast majority."

"How many men in this here camp can spell good enough to git into a spellin' bee?" says I.

"I'm confident they's at least thirty-five men in this camp which can read and write," says Gooseneck. "That's plenty. But we got to find somebody to give out the words. It wouldn't look right for me – it'd be beneath my offishul dignity. Who's educated enough for the job?"

"I am!" says Jerry Brennon and Bill Garrison simultaneous. They then showed their teeth at each other. They warn't friends nohow.

"Cain't but one git the job," asserted Gooseneck. "I tests yore ability. Can either one of you spell Constantinople?"

"K-o-n –" begun Garrison, and Brennon burst into a loud and mocking guffaw, and said something pointed about ignoramuses.

"You $%#&*!" says Garrison bloodthirstily.

"Gentlemen!" squawked Gooseneck – and then ducked as they both went for their guns.

They cleared leather about the same time. When the smoke oozed away Gooseneck crawled out from under the roulette table and cussed fervently.

"Two more reliable voters gone to glory!" he raged. "Breckinridge, whyn't you stop 'em?"

"T'warn't none of my business," says I, reching for another drink, because a stray bullet had knocked my glass outa my hand. "Hey!" I addressed the barkeep sternly. "I see you fixin' to chalk up that there spilt drink agen me. Charge it to Jerry Brennon. He spilt it."

"Dead men pays no bills," complained the bartender.

"Cease them petty squabbles!" snarled Gooseneck. "You argys over a glass of licker when I've jest lost two good votes! Drag 'em out, boys," he ordered the other members of the organization which was emerging from behind the bar and the whiskey barrels where they'd took refuge when the shooting started. "Damn!" says Gooseneck with bitterness. "This here is a deadly lick to my campaign! I not only loses two more votes, but them was the best educated men in camp, outside of me. Now who we goin' to git to conduck the spellin' match?"

"Anybody which can read can do it," says Lobo Harrison, a hoss thief with a mean face and a ingrown disposition. He'd go a mile out of his way jest to kick a dog. "Even Elkins there could do it."

"Yeah, if they was anything to read from," snorted Gooseneck. "But they ain't a line of writin' in camp except on whiskey bottles. We got to have a man with a lot of long words in his head. Breckinridge, dammit, jest because I told the barkeep to charge yore drinks onto campaign expenses ain't no reason for you to freeze onto that bar permanent. Ride over to Alderville and git us a educated man."

"How'll he know whether he's educated or not?" sneered Lobo, which seemed to dislike me passionately for some reason or another.

"Make him spell Constantinople," says Gooseneck.

"He cain't go over there," says Soapy Jackson. "The folks has threatened to lynch him for cripplin' their sheriff."

"I didn't cripple their fool sheriff," I says indignantly. "He crippled hisself fallin' through a wagon wheel when I give him a kind of a push with a rock. How you spell that there Constance Hopple word?"

Well, he spelt it thirty or forty times till I had it memorized, so I rode over to Alderville. When I rode into town the folks looked at me coldly and bunched up and whispered amongst theirselves, but I paid no attention to 'em. I never seen the deputy sheriff, unless that was him I seen climbing a white oak tree as I hove in sight. I went into the White Eagle saloon and drunk me a dram, and says to the barkeep, "Who's the best educated man in Alderville?"

Says he, "Snake River Murgatroyd, which deals monte over to the Elite Amusement Palace." So I went over there and jest as I went through the door I happened to remember that Snake River had swore he was going to shoot me on sight next time he seen me, account of some trouble we'd had over a card game. But sech things is too trivial to bother about. I went up to where he was setting dealing monte, and I says, "Hey!"

"Place your bet," says he. Then he looked up and said, "You! $#%&*@!" and reched for his gun, but I got mine out first and shoved the muzzle under his nose.

"Spell Constantinople!" I tells him.

He turnt pale and said, "Are you crazy?"

"Spell it!" I roared, and he says, "C-o-n-s-t-a-n-t-i-n-o-p-l-e! What the hell?"

"Good," I said, throwing his gun over in the corner out of temptation's way. "We wants you to come over to Yeller Dog and give out words at a spellin' match."

Everybody in the place was holding their breath. Snake River moved his hands nervous-like and knocked a jack of diamonds off onto the floor. He stooped like he was going to pick it up, but instead he jerked a bowie out of his boot and tried to stab me in the belly. Well, much as I would of enjoyed shooting him, I knowed it would spile the spelling match, so merely taken the knife away from him, and held him upside down to shake out whatever other weppins he might have hid, and he begun to holler, "Help! Murder! Elkins is killin' me!"

"It's a Yeller Dog plot!" somebody howled, and the next instant the air was full of beer mugs and cuspidors. Some of them spittoons was quite heavy, and when one missed me and went *bong* on Snake River's head, he curled up like a angleworm which has been tromped on.

"Lookit there!" they hollered, like it was my fault. "He's tryin' to kill Snake River! Git him, boys!"

They then fell on me with billiard sticks and chair laigs in a way which has made me suspicious of Alderville's hospitality ever since.

Argyment being useless, I tucked Snake River under my left arm and started knocking them fool critters right and left with my right fist, and I reckon that was how the bar got wrecked. I never seen a bar a man's head would go through easier'n that'n. So purty soon the survivors abandoned the fray and run out of the door hollering, "Help! Murder! Rise up, citizens! Yeller Dog is at our throats! Rise and defend yore homes and loved ones!"

You would of thought the Apaches was burning the town, the way folks was hollering and running for their guns and shooting at me, as I clumb aboard Cap'n Kidd and headed for Yeller Dog. I left the main road and headed through the bresh for a old trail I knowed about, because I seen a whole army of men getting on their hosses to lick out after me, and while I knowed they couldn't catch Cap'n Kidd, I was afeared they might hit Snake River with a stray bullet if they got within range. The bresh was purty thick and I reckon it was the branches slapping him in the face which brung him to, because all to onst he begun hollering blue murder.

"You ain't takin' me to Yeller Dog!" he yelled. "You're takin' me out in the hills to murder me! Help! Help!"

"Aw, shet up," I snorted. "This here's a short cut."

"You can't get across Apache River unless you follow the road to the bridge," says he.

"I can, too," I says. "We'll go acrost on the footbridge."

With that he give a scream of horror and a convulsive wrench which tore hisself clean out of his shirt which I was holding onto. The next thing I knowed all I had in my hand was a empty shirt and he was on the ground and scuttling through the bushes. I taken in after him, but he was purty tricky dodging around stumps and trees, and I begun to believe I was going to have to shoot him in the hind laig to catch him, when he made the mistake to trying to climb a tree. I rode up onto him before he could get out of rech, and reched up and got him by the laig and pulled him down, and his langwidge was painful to hear.

It was his own fault he slipped outa my hand, he kicked so vi'lent. I didn't go to drop him on his head.

But jest as I was reching down for him, I heard hosses running, and looked up and here come that derned Alderville posse busting through the bresh right on me. I'd lost so much time chasing Snake River they'd catched up with me. So I scooped him up and hung him over my saddle horn, because he was out cold, and headed for Apache River. Cap'n Kidd drawed away from them hosses like they was hobbled, so they warn't scarcely in pistol range of us when we busted out on the east bank. The river was up, jest a-foaming and a-b'ling, and the footbridge warn't nothing only jest a log.

But Cap'n Kidd's sure-footed as a billy goat. We started acrost it, and everything went all right till we got about the middle of it, and then Snake River come to and seen the water booming along under us. He lost his head and begun to struggle and kick and holler, and his spurs scratched Cap'n Kidd's hide. That made Cap'n Kidd mad, and he turnt his head and tried to bite my laig, because he always blames me for everything that happens, and lost his balance and fell off.

That would of been all right, too, because as we hit the water I got hold of Cap'n Kidd's tail with one hand, and Snake River's undershirt with the other'n, and Cap'n Kidd hit out for the west bank. They is very few streams he cain't swim, flood or not. But jest as we was nearly acrost the posse appeared on the hind bank and started shooting at me, and they was apparently in some doubt as to which head in the water was me, because some of 'em shot at Snake River, too, jest to make sure. He opened his mouth to holler at 'em, and got it full of water and dern near strangled.

Then all to onst somebody in the bresh on the west shore opened up with a Winchester, and one of the posse hollered, "Look out, boys! It's a trap! Elkins has led us into a ambush!"

They turnt around and high-tailed it for Alderville.

Well, what with the shooting and a gullet full of water, Snake River was having a regular fit and he kicked and thrashed so he kicked hisself clean out of his undershirt, and jest as my feet hit bottom, he slipped out of my grip and went whirling off downstream.

I jumped out on land, ignoring the hearty kick Cap'n Kidd planted in my midriff, and grabbed my lariat off my saddle. Gooseneck Wilkerson come prancing outa the bresh, waving a Winchester and yelling, "Don't let him drownd, dang you! My whole campaign depends on that spellin' bee! Do somethin'!"

I run along the bank and made a throw and looped Snake River around the ears. It warn't a very good catch, but the best I could do under the circumstances, and skin will always grow back onto a man's ears.

I hauled him out of the river, and it was plumb ungrateful for him to accuse me later of dragging him over them sharp rocks on purpose. I like to know how he figgered I could rope him outa Apache River without skinning him up a little. He'd swallered so much water he was nigh at his last gasp. Gooseneck rolled him onto his belly and jumped up and down on his back with both feet to git the water out; Gooseneck said that was artifishul respiration, but from the way Snake River hollered I don't believe it done him much good.

Anyway, he choked up several gallons of water. When he was able to threaten our lives betwixt cuss words, Gooseneck says, "Git him on yore hoss and le's git started. Mine run off when the shootin' started. I jest suspected you'd be pursued by them dumb wits and would take the shortcut. That's why I come to meet you. Come on. We got to git Snake River some medical attention. In his present state he ain't in no shape to conduck no spellin' match."

Snake River was too groggy to set in the saddle, so we hung him acrost it like a cow-hide over a fence, and started out, me leading Cap'n Kidd. It makes Cap'n Kidd very mad to have anybody but me on his back, so we hadn't went more'n a mile when he reched around and sot his teeth in the seat of Snake River's pants. Snake River had been groaning very weak and dismal and commanding us to stop and let him down so's he could utter his last words, but when Cap'n Kidd bit him he let out a remarkable strong yell and bust into langwidge unfit for a dying man.

"$%/#&¢!" quoth he passionately. "Why have I got to be butchered for a Yeller Dog holiday?"

We was reasoning with him, when Old Man Jake Hanson hove out of the bushes. Old Jake had a cabin a hundred yards back from the trail. He was about the width of a barn door, and his whiskers was marvelous to behold. "What's this ungodly noise about?" he demanded. "Who's gittin' murdered?"

"I am!" says Snake River fiercely. "I'm bein' sacrificed to the passions of the brutal mob!"

"You shet up," said Gooseneck severely. "Jake, this is the gent we've consented to let conduck the spellin' match."

"Well, well!" says Jake, interested. "A educated man, hey? Why, he don't look no different from us folks, if the blood war wiped offa him. Say, lissen, boys, bring him over to my cabin! I'll dress his wounds and feed him and take keer of him and git him to the city hall tomorrer night in time for the spellin' match. In the meantime he can teach my datter Salomey her letters."

"I refuse to tutor a dirty-faced cub – " began Snake River when he seen a face peeking eagerly at us from the trees. "Who's that?" he demanded.

"My datter Salomey," says Old Jake. "Nineteen her last birthday and cain't neither read nor write. None of my folks ever could, far back as family history goes, but I wants her to git some education."

"It's a human obligation," says Snake River. "I'll do it!"

So we left him at Jake's cabin, propped up on a bunk, with Salomey feeding him spoon-vittles and whiskey, and me and Gooseneck headed for Yeller Dog, which warn't hardly a mile from there.

Gooseneck says to me, "We won't say nothin' about Snake River bein' at Jake's shack. Bull Hawkins is sweet on Salomey and he's so dern' jealous-minded it makes him mad for another man to even stop there to say hello to the folks. We don't want nothin' to interfere with our show."

"You ack like you got a lot of confidence in it," I says.

"I banks on it heavy," says he. "It's a symbol of civilization."

Well, jest as we come into town we met Mule McGrath with fire in his eye and corn juice on his breath. "Gooseneck, lissen!" says he. "I jest got wind of a plot of Hawkins and Jack Clanton to git a lot of our voters so drunk election day that they won't be able to git to the polls. Le's call off the spellin' match and go over to the Red Tomahawk and clean out that rat nest!"

"Naw," says Gooseneck, "we promised the mob a show, and we keeps our word. Don't worry; I'll think of a way to circumvent the heathen."

Mule headed back for the Silver Saddle, shaking his head, and Gooseneck sot down on the aidge of a hoss trough and thunk deeply. I'd begun to think he'd drapped off to sleep, when he riz up and said, "Breck, git hold of Soapy Jackson and tell him to sneak out of camp and stay hid till the mornin' of the eleventh. Then he's to ride in jest before the polls open and spread the news that they has been a big gold strike over in Wild Hoss Gulch. A lot of fellers will stampede for there without waitin' to vote. Meanwhile you will have circulated amongst the men you know air goin' to vote for me, and let 'em know we air goin' to work this campaign strategy. With all my men in camp, and most of Bull's headin' for Wild Hoss Gulch, right and justice triumphs and I wins."

So I went and found Soapy and told him what Gooseneck said, and on the strength of it he imejitly headed for the Silver Saddle, and begun guzzling on campaign credit. I felt it was my duty to go along with him and see that he didn't get so full he forgot what he was supposed to do, and we was putting down the sixth dram apiece when in come Jack McDonald, Jim Leary, and Tarantula Allison, all Hawkins men. Soapy focused his wandering eyes on 'em, and says, "W-who's this here clutterin' up the scenery? Whyn't you mavericks stay over to the Red Tomahawk whar you belong?"

"It's a free country," asserted Jack McDonald. "What about this here derned spellin' match Gooseneck's braggin' about all over town?"

"Well, what about it?" I demanded, hitching my harness for'ard. The political foe don't live which can beard a Elkins in his lair.

"We demands to know who conducks it," stated Leary. "At least half the men in camp eligible to compete is in our crowd. We demands fair play!"

"We're bringin' in a cultured gent from another town," I says coldly.

"Who?" demanded Allison.

"None of yore dang business!" trumpeted Soapy, which gets delusions of valor when he's full of licker. "As a champion of progress and civic pride I challenges the skunk-odored forces of corrupt politics, and – "

Bam! McDonald swung with a billiard ball and Soapy kissed the sawdust.

"Now look what you done," I says peevishly. "If you coyotes cain't ack like gents, you'll oblige me by gittin' to hell outa here."

"If you don't like our company suppose you tries to put us out!" they challenged.

So when I'd finished my drink I taken their weppins away from 'em and throwed 'em headfirst out the side door. How was I to know somebody had jest put up a new cast-iron hitching rack out there? Their friends carried 'em over to the Red Tomahawk to sew up their sculps, and I went back into the Silver Saddle to see if Soapy had come to yet. Jest as I reched the door he come weaving out, muttering in his whiskers and waving his six-shooter.

"Do you remember what all I told you?" I demanded.

"S-some of it!" he goggled, with his glassy eyes wobbling in all directions.

"Well, git goin' then," I urged, and helped him up onto his hoss. He left town at full speed, with both feet outa the stirrups and both arms around the hoss' neck.

"Drink is a curse and a delusion," I told the barkeep in disgust. "Look at that sickenin' example and take warnin'! Gimme a bottle of rye."

Well, Gooseneck done a good job of advertising the show. By the middle of the next afternoon men was pouring into town from claims all up and down the creek. Half an hour before the match was sot to begin the hall was full. The benches was moved back from the front part, leaving a space clear all the way acrost the hall. They had been a lot of argyment about who was to compete, and who was to choose sides, but when it was finally settled, as satisfactory as anything ever was settled in Yeller Dog, they was twenty men to compete, and Lobo Harrison and Jack Clanton was to choose up.

By a peculiar coincidence, half of that twenty men was Gooseneck's, and half was Bull's. So naturally Lobo choosed his pals, and Clanton chosed his'n.

"I don't like this," Gooseneck whispered to me. "I'd ruther they'd been mixed up. This is beginnin' to look like a contest between my gang and Bull's. If they win, it'll make me look cheap. Where the hell is Snake River?"

"I ain't seen him," I said. "You ought to of made 'em take off their guns."

"Shucks," says he. "What could possibly stir up trouble at sech a lady-like affair as a spellin' bee. Dang it, where is Snake River? Old Jake said he'd git him here on time."

"Hey, Gooseneck!" yelled Bull Hawkins from where he sot amongst his coharts. "Why'n't you start the show?"

Bull was a big broad-shouldered hombre with black mustashes like a walrus. The crowd begun to holler and cuss and stomp their feet and this pleased Bull very much.

"Keep 'em amused," hissed Gooseneck. "I'll go look for Snake River."

He snuck out a side door and I riz up and addressed the throng. "Gents," I said, "be patient! They is a slight delay, but it won't be long. Meantime I'll be glad to entertain you all to the best of my ability. Would you like to hear me sing *Barbary Allen*?"

"No, by grab!" they answered in one beller.

"Well, yo're a-goin' to!" I roared, infuriated by this callous lack of the finer feelings. "I will now sing," I says, drawing my .45s, "and I blows the brains out of the first coyote which tries to interrupt me."

I then sung my song without interference, and when I was through I bowed and waited for the applause, but all I heard was Lobo Harrison saying, "Imagine what the pore wolves on Bear Creek has to put up with!"

This cut me to the quick, but before I could make a suitable reply, Gooseneck slid in, breathing heavy. "I can't find Snake River," he hissed. "But the barkeep gimme a book he found somewheres. Most of the leaves is tore out, but there's plenty left. I've marked some of the longest words, Breck. You can read good enough to give 'em out. You got to! If we don't start the show right away, this mob'll wreck the place. Yo're the only man not in the match which can even read a little, outside of me and Bull. It wouldn't look right for me to do it, and I shore ain't goin' to let Bull run my show."

I knew I was licked.

"Aw, well, all right," I said. "I might of knew I'd be the goat. Gimme the book."

"Here it is," he said. " 'The Adventures of a French Countess.' Be dern shore you don't give out no words except them I marked."

"Hey!" bawled Jack Clanton. "We're gittin' tired standin' up here. Open the ball."

"All right," I says. "We commences."

"Hey!" said Bull. "Nobody told us Elkins was goin' to conduck the ceremony. We was told a cultured gent from outa town was to do it."

"Well," I says irritably, "Bear Creek is my home range, and I reckon I'm as cultured as any snake hunter here. If anybody thinks he's better qualified than me, step up whilst I stomp his ears off."

Nobody volunteered, so I says, "All right. I tosses a dollar to see who gits the first word." It fell for Harrison's gang, so I looked in the book at the first word marked, and it was a gal's name.

"Catharine," I says.

Nobody said nothing.

"Catharine!" I roared, glaring at Lobo Harrison.

"What you lookin' at me for?" he demanded. "I don't know no gal by that name."

"%$&*@!" I says with passion. "That's the word I give out. Spell it, dammit!"

"Oh," says he. "All right. K-a-t-h-a-r-i-n-n."

"That's wrong," I says.

"What you mean wrong?" he roared. "That's right!"

" 'Tain't accordin' to the book," I said.

"Dang the book," says he. "I knows my rights and I ain't to be euchered by no ignorant grizzly from Bear Creek!"

"Who you callin' ignorant?" I demanded, stung. "Set down! You spelt it wrong."

"You lie!" he howled, and went for his gun. But I fired first.

When the smoke cleared away I seen everybody was on their feet preparing for to stampede, sech as warn't trying to crawl under the benches, so I said, "Set down, everybody. They ain't nothin' to git excited about. The spellin' match continues – an I'll shoot the first scoundrel which tries to leave the hall before the entertainment's over."

Gooseneck hissed fiercely at me, "Dammit, be careful who you shoot, cain't'cha? That was another one of my voters!"

"Drag him out!" I commanded, wiping off some blood where a slug had notched my ear. "The spellin' match is ready to commence again."

They was a kind of tension in the air, men shuffling their feet and twisting their mustashes and hitching their gun belts, but I give no heed. I now approached the other side, with my hand on my pistol, and says to Clanton, "Can you spell Catharine?"

"C-a-t-h-a-r-i-n-e!" says he.

"Right, by golly!" I says, consulting *The French Countess*, and the audience cheered wildly and shot off their pistols into the roof.

"Hey!" says Bill Stark, on the other side. "That's wrong. Make him set down! It spells with a 'K'!"

"He spelt it jest like it is in the book," I says. "Look for yoreself."

"I don't give a damn!" he yelled, rudely knocking *The French Countess* outa my hand. "It's a misprint! It spells with a 'K' or they'll be more blood on the floor! He spelt it wrong and if he don't set down I shoots him down!"

"I'm runnin' this show!" I bellered, beginning to get mad. "You got to shoot me before you shoots anybody else!"

"With pleasure!" snarled he, and went for his gun . . . Well, I hit him on the jaw with my fist and he went to sleep amongst a wreckage of busted benches. Gooseneck jumped up with a maddened shriek.

"Dang yore soul, Breckinridge!" he squalled. "Quit cancelin' my votes! Who air you workin' for – me or Hawkins?"

"Haw! haw! haw!" bellered Hawkins. "Go on with the show! This is the funniest thing I ever seen!"

Wham! The door crashed open and in pranced Old Jake Hanson, waving a shotgun.

"Welcome to the festivities, Jake," I greeted him. "Where's – "

"You son of a skunk!" quoth he, and let go at me with both barrels. The shot scattered remarkable. I didn't get more'n five or six of 'em and the rest distributed freely amongst the crowd. You ought to of heard 'em holler – the folks, I mean, not the buckshot.

"What in tarnation air you doin'?" shrieked Gooseneck. "Where's Snake River?"

"Gone!" howled Old Jake. "Run off! Eloped with my datter!"

Bull Hawkins riz with a howl of anguish, convulsively clutching his whiskers.

"Salomey?" he bellered. "Eloped?"

"With a cussed gambolier they brung over from Alderville!" bleated Old Jake, doing a war-dance in his passion. "Elkins and Wilkerson persuaded me to take that snake into my boozum! In spite of my pleas and protests they forced him into my peaceful $#%*¢ household, and he stole the pore, mutton-headed innercent's blasted heart with his cultured airs and his slick talk! They've run off to git married!"

"It's a political plot!" shrieked Hawkins, going for his gun. "Wilkerson done it a-purpose!"

I shot the gun out of his hand, but Jack Clanton crashed a bench down on Gooseneck's head and Gooseneck kissed the floor. Clanton come down on top of him, out cold, as Mule McGrath swung with a pistol butt, and the next instant somebody lammed Mule with a brick bat and he flopped down acrost Clanton. And then the fight was on. Them rival political factions jest kind of riz up and rolled together in a wave of profanity, gunsmoke and splintering benches.

I have always noticed that the best thing to do in sech cases is to keep yore temper, and that's what I did for some time, in spite of the efforts of nine or ten wild-eyed Hawkinites. I didn't even shoot one of 'em; I kept my head and battered their skulls with a joist I tore outa the floor, and when I knocked 'em down I didn't stomp 'em hardly any. But they kept coming, and Jack McDonald was obsessed with the notion that he could ride me to the floor by jumping up astraddle of my neck. So he done it, and having discovered his idee was a hallucination, he got a fistful of my hair with his left, and started beating me in the head with his pistol barrel.

It was very annoying. Simultaneous, several other misfits got hold of my laigs, trying to rassle me down, and some son of Baliol stomped severely on my toe. I had bore my afflictions as patient as Job up to that time, but this perfidy maddened me.

I give a roar which loosened the shingles on the roof, and kicked the toe-stomper in the belly with sech fury that he curled up on the floor with a holler groan and taken no more interest in the proceedings. I likewise busted my timber on somebody's skull, and reched up an pulled Jack McDonald off my neck like pulling a tick off a bull's hide, and hev him through a convenient winder. He's a liar when he says I aimed him deliberate at that rain barrel. I didn't even know they was a rain barrel till I heard his head crash through the staves. I then shaken nine or ten idjits loose from my shoulders and shook the blood outa my eyes and preceived that Gooseneck's men was getting the worst of it, particularly including Gooseneck hisself. So I give another roar and prepared to wade through them fool Hawkinites like a b'ar through a pack of hound dogs, when I discovered that some perfidious sidewinder had got my spur tangled in his whiskers.

I stooped to ontangle myself, jest as a charge of buckshot ripped through the air where my head had been a instant before. Three or four critters was rushing me with bowie knives, so I give a wrench and tore loose by main force. How could I help it if most of the whiskers come loose too? I grabbed me a bench to use for a club, and I mowed the whole first rank down with one swipe, and then as I drawed back for another lick, I heard somebody yelling above the melee.

"Gold!" he shrieked.

Everybody stopped like they was froze in their tracks. Even Bull Hawkins shook the blood outa his eyes and glared up from where he was kneeling on Gooseneck's wishbone with one hand in Gooseneck's hair and a bowie in the other'n. Everybody quit fighting everybody else, and looked at the door – and there was Soapy Jackson, a-reeling and a-weaving with a empty bottle in one hand, and hollering.

"Big gold strike in Wild Hoss Gulch," he blats. "Biggest the West ever seen! Nuggets the size of osteridge aigs – *gulp!*"

He disappeared in a wave of frenzied humanity as Yeller Dog's population abandoned the fray and headed for the wide open spaces. Even Hawkins ceased his efforts to sculp Gooseneck alive and j'ined the stampede. They tore the whole front out of the city hall in their flight, and even them which had been knocked stiff come to at the howl of "Gold!" and staggered wildly after the mob, shrieking pitifully for their picks, shovels and jackasses. When the dust had settled and the thunder of boot heels had faded in the distance, the only human left in the city hall was me and Gooseneck, and Soapy Jackson, which riz unsteadily with the prints of hobnails all over his homely face. They shore trompled him free and generous in their rush.

Gooseneck staggered up, glared wildly about him, and went into convulsions. At first he couldn't talk at all; he jest frothed at the mouth. When he found speech his langwidge was shocking.

"What you spring it this time of night for?" he howled. "Breckinridge, I said tell him to bring the news in the mornin', not tonight!"

"I did tell him that," I says.

"Oh, so that was what I couldn't remember!" says Soapy. "That lick Mc-Donald gimme so plumb addled my brains I knowed they was somethin' I forgot, but couldn't remember what it was."

"Oh sole mio!" gibbered Gooseneck, or words to that effeck.

"Well, what you kickin' about?" I demanded peevishly, having jest discovered that somebody had stabbed me in the hind laig during the melee. My boot was full of blood, and they was brand new boots. "It worked, didn't it?" I says. "They're all headin' for Wild Hoss Gulch, includin' Hawkins hisself, and they cain't possibly git back afore day after tomorrer."

"Yeah!" raved Gooseneck. "They're *all* gone, includin' my gang! The damn' camp's empty! How can I git elected with nobody here to hold the election, and nobody to vote?"

"Oh," I says. "That's right. I hadn't thunk of that."

He fixed me with a awful eye.

"Did you," says he in a blood-curdling voice, "did you tell my voters Soapy was goin' to enact a political strategy?"

"By golly!" I said. "You know it plumb slipped my mind! Ain't that a joke on me?"

"Git out of my life!" says Gooseneck, drawing his gun.

That was a genteel way for him to ack, trying to shoot me after all I'd did for him! I taken his gun away from him as gentle as I knowed how and it was his own fault he got his arm broke. But to hear him rave you would of thought he considered I was to blame for his misfortunes or something. I was so derned disgusted I clumb onto Cap'n Kidd and shaken the dust of that there camp offa my boots, because I seen they was no gratitude in Yeller Dog.

I likewise seen I wasn't cut out for the skullduggery of politics. I had me a notion one time that I'd make a hiyu sheriff but I learnt my lesson. It's like my pap says, I reckon.

"All the law a man needs," says he, "is a gun tucked into his pants. And the main l'arnin' he needs is to know which end of that gun the bullet comes out of."

What's good enough for Pap, gents, is good enough for me.

"No Cowherders Wanted"

I hear a gang of buffalo hunters got together recently in a saloon in Dodge City to discuss ways and means of keeping their sculps onto their heads whilst collecting pelts, and purty soon one of 'em riz and said, "You mavericks make me sick. For the last hour you been chawin' wind about the soldiers tryin' to keep us north of the Cimarron, and bellyachin' about the Comanches, Kiowas and Apaches which yearns for our hair. You've took up all that time jawin' about sech triflin' hazards, and plannin' steps to take agen 'em, but you ain't makin' no efforts whatsoever to pertect yoreselves agen the biggest menace they is to the entire buffalo huntin' clan – which is Breckinridge Elkins!"

That jest shows how easy prejudiced folks is. You'd think I had a grudge agen buffalo hunters, the way they takes to the bresh whenever they sees me coming. And the way they misrepresents what happened at Cordova is plumb disgustful. To hear 'em talk you'd think I was the only man there which committed any vi'lence.

If that's so, I'd like to know how all them bullet holes got in the Diamond Bar saloon which I was usin' for a fort. Who throwed the mayor through that board fence? Who sot fire to Joe Emerson's store, jest to smoke me out? Who started the row in the first place by sticking up insulting signs in publick places? They ain't no use in them fellers tryin' to ack innercent. Any unbiased man which was there, and survived to tell the tale, knows I acted all the way through with as much dignerty as a man can ack which is being shot at by forty or fifty wild-eyed buffalo skinners.

I had never even saw a buffalo hunter before, because it was the first time I'd ever been that far East. I was takin' a pasear into New Mexico with a cowpoke by the name of Glaze Bannack which I'd met in Arizona. I stopped in Albuquerque, and he went on, heading for Dodge City. Well, I warn't in Albuquerque as long as I'd aimed to be, account of goin' broke quicker'n I expected. I had jest one dollar left after payin' for having three fellers sewed up which had somehow got afoul of my bowie knife after crittersizin' the Democratic party. I ain't the man to leave my opponents on the publick charge.

Well, I pulled out of town and headed for the cow camps on the Pecos, aimin' to git me a job. But I hadn't went far till I met a waddy ridin' in, and he taken a good look at me and Cap'n Kidd, and says, "You must be him. Wouldn't no other man fit the description he gimme."

"Who?" I said.

"Glaze Bannack," says he. "He gimme a letter to give to Breckinridge Elkins."

So I says, "Well, all right, gimme it." So he did, and it read as follers:

Dere Breckinridge:

I am in jail in Panther Springs for nothin all I done was kind of push the deperty sheriff with a little piece of scrap iron could I help it if he fell down and fraktured his skull Breckinridge. But they say I got to pay $Ten dolars fine and I have not got no sech money Breckinridge. But old man Garnett over on Buck Creek owes me ten bucks so you colleck from him and come and pay me out of this hen coop. The food is terrible Breckinridge. Hustle.

Yore misjedged friend,

Glaze Bannack, Eskwire.

Glaze never could stay out of trouble, not being tactful like me, but he was a purty good sort of hombre. So I headed for Buck Creek and collected the money off of Old Man Garnett, which was somewhat reluctant to give up the dough. In fact he bit me severely in the hind laig whilst I was setting on him prying his fingers loose from that there ten spot, and when I rode off down the road with the dinero, he run into his shack and got his buffalo gun and shot at me till I was clean out of sight.

But I ignored his lack of hospitality. I knowed he was too dizzy to shoot straight account of him having accidentally banged his head on a fence post which I happened to have in my hand whilst we was rassling.

I left him waving his gun and howling damnation and destruction, and I was well on the road for Panther Springs before I discovered to my disgust that my shirt was a complete rooin. I considered going back and demanding that Old Man Garnett buy me a new one, account of him being the one which tore it. But he was sech a onreasonable old cuss I decided agen it and rode on to Panther Springs, arriving there shortly after noon.

The first critter I seen was the purtiest gal I'd saw in a coon's age. She come out of a store and stopped to talk to a young cowpuncher she called Curly. I reined Cap'n Kidd around behind a corn crib so she wouldn't see me in my scarecrow condition. After a while she went on down the street and went into a cabin with a fence around it and a front porch, which showed her folks was wealthy, and I come out from behind the crib and says to the young buck which was smirking after her and combing his hair with the other hand, I says, "Who is that there gal? The one you was jest talkin' to."

"Judith Granger," says he. "Her folks lives over to Sheba, but her old man brung her over here account of all the fellers over there was about to cut each other's throats over her. He's makin' her stay a spell with her Aunt Henrietta, which is a war-hoss if I ever seen one. The boys is so scairt of her they don't dast try to spark Judith. Except me. I persuaded the old mudhen to let me call on Judith and I'm goin' over there for supper."

"That's what you think," I says gently. "Fact is, though, Miss Granger has got a date with me."

"She didn't tell me – " he begun scowling.

"She don't know it herself, yet," I says. "But I'll tell her you was sorry you couldn't show up."

"Why, you – " he says bloodthirsty like, and started for his gun, when a feller who'd been watchin' us from the store door, he hollered, "By golly, if it ain't Breckinridge Elkins!"

"Breckinridge Elkins?" gasped Curly, and he dropped his gun and keeled over with a low gurgle.

"Has he got a weak heart?" I ast the feller which had recognized me, and he saw, "Aw, he jest fainted when he realized how clost he come to throwin' a gun on the terror of the Humbolts. Drag him over to the hoss trough, boys, and throw some water on him. Breckinridge, I owns that grocery store there, and yore paw knows me right well. As a special favor to me will you refrain from killin' anybody in my store?"

So I said all right, and then I remembered my shirt was tore too bad to call on a young lady in. I generally has 'em made to order, but they warn't time for that if I was going to eat supper with Miss Judith, so I went into the general store and bought me one. I dunno why they don't make shirts big enough to fit reasonable sized men like me. You'd think nobody but midgets wore shirts. The biggest one in the store warn't only eighteen in the collar, but I didn't figger on buttoning the collar anyway. If I'd tried to button it it would of strangled me.

So I give the feller five dollars and put it on. It fit purty clost, but I believed I could wear it if I didn't have to expand my chest or something. Of course, I had to use some of Glaze's dough to pay for it with but I didn't reckon he'd mind considerin' all the trouble I was going to gittin' him out of jail.

I rode down the alley behind the jail and come to a barred winder and said, "Hey!"

Glaze looked out, kinda peaked, like his grub warn't settin' well with him, but he brightened up and says, "Hurray! I been on aidge expectin' you. Go on around to the front door, Breck, and pay them coyotes the ten spot, and let's go. The grub I been gittin' here would turn a lobo's stummick!"

"Well," I says, "I ain't exactly got the ten bucks, Glaze. I had to have a shirt, because mine got tore, so – "

He give a yelp like a stricken elk and grabbed the bars convulsively.

"Air you crazy?" he hollered. "You squanders my money on linens and fine raiment whilst I languishes in a prison dungeon?"

"Be ca'm," I advised. "I still got five bucks of yore'n, and one of mine. All I got to do is step down to a gamblin' hall and build it up."

"Build it up!" says he fiercely. "Lissen, blast your hide! Does you know what I've had for breakfast, dinner and supper ever since I was throwed in here? Beans! Beans! Beans!"

Here he was so overcome by emotion that he choked on the word. "And they ain't even first-class beans, neither," he said bitterly, when he could talk again. "They're full of grit and wormholes, and I think the Mex cook washes his feet in the pot he cooks 'em in."

"Well," I says, "sech cleanliness is to be encouraged, because I never heard of one before which washed his feet in anything. Don't worry. I'll git in a poker game and win enough to pay yore fine and plenty over."

"Well, git at it," he begged. "Git me out before supper time. I wants a steak with ernyuns so bad I can smell it."

So I headed for the Golden Steer saloon.

They warn't many men in there jest then, but they was a poker game going on, and when I told 'em I craved to set in they looked me over and made room for me. They was a black-whiskered cuss which said he was from Cordova which was dealing, and the first thing I noticed was he was dealing his own hand off of the bottom of the deck. The others didn't seem to see it, but us Bear Creek folks has got eyes like hawks, otherwise we'd never live to git grown.

So I says, "I dunno what the rules is in these parts, but where I come from we almost always deals off of the top of the deck."

"Air you accusin' me of cheatin'?" he demanded passionately, fumbling for his weppins and in his agitation dropping three or four extra aces out of his sleeves.

"I wouldn't think of sech a thing," I says. "Probably them marked kyards I see stickin' out of yore boot tops is merely soovernears."

For some reason this seemed to infuriate him to the p'int of drawing a bowie knife, so I hit him over the head with a brass cuspidor and he fell under the table with a holler groan.

Some fellers run in and looked at his boots sticking out from under the table, and one of 'em said, "Hey! I'm the Justice of the Peace. You can't do that. This is a orderly town."

And another'n said, "I'm the sheriff. If you cain't keep the peace I'll have to arrest you!"

This was too much even for a mild-mannered man like me.

"Shet yore fool heads!" I roared, brandishing my fists. "I come here to pay Glaze Bannack's fine, and git him outa jail, peaceable and orderly, and I'm tryin' to raise the dough like a 3/4 $%&*! gentleman! But by golly, if you hyenas pushes me beyond endurance, I'll tear down the cussed jail and snake him out without payin' no blasted fine."

The J.P. turned white. He says to the sheriff, "Let him alone! I've already bought these here new boots on credit on the strength of them ten bucks we gits from Bannack."

"But – " says the sheriff dubiously, and the J. P. hissed fiercely, "Shet up, you blame fool. I jest now reckernized him. That's Breckinridge Elkins!"

The sheriff turnt pale and swallered his adam's apple and says feebly,

"Excuse me – I – uh – I ain't feelin' so good. I guess it's somethin' I et. I think I better ride over to the next county and git me some pills."

But I don't think he was very sick from the way he run after he got outside the saloon. If they had been a jackrabbit ahead of him he would of trompled the gizzard out of it.

Well, they taken the black whiskered gent out from under the table and started pouring water on him, and I seen it was now about supper time so I went over to the cabin where Judith lived.

I was met at the door by a iron-jawed female about the size of a ordinary barn, which give me a suspicious look and says, "Well, what's *you* want?"

"I'm lookin' for yore sister, Miss Judith," I says, taking off my Stetson perlitely.

"What you mean, my sister?" says she with a scowl, but a much milder tone. "I'm her aunt."

"You don't mean to tell me!" I says, looking plumb astonished. "Why, when I first seen you, I thought you was her herself, and couldn't figger out how nobody but a twin sister could have sech a resemblance. Well, I can see right off that youth and beauty is a family characteristic."

"Go 'long with you, you young scoundrel," says she, smirking, and giving me a nudge with her elbow which would have busted anybody's ribs but mine. "You cain't soft-soap me – come in! I'll call Judith. What's yore name?"

"Breckinridge Elkins, ma'am," I says.

"So!" says she, looking at me with new interest. "I've heard tell of you. But you got a lot more sense than they give you credit for. Oh, Judith!" she called, and the winders rattled when she let her voice go. "You got company."

Judith come in, lookin' purtier than ever, and when she seen me she batted her eyes and recoiled vi'lently.

"Who – who's that?" she demanded wildly.

"Mister Breckinridge Elkins of Bear Creek, Nevader," says her aunt. "The only young man I've met in this whole dern town which has got any sense. Well, come on in and set. Supper's on the table. We was jest waitin' for Curly Jacobs," she says to me, "but if the varmint cain't git here on time, he can go hongry."

"He cain't come," I says. "He sent word by me he's sorry."

"Well, I ain't," snorted Judith's aunt. "I give him permission to call jest because I figgered even a bodacious flirt like Judith wouldn't cotton to sech a sapsucker, but – "

"Aunt Henrietta!" protested Judith, blushing.

"I cain't abide the sigh of sech weaklins," says Aunt Henrietta, settling herself carefully into a rawhide-bottomed chair which groaned under her weight. "Drag up that bench, Breckinridge. It's the only thing in the house which has a chance of holdin' yore weight outside of the sofie in the front room. Don't argy with me, Judith! I says Curly Jacobs ain't no fit man for a gal like you. Didn't I see him strain his fool back tryin' to lift that there barrel of salt I wanted fotched to the smoke house? I finally had to tote it myself. What makes young men so blame spindlin' these days?"

"Pap blames the Republican party," I says. "Haw! Haw! Haw!" says she in a guffaw which shook the doors on their hinges and scairt the cat into convulsions. "Young man, you got a great sense of humor. Ain't he, Judith?" says she, cracking a beef bone betwixt her teeth like it was a pecan.

Judith says yes kind of pallid, and all during the meal she eyed me kind of nervous like she was expecting me to go into a war-dance or somethin'. Well, when we was through, and Aunt Henrietta had et enough to keep a tribe of Sioux through a hard winter, she riz up and says, "Now clear out of here whilst I washes the dishes."

"But I must help with 'em," says Judith.

Aunt Henrietta snorted. "What makes you so eager to work all of a sudden? You want yore guest to think you ain't eager for his company? Git out of here."

So she went, but I paused to say kind of doubtful to Aunt Henrietta, "I ain't shore Judith likes me much."

"Don't pay no attention to her whims," says Aunt Henrietta, picking up the water barrel to fill her dish pan. "She's a flirtatious minx. I've took a likin' to you, and if I decide yo're the right man for her, yo're as good as hitched. Nobody couldn't never do nothin' with her but me, but she's learnt who her boss is – after havin' to eat her meals off of the mantel board a few times. Gwan in and court her and don't be backward!"

So I went on in the front room, and Judith seemed to kind of warm up to me, and ast me a lot of questions about Nevada, and finally she says she's heard me spoke of as a fighting man and hoped I ain't had no trouble in Panther Springs.

I told her no, only I had to hit one black whiskered thug from Cordova over the head with a cuspidor.

At that she jumped up like she'd sot on a pin.

"That was my uncle Jabez Granger!" she hollered. "How dast you, you big bully! You ought to be ashamed, a great big man like you pickin' on a little feller like him which don't weigh a ounce over two hundred and fifteen pounds!"

"Aw, shucks," I said contritely. "I'm sorry, Judith."

"Jest as I was beginnin' to like you," she mourned. "Now he'll write to Pap and prejudice him agen you. You jest got to go and find him and apologize to him and make friends with him."

"Aw, heck," I said.

But she wouldn't listen to nothin' else, so I went out and clumb onto Cap'n Kidd and went back to the Golden Steer, and when I come in everybody crawled under the tables.

"What's the matter with you all?" I says fretfully. "I'm looking for Jabez Granger."

"He's left for Cordova," says the barkeep, sticking his head up from behind the bar.

Well, they warn't nothing to do but foller him, so I rode by the jail and Glaze was at the winder looking out eagerly.

"Air you ready to pay me out?" he asks.

"Be patient, Glaze," I says. "I ain't got the dough yet, but I'll git it somehow as soon as I git back from Cordova."

"What?" he shrieked.

"Be ca'm like me," I advised. "You don't see *me* gittin' all het up, do you? I got to go catch Judith Granger's Uncle Jabez and apolergize to the old illegitimate for bustin' his conk with a spittoon. I'll be back tomorrer or the next day at the most."

Well, his langwidge was scandalous, considering all the trouble I was going to jest to git him out of jail, but I refused to take offense. I headed back for the Granger cabin and Judith was on the front porch.

I didn't see Aunt Henrietta; she was back in the kitchen washing dishes and singing, "They've laid Jesse James in his grave!" in a voice which loosened the shingles on the roof. So I told Judith where I was going and ast her to take some pies and cakes and things to the jail for Glaze, account of the beans was rooinin' his stummick, and she said she would. So I pulled stakes for Cordova.

It laid quite a ways to the east, and I figgered to catch up with Uncle Jabez before he got there, but he had a long start and was on a mighty good hoss, I reckon. Anyway, Cap'n Kidd got one of his hell-fire streaks and insisted on stopping every few miles to buck all over the landscape, till I finally got sick of his muleishness and busted him over the head with my pistol butt. By this time we'd lost so much time that I never overtaken Uncle Jabez at all and it was gittin' daylight before I come in sight of Cordova.

Well, about sunup I come onto a old feller and his wife in a ramshackle wagon drawed by a couple of skinny mules with a hound dawg. One wheel had run off into a sink hole and the mules was so pore and good-for-nothin' they couldn't pull it out, so I got off and laid hold on the wagon, and the old man said, "Wait a minute, young feller, whilst me and the old lady gits out to lighten the load."

"What for?" I ast. "Set still."

So I h'isted the wheel out, but if it had been stuck any tighter I might of had to use both hands.

"By golly!" says the old man. "I'd of swore nobody but Breckinridge Elkins could do that!"

"Well, I'm him," I says, and they both looked at me with reverence, and I ast 'em was they going to Panther Springs.

"We aim to," says the old woman, kind of hopeless. "One place is as good as another'n to old people which has been robbed out of their life's savins." "You all been robbed?" I ast, shocked.

"Well," says the old man, "I ain't in the habit of burdenin' strangers with my woes, but as a matter of fact, we has. My name's Hopkins. I had a ranch down on the Pecos till the drouth wiped me out and we moved to Panther Springs with what little we saved from the wreck. In a ill-advised moment I started speculatin' on buffler hides. I put in all my cash buyin' a load over on the Llano Estacado which I aimed to freight to Santa Fe and sell at a fat profit – I happen to know they're fetchin' a higher price there jest now than they air at Dodge City – and last night the whole blame cargo disappeared into thin air, as it were.

"We was stoppin' at Cordova for the night, and the old lady was sleepin' in the hotel and I was camped at the aidge of town with the wagon, and sometime durin' the night somebody snuck up and hit me over the head. When I come to this mornin' hides, wagon and team was all gone, and no trace. When I told the city marshal he jest laughed in my face and ast me how I'd expect him to track down a load of buffalo hides in a town which was full of 'em. Dang him! They was packed and corded neat with my old brand, which was the Circle A, marked onto 'em in red paint.

"Joe Emerson, which owns the saloon and most all the town, taken a mortgage on our little shack in Panther Springs and loaned me enough money to buy this measly team and wagon. If we can git back to Panther Springs maybe I can git enough freightin' to do so we can kind of live, anyway."

"Well," I said, much moved by the story, "I'm goin' to Cordova, and I'll see if I cain't find yore hides."

"Thankee kindly, Breckinridge," says he. "But I got a idee them hides is already far on their way to Dodge City. Well, I hopes you has better luck in Cordova than we did."

So they driv on west and I rode east, and got to Cordova about a hour after sunup. As I come into the aidge of town I seen a sign board about the size of a door stuck up which says on it, in big letters, "No cowherders allowed in Cordova."

"What the hell does that mean?" I demanded wrathfully of a feller which had stopped by it to light him a cigaret. And he says, "Jest what it says! Cordova's full of buffler hunters in for a spree and they don't like cowboys. Big as you be, I'd advise you to light a shuck for some where else. Bull Croghan put that sign up, and you ought to seen what happened to the last puncher which ignored it!"

"3/4$%&*¢!" I says in a voice which shook the beans out of the mesquite trees for miles around. And so saying I pulled up the sign and headed for main street with it in my hand. I am as peaceful and mildmannered a critter as you could hope to meet, but even with me a man can go too damned far. This here's a free country and no derned hairy-necked buffalo

skinner can draw boundary lines for us cowpunchers and git away with it
– not whilst I can pull a trigger.

They was very few people on the street and sech as was looked at me
surprised-like.

"Where the hell is them fool buffalo hunters?" I roared, and a feller
says, "They're all gone to the race track east of town to race hosses, except
Bull Croghan, which is takin' hisself a dram in the Diamond Bar."

So I lit and stalked in the Diamond Bar with my spurs ajingling and
my disposition gitting thornier every second. They was a big hairy critter
in buckskins and moccasins standing at the bar drinking whiskey and
talking to the barkeep and a flashy-dressed gent with slick hair and a
diamond hoss shoe stickpin. They all turned and gaped at me, and the
buffalo hunter reched down for his belt where he was wearin' the longest
knife I ever seen.

"Who air you?" he gasped.

"A cowman!" I roared, brandishing the sign. "Air you Bull Croghan?"

"Yes," says he. "What about it?"

So I busted the sign board over his head and he fell onto the floor yellin'
bloody murder and trying to draw his knife. The board was splintered, but
the stake it had been fastened to was a purty good-sized post, so I took
and beat him over the head with it till the bartender tried to shoot me with
a sawed-off shotgun.

I grabbed the barrel and the charge jest busted a shelfload of whiskey
bottles and I throwed the shotgun through a nearby winder. As I neglected
to git the bartender loose from it first, it appears he went along with
it. Anyway, he picked hisself up off of the ground, bleeding freely, and
headed east down the street shrieking, "Help! Murder! A cowboy is killin'
Croghan and Emerson!"

Which was a lie, because Croghan had crawled out the front door on his
all-fours whilst I was tending to the barkeep, and if Emerson had showed
any jedgment he wouldn't of got his sculp laid open to the bone. How did
I know he was jest tryin' to hide behind the bar? I thot he was goin' for a
gun he had hid back there. As soon as I realized the truth I dropped what
was left of the bungstarter and commenced pourin' water on Emerson,
and purty soon he sot up and looked around wild-eyed with blood and
water dripping off of his head.

"What happened?" he gurgled.

"Nothin' to git excited about," I assured him, knocking the neck off of a bottle of whiskey. "I'm lookin' for a gent named Jabez Granger."

It was at this moment that the city marshal opened fire on me through the back door. He grazed my neck with his first slug and would probably of hit me with the next if I hadn't shot the gun out of his hand. He then run off down the alley. I pursued him and catched him when he looked back over his shoulder and hit a garbage can.

"I'm a officer of the law!" he howled, tryin' to git his neck out from under my foot so as he could draw his bowie. "Don't you dast assault no officer of the law."

"I ain't," I snarled, kicking the knife out of his hand, and kind of casually swiping my spur acrost his whiskers. "But a officer which lets a old man git robbed of his buffalo hides and then laughs in his face ain't deservin' to be no officer. Gimme that badge! I demotes you to a private citizen!"

I then hung him onto a nearby hen-roost by the seat of his britches and went back up the alley, ignoring his impassioned profanity. I didn't go in at the back door of the saloon, because I figgered Joe Emerson might be layin' to shoot me as I come in. So I went around the saloon to the front and run smack onto a mob of buffalo hunters which had evidently been summoned from the race track by the barkeep. They had Bull Croghan at the hoss trough and was trying to wash the blood off of him, and they was all yellin' and cussin' so loud they didn't see me at first.

"Air we to be defied in our own lair by a 3/4$%&*¢! cowsheperd?" howled Croghan. "Scatter and comb the town for him! He's hidin' down some back alley, like as not. We'll hang him in front of the Diamond Bar and stick his sculp onto a pole as a warnin' to all his breed! Jest lemme lay eyes onto him agen – "

"Well, all you got to do is turn around," I says. And they all whirled so quick they dropped Croghan into the hoss trough. They gaped at me with their mouths open for a second. Croghan riz out of the water snortin' and splutterin', and yelled, "Well, what you waitin' on? Grab him!"

It was in trying to obey his instructions that three of 'em got their skulls fractured, and whilst the others was stumblin' and fallin' over 'em, I back into the saloon and pulled my six-shooters and issued a defiance to the world at large and buffalo hunters in particular.

They run for cover behind hitch racks and troughs and porches and fences, and a feller in a plug hat comes out and says, "Gentlemen! Le's don't have no bloodshed within the city limits! As mayor of this fair city, I – "

It was at this instant that Croghan picked him up and throwed him through a board fence into a cabbage patch where he lay till somebody revived him a few hours later.

The hunters then all started shootin' at me with .50 caliber Sharps' buffalo rifles. Emerson, which was hidin' behind a Schlitz sign board, hollered something amazing account of the holes which was being knocked in the roof and walls. The big sign in front was shot to splinters, and the mirror behind the bar was riddled, and all the bottles on the shelves and the hanging lamps was busted. It's plumb astonishing the damage a bushel or so of them big slugs can do to a saloon.

They went right through the walls. If I hadn't kept moving all the time I'd of been shot to rags, and I did git several bullets through my clothes and three or four grazed some hide off. But even so I had the aidge, because they couldn't see me only for glimpses now and then through the winders and was shooting more or less blind because I had 'em all spotted and slung lead so far and clost they didn't dast show theirselves long enough to take good aim.

But my ca'tridges begun to run short so I made a sally out into the alley jest as one of 'em was trying to sneak in at the back door. I hear tell he is very bitter toward me about his teeth, but I like to know how he expects to git kicked in the mouth without losing some fangs.

So I jumped over his writhing carcase and run down the alley, winging three or four as I went and collectin' a pistol ball in my hind laig. They was hidin' behind board fences on each side of the alley but them boards wouldn't stop a .45 slug. They all shot at me, but they misjedged my speed. I move a lot faster than most folks expect.

Anyway, I was out of the alley before they could git their wits back. And as I went past the hitch rack where Cap'n Kidd was champin' and snortin' to git into the fight, I grabbed my Winchester .45–90 off of the saddle, and run acrost the street. The hunters which was still shootin' at the front of the Diamond Bar seen me and that's when I got my spurs shot off, but I ducked into Emerson's General Store whilst the clerks all run shrieking out the back way.

As for that misguided hunter which tried to confiscate Cap'n Kidd, I ain't to blame for what happened to him. They're going around now sayin' I trained Cap'n Kidd special to jump onto a buffalo hunter with all four feet after kicking him through a corral fence. That's a lie. I didn't have to train him. He thot of it hisself. The idjit which tried to take him ought to be thankful he was able to walk with crutches inside of ten months.

Well, I was now on the same side of the street as the hunters was, so as soon as I started shootin' at 'em from the store winders they run acrost the street and taken refuge in a dance hall right acrost from the store and started shootin' back at me, and Joe Emerson hollered louder'n ever, because he owned the dance hall too. All the citizens of the town had bolted into the hills long ago, and left us to fight it out.

Well, I piled sides of pork and barrels of pickles and bolts of calico in the winders, and shot over 'em, and I built my barricades so solid even them buffalo guns couldn't shoot through 'em. They was plenty of Colt and Winchester ammunition in the store, and whiskey, so I knowed I could hold the fort indefinite.

Them hunters could tell they warn't doin' no damage, so purty soon I heard Croghan bellerin', "Go git that cannon the soldiers loaned the folks to fight the Apaches with. It's over behind the city hall. Bring it in at the back door. We'll blast him out of his fort, by golly!"

"You'll ruin my store!" screamed Emerson.

"I'll rooin' yore face if you don't shet up," opined Croghan. "Gwan!"

Well, they kept on shootin' and so did I, and I must of hit some of 'em, jedging from the blood-curdlin' yells that went up from time to time. Then a most remarkable racket of cussin' busted out, and from the remarks passed, I gathered that they'd brung the cannon and somehow got it stuck in the back door of the dance hall. The shootin' kind of died down whilst they rassled with it and in the lull I heard me a noise out behind the store.

They warn't no winders in the back, which is why they hadn't shot at me from that direction. I snuck back and looked through a crack in the door and I seen a feller in the dry gully which run along behind the store, and he had a can of kerosine and some matches and was settin' the store on fire.

I jest started to shoot when I recognized Judith Granger's Uncle Jabez. I laid down my Winchester and opened the door soft and easy and pounced out on him, but he let out a squawk and dodged and run down the gully. The shootin' acrost the street broke out agen, but I give no heed, because I warn't goin' to let him git away from me agen. I run him down the gully about a hundred yards and catched him, and taken his pistol away from him, but he got hold of a rock which he hammered me on the head with till I nigh lost patience with him.

But I didn't want to injure him account of Judith, so I merely kicked him in the belly and then throwed him before he could git his breath back, and sot on him, and says, "Blast yore hide, I apolergizes for lammin' you with that there cuspidor. Does you accept my apolergy, you potbellied hoss thief?"

"Never!" says he rampacious. "A Granger never forgits!"

So I taken him by the ears and beat his head agen a rock till he gasps. "Let up! I accepts yore apolergy, you 3/4$%&*¢!"

"All right," I says, arising and dusting my hands, "and if you ever goes back on yore word, I'll hang yore mangy hide to the – "

It was at that moment that Emerson's General Store blew up with a ear-splitting bang.

"What the hell?" shrieked Uncle Jabez, staggering, as the air was filled with fragments of groceries and pieces of flying timber.

"Aw," I said disgustedly, "I reckon a stray bullet hit a barrel of gunpowder. I aimed to move them barrels out of the line of fire, but kind of forgot about it – "

But Uncle Jabez had bit the dust. I hear tell he claims I hit him onexpected with a wagon pole. I didn't do no sech thing. It was a section of the porch roof which fell on him, and if he'd been watching, and ducked like I did, it wouldn't of hit him.

I clumb out of the gully and found myself opposite from the Diamond Bar. Bull Croghan and the hunters was pouring out of the dance hall whooping and yellin', and Joe Emerson was tearin' his hair and howlin' like a timber wolf with the belly ache because his store was blowed up and his saloon was shot all to pieces.

But nobody paid no attention to him. They went surging acrost the street and nobody seen me when I crossed it from the other side and went into the alley behind the saloon. I run on down it till I got to the dance hall, and sure enough the cannon was stuck in the back door. It warn't wide enough for the wheels to git through.

I heard Croghan roaring acrost the street, "Poke into the debray, boys! Elkins' remains must be here somewheres, unless he was plumb dissolved! That – "

Crash!

They was a splinterin' of planks, and somebody yelled, "Hey! Croghan's fell into a well or somethin'!"

I heard Joe Emerson shriek, "Dammit, stay away from there! Don't – "

I tore away a section of the wall and got the cannon loose and run it up to the front door of the dance hall and looked out. Them hunters was all ganged up with their backs to the dance hall, all bent over whilst they was apparently trying to pull Croghan out of some hole he'd fell into headfirst. His cussin' sounded kinda muffled. Joe Emerson was having a fit at the aidge of the crowd.

Well, they'd loaded that there cannon with nails and spikes and lead slugs and carpet tacks and sech like, but I put in a double handful of beer bottle caps jest for good measure, and touched her off. It made a noise like a thunder clap and the recoil knocked me about seventeen foot, but you should of heard the yell them hunters let out when that hurreycane of scrap iron hit 'em in the seat of the britches. It was amazing!

To my disgust, though, it didn't kill none of 'em. Seems like the charge was too heavy for the powder, so all it done was knock 'em off their feet and tear the britches off of 'em. However, it swept the ground clean of 'em like a broom, and left 'em all standing on their necks in the gully behind where the store had been, except Croghan whose feet I still perceived sticking up out of the ruins.

Before they could recover their wits, if they ever had any, I run acrost the street and started beatin' 'em over the head with a pillar I tore off of the saloon porch. Some sech as was able ariz and fled howling into the desert. I hear tell some of 'em didn't stop till they got to Dodge City, having run right through a Kiowa war party and scairt them pore Injuns till they turnt white.

Well, I laid holt of Croghan's laigs and hauled him out of the place he had fell into, which seemed to be a kind of cellar which had been under the floor of the store. Croghan's conversation didn't noways make sense, and every time I let go of him he fell on his neck.

So I abandoned him in disgust and looked down into the cellar to see what was in it that Emerson should of took so much to keep it hid. Well, it was plumb full of buffalo hides, all corded into neat bundles! At that Emerson started to run, but I grabbed him, and reached down with the other hand and hauled a bundle out. It was marked with a red Circle A brand.

"So!" I says to Emerson, impulsively busting him in the snout. "You stole old man Hopkins' hides yoreself! Perjuice that mortgage! Where's the old man's wagon and team?"

"I got 'em hid in my livery stable," he moaned.

"Go hitch 'em up and bring 'em here," I says. "And if you tries to run off, I'll track you down and sculp you alive!"

I went and got Cap'n Kidd and watered him. When I got back, Emerson come up with the wagon and team, so I told him to load on them hides.

"I'm a ruined man!" sniveled he. "I ain't able to load no hides."

"The exercize'll do you good," I assured him, kicking the seat loose from his pants, so he give a harassed howl and went to work. About this time Croghan sot up and gaped at me weirdly.

"It all comes back to me!" he gurgled. "We was going to run Breckinridge Elkins out of town!"

He then fell back and went into shrieks of hysterical laughter which was most hair-raising to hear.

"The wagon's loaded," panted Joe Emerson. "Take it and git out and be quick!"

"Well, let this be a lesson to you," I says, ignoring his hostile attitude. "Honesty's always the best policy!"

I then hit him over the head with a wagon spoke and clucked to the hosses and we headed for Panther Springs.

Old man Hopkins' mules had give out halfway to Panther Springs. Him and the old lady was camped there when I drove up. I never seen folks so happy in my life as they was when I handed the team, wagon, hides and mortgage over to 'em. They both cried and the old lady kissed me, and the old man hugged me, and I thot I'd plumb die of embarrassment before I could git away. But I did, finally, and headed for Panther Springs again, because I still had to raise the dough to git Glaze out of jail.

I got there about sun-up and headed straight for Judith's cabin to tell her I'd made friends with Uncle Jabez. Aunt Henrietta was cleaning a carpet on the front porch and looking mad. When I come up she stared at me and said, "Good land, Breckinridge, what happened to you?"

"Aw, nothin'," I says. "Jest a argyment with them fool buffalo hunters over to Cordova. They'd cleaned a old gent and his old lady of their buffalo hides, to say nothin' of their hosses and wagon. So I rid on to see what I could do about it. Them hairy-necked hunters didn't believe me when I said I wanted them hides, so I had to persuade 'em a leetle. O'ny thing is they is sayin' now that I was to blame fer the hull affair. I apolergized to Judith's uncle, too. Had to chase him from here to Cordova. Where's Judith?"

"Gone!" she says, stabbing her broom at the floor so vicious she broke the handle off. "When she taken them pies and cakes to yore fool friend down to the jail house, she taken a shine to him at first sight. So she borrored the money from me to pay his fine – said she wanted a new dress to look nice in for you, the deceitful hussy! If I'd knowed what she wanted it for she wouldn't of got it – she'd of got somethin' acrost my knee! But she paid him out of the jug, and – "

"And what happened then?" I says wildly.

"She left me a note," snarled Aunt Henrietta, giving the carpet a whack that tore it into six pieces. "She said anyway she was afeared if she didn't marry him I'd make her marry you. She must of sent you off on that wild goose chase a purpose. Then she met him, and – well, they snuck out and got married and air now on their way to Denver for their honeymoon – Hey, what's the matter, Breckinridge? Air you sick?"

"I be," I gurgled. "The ingratitude of mankind cuts me to the gizzard! After all I'd did for Glaze Bannack! Well, by golly, this is a lesson to me! I bet I don't never work my fingers to the quick gittin' another ranny out of jail!"

The Conquerin' Hero of the Humbolts

I was in Sundance enjoying myself a little after a long trail-drive up from the Cimarron, when I got a letter from Abednego Raxton which said as follers:

Dear Breckinridge:

That time I paid yore fine down in Tucson for breaking the county clerk's laig you said you'd gimme a hand anytime I ever need help. Well Breckinridge I need yore assistance right now the rustlers is stealing me ragged it has got so I nail my bed-kivers to the bunk every night or they'd steal the blankets right offa me Breckinridge. Moreover a stumbling block on the path of progress by the name of Ted Bissett is running sheep on the range next to me this is more'n a man can endure Breckinridge. So I want you to come up here right away and help me find out who is stealing my stock and bust Ted Bissett's hed for him the low-minded scunk. Hoping you air the same I begs to remane as usual,

Yore abused frend,

A. Raxton, Esq.

P.S. That sap-headed misfit Johnny Willoughby which used to work for me down on Green River is sheriff here and he couldn't ketch flies if they was bogged down in merlasses.

Well, I didn't feel it was none of my business to mix into any row Abednego might be having with the sheepmen, so long as both sides fit fair, but rustlers was a different matter. A Elkins detests a thief. So I mounted Cap'n Kidd, after the usual battle, and headed for Lonesome Lizard, which was the nighest town to his ranch.

I found myself approaching this town a while before noon one blazing hot day, and as I crossed a right thick timbered creek, shrieks for aid and assistance suddenly bust the stillness. A hoss also neighed wildly, and Cap'n Kidd begun to snort and champ like he always does when they is a b'ar or a cougar in the vicinity. I got off and tied him, because if I was going to have to fight some critter like that, I didn't want him mixing into the scrap; he was jest as likely to kick me as the varmint. I then went on foot in the direction of the screams, which was growing more desperate every minute, and I presently come to a thicket with a big tree in the middle of it, and there they was. One of the purtiest gals I ever seen was roosting in the tree and screeching blue murder, and they was a cougar climbing up after her.

"Help!" says she wildly. "Shoot him!"

"I jest wish some of them tenderfoots which calls theirselves naturalists could see this," I says, taking off my Stetson. A Elkins never forgits his manners. "Some of 'em has tried to tell me cougars never attacks human beings nor climbs trees, nor prowls in the daytime. I betcha this would make 'em realize they don't know it all. Jest like I said to that'n which I seen in War Paint, Nevada, last summer – "

"Will you stop talkin' and do somethin'?" she says fiercely. "Ow!"

Because he had reched up and made a pass at her foot with his left paw. I seen this had went far enough, so I told him sternly to come down, but all he done was look down at me and spit in a very insulting manner. So I reched up and got him by the tail and yanked him down, and whapped him agen the ground three or four times, and when I let go of him he run off a few yards, and looked back at me in a most pecooliar manner. Then he shaken his head like he couldn't believe it hisself, and lit a shuck as hard as he could peel it in the general direction of the North Pole.

"Whyn't you shoot him?" demanded the gal, leaning as far out as she could to watch him.

"Aw, he won't come back," I assured her. "Hey, look out! That limb's goin' to break – "

Which it did jest as I spoke and she come tumbling down with a shriek of despair. She still held onto the limb with a desperate grip, however, which is why it rapped me so severe on the head when I catched her.

"Oh!" says she, letting go of the limb and grabbing me. "Am I hurt?"

"I dunno," I says. "You better let me carry you to wherever you want to go."

"No," says she, gitting her breath back. "I'm all right. Lemme down."

So I done so, and she says, "I got a hoss tied over there behind that fir.

I was ridin' home from Lonesome Lizard and stopped to poke a squirrel out of a holler tree. It warn't a squirrel, though. It was that dang lion. If you'll git my hoss for me, I'll be ridin' home. Pap's ranch is jest over that ridge to the west. I'm Margaret Brewster."

"I'm Breckinridge Elkins, of Bear Creek, Nevada," I says. "I'm headin' for Lonesome Lizard, but I'll be ridin' back this way before long. Can I call on you?"

"Well," she says, "I'm engaged to marry a feller, but it's conditional. I got a suspicion he's a spineless failure, and I told him flat if he didn't succeed at the jobs he's workin' on now, not to come back. I detests a failure. That's why I likes yore looks," says she, giving me a admiring glance. "A man which can rassle a mountain lion with his b'ar hands is worth any gal's time. I'll send you word at Lonesome Lizard; if my fiansay flops like it looks he's goin' to do, I'd admire to have you call."

"I'll be awaitin' yore message with eager heart and honest devotion," I says, and she blushed daintily and clumb on her hoss and pulled her freight. I watched her till she was clean out of sight, and then hove a sigh that shook the acorns out of the surrounding oaks, and wended my way back to Cap'n Kidd in a sort of rose-colored haze. I was so entranced I started to git onto Cap'n Kidd on the wrong end and never noticed till he kicked me vi'lently in the belly.

"Love, Cap'n Kidd," I says to him dreamily, batting him between the eyes with my pistol butt, "is youth's sweet dream."

But he made no response, outside of stomping on my corns; Cap'n Kidd has got very little sentiment.

So I mounted and pulled for Lonesome Lizard, which I arriv at maybe a hour later. I put Cap'n Kidd in the strongest livery stable I could find and seen he was fed and watered, and warned the stable hands not to antagonize him, and then I headed for the Red Warrior saloon. I needed a little refreshments before I started for Abednego's ranch.

I taken me a few drams and talked to the men which was foregathered there, being mainly cowmen. The sheepmen patronized the Bucking Ram, acrost the street. That was the first time I'd ever been in Montana, and them fellers warn't familiar with my repertation, as was showed by their manner.

Howthesomever, they was perlite enough, and after we'd downed a few fingers of corn scrapings, one of 'em ast me where I was from, proving they considered me a honest man with nothing to conceal. When I told 'em, one of 'em said, "By golly, they must grow big men in Nevada, if yo're a sample. Yo're the biggest critter I ever seen in the shape of a human."

"I bet he's as stout as Big Jon," says one, and another'n says, "That cain't be. This gent is human, after all. Big Jon ain't."

I was jest fixing to ast 'em who this Jon varmint was, when one of 'em cranes his neck toward the winder and says, "Speak of the devil and you gits a whiff of brimstone! Here comes Jon acrost the street now. He must of seen this gent comin' in, and is on his way to make his usual challenge. The sight of a man as big as him is like wavin' a red flag at a bull."

I looked out the winder and seen a critter about the size of a granary coming acrost the street from the Bucking Ram, follered by a gang of men which looked like him, but not nigh as big.

"What kind of folks air they?" I ast with interest. "They ain't neither Mexicans nor Injuns, but they sure ain't white men, neither."

"Aw, they're Hunkies," says a little sawed-off cowman. "Ted Bissett brung 'em in here to herd sheep for him. That big 'un's Jon. He ain't got no sense, but you never seen sech a hunk of muscle in yore life."

"Where they from?" I ast. "Canader?"

"Naw," says he. "They come originally from a place called Yurrop. I dunno where it is, but I jedge it's somewhere's east of Chicago." But I knowed them fellers never originated nowheres on this continent. They was rough-dressed and wild-looking, with knives in their belts, and they didn't look like no folks I'd ever saw before. They come into the barroom and the one called Jon bristled up to me very hostile with his little beady black eyes. He stuck out his chest about a foot and hit it with his fist which was about the size of a sledge hammer. It sounded like a man beating a bass drum.

"You strong man," says he. "I strong too. We rassle, eh?"

"Naw," I says. "I don't care nothin' about rasslin'."

He give a snort which blowed the foam off of every beer glass on the bar, and looked around till he seen a iron rod laying on the floor. It looked like the handle of a branding iron, and was purty thick. He grabbed this and bent it into a V, and throwed it down on the bar in front of me, and all the other Hunkies jabbered admiringly.

This childish display irritated me, but I controlled myself and drunk another finger of whiskey, and the bartender whispered to me, "Look out for him! He aims to prod you into a fight. He's nearly kilt nine or ten men with his b'ar hands. He's a mean 'un."

"Well," I says, tossing a dollar onto the bar and turning away, "I got more important things to do than rassle a outlandish foreigner in a barroom. I got to eat my dinner and git out to the Raxton ranch quick."

But at that moment Big Jon chose to open his bazoo. There are some folks which cain't never let well enough alone.

" 'Fraid!" jeered he. "Yah, yah!"

The Hunkies all whooped and guffawed, and the cattlemen scowled.

"What you mean, afraid?" I gasped, more dumbfounded than mad. It'd been so long since anybody's made a remark like that to me I was plumb flabbergasted. Then I remembered I was amongst strangers which didn't know my repertation, and I realized it was my duty to correct that there oversight before somebody got hurt on account of ignorance.

So I said, "All right, you dumb foreign muttonhead, I'll rassle you."

But as I went up to him, he doubled up his fist and hit me severely on the nose, and them Hunkies all bust into loud, rude laughter. That warn't wise. A man had better twist a striped thunderbolt's tail than hit a Elkins onexpected on the nose. I give a roar of irritation and grabbed Big Jon and started committing mayhem on him free and enthusiastic. I swept all the glasses and bottles off of the bar with him, and knocked down a hanging lamp with him, and fanned the floor with him till he was limp, and then I throwed him the full length of the barroom. His head went through the panels of the back door, and the other Hunkies, which had stood petrified, stampeded into the street with howls of horror. So I taken the branding iron handle and straightened it out and bent it around his neck, and twisted the ends together in a knot, so he had to get a blacksmith to file it off after he come to, which was several hours later.

All them cowmen was staring at me with their eyes popped out of their heads, and seemed plumb incapable of speech, so I give a snort of disgust at the whole incerdent, and strode off to git my dinner. As I left I heard one feller, which was holding onto the bar like he was too weak to stand alone, say feebly to the dumbfounded bartender, "Gimme a drink, quick! I never thunk I'd live to see somethin' I couldn't believe when I was lookin' right smack at it."

I couldn't make no sense out of this, so I headed for the dining room of the Montana Hotel and Bar. But my hopes of peace and quiet was a illusion. I'd jest started on my fourth beefsteak when a big maverick in Star-top boots and store-bought clothes come surging into the dining room and bellered, "Is your name Elkins?"

"Yes, it is," I says. "But I ain't deef. You don't have to yell."

"Well, what the hell do you mean by interferin' with my business?" he squalled, ignoring my reproof.

"I dunno what yo're talkin' about," I growled, emptying the sugar bowl into my coffee cup with some irritation. It looked like Lonesome Lizard was full of maneyacks which craved destruction. "Who air you, anyhow?"

"I'm Ted Bissett, that's who!" howled he, convulsively gesturing toward his six-shooter. "And I'm onto you! You're a damn' Nevada gunman old Abed' Raxton's brought up here to run me off the range! He's been braggin' about it all over town! And you starts your work by runnin' off my sheepherders!"

"What you mean, I run yore sheepherders off?" I demanded, amazed.

"They ran off after you maltreated Big Jon," he gnashed, with his face convulsed. "They're so scared of you they won't come back without double pay! You can't do this to me, you #$%&*!"

The man don't live which can call me that name with impunity. I impulsively hit him in the face with my fried steak, and he give a impassioned shriek and pulled his gun. But some grease had got in his eyes, so all he done with his first shot was bust the syrup pitcher at my elbow, and before he could cock his gun again I shot him through the arm. He dropped his gun and grabbed the place with his other hand and made some remarks which ain't fitten for to repeat.

I yelled for another steak, and Bissett yelled for a doctor, and the manager yelled for the sheriff.

The last-named individual didn't git there till after the doctor and the steak had arrove and was setting Bissett's arm – the doctor, I mean, and not the steak, which a trembling waiter brung me. Quite a crowd had gathered by this time and was watching the doctor work with great interest, and offering advice which seemed to infuriate Bissett, jedging from his langwidge. He also discussed his busted arm with considerable passion, but the doctor warn't a bit worried. You never seen sech a cheerful gent. He was jovial and gay, no matter how loud Bissett yelled. You could tell right off he was a man which could take it.

But Bissett's friends was very mad, and Jack Campbell, his foreman, was muttering something about 'em taking the law into their own hands, when the sheriff come prancing in, waving a six-shooter and hollering, "Where is he? P'int out the scoundrel to me!"

"There he is!" everybody yelled, and ducked, like they expected gunplay, but I'd already recognized the sheriff, and when he seen me he recoiled and shoved his gun out of sight like it was red hot or something.

"Breckinridge Elkins!" says he. Then he stopped and studied a while, and then he told 'em to take Bissett out to the bar and pour some licker down him. When they'd went he sot down at the table, and says, "Breck, I want you to understand that they ain't nothin' personal about this, but I got to arrest you. It's agen the law to shoot a man inside of the city limits."

"I ain't got time to git arrested," I told him. "I got to git over to old Abed' Raxton's ranch."

"But lissen, Breck," argyed the sheriff – it was Johnny Willoughby, jest like old Abed' said – "what'll folks think if I don't jail you for shootin' a leadin' citizen? Election's comin' up and my hat's in the ring," says he, gulping my coffee.

"Bissett shot at me first," I said. "Whyn't you arrest him?"

"Well, he didn't hit you," says Johnny, absently cramming half a pie into his mouth and making a stab at my pertaters. "Anyway, he's got a busted arm and ain't able to go to jail jest now. Besides, I needs the sheepmen's votes."

"Aw, I don't like jails," I said irritably, and he begun to weep.

"If you was a friend to me," sobs he, "you'd be glad to spend a night in jail to help me git re-elected. I'd do as much for you! The whole county's givin' me hell anyway, because I ain't been able to catch none of them cattle rustlers, and if I don't arrest you I won't have a Chinaman's chance at the polls. How can you do me like this, after the times we had together in the old days – "

"Aw, stop blubberin'," I says. "You can arrest me, if you want to. What's the fine?"

"I don't want to collect no fine, Breck," says he, wiping his eyes on the oilcloth table cover and filling his pockets with doughnuts. "I figgers a jail sentence will give me more prestige. I'll let you out first thing in the mornin'. You won't tear up the jail, will you, Breck?"

I promised I wouldn't, and then he wants me to give up my guns, and I refuses.

"But good gosh, Breck," he pleaded. "It'd look awful funny for a prisoner to keep on his shootin' irons."

So I give 'em to him, jest to shet him up, and then he wanted to put his handcuffs onto me, but they warn't big enough to fit my wrists. So he said if I'd lend him some money he could have the blacksmith to make me some laig-irons, but I refused profanely, so he said all right, it was jest a suggestion, and no offense intended, so we went down to the jail. The jailer was off sleeping off a drunk somewheres, but he'd left the key hanging on the door, so we went in. Purty soon along come Johnny's deperty, Bige Gantry, a long, loose-j'inted cuss with a dangerous eye, so Johnny sent him to the Red Warrior for a can of beer, and whilst he was gone Johnny bragged on him a heap.

"Why," says he, "Bige is the only man in the county which has ever got within shootin' distance of them dern' outlaws. He was by hisself, wuss luck. If I'd been along we'd of scuppered the whole gang."

I ast him if he had any idee who they was, and he said Bige believed they was a gang up from Wyoming. So I said well, then, in that case they got a hangout in the hills somewheres, and ought to be easier to run down than men which scattered to their homes after each raid.

Bige got back with the beer about then, and Johnny told him that when I got out of jail he was going to depertize me and we'd all go after them outlaws together. So Bige said that was great, and looked me over purty sharp, and we sot down and started playing poker. Along about supper time the jailer come in, looking tolerable seedy, and Johnny made him cook us some supper. Whilst we was eating the jailer stuck his head into my cell and said, "A gent is out there cravin' audience with Mister Elkins."

"Tell him the prisoner's busy," says Johnny.

"I done so," says the jailer, "and he says if you don't let him in purty dern quick, he's goin' to bust in and cut yore throat."

"That must be old Abed' Raxton," says Johnny. "Better let him in – Breck," says he, "I looks to you to pertect me if the old cuss gits mean."

So old Abed' come walzing into the jail with fire in his eye and corn licker on his breath. At the sight of me he let out a squall which was painful to hear.

"A hell of a help you be, you big lummox!" he hollered. "I sends for you to help me bust up a gang of rustlers and sheepherders, and the first thing you does is to git in jail!"

"T'warn't my fault," I says. "Them sheepherders started pickin' on me."

"Well," he snarls, "whyn't you drill Bissett center when you was at it?"

"I come up here to shoot rustlers, not sheepherders," I says.

"What's the difference?" he snarled.

"Them sheepmen has probably got as much right on the range as you cowmen," I says.

"Cease sech outrageous blasphermy," says he, shocked. "You've bungled things so far, but they's one good thing – Bissett had to hire back his derned Hunkie herders at double wages. He don't no more mind spendin' money than he does spillin' his own blood, the cussed tightwad. Well, what's yore fine?"

"Ain't no fine," I said. "Johnny wants me to stay in jail a while."

At this old Abed' convulsively went for his gun and Johnny got behind me and hollered, "Don't you dast shoot a ossifer of the law!"

"It's a spite trick!" gibbered old Abed'. "He's been mad at me ever since I fired him off'n my payroll. After I kicked him off'n my ranch he run for sheriff, and the night of the election everybody was so drunk they voted for him by mistake, or for a joke, or somethin', and since he's been in office he's been lettin' the sheepmen steal me right out of house and home."

"That's a lie," says Johnny heatedly. "I've give you as much pertection as anybody else, you old buzzard! I jest ain't been able to run any of them critters down, that's all. But you wait! Bige is on their trail, and we'll have 'em behind the bars before the snow falls."

"Before the snow falls in Guatemala, maybe," snorted old Abed'. "All right, blast you, I'm goin', but I'll have Breckinridge outa here if I have to burn the cussed jail! A Raxton never forgits!" So he stalked out sulphurously, only turning back to snort, "Sheriff! Bah! Seven murders in the county unsolved since you come into office! You'll let the sheepmen murder us all in our beds! We ain't had a hangin' since you was elected!"

After he'd left, Johnny brooded a while, and finally says, "The old lobo's right about them murders, only he neglected to mention that four of 'em was sheepmen. I know it's cattlemen and sheepmen killin' each other, each side accusin' the other'n of rustlin' stock, but I cain't prove nothin'. A hangin' *would* set me solid with the voters." Here he eyed me hungrily, and ventured, "If somebody'd jest up and confess to some of them murders – "

"You needn't to look at me like that," I says. "I never kilt nobody in Montana."

"Well," he argyed, "nobody could *prove* you never done 'em, and after you was hanged – "

"Lissen here, you," I says with some passion, "I'm willin' to help a friend git elected all I can, but they's a limit!"

"Oh, well, all right," he sighed. "I didn't much figger you'd be willin', anyway; folks is so dern selfish these days. All they thinks about is theirselves. But lissen here: if I was to bust up a lynchin' mob it'd be nigh as good a boost for my campaign as a legal hangin'. I tell you what – tonight I'll have some of my friends put on masks and come and take you out and pretend like they was goin' to hang you. Then when they got the rope around yore neck I'll run out and shoot in the air and they'll run off and I'll git credit for upholdin' law and order. Folks always disapproves of mobs, unless they happens to be in 'em."

So I said all right, and he urged me to be careful and not hurt none of 'em, because they was all his friends and would be mine. I ast him would they bust the door down, and he said they warn't no use in damaging property like that; they could hold up the jailer and take the key off'n him. So he went off to fix things, and after a while Bige Gantry left and said he was on the trace of a clue to them cattle rustlers, and the jailer started drinking hair tonic mixed with tequila, and in about a hour he was stiffer'n a wet lariat.

Well, I laid down on the floor on a blanket to sleep, without taking my boots off, and about midnight a gang of men in masks come and they didn't have to hold up the jailer, because he was out cold. So they taken the key off'n him, and all the loose change and plug tobaccer out of his pockets too, and opened the door, and I ast, "Air you the gents which is goin' to hang me?" And they says, "We be!"

So I got up and ast them if they had any licker, and one of 'em gimme a good snort out of his hip flask, and I said, "All right, le's git it over with, so I can go back to sleep."

He was the only one which done any talking, and the rest didn't say a word. I figgered they was bashful. He said, "Le's tie yore hands behind you so's to make it look real," and I said all right, and they tied me with some rawhide thongs which I reckon would of held the average man all right.

So I went outside with 'em, and they was a oak tree right clost to the jail nigh some bushes. I figgered Johnny was hiding over behind them bushes.

They had a barrel for me to stand on, and I got onto it, and they throwed a rope over a big limb and put the noose around my neck, and the feller says, "Any last words?"

"Aw, hell," I says, "this is plumb silly. Ain't it about time for Johnny – "

At this moment they kicked the barrel out from under me.

Well, I was kind of surprised, but I tensed my neck muscles, and waited for Johnny to rush out and rescue me, but he didn't come, and the noose began to pinch the back of my neck, so I got disgusted and says, "Hey, lemme down!"

Then one of 'em which hadn't spoke before says, "By golly, I never heard a man talk after he'd been strung up before!"

I recognized that voice; it was Jack Campbell, Bissett's foreman! Well, I have got a quick mind, in spite of what my cousin Bearfield Buckner says, so I knowed right off something was fishy about this business. So I snapped the thongs on my wrists and reched up and caught hold of the rope I was hung with by both hands and broke it. Them scoundrels was so surprised they didn't think to shoot at me till the rope was already broke, and then the bullets all went over me as I fell. When they started shooting I knowed they meant me no good, and acted according.

I dropped right in the midst of 'em, and brung three to the ground with me, and during the few seconds to taken me to choke and batter them unconscious the others was scairt to fire for fear of hitting their friends, we was so tangled up. So they clustered around and started beating me over the head with their gun butts, and I riz up like a b'ar amongst a pack of hounds and grabbed four more of 'em and hugged 'em till their ribs cracked. Their masks came off during the process, revealing the faces of Bissett's friends; I'd saw 'em in the hotel.

Somebody prodded me in the hind laig with a bowie at that moment, which infuriated me, so I throwed them four amongst the crowd and hit out right and left, knocking over a man or so at each lick, till I seen a wagon spoke on the ground and stooped over to pick it up. When I done that somebody throwed a coat over my head and blinded me, and six or seven men then jumped onto my back. About this time I stumbled over some feller which had been knocked down, and fell onto my belly, and they all started jumping up and down on me enthusiastically. I reched around and grabbed one and dragged him around to where I could rech his left ear with my teeth. I would of taken it clean off at the first snap, only I had to bite through the coat which was over my head, but as it was I done a good job, jedging from his awful shrieks.

He put forth a supreme effort and tore away, taking the coat with him, and I shaken off the others and riz up in spite of their puny efforts, with the wagon spoke in my hand.

A wagon spoke is a good, comforting implement to have in a melee, and very demoralizing to the enemy. This'n busted all to pieces about the fourth or fifth lick, but that was enough. Them which was able to run had all took to their heels, leaving the battlefield strewed with moaning and cussing figgers.

Their remarks was shocking to hear, but I give 'em no heed. I headed for the sheriff's office, mad clean through. It was a few hundred yards east of the jail, and jest as I rounded the jail house, I run smack into a dim figger which come sneaking through the bresh making a curious clanking noise. It hit me with what appeared to be a iron bar, so I went to the ground with it and choked it and beat its head agen the ground, till the moon come out from behind a cloud and revealed the bewhiskered features of old Abednego Raxton!

"What the hell?" I demanded of the universe at large. "Is everybody in Montaner crazy? What air you doin' tryin' to murder me in my sleep?"

"I warn't, you jack-eared lunkhead," snarled he, when he could talk.

"Then what'd you hit me with that there pinch bar for?" I demanded.

"I didn't know it was you," says he, gitting up and dusting his britches. "I thought it was a grizzly b'ar when you riz up out of the dark. Did you bust out?"

"Naw, I never," I said. "I told you I was stayin' in jail to do Johnny a favor. And you know what that son of Baliol done? He framed it up with Bissett's friends to git me hung. Come on. I'm goin' over and interview the dern skunk right now."

So we went over to Johnny's office, and the door was unlocked and a candle burning, but he warn't in sight.

They was a small iron safe there, which I figgered he had my guns locked up in, so I got a rock and busted it open, and sure enough there my shooting-irons was. They was also a gallon of corn licker there, and me and Abed' was discussing whether or not we had the moral right to drink it, when I heard somebody remark in a muffled voice, "Whumpff! Gfuph! *Oompg!*"

So we looked around and I seen a pair of spurs sticking out from under a camp cot over in the corner. I grabbed hold of the boots they was on, and pulled 'em out, and a human figger come with 'em. It was Johnny. He was tied hand and foot and gagged, and he had a lump onto his head about the size of a turkey aig.

I pulled off the gag, and the first thing he says was, "If you sons of Perdition drinks my private licker I'll have yore hearts' blood!"

"You better do some explainin'," I says resentfully. "What you mean, siccin' Bissett's friends onto me?"

"I never done no sech!" says he heatedly. "Right after I left the jail I come to the office here, and was jest fixin' to git hold of my friends to frame the fake necktie party, when somebody come in at the door and hit me over the head. I thought it was Bige comin' in and didn't look around, and then whoever it was clouted me. I jest while ago come to myself, and I was tied up like you see."

"If he's tellin' the truth," says old Abed' – "which he seems to be, much as I hates to admit it – it looks like some friend of Bissett's overheard you all talkin' about this thing, follered Johnny over and put him out of the way for the time bein', and then raised a mob of his own, knowin' Breck wouldn't put up any resistance, thinkin' they was friends. I told you – who's that?"

We all drawed our irons, and then put 'em up as Bige Gantry rushed in, holding onto the side of his head, which was all bloody.

"I jest had a bresh with the outlaws!" he hollered. "I been trailin' 'em all night! They waylaid me a while ago, three miles out of town! They nearly shot my ear off! But if I didn't wing one of 'em, I'm a Dutchman!"

"Round up a posse!" howled Johnny, grabbing a Winchester and cartridge belt. "Take us back to where you had the scrape, Bige – "

"Wait a minute," I says, grabbing Bige. "Lemme see that ear!" I jerked his hand away, disregarding the spur he stuck into my laig, and bellered, "Shot, hell! That ear was chawed, and I'm the man which done it! You was one of them illegitimates which tried to hang me!"

He then whipped out his gun, but I knocked it out of his hand and hit him on the jaw and knocked him through the door. I then follered him outside and taken away the bowie he drawed as he rose groggily, and throwed him back into the office, and went in and throwed him out again, and went out and throwed him back in again.

"How long is this goin' on?" he ast.

"Probably all night," I assured him. "The way I feel right now I can keep heavin' you in and out of this office from now till noon tomorrer."

"Hold up!" gurgled he. "I'm a hard nut but I know when I'm licked! I'll confess! I done it!"

"Done what?" I demanded.

"I hit Johnny on the head and tied him up!" he howled, grabbing wildly for the door jamb as he went past it. "I rigged the lynchin' party! I'm in with the rustlers!"

"Set him down!" hollered Abed', grabbing holt of my shirt. "Quick, Johnny! Help me hold Breckinridge before he kills a valurebull witness!"

But I shaken him off impatiently and sot Gantry onto his feet. He couldn't stand, so I helt him up by the collar and he gasped, "I lied about tradin' shots with the outlaws. I been foolin' Johnny all along. The rustlers ain't no Wyoming gang; they all live around here. Ted Bissett is the head chief of 'em – "

"Ted Bissett, hey?" whooped Abed', doing a war-dance and kicking my shins in his glee. "See there, you big lummox? What'd I tell you? What you think now, after showin' so dern much affection for them cussed sheepmen? Jest shootin' Bissett in the arm, like he was yore brother, or somethin'! S'wonder you didn't invite him out to dinner. You ain't got the – "

"Aw, shet up!" I said fretfully. "Go on, Gantry."

"He ain't a legitimate sheepman," says he. "That's jest a blind, him runnin' sheep. Ain't no real sheepmen mixed up with him. His gang is jest the scrapins of the country, and they hide out on his ranch when things gits hot. Other times they scatters and goes home. They're the ones which has been killin' honest sheepmen and cattlemen – tryin' to set the different factions agen each other, so as to make stealin' easier. The Hunkies ain't in on the deal. He jest brung 'em out to herd his sheep, because his own men wouldn't do it, and he was afeared if he hired local sheepherders, they'd ketch onto him. Naturally we wanted you outa the way, when we knowed you'd come up here to run down the rustlers, so tonight I seen my chance when Johnny started talkin' about stagin' that fake hangin'. I follered Johnny and tapped him on the head and tied him up and went and told Bissett about the business, and we got the boys together, and you know the rest. It was a peach of a frame-up, and it'd of worked, too, if we'd been dealing with a human bein'. Lock me up. All I want right now is a good, quiet penitentiary where I'll be safe."

"Well," I said to Johnny, after he'd locked Gantry up, "all you got to do is ride over to Bissett's ranch and arrest him. He's laid up with his arm, and most of his men is crippled. You'll find a number of 'em over by the jail. This oughta elect you."

"It will!" says he, doing a war-dance in his glee. "I'm as good as elected right now! And I tell you, Breck, t'ain't the job alone I'm thinkin' about. I'd of lost my gal if I'd lost the race. But she's promised to marry me if I ketched them rustlers and got re-elected. And she won't go back on her word, neither!"

"Yeah?" I says with idle interest, thinking of my own true love. "What's her name?"

"Margaret Brewster!" says he.

"*What?*" I yelled, in a voice which knocked old Abed' over on his back like he'd been hit by a cyclone. Them which accuses me of vi'lent and onusual conduck don't consider how my emotions was stirred up by the knowledge that I had went through all them humiliating experiences jest to help a rival take my gal away from me. Throwing Johnny through the office winder and kicking the walls out of the building was jest a mild expression of the way I felt about the whole dern affair, and instead of feeling resentful, he ought to have been thankful I was able to restrain my natural feelings as well as I done.

A Gent from the Pecos

I was in the Buckhorn Saloon in San Antonio, jest h'isting a schooner of Pearl XXX, when my brother Kirby come staggering in all caked with dust and sweat, and stuck out a letter at me.

"Pap sent it," he gasped. "I've rode day and night to find you!"

He then collapsed onto the floor where he lay till I picked him up and laid him on the bar and started the barkeep to pouring licker down his throat. It's a long way from our cabin to Santone, and he must of had a hard ride. I figgered the letter he brung must be arful important, so after I'd drunk my beer and et me a sandwich offa the free lunch counter, I onfolded it and read it. It was from Aunt Navasota Hawkins, over in East Texas, and it was addressed to Mister Judson Bearfield, Wolf Mountain, Texas, which is Pap, and it said:

Dear Jud:

We air in awful trouble. Somethin happened none of us never drempt could happen. Uncle Joab Hudkins has took to stealin hawgs! You won't believe this I know Judson because none of the family never stole nothin in their life before but it's the truth. The Watsons ketched him in their pigpen tother night and filled his britches with bird-shot and I will not repeat his langwidge whilst we was picking them shot out of his hide Judson. The whole clan gathered around and argyed with him Judson but we wouldn't move him all he said was he wisht we would mind our own dadburned business. He was very cantankerus Judson and you ought to of heard what he called Uncle Saul Hawkins when Uncle Saul told him he had disgraced the family. We could not do nothin with him so we left Cousin Esau Harrison to see he didn't git out of the house till we could decide what to do. But he hit Cousin Esau over the head with the axe handle I use to stir hominy with and has run off into the woods Judson it is tarrible we don't know what he's up to but we suspects the wust. We have apolergized to the Watsons and offered to pay them for any damage he done but you know how them Watsons is Judson they say nothin will wipe out the insult but blood. It looks like they air goin to force a feud onto us we have got enough feuds as it is Judson. And so will you please send Pikeston over here to help find Uncle Joab and settle them Watsonses' hash.

Yore lovin Ant Navasota Hawkins

On the bottom of her letter Pap had writ, "Pike, pull for Choctaw Bayou as fast as you can peel it and don't take no sass from them cussed Watsons."

Well, I was so overcame for a few minutes all I could do was lean on the bar and drink a pint of tequila. To think as a relative of mine would stoop to pig stealing! Why, us Bearfields was that proud we wouldn't even steal a hoss. I dunno when I ever felt so low and wolfish in my spirits. I felt like the whole world knowed our shame and was p'inting the finger of scorn at us.

When Kirby come to he said he felt the same, and he said he aimed to shoot the first illegitimate which even said "hawg" at him. But I cautioned him to guard our arful secret with his life, and I told him to go around to the wagon yard where my hoss Satanta was, and arrange for his board whilst I was gone.

I then bought me a ticket for Houston and clumb aboard the train without telling my friends good-by; I was too ashamed to look 'em in the face with a pig thief in the family.

That was a irksome journey. All I could think of was pigs and when I dozed in my seat I dreampt about pigs. It was a dark hour for the Bearfield pride, and I got tetchier every minute.

When I got to Houston I imejitly went to a livery stable to rent me a hoss, and there I run into the same difficulty I always run into whenever I gits east of the Trinity. They warn't a hoss in town which was big enough and strong enough to tote my weight any distance. I dunno why them folks raises sech spindly critters. They claims their hosses is all right, and I'm jest bigger'n a human being ought to be. Well, I ain't considered onusually gigantic on Wolf Mountain, but I have already noticed that men on Wolf Mountain grows bigger'n they does in most places. So I reckon I do look kind of prominent to strangers, being as I stand six foot nine in my socks and weigh two hundred and ninety-five pounds, all bone and muscle. In addition to which modesty forces me to remark that I'm jest about the best man in a free-for-all on Wolf Mountain or anywheres else that I ever been, either.

Anyway, I finally pitched on a squint-eyed mule named Sinclair's Defeat, which was big enough even for me, and I forked him and headed for the home-range of my erring relative. I was in the piney-woods by now, and I felt plumb smothered with all them trees and sloughs and swamps, and no hills nor prickly pears nor prairies.

Them woods was full of razorback hawgs and every time I seen one it reminded me of the family shame, so I was in a regular welter of nervous irritation time I got to Sabineville, where my kinfolks does their trading. It was about noon, so I put Sinclair's Defeat in the wagon yard and seen he was fed and watered, and then I went to the restaurant. I hadn't been to Sabineville since I was a kid, and didn't know nobody there, but everybody I met stopped and gaped like they never seen a man my size before. They all had their guns on under their shirts and so did I, because I hid mine when we pulled into Houston.

I sot down in the restaurant and the waiter ast me what I'd have. I ast him what he had, and he says, "We got some nice roast pork!"

"Listen here, you!" I says, rising in wrath. "Maybe you think you can mock me with impunity because I'm a stranger in yore midst. But the man don't live which can throw the family scandal in my face and survive!"

"What air you talkin' about?" gasped he, recoiling.

"Don't try to ack innercent," I says bitterly. "I don't know you, and I don't know how come you to recognize me, but the best thing you can do is to pertend not to know me. Bring me a beefsteak smothered with onions and nine or ten bottles of beer, and lemme hear no more about pork if you values yore wuthless life!"

He done so in fear and trembling, and I heard him whisper to the cook that they was a homicidal maneyack outside; but I didn't see none.

I'd jest started on my steak when three big, rough-looking men come in. They give me a suspicious glance, but I paid 'em no heed and went on eating. So they sot down at the counter and ordered beans and coffee, and one of 'em said, "Have you swore out that warrant for old Joab Hudkins yet, Jabez?"

They all looked around at me on account of me strangling on my beer, and the oldest and meanest-looking one says, "I'm goin' over to the sheriff's office soon's we've et, Bill. This is the chance I been lookin' fur."

"Suits me," says Bill with a oath. "Hey, Joe?"

"Shore," says the third 'un. "But we better be keerful. Them Hudkinses and their kinfolks around here is bad enough, but the Bearfields, which lives out beyond the Pecos somewhere, is wuss yet."

"I ain't scairt of 'em," says Jabez. "Ain't us Watsons won all our feuds up to now? I don't keer nothin' about the hawgs, neither. But this here's my chance to git even with old Esau Hawkins for that whuppin' he give me over to the county seat fifteen year ago. I jest want to see his face when one of his kin goes to the pen for stealin' hawgs! . . . What was that?"

It was me, tying a knot in my steak fork in my struggle to control myself, but by a supreme effort I helt my peace.

"Well," says Bill, "I hopes for Hudkins gore! I jest wisht one of them tough Bearfields was here. I'd show him a thing or two, I betcha!"

"Well, git the exhibition started!" I said, heaving up so sudden I upsot my table and Joe fell off his stool. "I've stood all I can from you illegitimates."

"Who the devil air you?" gasped Jabez, jumping up, and I says, "I'm a Bearfield from the Pecos, and Joab Hudkins is my kin! I'm askin' you like a gent to refrain from swearin' out that warrant you all was talkin' about I'm here to see that he don't molest nobody else's hawgs, but I ain't goin' to see him tromped on, neither!"

"Oh, ain't you?" sneered Bill, fingering his pistol, whilst I seen Joe sneaking a bowie outa his boot. "Well, lemme tell *you* somethin', you dern mountain grizzly, we aims to put that there pig snatchin' uncle of yore'n behind the bars! How you like that, hey?"

"This is how much, you blasted swamp rat!" I roared, shattering my steak plate over his head.

He fell offa his stool howling bloody murder, and Joe made a stab at me but missed and stuck his knife in the table and whilst he was trying to pull it out I busted the catsup bottle over his head and he j'ined Bill on the floor. I then seen Jabez crouching at the end of the counter fixing to shoot me with his pistol, so I grabbed a case of canned tomaters and throwed it at him, and what happened to the waiter was his own fault. He oughta stayed outa the fight in the first place. If he hadn't been trying to git a shotgun he had behind the counter he wouldn't of run between me and Jabez jest as I heaved that case of vegetables. T'warn't my fault he got hit in the head, no more'n it was my fault he ketched old Jabez's bullet in his hind laig, neither. I kicked Jabez's pistol out of his hand before he could shoot again, and he run around behind the counter on his all-fours, jest as the cook come out of the kitchen with a iron skillet.

It always did make me mad to git hit over the head with a hot skillet; the grease always gits down the back of yore neck. So I grabbed the cook and went to the floor with him jest in time to duck the charge of buckshot old Jabez blazed at me with the waiter's shotgun from behind the counter. I then riz up and throwed the cook at him and they both crashed into the wall so hard they brung down all the shelves on it and the cans of beans and milk and corn and stuff fell down on top of Jabez till all I could see was his boots sticking out and his howls was arful to hear.

I was jest on the p'int of throwing the kitchen stove on top of the pile, because I was gitting mad by this time, when a feller hit the porch outside on the run, and stuck his head and a shotgun into the door and hollered, "Halt, in the name of the law!"

"Who the devil air you?" I demanded, rising up amidst a rooin of busted chairs, tables, canned goods and unconscious Watsons.

"I'm the sheriff," says he. "For the Lord's sake what's goin' on here? You must be one of John McCoy's men!"

"I'm Pike Bearfield of Wolf Mountain," I says, and he says, "Well, anyway, yo're under arrest!"

"If you was a fair-minded officer," I says, grinding my teeth slightly, "I wouldn't think of resistin' arrest. But I can see right off that yo're in league with the Watsons! This here's a plot to keep me from aidin' my pore misguided uncle. I see now why these scoundrels come in here and picked a fight with me. But I'll foil you, by gum! A Bearfield couldn't git jestice in yore jailhouse, and I ain't goin'!"

"You air, too!" he hollered, swinging up his shotgun. But I clapped my hand over the lock between the nipples and the hammers before he could pull the triggers, and I then taken hold of the barrels with my other hand and bent 'em at right angles.

"Now lemme see you try to shoot me with that gun," I says. "It'll explode and blow yore fool head off!"

He wept with rage.

"I'll git even with you, you cussed outlaw!" he promised. "Yore derned uncle has run off and j'ined John McCoy's bandits, and yo're one of his spies, I bet! You've defied the law and rooint my new shotgun, and I'll have revenge if I have to sue you in the county court!"

"Gah!" I retorted in disgust, and stalked out in gloomy grandeur, emerging onto the street so sudden-like that the crowd which had gathered outside stampeded in all directions howling bloody murder. I never seen sech skittish folks. You'd of thunk I was a tribe of Comanches.

I headed for the wagon yard, and it was a good thing I got there when I did, because Sinclair's Defeat had got to fighting with Tom Hanson the yard owner's saddle pony, and when Tom come out with a pitchfork he bit a chunk outa him and run him into a stall where they was a yoke of oxen. The oxes hooked Tom and every time he crawled out Sinclair's Defeat kicked him back in again and the oxes taken another swipe at him. You oughta heard him holler.

Well, Sinclair's Defeat was feeling so brash he thought he could lick me, too, so I give him a good punch on the nose and ontangled Tom from amongst the oxes. He bellyached plumb disgusting about gitting mule-bit, so to shet him up I give him my last ten dollar bill. He also wanted me to pay for his britches which the oxes had hooked the seat out of, but I refused profanely and as soon as Sinclair's Defeat come to, I clumb onto him and headed out along the Choctaw Bayou road.

I hadn't more'n got outa town when I met a old coot legging it up the road on foot, with his whiskers flying in the wind. As soon as he seen me he hollered, "Whar's the sheriff? I got work for him!"

"What kind of work?" I ast, hit by a sudden suspicion.

"Larceny, kidnapin' and a salt and batter," says he, stopping to git his breath whilst he fanned hisself with his old broad-brimmed straw hat. "Golly, I'm winded! My farm's three mile back in the piney woods and I've run every step of the way! You know what? While ago I heered a arful racket out to my pigpen and I run out and who should I see but old Joab Hudkins tryin' to rassle my prize Chester boar, Gen'ral Braddock, over the fence! I sung out: 'Drap that defenseless animal, you cussed outlaw!' and I'd no more'n got the words outa my mouth when old Joab up and hit me with a wagon spoke . . . Looka here!" he displayed a knot on his head about the size of a hen aig. "When I come to," he says, "Joab was gone and so was Gen'ral Braddock. Sech outrages ain't to be endured by American citerzens! I'm goin' after the sheriff!"

"Now wait," I says. "I dunno what's the matter with Uncle Joab, but le's see if we cain't straighten this out without draggin' in the law – "

"Don't speak to me if yo're kin of his'n!" squalled he, stooping for a rock. "Git outa my way! I'll have jestice if it's my last ack!"

"Aw, heck," I says. "I've knowed men to make less fuss over losin' a thousand head of steers than yo're makin' over one measly pig. I'll see that yo're paid for yore fool swine."

He hesitated.

"Show me the dough!" he demanded covetously.

"Well," I said, "I ain't got no money right now, but – "

"T'ain't the money, it's the principle of the thing!" he asserted. "I ain't to be tromped on! Stand aside! I'm goin' for the sheriff."

"Over my dead carcass!" I roared, losing patience. "Dang yore stubborn old hide! Yo're comin' with me till we find Uncle Joab and straighten this thing out – "

I leant down from my saddle and grabbed for him, and he give a squall and hit me in the head with his rock and turnt to run, but he stumped his toe and fell down, and that's when Sinclair's Defeat bit him in the seat of the britches. He's a liar when he says I told Sinclair's Defeat to bite him; it jest come natural for a mule. I reached down and grabbed him by the galluses – the old coot I mean, and not the mule – and heaved him up acrost the saddle horn in front of me, and he hollered, "Halp! Murder! The McCoy gang got me in the toils!"

Somebody echoed his howl, and I looked around and seen a barefooted kid with a fishing pole in his hand jest coming out of the footpath. His eyes was popping right out of his head.

"Run for the sheriff, boy!" squalled my captive. "Git a posse!"

So the kid scooted for town, howling, "Halp! Halp! A outlaw is kidnapin' old Ash Buckley!"

Well, I had a suspicion things would be a mite warm around there purty soon, so I kicked Sinclair's Defeat in the ribs and he done a smart piece of skedaddling up that road. I run for maybe four miles till Ash Buckley's howls got onbearable. I never seen a human which was harder to please than that old buzzard.

"Set me down and lemme die easy!" he gasped. "This cussed horn has pierced my vitals in front and I have got a mortal wound behind!"

"Aw," I said, "the mule jest bit off a little piece of hide, not any bigger'n yore hand. You ain't hurt."

"I'm dyin'," he maintained fiercely. "I'll git even, you big monkey! I'll come back and ha'nt you, that's what I'll do – hey!"

I also give a startled yell, because out of the bresh ambled the most pecooliar looking critter I ever seen in my life. I reached for my pistol, but old Ash give a yowl like he'd been stabbed.

"It's Gen'ral Braddock!" he shrieked. "They've shaved him!"

Then I seen that the critter was a hawg which had wunst been white, but now he was as naked as a newborn babe! They warn't a bristle onto him; it was plumb ondecent. I was so surprised I let old Ash fall onto the ground, and he jumped up and started for Gen'ral Braddock, saying, "Sooey! Sooey! Come here, boy – "

But Gen'ral Braddock give a squeal and curled his tail and lit a shuck through the bresh.

I jest sat my mule and looked. I couldn't move.

"He's plumb upsot," says old Ash, kinda stunned-like. "Whoever heard of sech doins?" Then he says, "Make room for me on that mule! I aim to find Joab if it takes the rest of my life! Shavin' a hawg is the craziest thing I ever heard of, and I won't rest easy till I know why he done it!"

I helped him on behind the saddle, and I says, "Where'll we look for him? No use tryin' to backtrack that pig. Neither hoss nor man could git through that thicket he come out of."

"I figger he's hidin' out somewheres over on the Choctaw," says Ash. "When he tried to steal the Watson hawgs I figgered he'd gone wild and j'ined the outlaws that hang out in the swamps over east of here, and was stealin' pigs for the McCoys. But he must be jest plain crazy."

"We'll head for Uncle Esau Hawkins," I says, "and round up all the kinfolks and start combin' the woods. By the way, who is these McCoys?"

"A gang of thieves and cutthroats which used to hang around here," says he. "They ain't been seen recent, and I figgers they've skipped over into Louisiana. They had a hang-out somewhere in the piney woods and nobody never could find it. They ambushed three or four posses which went in after 'em – What you stoppin' for?"

We was jest passing a path which crossed the road, and I seen hawg tracks going up it, and a man's tracks right behind, wide apart.

"Somebody chased a pig up that path right recent," I says, and turned up it at a lope.

We hadn't went more'n a mile till we heard a pig squealing. So I slipped off of Sinclair's Defeat and snuck through the bresh on foot till I come to a little clearing, and there was a white hawg tied up and laying on its side, and there was Uncle Joab Hudkins honing a butcher knife on his boot. A tub of soap suds stood nigh at hand.

"Uncle Joab, air you crazy?" I demanded.

Uncle Joab give a startled yell and fell over backwards into the tub. Sech langwidge you never heard as I hauled him out with soap bubbles in his eyes and ears and mouth. Ash run up jest then.

"That's Jake Peters' sow!" he hollered, dancing with excitement. "I tell you, he's as crazy as a mudhen! You better tie him up!"

"You ontie the hawg," I says. "I'll take keer of Uncle Joab."

"Don't you ontie that hawg!" howled Uncle Joab. "Gol-dern it, cain't a man tend to his own business without a passel of idjits buttin' in?"

"Be calm, Uncle Joab," I soothed. "I don't think this'll be permanent. Yore dad was wunst took like this, they say, and voted agen Sam Houston. But he recovered his sanity before the next election, and you probably will too. Jest when was you first seized with a urge to shave pigs?"

At this Uncle Joab begun to display symptoms of vi'lence, even to the extent of trying to stab me with his butcher knife. But I ignored his rudeness, also his biting me viciously in the hind laig whilst I was setting on him and twisting the knife outa his hand. I was as gentle as I could be with him, but he didn't have no gratitude, and his langwidge was plumb scandalous to hear.

"I've heered a lick on the head will often kyore insanity," says Ash

Buckley. " 'Twon't hurt to try, anyhow. You hold him whilst I bust him over the dome with a rock."

"Don't you tech me with no rock!" yelled Uncle Joab. "I ain't crazy, gosh – hang you! I got a good reason for shavin' them hawgs!"

"Well, why?" I demanded.

"None of yore business," he sulked.

"All right," I says with a sigh. "All I see to do is to tie you up and take you over to Uncle Esau Hawkins. He can git a doctor for you, or maybe send you to Austin for observation."

At that he give a convulsive heave and nearly got loose, but I sot on him and told Ash to go git my lariat off of my saddle.

"Hold on!" says Uncle Joab. "I know when I'm licked. I wanted all the loot for myself, but if you'll git off of me, I'll tell you everything."

"What loot?" I ast.

"The loot Cullen Baker's gang hid in Choctaw Bayou," says he.

Old Ash pricked up his ears at that.

"You mean to say yo're on the trail of that?" he demanded.

"I am!" asserted Uncle Joab. "Listen! We all know that a few months before Baker was kilt, he robbed a train jest over the Louisiana line. He then come over here and hid the gold – a hundred thousand dollars' wuth! – somewhar on Choctaw. Nobody knows whar, because right after that him and all the men which was with him when he hid it, got kilt over night. Jefferson, in 1869. They paid ten thousand dollars for his head in Little Rock.

"Well, I been lookin' for that plunder off and on for years, like everybody else around here, especially old Jeppard Wilkinson, which used to hold a grudge agen me account of me skinnin' him in a mule swap. But I got a letter from him the other day, from New Orleans, and he said he'd had a change of heart. He said before he left here he found where Baker's treasure was hid! But he was afeared to take it out, account of the McCoy gang which was huntin' it too, and always follerin' him around and spyin' on him, so he drawed a map of the place and was waitin' a chance to go back and git the loot, when he got run out of the country – you know, Ash, on account of the trouble he had with the Clantons – and now he says he wasn't never comin' back, so if I could find the map the loot would be mine. And he said he tattooed the map on a white hawg! He said he reckon it run off into the woods after he left the country."

"Well, whyn't you tell us all this in the first place?" yelled old Ash. "What air we waitin' on? Pike, you hold this critter whilst me and Joab scrapes the bristles off. This may be the very hawg."

Well, I felt plumb silly helping shave a pig, but them old coots was serious. They like to have fit right in the middle of the job when they got to argying how they'd divide the plunder. I told 'em they better wait till they found it before they divided it.

Well, they shaved that critter from stem to stern, but not one mark did they find that looked like a map. But they warn't discouraged.

"I've shaved six already," says Uncle Joab. "I aim to find that map if I have to shave every white hawg in the county. They ain't none been butchered since old Jeppard tattooed that'n, so it's bound to be somewheres in these woods. Listen: I been livin' in the old Sorley cabin over on the Choctaw. You all go over there with me, and we'll take up our camp there and work out from it. They ain't no settlements within a long ways of it, and all the pigs in the county comes over there to that oak grove about a mile from it to eat acorns. Won't be nobody to interfere with us, and we'll stay there and comb the woods till we finds the right hawg."

So we pulled out, taking turns riding and walking.

We went through mighty wild, tangled, uninhabited country to git to that there cabin, which stood a few hundred yards from the bank of the Choctaw. Mostly we follered pig trails through the thickets. On the way Uncle Joab told us the McCoys used to hang out in them parts, and he bet they'd show up again sometime when Louisiana got too hot for 'em, and start burning cabins and stealing and shooting folks from the bresh again. And Ash Buckley said he bet the sheriff of Sabineville wouldn't never catch 'em, and they got to talking about all the crimes them McCoys had committed, and I was plumb surprised to hear white men could ack like that. They was wuss'n Apaches. They shore wouldn't of lasted long on Wolf Mountain.

Well, we slept at the cabin that night and early next morning we scattered through the pine flats and cypress swamps looking for white hawgs. Uncle Joab told me not to git lost nor et up by a alligator. Shucks, you could lose a timber wolf as easy as a Bearfield, even in the piney woods, and the muskeeters worrit me more'n the alligators.

I didn't have no luck looking for white pigs. All I found was plain razorbacks. I finally got disgusted pulling through them swamps and thickets on foot, so about noontime I headed back for the cabin. And when I come out in the clearing I seen a man in the rail pen behind the cabin trying to rope Sinclair's Defeat. I hollered at him and he ducked and pulled a pistol out of his boot and taken a shot at me, and then ran off into the bresh.

Well, I instantly knowed it was one of them dern Watsons trying to run off our stock and set us afoot so they could snipe us off at their leisure, so I taken in after him. They must of tracked us from Sabineville.

He knowed the country better'n I did, and he stayed ahead of me for three miles, heading south, but he couldn't shake me off, because us Bearfields learnt tracking from the Yaquis. I gained on him and warn't but a few yards behind him when he come into a clearing in the middle of the dangedest thicket I ever seen. A path had been cut through it with axes, but if I hadn't been follering his tracks I probably wouldn't never have found it, the mouth was so well hid, and not even a razorback could git through anywheres else.

I taken a shot at him as he broke cover and legged it for a cabin in the clearing, and then I started after him; but three or four men opened up on me from the door with Winchesters, so I jumped back into the bresh. He ducked inside and they slammed the door.

It was a hundred yards from the bresh to the cabin, and no cover for a man to crawl up clost. They'd riddle him if he tried it. There warn't no winders, jest loopholes to shoot through, and the door looked arful thick. Leastways when I tried to shoot through it with my pistol the men inside hollered jeeringly and shot at me through the loopholes. The cabin was built up agen a big rock, the first of its size I'd saw in that country, so they warn't no chance of storming 'em from the rear. It looked like they jest warn't no way of coming to grips with them devils.

Then I seen smoke coming out of the top of the rock, and I knowed they had a fireplace built into the rock which formed the back wall of the cabin, and had tunneled out a chimney in the rock. I thought by golly, I bet if I was to climb up onto that rock from behind and drop a polecat down that chimney I could shoot all them Watsons as they run out.

So I fired a few shots at the door, and then ducked low and snuck off. I figgered they'd stay denned up till dark at least, thinking I was still laying for 'em outside, and by that time I could find me a skunk and git back with it. I was depending a lot on it. I notice the average man would rather run the risk of gitting shot than to stay denned up in a winderless cabin with a irritated polecat.

But I looked and looked, and didn't find none, and it begun to git late, and all at once I thought by golly, I bet a alligator would have the same effect. The nearest way to the bayou was back by our cabin, so I headed that way.

The cabin was empty when I went past it. Uncle Joab and Ash Buckley was still out looking for the tattooed hawg. I went on to the Bayou where I'd heard a big bull beller the night before, and waded out in the water to find him, which I presently did by him grabbing me by the hind laig. So I waded to shore with him, him being too stubborn to let go, and suffering from the illusion that he could pull me out into deep water.

Ain't it funny what fools some animals is? It's ideas like that proves their undoing.

When he realized his error we was already in the shallers, so I pried him loose and got him under my arm and started for the bank with him. He then started swinging his tail up and hitting me in the back of the head with it, and it was wuss'n being kicked by a mule. He knocked me down three times before I got out of the water, and nearly wiggled away from me each time, to say nothing of biting me severely in various places. They is nothing more stubborn than a old bull alligator.

Finally I got so disgusted with him I hauled off with my fist and busted him betwixt the eyes, and whilst he was stunned I broke some vines and tied his laigs, and then I could carry him better. I called him Jedge Peabody because he looked so much like a jedge back in my country which would of fined me for shooting Jack Rackston wunst, only I wouldn't stand for no sech interference with my personal liberty.

Well, I couldn't figger out no way to tie Jedge Peabody's tail, and he come to purty soon and started beating me in the neck with it again. It was gitting arful late by now, and I was afeared the Watsons would come out of their cabin and find me gone. So I decided to stop off at our cabin and then ride back instead of going afoot. I figgered to have some trouble with Sinclair's Defeat when I put Jedge Peabody on his back, but I 'lowed I could persuade him.

So I taken Jedge Peabody up to our cabin and laid him on my bunk to keep him safe till I saddled up. The sun was already outa sight behind the pines and the long shadders was streaming acrost the clearing. It was purty dark in the cabin and you could hardly see Jedge Peabody at all.

Well, I went to the hoss pen and grabbed my saddle, but before I could throw it on, I seen Uncle Joab cross the clearing from the east and go into the cabin. I started to call to him, but the next instant he give a arful screech and come busting out of there so fast he tripped and slid on his nose for about three yards.

"Halp! Murder! The Devil hisself's in that cabin!" he screamed, and bounced up and streaked for the tall timber.

"Uncle Joab, come back!" I yelled, jumping the pen fence and lighting out after him. "That ain't nobody but Jedge Peabody!"

But he jest yelled that much louder and put on more speed. I reckon Jedge Peabody did look kind of uncanny to come onto him unexpected in that dark corner where you couldn't see much but his big red eyes. Uncle Joab didn't even look back, and when he heard me crashing through the bresh right behind him, he evidently thought the devil was chasing him, because he let out some more arful screams and jest went a-kiting.

It was dark under the trees, and I reckon that's why he didn't see that gully in front of him, anyway, he suddenly vanished from sight with a crash and a howl. Then they busted out an arful squealing and out of the gully come the biggest white hawg I ever seen in my life. And Uncle Joab was astraddle of him, having evidently fell on him.

"Stop him!" howled Uncle Joab, hanging on for his life, afeared to let go and afeared to hold on. That hawg was headed back the way we'd come, and he went past me like a bullet. I grabbed for him, but all I done was tear off Uncle Joab's shirt. That hawg went through the bresh like a quarter hoss, and the way Uncle Joab hollered was a caution when the limbs scratched him and slapped him in the face.

Well, a Bearfield ain't to be outdid by man nor beast, so I sot myself to run down that fool hawg on foot. And I was gaining on him, too, when we reached the cabin. But as we busted into the clearing I heard a most amazing racket in the cabin and seen Ash Buckley perched in a tree, plumb wildeyed.

I was so astonished I didn't look where I was going and tripped over a root and nearly busted my brains out, and when I got up, Uncle Joab and the hawg was clean out of sight.

"What the devil?" I demanded profanely.

"I dunno!" hollered old Ash. "Jest as I come up awhile ago I seen a gang of men sneakin' into the cabin, so I hid and watched. They shet the door and I heard one of 'em holler: 'That must be him layin' on that bunk over there. Grab him!' Then that racket started. It's been goin' on for fifteen minutes. *What's that?*"

It sounded like a mule kicking slats out of a shed wall, but I knowed it was Jedge Peabody hitting the Watsons in the head with his tail. Them scoundrels had evidently come to raid our cabin, and Jedge Peabody had busted loose when they grabbed him, thinking he was me.

I run over to the door jest as it was busted down from inside, and a gang of men come piling out. I hit each one on the jaw as he come out, and throwed him to one side till I had seven men laying there, out cold. The last one to come out had Jedge Peabody hanging onto the seat of his britches, and when old Ash seen Jedge Peabody he give a shriek and fell outa the tree and would probably of broke his neck if his galluses hadn't catched on a limb.

The last Watson I knocked stiff had a scarred face and was about the meanest-looking cuss I ever seen. He was tough, too. I had to hit him twice. I was expecting a tussle with Jedge Peabody, too, but as soon as he seen me he let go of his victim's pants and scuttled for the creek as fast as he could go. I never seen a 'gator run like him.

Ash was yelling for me to help him down, but they was more important work to do, so I run and got my lariat and tied them Watsons up before they could come to and rolled 'em into the cabin. Then I started towards the tree to git Ash loose, when somebody says, "Hands up!" and whirled around and faced the sheriff and fifty men, all of which was aiming shotguns at me.

"Don't move!" says the sheriff, which was weighted down with handcuffs and laig-irons and chains till he couldn't hardly walk. "We got you kivered, Bearfield! Them guns is all loaded with buckshot and railroad spikes! We got you cold! Where's Ash Buckley?"

"Right up over yore fool heads," says Ash fiercely, which startled the posse so bad they nigh jumped outa their skins and four or five of 'em shot at him before they seen who it was. "Stop that, you nitwits!" he screamed. "Lemme down before I has a rush of blood to the head!"

"Warn't you kidnaped?" ast the sheriff, dumbfounded, and Ash snarled, "No, I warn't! Me and Pike and Joab come out here on private business!"

The sheriff cussed something fierce, but the posse started helping Ash down, when we heard somebody hollering for help off to the west, and they dropped Ash on his head and grabbed their guns and says, "Who's that?"

"It's Uncle Joab!" I bellered, and made a break for the bresh, with Ash right behind me. Some of 'em shot at me, but they missed, and jest then I heard one of 'em yell, "Sheriff, come here quick! The cabin's full of men tied hand and foot!"

Every second I expected to hear 'em pursuing us, but we didn't hear 'em, and purty soon we almost fell over Uncle Joab in the dusk. He was trying to rassle the white hawg over on its side, whilst squalling, "It's the one! I can see the tattoo marks through the bristles!"

Well, so could we, in spite of the dusk, and old Ash like to collapsed with excitement.

"Grab that hawg, Pike!" he screamed, lugging out a handful of matches. "Cullen Baker's loot is right in our meat hooks!"

So I helt the hawg and Uncle Joab made a swipe with his butcher knife, and panted, "Strike a match quick, Ash! 'Tain't a map – it's writin', but I cain't read it by this light! Strike a light!"

Ash struck a match and helt it clost whilst we jammed our three heads together to read what was tattooed on that hawg's hide. And then Ash and Uncle Joab give a howl that jolted the cones outa the pines. The words tattooed on that hawg was, "April fule! The joak's on you, you old jackass. JEPPARD WILKINSON."

I let go of the hawg and it went kiting and squealing off into the bresh, and we sot there in bitter silence for a long time.

This silence was busted by the sheriff suddenly sticking his head through the bushes, and saying, "What the devil air you all doin'?"

"Well, I ain't bein' arrested," I says vengefully, gitting to my feet and drawing my pistol. "I'll pay you for yore shotgun, but – "

"Then I got no charge," says he. "Bein' as you didn't kidnap Ash there, and as for the Watsons – "

"That reminds me," I interrupted. "I got seven of them skunks tied up back at the cabin. They tried to steal my mule and murder me in my sleep, but I won't make no charges agen 'em if they'll drop that pig stealin' case."

"Why, heck!" says he. "They've already dropped that charge! When old Jabez come to he 'lowed all he wanted with yore clan was peace, and plenty of it! He says they can lick the Hudkinses any day, but when they rings in a Bearfield on 'em, they got more'n enough! Them fellers you got tied up back there – and which the boys is now loadin' with the irons I brung for you – they ain't Watsons!"

"Well, who is they, then?"

"Oh," says he, taking a chaw of plug tobaccer, "nobody but John McCoy and his gang which recent come back from Louisiana! Son, you can have anything in this county! Hey, where you goin'?"

"Home," I says in disgust, "where a man can depend on a feud bein' fought to a finish, and one side don't back out jest because a few of 'em gits their heads busted!"

Gents on the Lynch

Blue Lizard, Colorado,
September 1, 1879.

Mister Washington Bearfield,
Antioch, Colorado.

Dear Brother Wash:

Well, Wash, I reckon you think you air smart persuading me to quit my job with the Seven Prong Pitchfork outfit and come way up here in the mountains to hunt gold. I knowed from the start I warn't no prospector, but you talked so much you got me addled and believing what you said, and the first thing I knowed I had quit my job and withdrawed from the race for sheriff of Antioch and was on my way. Now I think about it, it is a dern funny thing you got so anxious for me to go prospecting jest as elections was coming up. You never before showed no anxiety for me to git rich finding gold or no other way. I am going to hunt me a quiet spot and set down and study this over for a few hours, and if I decide you had some personal reason for wanting me out of Antioch, I aim to make you hard to ketch.

All my humiliating experiences in Blue Lizard is yore fault, and the more I think about it, the madder I git. And yet it all come from my generous nature which cain't endure to see a feller critter in distress onless I got him that way myself.

Well, about four days after I left Antioch I hove into the Blue Lizard country one forenoon, riding Satanta and leading my pack-mule, and I was passing through a canyon about three mile from the camp when I heard dawgs baying. The next minute I seen three of them setting around a big oak tree barking fit to bust yore eardrums. I rode up to see what they'd treed and I'm a Injun if it warn't a human being! It was a tall man without no hat nor gun in his scabbard, and he was cussing them dawgs so vigorous he didn't hear me till I rode up and says, "Hey, what you doin' up there?"

He like to fell out of the crotch he was setting in, and then he looked down at me very sharp for a instant, and said, "I taken refuge from them vicious beasts. I was goin' along mindin' my own business when they taken in after me. I think they got hyderphoby. I'll give you five bucks if you'll shoot 'em. I lost my gun."

"I don't want no five bucks," I says. "But I ain't goin' to shoot 'em. They're pecooliar lookin' critters, and they may be valurebul. I notice the funnier-lookin' a animal is, the more money they're generally wuth. I'll shoo 'em off."

So I got down and says, "Git!" and they immejitly laid holt of my laigs, which was very irritating because I didn't have no other boots but them. So I fotched each one of them fool critters a hearty kick in the rear, and they give a yowl and scooted for the tall timber.

"You can come down now," I says. "Dern it, them varmints has rooint my boots."

"Take mine!" says he, sliding down and yanking off his boots.

"Aw, I don't want to do that," I says, but he says, "I insists! It's all I can do for you. Witherington T. Jones always pays his debts, even in adversity! You behold in me a lone critter buffeted on the winds of chance, penniless and friendless, but grateful! Take my boots, kind stranger, do!"

Well, I was embarrassed and sorry for him, so I said all right, and taken his boots and give him mine. They was too big for him, but he seemed mighty pleased when he hauled 'em on. His'n was very handsome, all fancy stitching. He shaken my hand and said I'd made him very happy, but all to once he bust into tears and sobbed, "Pore Joe!"

"Pore who?" I ast.

"Joe!" says he, wiping his eyes on my bandanner. "My partner, up on our claim in the hills. I warned him agen drinkin' a gallon of corn juice to inoculate hisself agen snake bite – before the snake bit him – but he wouldn't listen, so now he's writhin' in the throes of delirium tremens. It would bust yore heart to hear the way he shrieks for me to shoot the polka-dotted rhinocerhosses which he thinks is gnawin' his toes. I left him tied hand and foot and howlin' that a striped elephant was squattin' on his bosom, and I went to Blue Lizard for medicine. I got it, but them cussed dawgs scairt my hoss and he got away from me, and it'll take me till midnight to git back to our claim afoot. Pore Joe'll be a ravin' corpse by then."

Well, I never heard of a corpse raving, but I couldn't stand the idee of a man dying from the d.t.'s, so I shucked my pack offa my mule, and said, "Here, take this mule and skeet for yore claim. He'll be better'n walkin'. I'd lend you Satanta only he won't let nobody but me ride him."

Mister Witherington T. Jones was plumb overcome by emotion. He shaken my hand again and said, "My noble friend, I'll never forget this!" And then he jumped on the mule and lit out, and from the way he was kicking the critter's ribs I reckoned he'd pull into his claim before noon, if it was anywheres within a hundred miles of there. He sure warn't wasting no time. I could see that.

I hung his boots onto my saddle horn and I had started gathering up my plunder when I heard men yelling and then a whole gang with Winchesters come busting through the trees, and they seen me and hollered, "Where is he?"

"We heard the dawgs bayin' over here," says a little short one. "I don't hear 'em now. But they must of had him treed somewheres clost by."

"Oh, Mr. Jones," I said. "Well, don't worry about him. He's all right. I druv the dawgs off and lent him my mule to git back to his claim."

At this they let forth loud frenzied yells. It was plumb amazing. Here I'd jest rescued a feller human from a pack of ferocious animals, and these hombres acted like I'd did a crime or something.

"He helped him git away!" they hollered. "Le's lynch him, the derned outlaw!"

"Who you callin' a outlaw?" I demanded. "I'm a stranger in these parts. I'm headin' for Blue Lizard to work me a claim."

"You jest helped a criminal to escape!" gnashed they, notably a big black-bearded galoot with a sawed-off shotgun. "This feller Jones as you call him tried to rob a stagecoach over on Cochise Mountain less'n a hour ago. The guard shot his pistol out of his hand, and his hoss got hit too, so he broke away on foot. We sot the dawgs on his trail, and we'd of had him by now, if you hadn't butted in! Now the dawgs cain't track him no more."

"Call 'em back and set 'em on the mule's trail," sejests a squint-eyed cuss. "As for you, you cussed Texas hillbilly, you keep on travelin'. We don't want no man like you in Blue Lizard."

"Go to the devil, you flat-nosed buzzard," I retort with typical Southern courtesy. "This here's a free country. I come up here to hunt gold and I aim to hunt it if I have to lick every prospector in Lizard Cañon! You cain't ride me jest because I made a honest mistake that anybody could of made. Anyway, I'm the loser, 'cause he got off with my mule."

"Aw, come on and le's find the dawgs," says a bowlegged gun-toter with warts. So they went off up the cañon, breathing threats and vengeance, and I taken my plunder on my shoulder and went on down the cañon, leading Satanta. I put on Mister Jones's boots first, and they was too small for me, of course, but I could wear 'em in a pinch. (That there is a joke, Wash, but I don't suppose you got sense enough to see the p'int.)

I soon come to the aidge of the camp, which was spread all over the place where the canyon widened out and shallowed, and the first man I seen was old Polk Williams. You remember him, Wash, we knowed him over to Trinidad when we first come to Colorado with the Seven Prong Pitchfork outfit. I hailed him and ast him where I could find a good claim, and he said all the good ones had been took. So I said, well, I'd strike out up in the hills and hunt me one, and he says, "What you know about prospectin'? I advises you to git a job of workin' some other man's claim at day wages till they's a new strike up in the hills somewheres. They's bound to be one any day, because the mountains is full of prospectors which got here too late to git in on this'n. Plenty of jobs here at big wages, because nobody wants to *work*. They all wants to wade creeks till they stub their fool toe on a pocket of nuggets."

"All right," I said. "I'll pitch my camp down on the creek."

"You better not," says he. "These mountains is full of hyderphoby skunks. They crawls in yore blankets at night and bites you, and you foam at the mouth and go bite yore best friends. Now, it jest happens I got a spare cabin which I ain't usin'. The feller who had it rented ain't with us this mornin' account of a extry ace in a poker game last night. I'll rent it to you dirt cheap – ten dollars a day. You'll be safe from them cussed skunks there."

So I said, "All right. I don't want to git hyderphoby."

So I give him ten dollars in advance and put my plunder in the cabin which was on a slope west of the camp, and hobbled Satanta to graze. He said I better look out or somebody would steal Satanta. He said Mustang Stirling and his outlaws was hiding in the hills clost by and terrorizing the camp which didn't even have a sheriff yet, because folks hadn't had time to elect one, but they was gittin so sick of being robbed all the time they probably would soon, and maybe organize a Vigilante Committee, too. But I warn't scairt of anybody stealing Satanta. A stranger had better take a cougar by the whiskers than to monkey with Satanta. That hoss has got a disposition like a sore-tailed rattlesnake.

Well, while we was talking I seen a gal come out from amongst the cluster of stores and saloons and things, and head up the canyon with a bucket in her hand. She was so purty my heart skipped a beat and my corns begun to throb. That's a sure sign of love at first sight.

"Who's that gal?" I ast.

"Hannah Sprague," says Polk. "The belle of Blue Lizard. But *you* needn't start castin' sheep's eyes at her. They's a dozen young bucks sparkin' her already. I think Blaze Wellington's the favorite to put his brand onto her, though. She wouldn't look twicet at a hillbilly like you."

"I might remove the compertition," I sejested.

"You better not try no Wolf Mountain rough stuff in Blue Lizard," warned he. "The folks is so worked up over all these robberies and killins they're jest in a mood to lynch somebody, especially a stranger."

But I give no heed. Folks is always wanting to lynch me, and quite a few has tried, as numerous tombstones on the boundless prairies testifies.

"Where's she goin' with that bucket?" I ast him, and he said, "She's takin' beer to her old man which is workin' a claim up the creek."

"Well, listen," I says. "You git over there behind that thicket and when she comes past you make a noise like a Injun."

"What kind of damfoolishness is this?" he demanded. "You want to stampede the hull camp?"

"Don't make a loud whoop," I says. "Jest make it loud enough for her to hear it."

"Air you crazy?" says he.

"No, dern it!" I said fiercely, because she was tripping along purty fast.

"Git in there and do like I say. I'll rush up from the other side and pertend to rescue her from the Injuns, and that'll make her like me."

"I mistrusts you're a blasted fool," he grumbled. "But I'll do it jest this oncet."

He snuck into the thicket which she'd have to pass on the other side, and I circled around so she couldn't see me till I was ready to rush out and save her from being sculped. Well, I warn't hardly in place when I heard a kind of mild war-whoop and it sounded jest like a Blackfoot, only not so loud. But immejitly there come the crack of a pistol and another yell which warn't subdued like the first. It was lusty and energetic.

I run towards the thicket, but before I could git into the open trail old Polk come b'ilin' out of the back side of the clump with his hands to the seat of his britches.

"You planned this a-purpose, you snake in the grass!" he squalled. "Git outa my way!"

"Why, Polk!" I says. "What happened?"

"I bet you knowed she had a derringer in her stocking," he howled as he run past me with his pants smoking. "It's all yore fault! When I whooped she pulled it and shot into the bresh! Don't speak to me! I'm lucky that I warn't hit in a vital spot. I'll git even with you for this if it takes a hundred years!"

He headed on into the deep bresh, and I run around the thicket and seen Hannah Sprague peering into it with her gun smoking in her hand. She looked up as I come onto the trail, and I taken off my hat and said perlite, "Howdy, Miss. Can I be of no assistance to you?"

"I jest shot a Injun," says she. "I heard him holler. You might go in there and git the sculp, if you don't mind. I'd like to have it for a soovenear."

"I'll be glad to, Miss," I says gallantly. "I'll likewise kyore and tan it for you myself."

"Oh, thank you, sir!" she says, dimpling. "It's a pleasure to meet a real gent like you!"

"The pleasure's all mine," I assured her, and went into the bresh and stomped around a little, and then come out and says, "I'm arful sorry, Miss, but the varmint ain't nowheres to be found. You must of jest winged him. If you want me to, I'll take his trail and run him down."

"Oh, I wouldn't think of puttin' you to sech trouble," she says, much to my relief, because I was jest thinking that if she did demand a sculp, the only thing I could do would be to ketch old Polk and sculp him, and I'd hate to have to do that. I bet it would of made him arful mad.

But she looked me over admiringly and says, "I'm Hannah Sprague. Who're you?"

"I knowed you the minute I seen you," I says. "The fame of yore beauty has reached clean to Wolf Mountain, Texas. I'm Pike Bearfield."

"Glad to meetcha, Mister Bearfield," says she. "They must grow big men in Texas. Well, I got to go now. Pap gits arful tetchy if he don't git his beer along with his dinner."

"I'd admire powerful to call on you this evenin'," I says, and she says, "Well, I dunno. Mister Blaze Wellington was goin' to call – "

"He cain't come," I says.

"Why, how do you know?" she ast surprised. "He said – "

"A unforeseen circumstance," I says gently. "It ain't happened to him yet, but it's goin' to right away."

"Well," she says, kind of confused, "I reckon in that case you can come on, if you want. We live in that cabin down yonder by that big fir. But when you git within hearin' holler and tell us who you be, if it's after dark. Pap is arful nervous account of all these outlaws which is robbin' people."

So I said I would, and she went on, and I headed for the camp. People give me some suspicious looks, and I heard a lot of folks talking about this here Mustang Stirling and his gang. Seems like them critters hid in the hills and robbed somebody nearly every day and night, and nobody could hardly git their gold out of camp without gittin' stuck up. But I didn't have no gold yet, and wouldn't of been scairt of Mustang Stirling if I had, so I went on to the biggest saloon, which they called the Belle of New York. I taken a dram and ast the bartender if he knowed Blaze Wellington. He said sure he did, and I ast him where Blaze Wellington was, and he p'inted out a young buck which was setting at a table with his head down on his hands like he was trying to study out something. So I went over and sot down opposite him, and he looked up and seen me, and fell out of his chair backwards hollering, "Don't shoot!"

"Why, how did you know?" I ast, surprised.

"By yore evil face," he gibbered. "Go ahead! Do yore wust!"

"They ain't no use to git highsterical," I says. "If you'll be reasonable nobody won't git hurt."

"I won't tell you whar it's hid!" he defied, gitting onto his feet and looking like a cornered wharf-rat.

"Where what's hid?" I ast in amazement.

At this he looked kind of dumfounded.

"Say," says he cautiously, "ain't you one of Mustang Stirling's spies, after the gold?"

"Naw, I ain't," I says angrily. "I jest come here to ast you like a gent not to call on Hannah Sprague tonight."

"What the devil?" says he, looking kind of perplexed and relieved and mad all at the same time. "What you mean, not call on Hannah?"

"Because I am," I says, hitching my guns for'ard.

"Who the devil air you?" he demanded, convulsively picking up a beer mug like he aimed to throw it at me.

"Pike Bearfield of Wolf Mountain," I says, and he says, "Oh!" and after a minute he puts the beer mug down and stood there studying a while.

Then he says, "Why, Bearfield, they warn't no use in you threatenin' me. I bet you think I'm in love with Hannah Sprague! Well, I ain't. I'm a friend of her old man, that's all. I been keepin' his gold over to my shack, guardin' it for him, so Mustang Stirling's outlaws wouldn't git it, and the old man is so grateful he wants me to marry the gal. But I don't keer nothin' about her.

"To tell you the truth, if it warn't that I like the old man, I'd throw up the job, it's so dangerous. Mustang Stirling has got spies in the camp, and they dogs me night and day. I thought you was one of 'em when I seen yore arful face . . . Well, I'm glad the old man's goin' to send it out on the stage tomorrer. It's been an arful strain on me and my partner, which is over at the shack now. Somebody's got to stay there on guard all the time, or them cussed outlaws would come right in and tear the shack apart and find where I got it hid. Tonight'll be the wust. They'll make a desprut effort to git it before mornin'."

"You mean old man Sprague wants you to marry Hannah because yo're guardin' his gold?" I ast, and he says yes, but the responsibility was aging him prematurely. I says, "Looky here! Lemme take this job off'n yore hands! Lemme guard the gold tonight! I hates to see a promisin' young man like you wore down to a nubbin by care and worry."

"I hate to do that," he demurred, but I said, "Come on, be a good feller! I'll do as much for you, some time."

He thought it over a while, shaking his head, whilst I was on needles and pins, and then he stuck out his hand and said, "I'll do it! Shake! But don't tell nobody. I wouldn't do it for nobody but you . . . What's that noise?"

Because we heard a lot of men running up the street and yelling, "Git yore guns ready, boys! We're right on his trail!"

Somebody hollered "Who?" And somebody else yelled, "Jones! The hounds picked up his foot-tracks whilst we was tryin' to git 'em after the mule's! He musta jumped offa the mule and doubled back afoot! We've trailed him right down Main Street!"

Then somebody else whooped, "They're goin' into the Belle of New York! We got him cornered! Don't let him git away!"

The next minute here come them three fool bloodhounds b'ilin' in at the front door and grabbed me by the hind laig again. It was most ann'ying. I dunno when I was ever so sick of a pack of hounds in my life. But I controlled my temper and merely jerked 'em loose from my laig and throwed 'em out the winder, and they run off. Then a crowd of faces jammed in the door and looked at me wildly and said, "You again!"

I recognized Black-Beard and Squint-Eye and Shorty and Warts and the rest of the men which was in the posse chasing Mister Jones, and I said fretfully, "Gol-dern it, whyn't you all lemme alone?"

But they ignored my remark, and Squint-Eye said, "I thought we told you not to stop in Blue Lizard!"

Before I could think of anything insulting enough to say in response, Warts give a yelp and p'inted at my laigs.

"Look there!" he howled. "He's got on Jones's boots! I was on the stagecoach when Jones tried to hold it up, and he had on a mask, but I remember them boots! Don't you remember – this hillbilly didn't have on no boots when we seen him before! He traded boots with Jones to fool the dawgs! No wonder they wouldn't foller the mule! He's a derned outlaw! He knowed what Jones's name was! He's one of Stirling's spies! Git him!"

I started to tell Blaze to tell 'em I was all right, but at this moment Shorty was so overcome by excitement that he throwed a cuspidor at me. I ducked and it hit Blaze betwixt the eyes and he curled up under the table with a holler gasp.

"Now look what you done!" I says wrathfully, but all Shorty says is to holler, "Grab him, boys! Here's where we starts cleaning' up this camp right now! Let the hangins commence!"

If he hadn't made that last remark, I probably wouldn't of broke his arm when he tried to stab me with his bowie, but I'm kind of sensitive about being hung. I would of avoided vi'lence if I could of, but sech remarks convinced me that them idjits was liable to do me bodily harm, especially when some of 'em grabbed me around the laigs and five or six more tried to twist my arms around behind my back. So I give a heave and slung them loose from me which was hanging onto my arms, and then I ast the others ca'mly and with dignity to let go of me before I injured 'em fatally, but they replied profanely that I was a dadgasted outlaw and they was going to hang me if it was the last thing any of 'em done. They also tried to rassle me off my feet and Black-Beard hit me over the head with a beer bottle.

This made me mad, so I walked over to the bar with nine or ten of 'em hanging onto me and bracing their feet in a futile effort to stop me, and I stooped and tore up a ten-foot section of brass rail, and at the first swipe I laid out Black-Beard and Squint-Eye and Warts, and at the second I laid out four more gents which was perfect strangers to me, and when I heaved her up for the third swipe they warn't nobody in the saloon but me and them on the floor. It is remarkable the number of men you can fotch at one lick with a ten foot section of brass railing. The way the survivors stampeded out the front door yelling blue murder you'd of thought it was the first time anybody had ever used a brass rail on 'em.

Blaze was beginning to come to, so I hauled him out from under the table, and lugged him out onto the street with me. Some fellers on the other side of the street immejitly started shooting at me, so I drawed my pistols and shot back at 'em, and they broke and run every which a way. So I got Blaze onto my back and started up the street with him, and after I'd went a few hundred yards he could walk hisself, though he weaved considerable, and he taken the lead and led me to his cabin which was back of some stores and clost to the bank of the creek. They warn't nobody in sight but a loafer setting under a tree on the bank fishing, with his slouch hat pulled down to shade his eyes. The door was shet, so Blaze hollered, still kind of dizzy, "It's me, Branner; open up!"

So another young feller opened the door and looked out cautious with a double-barreled shotgun, and Blaze says to me, "Wait here whilst I go in and git the gold."

So I did and after a while he come out lugging a good-sized buckskin poke which I jedged from the weight they must be several thousand dollars worth of nuggets in there.

"I'll never forget this," I said warmly. "You go tell Hannah I cain't come to see her tonight because I'm guardin' her old man's gold. I'll see her tomorrer after the stagecoach has left with it."

"I'll tell her, pal," says he with emotion, shaking my hand, so I headed for my cabin, feeling I had easily won the first battle in the campaign for Hannah Sprague's hand. Imagine that pore sap Blaze throwing away a chance like that! I felt plumb sorry for him for being so addle-headed.

The sun was down by the time I got back to my cabin, and oncet I thought somebody was follering me, and I looked around, but it warn't nobody but the feller I'd seen fishing, trudging along about a hundred yards behind me with his pole onto his shoulder.

Well, when I arriv' at my cabin, I seen a furtive figger duck out the back way. It looked like old Polk, so I called to him, but he scooted off amongst the trees. I decided I must of been mistook, because likely old Polk was still off somewheres sulking on account of gitting shot in the britches. He was a onreasonable old cuss.

I went in and throwed the buckskin poke on the table and lit a candle, and jest then I heard a noise at the winder and wheeled quick jest in time to see somebody jerk his face away from the winder. I run to the door, and seen somebody sprinting off through the trees, and was jest fixing to take a shot at him when I recognized that old slouch hat. I wondered what that fool fisherman had follered me and looked in at my winder for, and I wondered why he run off so fast, but I'd already found out that Blue Lizard was full of idjits, so I give the matter no more thought. I ain't one of these here fellers which wastes their time trying to figger out why things is like they is, and why people does things like they does. I got better employment for my spare time, sech as sleeping.

Satanta come up to the door and nickered, and I give him some oats, and then I built a fire in the fireplace and cooked some bacon and made some coffee, and I'd jest got through eating and cleaned up the pot and skillet when somebody hailed me outside.

I quick blowed out the candle and stepped to the door with a gun in each hand. I could see a tall figger standing in the starlight, so I ast who the devil he was and what he wanted.

"A friend of Old Man Sprague's," says he. "Huddleston is the name, my enormous young friend, Carius Z. Huddleston. Mister Sprague sent me over to help you guard his gold tonight."

That didn't set well with me, because it looked like Old Man Sprague didn't think I was capable of taking care of it by myself, and I said so right out.

"Not at all," says Mister Huddleston. "He's so grateful to you for assumin' the responsibility that he said he couldn't endure it if you come to any harm on account of it, so he sent me to help you."

Well, that was all right. It looked like Old Man Sprague had took a fancy to me already, even before he'd saw me, and I felt that I was nigh as good as married to Hannah already. So I told Mr. Huddleston to come in, and I lit the candle and shet the door. He was a tall man with the biggest black mustache I ever seen, and he had on a frock tail coat and a broad-brim hat. I seen two ivory-handled six-shooters under his coattails. His eyes kind of bulged in the candlelight when he seen the big poke on the table and he ast me was that the gold and I said yes. So he hauled out a bottle of whiskey and said, "Well, my gigantic young friend, le's drink to Old Man Sprague's gold, may it arrive at its proper destination."

So we had a drink and we sot down on the bench and he sot on a rawhide bottomed chair, and he got to telling me stories, and he knowed more things about more people than I ever seen. He told me about a feller named Paul Revere which thrived during the Revolution when we licked the Britishers, and I got all het up hearing about him. He said the Britishers was going to sneak out of a town named Boston which I jedge must of been a right sizable cowtown or mining camp or something, and was going to fall on the people unawares and confiscate their stills and weppins and steers and things, but one of Paul's friends signaled him what was going on by swinging a lantern, and Paul forked his cayuse and fogged it down the trail to warn the folks.

When he was telling about Paul's friend signaling him Mister Huddleston got so excited he grabbed the candle and went over to the west winder and waved the candle back and forth three times to show me how it was done. It was a grand story, Wash, and I got goose bumps on me jest listening to it.

Well, it was gitting late by now, and Mister Huddleston ast me if I warn't sleepy. I said no, and he said, "Go ahead and lay down and sleep. I'll stand guard the rest of the night."

"Shucks," I said. "I ain't sleepy. You git some rest."

"We'll throw dice to see who sleeps first," says he, hauling out a pair, but I says, "No, sir! It's my job. I'm settin' up with the gold. You go on and lay down on that bunk over there if you wanta."

Well, for a minute Mister Huddleston got a most pecooliar expression onto his face, or it might of been the way the candlelight shined on it, because for a minute he looked jest like I've seen men look who was ready to pull out their pistol on me. Then he says, "All right. I believe I will take a snooze. You might as well kill the rest of that whisky. I got all I want."

So he went over to the bunk which was in a corner where the light didn't shine into very good, and he sot down on it to take off his boots. But he'd no sooner sot than he give a arful yell and bounded convulsively out into the middle of the room, clutching at his rear, and I seen a b'ar trap hanging onto the seat of his britches! I instantly knowed old Polk had sot it in the bunk for me, the revengeful old polecat.

From the way Mr. Huddleston was hollering I knowed it warn't only pants which was nipped betwixt the jaws; they was quite a chunk of Mister Huddleston betwixt 'em too. He went prancing around the cabin like one of them whirling derfishes and his langwidge was plumb terrible.

"Git it off, blast you!" he howled, but he was circling the room at sech speed I couldn't ketch him, so I grabbed the chain which dangled from the trap and give a heave and tore it loose from him by main strength. The seat of his pants and several freckles come with it, and the howls he'd let out previous warn't a circumstance to the one which he emitted now, also bounding about seven foot in the air besides.

"You – !" screamed he, and I likewise give a beller of amazement because his mustash had come off and revealed a familiar face!

"Witherington T. Jones!" I roared, dumfounded. "What the devil you doin' here in disguise?"

"Now!" says he, pulling a gun. "Hands up, curse you, or – "

I knocked the gun out of his hand before he could pull the trigger, and I was so overcome with resentment that I taken him by the neck and shaken him till his spurs flew off.

"Is this any way to treat a man as risked his repertation to rescue you from bloodhounds?" I inquired with passion. "Where's my mule, you ornery polecat?"

I had forgot about his other gun, but he hadn't. But I was shaking him so energetic that somehow he missed me even when he had the muzzle almost agen my belly. The bullet tore the hide over my ribs and the powder burnt me so severe that I lost my temper.

"So you tries to murder me after obtainin' my mule under false pretenses!" I bellered, taking the gun away from him and impulsively slinging him acrost the cabin. "You ain't no friend of Old Man Sprague's."

At this moment he got hold of a butcher knife I used to slice bacon with and come at me, yelling, "Slim! Mike! Arizona! Jackson! Where'n hell air you?"

I taken the blade in my arm muscles and then grabbed him and we was rassling all over the place when six men come storming through the door with guns in their hands. One of them yelled, "I thought you said you'd wait till he was asleep or drunk before you signaled us!"

"He wouldn't go to sleep!" howled Mister Jones, spitting out a piece of my ear he'd bit off. "Dammit, do somethin'! Don't you see he's killin' me?"

But we was so tangled up they couldn't shoot me without hitting him, so they clubbed their pistols and come for me, so I swung Mister Jones off his feet and throwed him at 'em. They was all in a bunch and he hit 'em broadside and knocked 'em all over and they crashed into the table and upset it and the candle went out. The next minute they was a arful commotion going on as they started fighting each other in the dark, each one thinking it was me he had holt of.

I was feeling for 'em when the back door busted open and I had a brief glimpse of a tall figger darting out, and it was carrying something on its shoulder. Then I remembered that the poke had been on that table. Mister Jones had got holt of the gold and was skedaddling with it!

I run out of the back door after him jest as a mob of men come whooping and yelling up to the front door with torches and guns and ropes. I heard one of 'em yell, "Somebody's fightin' in there! Listen at 'em!"

Somebody else yelled, "Maybe the whole gang's in there with the hillbilly! Git 'em!" So they went smashing into the cabin jest as I run in amongst the trees after Mister Jones.

And there I was stumped. I couldn't see where he went and it was too dark to find his trail. Then all to oncet I heard Satanta squeal and a man yelled for help, and they come a crash like a man makes when a hoss bucks him off into a blackjack thicket. I run in the direction of the noise and by the starlight I seen Satanta grazing and a pair of human laigs sticking out of the bresh. Mister Jones had tried to git away on Satanta.

"I told you he wouldn't let nobody but me ride him," I says as I hauled him out, but his langwidge ain't fit to be repeated. The poke was lying clost by, busted open. When I picked it up, it didn't look right. I struck a match and looked.

That there poke was full of nothing but scrap iron!

I was so stunned I didn't hardly know what I was doing when I taken the poke in one hand and Mister Jones' neck in the other'n, and lugged 'em back to the cabin. The mob had Mister Jones's six men outside tied up, and was wiping the blood off 'em, and I seen Shorty and Black-Beard and Squint-Eye and the others, and about a hundred more.

"They're Stirling's men all right," says Warts. "But where's Mustang, and that hillbilly? Anyway, le's string these up right here."

"You ain't," says Black-Beard. "You all elected me sheriff before we come up here, and I aims to uphold the law . . . Who's that?"

"It's Old Man Sprague," says somebody, as a bald-headed old coot come prancing through the crowd waving a shotgun.

"What you want?" says Black-Beard. "Don't you see we're busy?"

"I demands jestice!" howled Old Man Sprague. "I been abused!"

At this moment I shouldered through the crowd with a heavy heart, and slang the poke of scrap iron down in front of him.

"There it is," I says, "and I'll swear it ain't been monkeyed with since Blaze Wellington gave it to me!"

"Who's that?" howled Sprague.

"The hillbilly!" howled the mob. "Grab him!"

"No, you don't!" I roared, drawing a gun. "I've took enough offa you Blue Lizard jackasses! I'm a honest man, and I've brung back Mister Jones to prove it."

I then flang him down in front of them, and Warts give a howl and pounced on him. "Jones, nothing!" he yelled. "That's Mustang Stirling!"

"I confesses," says Mustang groggily. "Lock me up where I can be safe from that hillbilly! The critter ain't human."

"Somebody listen to me!" howled Old Man Sprague, jumping up and down. "I demands to be heard!"

"I done the best I could!" I roared, plumb out of patience. "When Blaze Wellington give me yore gold to guard – "

"What the devil air you talkin' about?" he squalled. "That wuthless scoundrel never had no gold of mine."

"*What!*" I hollered, going slightly crazy. Jest then I seen a feller in the crowd I recognized. I made a jump and grabbed him.

"Branner!" I roared. "You was at Wellington's shack when he give me that poke! You tell me quick what this is all about, or – "

"Leggo!" he gasped. "It warn't Sprague's gold we hid. It was our'n. We couldn't git it outa camp because we knowed Stirling's spies was watchin' us all the time. When you jumped Blaze in the Belle of New York, he seen a chance to git 'em off our necks. He filled that poke with scrap iron and give it to you where the spy could see it and hear what was said. The spy didn't know whether it was our gold or Sprague's, but we knowed if he thought you had it, Stirling would go after you and let us alone. He did, too, and that give Blaze a chance to sneak out early tonight with it."

"And that ain't all!" bellered Old Man Sprague. "*He taken Hannah with him! They've eloped!*"

My yell of mortal agony drownded out his demands for the sheriff to pursue 'em. Hannah! Eloped! It was too much for a critter to endure!

"Aw, don't you keer, partner," says Shorty, slapping me on the back with the arm I hadn't busted. "You been vindicated as a honest citizen! You're the hero of the hour!"

"Spare yore praise," I says bitterly. "I'm the victim of female perfidy. I have lost my faith in my feller man and my honest heart is busted all to perdition! Leave me to my sorrer!"

So they gathered up their prisoners and went away in awed silence. I am a rooint man. All I want to do is to become a hermit and forgit my aching heart in the untrodden wilderness.

Your pore brother,

PIKE

P.S. – The Next Morning. I have jest learnt that after I withdrawed from the campaign and left Antioch, you come out for sheriff and got elected. So that's why you persuaded me to come up here. I am heading for Antioch and when I git there I am going to whup you within a inch of yore wuthless life, I don't care if you air sheriff of Antioch. I am going to kick the seat of yore britches up around yore neck and sweep the streets with you till you don't know whether yo're setting or standing. Hoping this finds you in good health and spirits, I am,

Yore affectionate brother,

P. BEARFIELD ESQUIRE.

The Riot at Bucksnort

THE SAN SIMEON BRANDING IRON   April 6, 1885
Editorial

It has lately been brought to our notice by some of the less fastidious of our citizens who, presumably, have been amusing themselves by a slumming tour which naturally included a visit to our neighboring city of Bucksnort, that a campaign for sheriff is now raging in that aforesaid Hellhole of Iniquity. The candidates, as they were informed by such of Bucksnort's citizens as were out of jail and sober enough to talk lucidly, are the present Sheriff of Papago County, John Donaldson, and the City Marshal of Bucksnort, Cheyenne Campbell, whose term of office evidently expires about election time. Not, however, that the undemocratic spectacle of a man holding one office and simultaneously running for another would create any impression on the stunted sensibilities of the denizens of that Miners' Bedlam, that Blot on the Desert, that reeking Cesspool of Infamy, BUCKSNORT!

Each of the candidates seems to be straining nerve and sinew (we had almost said *brain!*) to distinguish himself in some spectacular manner which will catch the alcohol-soaked fancy of the citizenry. While we would no more descend to mingle into Bucksnort's politics than we would dip our hands in any other mud puddle, we humbly suggest to whichever candidate may be elected, that he devote less time to persecuting innocent citizens of San Simeon, whom misfortune catches in Bucksnort, and more to the pursuit of that notorious scourge of the Border, Raphael Garcia, or El Lobo, the bandit, whose depredations are a thorn in the flesh of all honest men, and who, incidentally, seems to be reaping the larger proceeds of the mines of which Bucksnort is so proud. Within the last few months his robberies of stagecoaches, ore-trains, and company offices have cost the mine owners several hundred thousand dollars. This is of no consequence to San Simeon, the fair queen-city of the cow country, but doubtless is to the muckgrubbers of Bucksnort.

We close this column with the remark that if anyone in the alleged town of Bucksnort wishes to physically resent any of the just statements here above made, that the editor of *The Branding Iron* is at his desk every day, hot or cold, rain or shine, drunk or sober, that the editor's bench-legged English bulldog is always on the job, and that the editorial shotgun is loaded with turkey shot and ten-penny nails. Liberty, Law, Order and Democracy!

THE BUCKSNORT CHRONICLE   April 9, 1885

Editorial Note

We notice that our esteemed contemporary, the editor of that filthy rag, *The San Simeon Branding Iron*, has emerged from his habitual state of drunken stupor long enough to direct at our beautiful city an unprovoked blast which sounds much like the well-known braying of that individual's not-too-distant ancestor. We scorn to bend to his level by replying. The accompanying notice is Bucksnort's official retort to the cow-chasing scum of San Simeon and all Hualpai County! Loyal citizens please peruse.

NOTICE!   (Personal Insertion)

There has been a lot of loose talk going on over to San Simeon about the way the campaign for Sheriff of Papago County is being ran. It is none of their blasted business and we do not want none of their company. Bucksnort is the leading mining town of the Territory and is sufficient unto herself. We have took enough off of the bat-legged cowpokes which infest San Simeon. As marshal of our thriving city I have placed a sign at the edge of town reading as per follows, "Horse thieves, cow rustlers, Injuns and other varmints, particularly including folks from San Simeon, stay out of Bucksnort!" I aim to enforce that edict. That ought to settle their hash, and when you, the citizens of this desert metropolis, go to the polls to exercise your inalienable privilege as American citizens, please remember that it is because of the zeal and patriotism of your favorite candidate that you are not now harassed with vermin from San Simeon! Yours for better government, law, order and personal liberty.

Cheyenne Campbell,
City Marshal

Bucksnort, Arizona,
1 P. M., April 9, 1885.

Mr. Sam Abercrombie,
c/o Hualpai County Jail,
San Simeon, Arizona

Dear Sam:

Campbell has put over a fast one by ordering San Simeonites to stay out of Bucksnort. Ever since the editor of the *Branding Iron* wrote that editorial about Bucksnort last week, the folks over here froth at the sight of a man from San Simeon. Campbell's order made a big hit with them. Why the devil didn't we think of it first? You're a fine campaign manager. You better think up something in a hurry. You know the mine owners are sore at me anyway, because I haven't been able to catch El Lobo. A big help you be. What you want to punch old judge Clanton's nose for in his own court? You might of knowed he was just itching for a excuse to throw you into the calaboose for contempt of court. You just would go over into Hualpai County to defend a horse thief just when the campaign was at its hottest. It we don't do something to match Campbell's latest move, we're as good as licked. But whatever you do, be careful. Jack Harrigan, one of Campbell's campaign managers, is snooping around over in San Simeon. I hope one of them cowpunchers shoots him. Do you want some of the boys to come over and bust you out of jail?

Yours in haste,
John Donaldson, Sheriff

San Simeon, Arizona,
County Jail, 6 P. M.,
April 9, 1885.

Dear John:

Don't send the boys. The jailer and I have been playing draw poker and I can't leave till I win back my pants at least. Anyway, a great legal mind can work as good in jail as anywhere else. The associations are congenial, if you get what I mean. I've already solved your problem, my boy. A Texas man by the name of Pike Bearfield is due here tomorrow to pay a fine for one of the Triple Arrow cow punchers, who's in jail for the minor offense of shooting the city marshal in the leg.

Bearfield's got the reputation of being a fire-eater, and no more brains than the law allows. I'll engage him in conversation and get him all worked up about Bucksnort ordering San Simeon people to keep away. All the cowpunchers in Hualpai County consider themselves citizens of San Simeon, and their civic pride is ardent and homicidal. I'll prod him about San Simeon being afraid of Bucksnort, and if he's like all the other Texans I've ever seen, he'll fork his horse and come fogging over there, just to show the world that Bucksnort can't give orders to a San Simeon warrior. From what I've heard of Bearfield, Campbell's warning will be like waving a red flag at a bull. Now you be on the watch and grab him as soon as he shows up. Be smart this time and don't let Cheyenne get ahead of you and arrest him first. Station one of your deputies at the edge of town to watch for him and give you warning as he comes into town.

I'm sending this letter by the same fellow who brought yours. You'll get it by midnight, at the latest. That will give you plenty of time to get ready for Bearfield. He'll probably come to the jail early tomorrow morning, and if my silver tongue has lost none of its charm, he'll be fogging it for Bucksnort pronto thereafter.

When you get him in the calaboose, tell the editor of the Chronicle to play it up big. He will if you'll slip him a ten-spot. Play it up as the arrest of a dangerous outlaw from Texas, come to shoot up the town! Let it look like Campbell wasn't big enough to handle him and had to call in the county officers. Better try to get Campbell out of town on some fake call or other before Bearfield gets there. Anyway, don't let Campbell be the one to arrest him! This is our chance to put you over big with the voters.

Yours for honest politics,
Samuel Trueheart Abercrombie,
Attorney.

Telegram
SAN SIMEON ARIZONA
9 AM
APRIL 10 1885

CHEYENNE CAMPBELL
BUCKSNORT ARIZONA

THEY ARE FIXING TO PUT ONE OVER STOP A HORSE THIEF WHO JUST
GOT OUT OF JAIL TOLD ME HE HEARD SAM ABERCROMBIE PRIMING A
TEXAS GUNFIGHTER NAMED BEARFIELD TO COME OVER AND CLEAN
OUT BUCKSNORT STOP DONALDSON AIMS TO ARREST HIM STOP THIS
WILL MAKE YOU LOOK BAD STOP BE ON THE JOB AND GRAB HIM
BEFORE DONALDSON DOES STOP

JACK HARRIGAN

Telegram
BUCKSNORT ARIZONA
11 15 AM
APRIL 10 1885

COMMANDING OFFICER
FT CROOK ARIZONA

FOR GOSH SAKE RUSH ALL THE SOLDIERS YOU GOT OVER HERE STOP
A MANIAC FROM TEXAS NAMED BEARFIELD IS TEARING THE TOWN
APART STOP HUSTLE STOP

EPHRAIM L WHITTAKER MAYOR

The Riot at Bucksnort

PHYSICIAN'S MEMORANDUM,

AFTERNOON OF APRIL 10, 1885.

D. V. RICHARDS, M.D.

Treatment administered at the Golconda Gold Mining Company's Emergency Hospital, as follows:

Bullets removed and treated for gunshot wounds: Sheriff John Donaldson, City Marshal Cheyenne Campbell, Deputies Gonzales, Keene, Wilkinson, McDonald and Jones; J. G. Smithson, County Clerk; Thomas Corbett, Tax Collector; Harrison, Jeppart, Wiltshaw and O'Toole, miners; Joe O'Brien, teamster.

Knife wounds: Ace Tremayne, gambler; nineteen stitches.

Iron beer keg hoops removed from neck of Michael Grogan, bartender, with aid of hacksaw.

The following were treated for contusions resulting from being struck with some blunt instrument such as the butt of a Sharps' buffalo rifle: Sergeant O'Hara, fractured skull; Brogart, Olson, DeBose, Williams, Watson, Jackson, Emerson, miners. Six unidentified men now being revived.

Miscellaneous: Big Jud Pritchard, blacksmith – set broken arm and wired up fractured jaw, impossible to replace ear. Seventeen other men treated for minor lacerations and abrasions, apparently resulting from having been stepped on by a large horse.

Bucksnort, Arizona,
April 14, 1885.

Honorable Governor of Arizona,
Phoenix, Arizona

Honorable Sir:

I am writing to you to ast you to please see that jestice is did and stop an innercent man from being hounded by his enemies before he loses his patience and injures some of them fatally. I am referring to my pore persecuted brother, Pike Bearfield, of Wolf Mountain, Texas, now a fugitive from jestice and subsisting on prickly pears and horned toads somewheres in the Guadalupe Mountains. That ain't no fitten diet for a white man, Yore Honor.

You have maybe saw the pack of lies which was writ about him in that dang newspaper *The Bucksnort Chronicle* which the only reason I ain't shot the editor is because I am a peaceful and law-abiding man same as all us Bearfields, especially Pike. But let him beware! The editor, I mean. Truth is mighty and will prevail!

In that article about Pike, which was writ as soon as the editor sobered up on the morning of the 11th (he claims he was knocked cold by Pike the day before but it's my opinion he was jest drunk) he claims Pike come out of his way jest to make trouble in Bucksnort. That's a lie. Pike had been to San Simeon to pay a fine for a friend of his'n and was on his way back to the Triple Arrer ranch where we've both worked ever since we come out from Texas. He went by Bucksnort on his way to the ranch. Maybe you will say what the devil was he going by Bucksnort for, that is in the oppersite direction from the ranch, but Pike is very sociable and will go a long way out of his way jest to visit a town and meet folks and buy them drinks. As for that story about him storming out of San Simeon on the morning of April 10th spurring like a Comanche and waving his guns and announcing that he'd show them Bucksnort illegitimates whether they could keep San Simeon folks out of their dad-blasted town well, shucks, maybe he did holler and shoot off his pistols a little as he rode out, but that was jest high spirits. You know how us cowboys is, always full of fun and frolic.

His enemies has tried to make something out of the fack that he made the ride from San Simeon to Bucksnort in about a hour when it ordinarily takes a man about four hours to ride it. They say why was he splitting the road like that if he warn't coming with war-like intention. But they don't know Pike's hoss, Satanta, which Pike ketched wild out of a Kiowa hoss herd and broke hisself, at the risk of his life. Satanta can outrun any critter in the Territory and he generally goes at a high lope. He ain't careful about stepping around anything which happens to git in his way, neither, and probably Pike was shooting to warn them folks which he met to git out of his way, so they wouldn't git tromped on. Pike has got a arful soft heart that way and don't want to see nobody git hurt. They warn't no use for them to take to the bresh and later accuse him of trying to murder them. If he'd been trying to hit them he would of, instead of jest knocking their hats off.

As for what actually happened at Bucksnort when he got there, they has been so many lies told about it that it plumb discourages a honest man. But this here is a plain, unvarnished account which I hope you will forgit all them yarns which Pike's enemies has been telling, they air all prejudiced and anyway some of them air still addled in the brains and not responsible. Well, this is the way it was:

They is, or was, a very insulting sign at the aidge of Bucksnort which warned folks from San Simeon to keep out of the derned town. It now appears that it was shot all to pieces on the morning of the 10th, and folks air accusing Pike of doing it as he rode into town. Well, maybe he did kind of empty his pistol into the sagebrush, but they ain't no use in abusing him because their derned sign happened to be where he was shooting. He didn't put it there. Us cowboys frequently shoots into the air as we comes into town. It's a kind of salute to the town, and a mark of respeck. As for that there deperty who got his hat shot off account of Pike seeing it sticking up in the sagebresh, why, that was jest a friendly joke. Pike was jest trying to be sociable. It hurt Pike's feelings when the deperty ran off hollering halp murder and that's why he shot the feller's suspender buttons off – if the deperty didn't bust them off hisself running through the sagebresh. He didn't have no business hiding out there in the first place.

Pike then went on into town and tied his hoss, as quiet and peaceable as you please, and went into the Miners' Delight Saloon. How do I know why the folks in the saloon all left by way of the back door as he come in at the front? Maybe they had to go home to dinner or something. The bartender was one of these hot-tempered, overbearing cusses which don't deserve no sympathy. It appears they was some shots fired by somebody which cracked the mirror behind the bar and busted all the ceiling lamps, and the bartender seems to have blamed it on Pike. But he had no business making a play at Pike with a sawed-off shotgun. I reckon a man has a right to pertect hisself, which is why Pike kind of tapped him with a beer kag to shake his aim. I cain't see as it was Pike's fault that the bartender's head went through the kag.

It now appears that the sheriff and the marshal was both expecting Pike, and it looks to me like they is something crooked about that. You cain't trust these Bucksnort coyotes. Anyway, the deperty Pike met at the aidge of town was supposed to let the sheriff know the minute Pike hit town, and the marshal had bribed the deperty to tell *him* before he told the sheriff. Anyway, they was both depending onto that deperty to let 'em know when Pike come, but he run off into the desert when Pike shot at him, so the first thing they knowed about it was when they heard the shooting in the Miners' Delight. The sheriff started for there on the run, and the marshal come up from the other direction.

But before they got there Pike had left. They warn't nobody left in the Miners' Delight but the bartender and he was unconscious, and Pike is that sociable he likes crowds of people around him. So he went acrost the street to the Bear Claw Saloon and Gambling Hall, and imejitly all them miners started picking on him. They ain't no use in them trying to pertend that he started it. They say he was war-like and boastful, and try to prove this lie by bearing down on the fack of him announcing that he was a woolly wolf from the Hard Water Fork of Bitter Creek as he come through the door. But that warn't no brag. It was jest a plain statement of fack, as anybody knows who is acquainted with Pike.

As for that roulette wheel, it ought to have been shot apart long ago. Pike probably knowed it was crooked, and jest couldn't endure to see the men losing their hard-earned dough on it. He is arful soft-hearted. But that gambler, Ace Tremayne, he couldn't take a joke, and mild-mannered as Pike is, he aint the man to endure being shot at with .41 caliber derringers at a distance of four foot. Ace somehow got cut right severe whilst him and Pike was rassling around on the floor. I reckon Pike's bowie must of fell out of his boot and Ace rolled on it or something.

But several of them overbearing Bucksnort bullies taken the matter to heart, notably Jud Pritchard the blacksmith, and he ought to of knowed better'n to lay holt of Pike like he done. I reckon a man has got a right to defend hisself. Jud thinks he is a whole lot of man because he is six and a half foot tall and has licked most of them miners, but when you stack him up agen Pike he don't look so big neither in size nor in fighting capacity. Pike allus fights a man like the man wants to fight, so he waded into Jud bar' – handed and Jud begun to holler halp murder the cow puncher is killing me. So several miners jumped in and taken a hand and Pike was dealing with them when the sheriff and marshal come running up.

They met on the street outside of the Bear Claw and the marshal said to the sheriff, "Where the devil do you think yo're goin'?"

And the sheriff said to the marshal, "I'm goin' in there to arrest a desperate criminal from Texas!"

And the marshal said, "How do you know he's from Texas? I'm onto you, but you cain't cut it! So git outa the way. This here's my job! You tend to the county jobs and let city doins alone."

"Air you tryin' to tell me where to head in?" says the sheriff. "Pull in yore horns before I clip 'em! I'm runnin' Papago County!"

"And I'm runnin' Bucksnort!" says the marshal, and they slapped leather simultaneous, and both of 'em kissed the board sidewalk with lead in various parts of their carcasses.

Their deperties was jest fixing to carry on the war, when Pike come out to see what the shooting was about and a number of folks come out ahead of him. It was them which stampeded over the sheriff and the marshal as they laid in front of the Bear Claw. They later claimed Pike was making so much noise inside they didn't bear the shooting which was going on outside, and they further claimed they was trying to escape from Pike when they stampeded out the front door. But they air sech liars I hope you won't pay no attention to them, Yore Honor.

Anyway, it appears that the mayor had got severely trompled in the rush, and he hollered to the deperty sheriffs and deperty marshals and said, "Stop fightin' each other, you jack-eared illegitimates and git this maneyack before he wrecks the town!"

That was a purty way for a mayor to talk about a pore, friendless stranger in their midst. They needn't to never brag about Bucksnort hospitality no more. It'd serve them right if Pike *never* went there again.

Anyway, the deperties was jest as narrer-minded as the mayor, so they all started shooting at Pike, and he retreated into the French Queen Dancing Hall with a Sharps' Buffalo rifle he'd taken away from one of the deperties, being afeared the deperty'd hurt somebody with his wild shooting. It appears the deperty's cartridge belt come off in the scuffle, so Pike had it when he come into the Dance Hall.

By this time they was a mob milling in the street and talking about hanging Pike – that jest shows how lawless them Bucksnort devils is! – and sech deperties as warn't unconscious and a lot of miners was shooting at him from every direction from behind signboards and hoss troughs and out of houses, so Pike begun shooting into the air to scare 'em off. But you know how bullets glance, and it appears that nine or ten men got hit. But it's plumb unjest to blame Pike because his bullets glanced.

But the mayor lost his head and sent for soldiers, and a whole company rode out from the fort. By the time they got there somebody had sot the dance hall on fire, and Pike was about out of cartridges and his boots was burnt clean off of him account of him trying to stomp out the fire. I dunno what would of happened to him, but when Satanta, which was tied over beside the Miners' Delight, seen the soldiers' hosses, he bust loose and come charging over to fight them. He is the fightingest hoss you ever seen.

He galloped up to the front of the hall, right behind the soldiers which was fixing to bust down the front door, and Pike seen him. So Pike made a break and busted through the crowd, gently shoving Sergeant O'Hara out of his way, and I cain't imagine how the sergeant got his skull fractured from a little push like that. But men is sech softies then days. Anyway, Pike got to Satanta and got onto him, meaning to ride quietly out of town, but Satanta got the bit in his teeth or something and bolted right through the crowd knocking down sixteen or seventeen, men and trompling them. Some more men tried to ketch holt of his bridle, but Pike was scairt they'd git stepped on and hurt like the others, so he kind of pushed them away with the butt of the Sharps. They ought to be grateful to him, instead of bellyaching about their noses and teeth and things.

He rode on out of town and was swinging back towards the San Simeon road, because he was beginning to get the idee that he warn't welcome in Bucksnort, when jedge his surprise when he seen the whole company of soldiers coming lickety-split after him! Well, he didn't have no cartridges left so he headed for the mountains south of there, and purty soon Satanta stumbled and the girth broke, account of somebody having slashed it nearly in two with a knife as they went through the crowd.

Pike was throwed over Satanta's head and would probably of broke a laig if it hadn't been for a big rock which he hit on headfirst and kind of cushioned his fall so's he didn't injure none of his limbs. The soldiers were crowding him so clost he didn't have time to ketch Satanta, so he jumped up and taken to the hills afoot, and you may not believe it, Yore Honor, but them soldiers pursued him like he was a coyote or something, and shot at him so dern reckless it looked like they didn't have a bit of regard for his safety. But they didn't hit him except in a few unimportant places and he taken to country so rough they couldn't foller on horseback, and finally he got away from them and taken refuge in the mountains. He's hiding up there right now, barefooted, hongry, without no knife nor cartridges, and soldiers and posses is combing the country for him, and he cain't git away in any direction except south without getting ketched. And the only thing south of him is Old Mexico. He don't want to go there Yore Honor, it would make him look like he was a outlaw or something.

As soon as I heard about this business I come down from the Triple Arrer and as soon as I got to Bucksnort they throwed me in jail jest because I am a Bearfield, so I ain't been able to look for Pike and help him. But he sent me a letter by a Mex sheepherder and explained how things was and told me his side of everything. So will you please make the soldiers quit persecuting him, he is as innercent as a newborn baby.

Please do something about this, he is powerful hongry and scairt to even eat with the sheepherder which slipped his letter in to me, for fear the Mex will pizen him for the reward they air offering.

Very trooly yoren,
Kirby Bearfield, Esquire

Gaudalupe Mountains, Arizony,
April 17, 1885.

Dear Kirby:

I am gitting purty dang tired of this business. The cactus hurts my feet and I have et jackrabbits and lizards till I feel like a Piute Injun. Tonight I am heading for Old Mexico by the way of Wolf Pass to git me some boots. It is a terrible note when a honest, respectable, law-abiding citerzen gits run out of the country by the soldiers which is supposed to perteck him, and has to take refuge in a furrin land. For three cents I'd stay in Old Mexico and leave the country flat. They is a limit to everything. The Mex will slip this note to you through the jail winder when they ain't nobody looking.

Yore persecuted brother,
Pike

El Lobo:

I send this note by a swift and trusted messenger. Now is the time to make one big raid on Bucksnort. All the officers are still in the hospital and the soldiers still hunt the fool *Tejano*, Bearfield, through the mountains. I have contrived to send them to the northwest on a wild goose chase, by telling them he was seen in that direction. They do not guess that Esteban, the handsome monte dealer, is El Lobo's spy! Now is the time to make a clean sweep, in force, to take all the gold on hand and burn the town, as you have long desired. Come swiftly tonight, with all your men, by way of Wolf Pass!

Esteban

THE BUCKSNORT CHRONICLE   April 18, 1885

EL LOBO CAPTURED

Raid Failed by Heroic Texan

A Misjudged Hero Vindicated

Last night will be long remembered in the history of this glorious if rugged, Territory, for it marked the elimination of a menace which has long hovered like a black cloud in the mountains of the South. For longer than honest men like to remember, the bloody bandit El Lobo has from time to time swooped down on isolated mining camps or on travelers, leaving death and desolation in his wake, and evading retribution by retiring across the Border. An Ishmael of the Border, with his crimson hand against all men, he further proved himself an implacable enemy of culture and progress by threatening, on more than one occasion, to forcibly detach the ears of the *Chronicle's* editor, because of unfavorable comment in these columns.

Last night, taking advantage of the recent unsettled conditions, he crossed the Border with a force estimated at a hundred men, and headed toward Bucksnort intending to crown his infamous career by an exploit of blood and destruction too sweeping to be regarded with anything but horror. In short he determined to wipe out the city of Bucksnort, and he had good reason to feel confident of success, as most of the soldiers from Fort Crook were away in the northwest corner of the county, and the natural defenders of the town, the officers of the law, had not yet recovered from a vulgar brawl which reflected little credit upon any of them. But he reckoned without Pike Bearfield, himself a fugitive from a misguided justice!

Mr. Bearfield, formerly of Wolf Mountain, Texas, but now claimed by Bucksnort as an honored son, will be remembered by citizens as a visitor in Bucksnort on the tenth of this month, at which date we understand some slight confusion arose as a result of a trivial misunderstanding between him and some of the officers.

Mr. Bearfield, who had been residing temporarily in the mountains just this side of the Border, due to the unfortunate misunderstanding above mentioned, evidently heard of the proposed raid, and with a heroism rare even in this Territory, went to meet the invaders single-handed. We have not been able to interview the hero, but from the accounts of the prisoners, we are able to reconstruct the scene as follows:

Arriving at Wolf Pass, on foot, at about midnight, our hero found the raiders already filing through the narrow gorge. Being without weapons he resorted to a breath-taking strategy. Turning aside, he climbed the almost sheer wall of the left-band cliff, and concealed himself on a jutting ledge of rock. Then when the head of the column was pawing directly under him, he hurled himself, barehanded, like a thunderbolt, down on the back of El Lobo himself!

Horse and man went to the earth under that impact, and El Lobo was knocked senseless. Instantly all was confusion, for in the darkness of the pass, the raiders could not see just what had happened, and evidently thought themselves ambushed by a large force. This illusion was heightened by Mr. Bearfield's action, for seizing the ivory-handled revolvers of the senseless bandit, he leaped back against the shadowed cliff where, invisible himself to his enemies, he poured a two-handed hail of lead at the figures on horseback etched dimly against the starlit sky.

This completed the rout. Their leader down, they themselves unnerved and panicked by the unexpected attack, they fired wildly in all directions, hitting nobody but their own companions, and then broke in ignominious flight, leaving five or six corpses behind them, and El Lobo.

A posse which, we are pained to say, was combing the canyons in search of Mr. Bearfield, a few miles to the east, heard the shooting and hurrying to the pass, found the senseless bandit chief and the bodies of his villainous followers. They also sighted Mr. Bearfield, who was just about to remove El Lobo's boots, but the modest hero hurried away without waiting for their congratulations.

His brother Kirby, an honored guest of the city, has been delegated to find Mr. Bearfield and bring him in to receive the grateful plaudits of an admiring citizenry. We hope he will prove as generous as he is valiant, and forget – as we have forgotten – the unfortunate affair of April 10th. If we have, at any time, seemed to criticize Mr. Bearfield in the columns of this paper, we sincerely apologize.

Mr. Bearfield's efforts in defense of Bucksnort shine more brightly than ever in contrast with the recent actions of the two candidates for the sheriff's office, whose political greed and ambition led them into a sordid brawl which incapacitated them at a time when the city most needed them. Let the citizens of Bucksnort consider that!

> Bucksnort, Arizona,
> April 18, 1885.

Dear Pike:

Come on in. Everything is hotsy-totsy and they air fixing a banquet in yore honor. Only jest don't let anybody know that you was tryin to git away into Old Mexico when you met El Lobo and his gang, and thought they was a posse after you, and was trying to git away by climbing the cliffs when you lost your holt and fell on El Lobo.

Yore brother,
Kirby

P. S. – They have jest now held a popular meeting and elected you sheriff of Papago County. I am sending yore badge by the Mex, also a pair of boots and a fried steak. You takes office jest as soon as they can git the governor to take the price off of yore head.

Knife River Prodigal

I had just sot down on my bunk and was fixing to pull off my boots, when Pap come out of the back room and blinked at the candle which was stuck onto the table.

Says he, "Well, Buckner, is they anything new over to Knife River?"

"They ain't never nothin' new there," I says, yawning. "They's a new gal slingin' hash in the Royal Grand resternt, but Bill Hopkins has already got hisself engaged to her, and 'lows he'll shoot anybody which so much as looks at her. They was a big poker game in back of the Golden Steer and Tunk winned seventy bucks and got carved with a bowie."

"The usual derned foolishness," grumbled Pap, turning around to go back to bed. "When I was a young buck, they was always excitement to be found in town – pervidin' you could find a town."

"Oh, yes," I says suddenly. "I just happened to remember. I shot a feller in the Diamond Palace Saloon."

Pap turned around and combed his beard with his fingers.

"Gittin' a mite absent-minded, ain't you, Buckner?" says he. "Did they identify the remains?"

"Aw, I didn't croak him," says I. "I just kinda shot him through the shoulder and a arm and the hind leg. He was a stranger in these here parts, and I thought maybe he didn't know no better."

"No better'n what?" demanded Pap. "What was the argyment?"

"I don't remember," I confessed. "It was somethin' about politics."

"What you know about politics?" snorted Pap.

"Nothin'," I says. "That's why I plugged him. I run out of argyments."

"Daw-gone it, Buckner," says Pap, "you got to be a little more careful how you go around shootin' people in saloons. This here country is gittin' civilized, what with britch-loadin' guns, and stagecoaches and suchlike. I don't hold with these here newfangled contraptions, but lots of people

223

does, and the majority rules – les'n yo're quicker on the draw than what they be.

"Now you done got the family into trouble again. You'll have that ranger, Kirby, onto yore neck. Don't you know he's in this here country swearin' he's goin' to bring in law and order if he has to smoke up every male citizen of Knife River County? If any one man can do it, he can, because he's the fastest gunman between the Guadalupe and the Rio Grande. More'n that, it ain't just him. He's got the whole ranger force behind him. The Grimes family has fit their private feuds as obstreperous as anybody in the State of Texas. But we ain't buckin' the rangers. And what we goin' to do now when Kirby descends on us account of yore action?"

"I don't think he's goin' to descend any time soon, Pap," I says.

"When I wants yore opinion I'll ast for it!" Pap roared. "Till then, shut up! Why don't you think he will?"

" 'Cause Kirby was the feller I shot," I says.

Pap stood still a while, combing his whiskers, with a most curious expression; then he laid hold onto my collar and the seat of my britches and begun to walk me toward the door.

"The time has come, Buckner," says he, "for you to go forth and tackle the world on yore own. Yo're growed in height, if not in bulk and mentality, and anyway, as I remarked while ago, the welfare of the majority has got to be considered. The Grimes family is noted for its ability to soak up punishment, but they's a limit to everything. When I recalls the family feuds, gunfights and range wars yore mental incapacity and lack of discretion has got us into ever since you was big enough to sight a gun, I looks with no enthusiasm onto a pitched battle with the rangers and probably the State milishy. No, Buckner, I think you better hit out for foreign parts."

"Where you want me to go, Pap?" I inquired.

"Californy," he answered, kicking the door open.

"Why Californy?" I asked.

"Because that's the fartherest-off place I can think of," he says, lifting me through the door with the toe of his boot. "Go with my blessin'!"

I pulled my nose out of the dirt and got up and hollered through the door which Pap had locked and bolted on the inside, "How long I oughta stay?"

"Not too long," says Pap. "Don't forgit yore pore old father and yore other relatives which will grieve for you. Come back in about forty or fifty years."

"Where 'bouts is Californy?" I asked.

"It's where they git gold," he says. "If you ride straight west long enough yo're bound to git there eventually."

I went out to the corral and saddled my horse – or rather, I saddled my brother Jim's horse – because his'n was better'n mine – and I hit out, feeling kinda funny, because I hadn't never been away from home no farther'n the town of Knife River. I couldn't head due west on account of that route would 'a' took me across "Old Man" Gordon's ranch, and he had give his punchers orders to shoot me on sight, account of me smoking up his three boys at a dance a few months before.

So I swung south till I got as near the Donnellys' range as I felt like I oughta, what with Joe Donnelly still limping on a crutch from a argyment him and me had in Knife River. So I turned west again and hit straight through the settlement of Broken Rope. None of the nine or ten citizens which was gunning for me was awake, so I rode peacefully through and headed into unknown country just as the sun come up.

Well, for a long time I rode through country which was inhabited very seldom. After I left the settlements on Knife River, there was a long stretch in which about the only folks I seen was Mexican sheep-herders which I was ashamed to ask 'em where I was, for fear they'd think I was ignerunt. Then even the sheep-herders played out, and I crossed some desert that me and Brother Jim's horse nearly starved on, but I knowed that if I kept heading west I'd fetch Californy finally.

So I rode for days and days and finally got into better-looking country again, and I decided I must be there, because I didn't see how anything could be any further from anything else than what I'd come. I was homesick and low in my spirits, and would 'a' sold my hopes of the future for ten cents.

Well, finally one day, along about the middle of the morning, I found myself in a well-watered, hilly country, a little like that around Knife River, only with the hills bigger, and they was right smart rocks. So I thought to myself, "I'm good and tired of this here perambulatin'; I'm goin' to stop right here and mine me some gold." I'd heard tell they found gold in rocks. So I tied brother Jim's horse to a tree, and I located me a likely boulder beside the trail, about as big as a barn, and begun knocking chips off it with a hunk of flint.

I was making so much noise I didn't hear the horses coming up the trail, and the first thing I knowed I wasn't alone.

Somebody said, "What in tarnation are you doin'?"

I turned around and there was a gang of five men on horses, hard-looking gents with skins about the color of old leather, and the biggest one was nigh as dark as a Indian with drooping whiskers. He twist these whiskers and scowled, and says, "Didn't you hear me? What you bustin' chunks off that rock for?"

"I'm prospectin' for gold," I says. He kinda turned purple, and his eyes got red and he snorted through his whiskers and says, "Don't you try to make no fool outa William Hyrkimer Hawkins! The boundless prairies is dotted with the bones of such misguided idjits. I ast you a civil question – "

"I done told you," I said. "I'm huntin' me some gold. I heard tell they git it outa rocks."

He looked kinda stunned, and the men behind him haw-hawed and said, "Don't shoot him, Bill, the blame hillbilly is on the level."

"By golly," he said, twisting his mustash, "I believe it. But he ain't no hillbilly. Who're you, and where you from, and where you goin'?"

"I'm Buckner Jeopardy Grimes," I says. "I'm from Knife River County, Texas, and I'm on my way to the gold fields of Californy."

"Well," says he, "you still got a long way to go."

"Ain't this Californy?" I says.

He says, "Naw, this here is New Mexico. Come on. We're ridin' to Smokeville. Climb on yore cayuse and trail with us."

"What you want this gangle-legged waddy grazin' around with us for?" demanded one of the fellers.

"He's good for a laugh," said Hawkins.

"If you like yore humor mixed up with gun smoke," opined a bald-headed old cuss which looked like a pessimistic timber wolf. "I've seen a lot of hombres outa Texas, and some was smart and some was dumb, but they was all alike in one respect: they was all pizen."

Hawkins snorted and I mounted onto my brother Jim's horse and we started for Smokeville, wherever that was. They was four men and Hawkins, and they called thereselves "Squint" and "Red" and "Curly" and "Arizona," and next to some of my relatives on Knife River, they was the toughest-looking gang of thugs I ever seen in my life.

Then after a while we come in sight of Smokeville. It wasn't as big as Knife River, but it had about as many saloons. They rode into town at a dead run, hollering and shooting off their pistols. I rode with 'em because I wanted to be polite, but I didn't celebrate none, because I was a long ways from home and low in my spirits.

All the folks taken to cover, and Hawkins rode his horse up on the porch of a saloon. There was a piece of paper tacked on the wall.

His men says, "What does it say, Bill? Read it to us!"

So he spit his tobaccer out on the porch, and read:

Us citizens of Smokeville has passed the follerin' laws which we aims to see enforced to the full extent of fines and imprisonment and being plugged with a .45 for resistin' arrest. It's agin' the law to shoot off pistols in saloons and resternts; it's agin' the law for gents to shoot each other inside the city limits; it's agin' the law to ride horses into saloons and shoot buttons off the bartender's coat. Signed: us citizens of Smokeville and Joe Clanton, sheriff.

Hawkins roared like a bull looking at a red bandanner.

"What air we a-comin' to?" he bellered. "What kind of a government air we livin' under? Air we men or air we jassacks? Is they no personal liberty left no more?"

"I dunno," I said. "I never heered of no such laws back in Texas."

"I warn't talkin' to you, you long-legged road-runner!" he snorted, ripping the paper off the wall. "Foller me, boys. We'll show 'em they can't tromple on the rights of free-born white men!"

So they surged into the saloon on their horses and the bartender run out the back way hollering, "Run, everybody! Hawkins is back in town!"

So the feller they called Squint got behind the bar and started servin' the drinks. They all got off of their cayuses so's they could drink easier, and Hawkins told me to take the horses out and tie 'em to the hitching rack.

I done it, and when I got back they'd dragged the sheriff out from under the bar where he was hiding, and was making him eat the paper Hawkins had tore off the wall. He was a fat man with a bald head and a pot belly, and they'd tooken his gun away, which he hadn't tried to use.

"A fine specimen you be!" said Hawkins fiercely, sticking his gun muzzle outa sight in the sheriff's quivering belly. "I oughta shoot you! Tryin' to persecute honest men! Tryin' to crush human liberty under the mailed fist of oppressive laws! Sheriff! Bah! We impeaches you!" He jerked off Clanton's star and kicked him heartily in the pants. "Git out! You ain't sheriff no more'n a jack rabbit." Clanton made for the door like he had wasps in his britches, and they shot the p'ints off his spurs as he run.

"The nerve of these coyotes!" snorted Hawkins, downing about a quart of licker at a snort and throwing the bottle through the nearest glass winder. "Sheriff! Ha!" He glared around till he spied me. Then he grinned like a timber wolf, and says, "Come here, you! I make *you* sheriff of Smokeville!" And he stuck the badge on my shirt, and everybody haw-hawed and shot their pistols through the roof.

I said, "I ain't never done no sheriffin' before. What am I supposed to do?"

"The first thing is to set up drinks for the house," said Red.

I said, "I ain't got but a dollar."

And Hawkins said, "Don't be a sap. None of my men ever pays for anything they get in Smokeville. I got a pocketful of money right now, but you don't see me handin' out none to these sissies, does you?"

So I said, "Oh, all right then, the drinks is on me."

And everybody yelled and hollered and shot holes in the mirror behind the bar and guzzled licker till it was astonishing to behold. After a while they scattered up and down the street, some into other saloons, and some into a dance hall.

So I taken brother Jim's horse down to the wagon yard and told the man to take care of him.

He looked at my badge very curious, but said he'd do it.

So I said, "I understand none of Mr. Hawkins' men has to pay for nothin' in Smokeville. Is that right?"

He kinda shivered and said that Mr. Hawkins was such a credit to the country that nobody had the heart to charge him for anything, and them which had was not now in the land of the living.

Well, this all seemed very strange to me, but Pap once told me that when I got outa Texas I would find folks in other parts had different customs. So I went back up the street. Hawkins' gang was still raising hell and very few folks was in sight. I never seen people so scared of five men in my life. I seen a resternt up toward the east end of the street, and I was hungry and went in. They was a awful purty gal in there.

I would 'a' beat a retreat, because I was awful bashful and scared of gals, but she seen me and kinda turned pale, and said, "What – what do you want?"

So I taken off my hat, and said, "I would like a steak and some aigs and 'taters and a few molasses if it ain't too much trouble, please, ma'am."

So I sot down and she went to work and slung the stuff together, and purty soon she looked at me kinda apprehensive, and says, "How – how long are you men going to stay in Smokeville?"

I said I jedged the gents would stay till all the whisky was gone, which wouldn't be long at the rate they was demolishing it, and I says, "You're a foreigner, ain't you, miss?"

And she says, "Why do you ask?"

"Well," I says, "I ain't never hear nobody talk like that before."

"I am from New York," she says.

So I says, "Where at is that?"

She says, "It's away back East."

"Oh," I says, "it must be somewheres on t'other side of the Guadalupe."

She just hove a sigh and shaken her head like she wished she was back there, and just then in come a old codger, with whiskers, which sot down and likewise hove a sigh, clean up from his boot tops. He said, "T'ain't no use, Miss Joan. I can't raise the dough. Them thievin' scoundrels has stole me plumb out. They got the last bunch the other night. All I got on my ranch is critters too old or too sorry for Bill Hawkins to bother to steal – "

She turned pale and whispered, "For Heaven's sake, be careful, Mr. Garfield; that's one of Hawkins' men sitting right there!"

He turned around and seen me, and he turned pale, too, under his whiskers, but he riz up and shaken his fist at me, and said, "Well, you heered what I said, and I ain't takin' it back! Bill Hawkins is a thief, and all his men air thieves! Everybody in this country knows they're thieves, only they're too skeered to say so! Now, go ahead and shoot me! You and yore gang of outlaws has stole me out and ruined me till I might as well be dead. Well, what you goin' to do?"

"I'm goin' to eat this here can of cling peaches if you'll quit yellin' at me," I said, and him and Miss Joan looked astonished, and he sot down and mumbled in his beard and she looked sorry for him and for herself, and I et my peaches.

When I got through, I said, "How much I owe you, miss?"

She looked like she'd just saw a ghost and said, "*What?*"

"How much, please, ma'am," I said.

She said, "I never heard of one of Hawkins' men *paying* for anything – but it's a dollar, if yo're not kidding me."

I laid down my dollar, and just then somebody shot off their gun outside. In come Hawkins' man Curly. He was drunk and weaving and he shot his pistol into the roof and yelled, "Gimme some grub and be quick about it!"

Old man Garfield turned white under his whiskers and doubled his fists like he yearned to do somebody vi'lence, and Miss Joan looked scared and started fixing the grub.

Curly seen me and he guffawed, "Howdy, sheriff, you long-legged Texas sage-rooster! Haw! Haw! Haw! That there was the funniest one Bill ever pulled!" So he sot down and breathed whisky fumes all over the place, and when Miss Joan brung his vittles, he grabbed her arm and leered like a cat eating prickly pears, and says, "Gimme a kiss, gal!"

She says, quick and scared, "Let me go! Please let me go!"

I got up then and says, "What you mean by such actions? I never heered of such doins in my life! You release go of her and apolergize!"

"Why, you long, ganglin' Texas lunkhead!" he yelped, reaching for his gun. "Set down and shet up before I pistol-whips the livin' daylights outa you!"

So I split open his scalp with my gun barrel, and he fell onto the floor and kicked a few times and layed still. I hauled him to the back door and throwed him down the steps. He fell, head first, into a garbage can which upsot and spilled garbage all over him. He laid there like a hawg in its trough, which was the proper place for him.

"Pap told me other places was different from Texas," I says fretfully, "but I never had no idee they was this different."

"I'm getting used to it," she says with a kinda hard laugh. "The people that live here are good folks, but every time Hawkins and his gang come into town I have to put up with such things as you just saw."

"How come you ever come out here in the first place?" I asked, because it was just dawning on me that she must be one of them Eastern tenderfoots I'd heard tell of.

"I was tired of slaving in a city," she said. "I saved my money and came West. When I got to Denver I read an advertisement in a newspaper about a man offering a restaurant for sale in Smokeville, New Mexico. I came here and spent every penny I had on it. It was all right, until Hawkins and his gang started terrorizing the town."

"I was all set to buy her out," said old man Garfield mournfully. "I used to be a cook before I was blame fool enough to go into the cattle business. A resternt in Smokeville for my declinin' years is my idee of heaven – exceptin' Hawkins and his gang. But I can't raise the dough. Them thieves has stole me out. Five hundred buys her, and I can't raise it."

"Five hundred would get me out of this place and back to some civilized country," said Miss Joan, with a kind of sob.

I was embarrassed because it always makes me feel bad to see a woman cry. I feel like a yaller dawg, even when it ain't my fault. I looked down, and all to onst my gaze fell onto the badge which Hawkins had pinned onto my shirt.

"Wait here!" I said suddenly, and I taken old man Garfield by the neck and shoved him down in a chair. "You all stay here till I get back," I says. "Don't go no place. I'll be back right away."

As I went out the front door, Curly come weaving around the building with egg shells in his ears and 'tater peelings festooned on him, and he was mumbling something about cuckoo clocks and fumbling for his gun. So I hit him under the jaw for good measure and he coiled up under a horse trough and layed there.

I heard a gun banging in the Eagle Saloon, which was about a block west of the resternt, and I went in. Sure enough, Bill Hawkins was striding up and down in solitary grandeur, amusing hisself shooting bottles off the shelves behind the bar.

"Where's the rest of the fellers?" I asked.

"In the Spanish Bar at the west end of town," he said. "What's it to you?"

"Nothin'," I says.

"Well," says he, "I'm goin' to the resternt and make that gal cook me some grub. I'm hungry."

"I reckon that's what's sp'ilin' yore aim," I says.

He jumped like he was stabbed and cussed. "What you mean, sp'ilin' my aim?" he roared.

"Well," I said, "I seen you miss three of them bottle tops. Back in Texas – "

"Shet up!" he bellered. "I don't want to hear nothin' about Texas. You say 'Texas' to me just once more and I'll blow yore brains out."

"All right," I said, "but I bet you can't write yore initials in that mirror behind the bar with yore six-guns."

"Huh!" he snorted, and begun blazing away with both hands.

"What you quittin' for?" I asked presently.

"My guns is empty," he said. "I got to reload."

"No, you don't," I says, shoving my right-hand gun in his belly. "Drop them empty irons!"

He looked as surprised as if a picture had clumb off the wall and bit him.

"What you mean?" he roared. "Is this here yore idee of a joke?"

"Drop them guns and h'ist yore hands," I commanded.

He turned purple, but he done so, and then dipped and jerked a bowie out of his boot, but I shot it outa his hand before he could straighten. He was white and shaking with rage.

"I arrests you for disturbin' the peace," I said.

"What you mean, you arrests me?" he bellered. "You ain't no sheriff!"

"I am, too," I said. "You gimme this here badge yoreself. They's a law against shootin' holes in saloon mirrors. I tries you and I finds you guilty, and I fines you a fine."

"How much you fines me?" he asked.

"How much you got?" I asked.

"None of yore cussed business!" he howled.

So I made him turn around with his hands in the air, and I pulled a roll outa his hip pocket big enough to choke a cow.

"This here dough," I said, "is the money you got from sellin' the steers you stole from pore old man Garfield. I know, from the remarks yore men let drop while we was ridin' to Smokeville. Stand still whilst I count it, and don't try no monkey business."

So I kept him covered with one hand and counted the dough with the other, and it was slow work, because I hadn't never seen that much money. But finally I announced, "I fines you five hundred bucks. Here's the rest." And I give him back a dollar and fifteen cents.

"You thief!" he howled. "You bandit! You robber! I'll have yore life for this."

"Aw, shet up," I says. "I'm goin' to lock you up in jail for the night. Some of yore gang can let you out after I'm gone. If I was to let you go now, I'd probably have some trouble with you before I could git outa town."

"You would!" he asserted bloodthirstily.

"And bein' a peaceful critter," I says, jabbing my muzzle into his back, "I takes this here precaution. Git goin' before I scatters yore remnants all over the floor."

The jail was a short distance behind the stores and things. I marched him out the back door, and his cussing was something terrible every step of the way. The jail was a small, one-roomed building and a big fat egg was sleeping in the shade. I give him a kick in the pants to wake him up.

He throwed up his hands and yelled, "Don't shoot! The key's hangin' on that nail by the door!" before he got his eyes open.

When he seen me and my prisoner his jaw fell down a foot or so.

"Be you the jailer?" I asked.

"I'm Reynolds, Clanton's deperty," he said in a small voice.

"Well," I says, "onlock that door. We got a prisoner."

"Wait a minute," he said. "Ain't that Bill Hawkins?"

"Sure it is," I said impatiently. "Hustle, will you?"

"But, gee whiz!" says he. "You ain't lockin' up Bill *Hawkins!*"

"Will you onlock that door and stop gabblin'?" I hollered in exasperation. "You want me to 'rest you for obstructin' justice?"

"It's agin' my better jedgment," he said, shaking his head as he done my bidding. "It'll cost us all our lives."

"And that ain't no lie!" agreed Hawkins bitterly. But I booted him into the jug, paying no attention to his horrible threats. I told Reynolds to guard him and not let him out till next morning, not on no conditions whatever. Then I headed back up the street for the resternt. Noises of revelry was coming from the Spanish Bar, way down at the west end of the street, and I figgered Hawkins' braves was still down there.

When I come into the resternt, Miss Joan and old man Garfield was still setting there where I left 'em, looking sorry. I shoved the wad I had took from Hawkins into old man Garfield's hands, and I says, "Count it!"

He looked dumfounded, but he done so, kind of mechanical, and I says, "How much is they?"

"Five hundred bucks even," he stuttered.

"That there is right," I said, yanking the roll out of his hands, and giving it to Miss Joan. "Old man Garfield is now owner of this here hash house. And you got dough enough to go back East."

"But I don't understand," said Miss Joan, kinda dazedly. "Whose money is this?"

"It's yourn," I said.

"Hold on," says old man Garfield. "Ain't them Bill Hawkins' ivory-handled guns you got stuck in yore belt?"

"Uh-huh," I says, laying 'em on the counter. "Why?"

He turned pale and his whiskers curled up and shuddered. "Is that Hawkins' dough?" he whispered. "Have you croaked him?"

"Naw," I says. "I ain't croaked him. He's in the jail house. And it wasn't his dough. He just thought it was."

"I'm too young to die," quavered old man Garfield. "I knowed they was bound to be a catch in this. You young catamount, don't you realize that when Hawkins gits outa jail, and finds me ownin' this resternt, he'll figger out that I put you up to robbin' him? He knows I ain't got no money. You mean well, and I'm plumb grateful, but you done put my aged neck in a sling. He'll tear this resternt j'int from rafter, and shoot me plumb full of holes."

"And me!" moaned Miss Joan, turning the color of chalk. "My Lord, what will he do to me?"

I was embarrassed and hitched my gun belt.

"Dawg-gone it," I says bitterly, "Pap was right. Everything I does is wrong. I never figgered on that. I'll just have to – "

"Sheriff!" hollered somebody on the outside. "Sheriff!"

Reynolds staggered in with blood streaming from a gash in his head.

"Run, everybody!" he bawled. "Hawkins is out! He pulled the bars outa the winder with his bare hands and hit me on the head with one, and he taken my gun, and he's headin' for the Spanish Bar to git his pards and take the town apart! He's nigh loco he's so mad, and ravin' and swearin' that he'll burn the town and kill every man in it!"

At that old man Garfield let out a wail of despair, and Miss Joan sank down behind the counter with a moan.

"Le's take to the hills," babbled Reynolds. "Clanton's hidin' out there somewhere, and – "

"Aw, shet up," I grunted. "You all stay here. I'm sheriff of this here town, and it's my job to pertect the citizens. Shet up and set down."

And, so saying, I hurried out the back door and turned west. As I passed the corner of the building I noticed that Curly was still laying where I left him, being overcome with licker and swats on the dome, though he was showing some signs of life.

I run along behind the backs of the buildings, dodging from one to the other. The Spanish Bar was on the same side of the street as the resternt, so I didn't have to cross the street to get to it. Evidently, word of the impending massacre must have spread, because the town was perfectly still and tense, except the racket that was goin' on in the Spanish Bar, where evidently the bold bandits was priming on raw licker and blasphemy for wholesale murder.

I ducked into the back door and was in the saloon before they knowed it, with a gun in each hand. They all whirled away from the bar and glared at me; there was Red, Squint, and Arizona. Hawkins wasn't there; I heard him bellering out in the street for Curly.

"Don't move," I cautioned 'em.

But as if my remark was a fuse to set off a explosion, they all yelled and went for their guns.

I killed Red before he could unleather his irons, and Squint only got in one shot which chipped my ear before I perforated his anatomy in three important places. Arizona missed me with his left-hand gun, but planted a slug in my thigh with his right, before giving up the ghost, hot lead proving harder than even his skull. It was short and deadly as a concentrated cyclone – guns roaring at close range – bullets spatting into flesh – men falling through the smoke. And just as Arizona dropped, Hawkins loomed in the door with Reynolds' gun in his hand.

He was big as a house anyhow, and he looked even bigger through the curling smoke, with his eyes blazing and his mustaches bristling. He roared like a hurricane through the mesquite, and we fired simultaneous. His bullet lodged in my shoulder, and the last slug in my right-hand gun knocked his pistol out of his hand, along with a finger or so.

He then give a maddened roar and come plunging at me bare-handed. I planted the last three bullets of my other gun in various necessary parts of his carcass as he come, but they just seemed to irritate him. The last shot went into his belly so close the powder burned his shirt. Every other man I ever shot that way imejitately bent double and dropped, but this New Mexican grizzly merely give a enraged beller, jerked the gun outa my hand, fell on me and started beating my brains out with the butt.

He derned near scalped me with that .45 stock. We rolled over and over across the bloodstained floor, bumping over corpses and splintering chairs and tables, him bellering like a bull and choking me with one hand and bashing my head with the gun handle in the other one, and me feeding my bowie to him free and generous in the groin, breast, neck, and belly. I fed it to him sixteen times before he stiffened and went limp. I could hardly believe I'd won. I'd begun to think he *couldn't* be croaked. I rize up groggily and shaken some of the blood outa my eyes, and pulled back a loose flap of scalp, and stared dizzily at that shambles –

Presently the awed citizens of Smokeville crept out of their refuges and looked in pallidly to where I sot amidst the ruins, with my bloody head in my hands, weeping bitterly. Old man Garfield was there, and Miss Joan, and Clanton and Reynolds, and a lot of others.

"G-good gosh!" hollored Clanton, wild-eyed. "Are we seein' things?"

"I reckon you want yore badge," I says sadly, pulling it off my shirt.

He waved it away with a shaking hand. "You keep it!" he says. "I think Smokeville has found herself a real sheriff at last! Hey, boys?"

"You bet!" they hollered. "Keep the badge and be our regular sheriff!"

"Naw," I gulped, wiping away some tears. "This ain't my game. I just mixed in to help some folks. You keep that dough, Miss Joan, and you keep the resternt, Mr. Garfield. It was yore dough by rights. I ain't no sheriff. I appreshiates yore trust, but if you all would just be so kind as to dig some of this here lead outa me, and sew my scalp back onto my skull in nine or ten places, I'll be on my way. I got to go to Californy. Pap told me to."

"But what you cryin' about?" they asked in awe.

"Aw, I'm just homesick," I sobbed, glancing around at the blood-smeared ruins. "This here reminds me so much of Knife River, way back in Texas!"

A Man-Eating Jeopard

I'm a peaceable man, as law-abiding as I can be without straining myself, and it always irritates me for a stranger to bob up from behind a rock and holler, "Stop where you be before I blow your fool head off!"

This having happened to me I sat still on my brother Bill's horse, because that's the best thing you can do when a feller is p'inting a cocked .45 at your wishbone. This feller was a mean-looking hombre in a sweaty hickory shirt with brass rivets in his leather hat band, and he needed a shave. He said, "Who are you? Where you from? Where you goin'? What you aimin' to do when you get there?"

I says, "I'm Buckner J. Grimes of Knife River, Texas, and I'm headin' for Californy."

"Well, what you turnin' south for?" he asked.

"Ain't this here the trail to Piute?" I inquired.

"Naw, 'tain't," he answered. "Piute's due west of here."

All at once he stopped and seemed to ponder, though his gun muzzle didn't waver none. I was watching it like a hawk.

Pretty soon he give a kinda forced leer which I reckon he aimed for a smile, and said, "I'm sorry, stranger. I took you for somebody else. Just an honest mistake. This here trail leadin' off to the west goes to Piute. T'other'n goes south to my claim. I took you for one of them blame claim jumpers." He lowered his gun but didn't put it back in the holster, I noticed.

"I didn't know they was any claims in Arizona," I says.

"Oh, yes," says he, "the desert is plumb full of 'em. For instance," says he, "I got a chunk of quartz in my pocket right now which is just bustin' with pure ore. Light," says he, fumbling in his pocket, "and I'll show you."

Well, I was anxious to see some ore, because Pap had told me that I was just likely to hit it rich in Californy; he said an idiot was a natural fool for luck, and I wanted to know what ore looked like when I seen some. So I clumb down off of brother Bill's horse, and the stranger hauled something out of his pocket, but as he poked it out toward me, it slipped off his palm and fell to the ground.

Naturally I leaned over to pick it up, and when I done so, something went *bam!* and I seen a million stars. At first I thought a cliff had fell on me, but almost simultaneous I realized the stranger had lammed me over the head with his pistol barrel.

The lick staggered me, but I didn't have to fall like I done. I done that instinctive hit on my side and tumbled over on my back and laid still, with my eyes so near shut he couldn't tell that I was watching him through the slits. The instant he'd hit me he lifted his gun quick to shoot me if I didn't drop, but my flop fooled him.

He looked down at me scornful, too proud of his smartness to notice that my limp hand was laying folded over a rock about the size of a muskmelon, and he says aloud to hisself, he says, "Another idiot from Texas! Huh! Think I'm goin' to let you go on to Piute and tell 'em about bein' turned back from the south trail, and mebbe give them devils an idee of what's cookin' up? Not much, I ain't. I ain't goin' to waste no lead on you, neither. I reckon I'll just naturally cut your throat with my bowie."

So saying, he shoved his gun back in its holster and drawed his knife out of his boot, and stooped over and started fumbling with my neck cloth, so I belted him free and hearty over the conk with my rock. I then pushed his limp carcass off me and rose.

"If you'd been raised in Texas like I was," I says to his senseless hulk more in sorrer than in anger, "you'd know just because a man falls it don't necessarily mean he's got his'n."

He didn't say nothing because he was out cold; the blood was oozing from his split scalp, and I knowed it would be hours before he come to hisself, and maybe days before he'd remember his own name.

I mounted brother Bill's horse, which I'd rode all the way from Texas because it was better'n mine, and I paused and ruminated. Right there a narrer trail split off from the main road and turned south through a deep cleft in the cliffs, and the stranger had been lurking there at the turn.

Well, thinks I, something shady is going on down that there trail, else why should he hold me up when he thought I was going down it? I warn't taking the south trail. I'd just stopped to rest my brother Bill's horse in the shadder of the cliffs, and this ambushed gent just thought I was going to turn off. That there indicates a guilty conscience. Then, when he was convinced I wasn't going south, he was going to cut my throat just so's I couldn't tell the folks at Piute about him stopping me. And he was lying about a claim. He didn't have no hunk of quartz; that thing he'd taken out of his pocket was a brass button.

Well, I very naturally turned off down the south trail to see why he didn't want me to. I went very cautious, with my gun in my right hand, because I didn't aim to get catched off guard again. The thought occurred to me that maybe he was being hunted by a sheriff's posse. Well, that wasn't none of my business, but Pap always said my curiosity would be the ruin of me.

I rode on for about a mile, till I come to a place where the trail went up over a saddleback with dense thickets on each side. I left the trail and pushed through the thickets to see what was on the other side of the ridge; around Knife River they was generally somebody waiting to shoot somebody else.

I looked down into a big holler, and in the middle they was a big cluster of boulders, bigger'n a house. I seen some horses sticking out from behind them boulders, and a horse tied under a tree a little piece away. He was a very bright-colored pinto with a silver-mounted bridle and saddle. I seen the sun flash on the trappings on 'em.

I knowed the men must be on the other side of them rocks, and I counted nineteen horses. Well, nineteen men was more'n I wanted to tackle, in case they proved hostile to strangers, which I had plenty of reason to believe they probably would. So I decided to backtrack.

Anyway, them men was probably just changing brands on somebody else's cows, or talking over the details of a stagecoach holdup, or some other private enterprise like that which wasn't nobody's business but their'n. So I turned around and went back up the trail to the forks again.

When I passed the stranger I had hit with the rock he was still out, and I kinda wondered if he'd *ever* come to. But that wasn't none of my business neither, so I just dragged him under bushes where he'd be in the shade in case he did, and rode on down the west trail. I figgered it couldn't be more'n a few miles to Piute, and I was getting thirsty.

And sure enough, after a few miles I come upon the aforesaid town baking in the sun on a flat with hills on all sides – just a cluster of dobe huts with Mexican women and kids littered all over the place – and dogs, and a store and a little restaurant and a big saloon. It wasn't much past noon and hotter'n hell.

I tied brother Bill's horse to the hitching rack alongside the other horses already tied there, in the shade of the saloon, and I went into the saloon myself. They was a good-sized bar and men drinking at it, others playing poker at tables.

Well, I judged it wasn't very usual that a stranger come to Piute, because when I come in everybody laid down their whisky glass or their hand of cards and stared at me without no expression on their faces, and I got fidgety and drunk five or six fingers of red licker to cover my embarrassment.

They was a kind of restless shuffling of boots on the floor, and spitting into the sawdust, and men tugging at their mustaches, and I wondered am I going to have to shoot my way out of this joint; what kind of a country is this anyway.

Just then a man lumbered up to the bar and the men drinking at the bar kinda surged around me and him, and some of them playing poker rose up from their tables and drifted over behind me, or would have, if I hadn't quick put my back against the bar. This feller was nigh as tall as me, and a lot heavier. He had a big mustache like a walrus.

"Who be you?" he inquired suspiciously.

"I'm Buckner J. Grimes," I said patiently. "I'm from Texas, and I'm just passin' through. I'm headin' for Californy."

"What's the 'J' for?" he asked.

"Jeopardy," I said.

"What's that mean?" he next demanded.

"I dunno," I confessed. "It come out of a book. I reckon it means somethin' pertainin' to a jeopard."

"Well, what's a jeopard?" he asked.

"It's a spotted critter like a panther," said one of the men. "I seen one in a circus once in Santa Fe."

The big feller studied over this for a while, and then he said have a drink, so we all drunk.

"Do you know Swag McBride?" he asked at last.

"I never heard tell of him," I said. Everybody was watching me when he asked me, and some of them had their hands on their guns. But when I said I didn't know him they kinda relaxed and went back to playing poker and drinking licker. I reckon they believed me; Pap always said I had a honest face; he said anybody could tell I didn't have sense enough to think up a lie.

"Set down," said the big man, easing his bulk ponderously into a chair and sinking his mustaches into a tub of beer. "I'm Navajo Beldon. I'm boss of Piute and all the surroundin' country, and don't let nobody tell you no different. Either a man is for me or he's against me, and if he's against me he's for Swag McBride and don't belong in this town at all."

"Who's Swag McBride?" I asked.

"A cross between a rattlesnake and a skunk," said Beldon, gulping his beer. "But don't say 'skunk' around him les'n you want to get killed. When the vigilantes run him outa Nevada they sent him down the trail with a dead polecat tied around his neck as a token of affection and respect. Skunks has been a sore spot with him ever since. If anybody even mentions one in his hearin' he takes it as a personal insult and acts accordingly. He's lightnin' with a gun, and when souls was handed out, Nature plumb forgot to give him one. He run this town till I decided to take it over."

He wiped his mustaches with the back of his hand, and said, "We had a showdown last week, and decreases in the population was sudden and generous. But we run them rats into the hills where they've been skulkin' ever since, if they ain't left the country entirely."

I thought about them fellers I seen up in the hills, but I didn't say nothing. I was raised in a country where keeping your mouth shut is an art practiced by everybody which wants to live to a ripe old age.

"This here country has to have a boss of some kind," says "Navajo," pouring me a drink. "Ain't no law here, and somebody's got to kinda run things. I ain't no saint, but I'm a lot better man than Swag McBride. If you don't believe it, go ask the citizens of Piute. Man's life is safe here with me runnin' things, long's he keeps his nose outa my business, and a woman can walk down the street without bein' insulted by some tough. Honest to gosh, if I was to tell you some of the things McBride and his devils has pulled – "

"Things looks peaceful enough now," I admitted.

"They are, while I'm in the saddle," says Beldon. "Say, how would you like to work for me?"

"Doin' what?" I ask.

"Well," he says, "I got considerable cattle, besides my interests in Piute. These men you see here ain't all the boys I got workin' for me, of course. They's a bunch now down near Eagle River, drivin' a herd up from the border, which ain't so terrible far from you, you know."

"You buy cattle in Mexico?" I ask.

"Well," he says, "I gets quite a lot of steers from across the line. I has to have men watchin' all the time to keep them greasers from comin' over and stealin' everything I got. What's that?"

Outside come a thunder of hoofs and a voice yelled, "Beldon! Beldon!"

"Who's that?" demanded Beldon, scrambling up and grabbing his gun.

"It's Richards!" called one of the men, looking out of the winder with a rifle. "He's foggin' it up the south trail like the devil was ridin' behind him."

Beldon started lumbering toward the door, but about that time the horse slid to a gravel-scattering halt at the edge of the porch, and a man come storming in, all plastered with sweat and dust.

"What's eatin' you, Richards?" demanded Navajo.

"The greasers!" yelped Richards. "Early this mornin' we run a herd of Diego Gonzales' cattle across the line, and you know what happened? We hadn't hardly more'n got back across the border when his blame vaqueros overtook us and shot up every man except me, and run them steers back home again!"

"*What?*" bellered Navajo, with his mustaches quivering in righteous wrath. "Why, them thievin', yeller polecats! Ain't they got *no* respect for law and order? What air we a-comin' to? Ain't they no honest men left besides me? Does they think they can treat *me* like that? Does they think we're in the the cow business for our health? Does they think they can tromple on us after we've went to the trouble and expense of stealin' them steers ourselves?

"Donnelly, take your men and light out! I'll show them greasers they can't steal my critters and get away with it. You fetch them cows back if you have to foller 'em right into Diego's patio – blast his thievin' soul!"

The feller he called Donnelly got up and told his men to come on, and they took a drink at the bar, and drawed up their gun belts and went stomping out toward the hitching rack. Richards went along to guide 'em.

"Don't you wanta go?" says Navajo to me, still snorting with his indignation. "The boys may need help, and I can tell from the way you wear your guns that you know how to handle 'em. I'll pay you well."

Well, if they is anything I despises it's a darned thief, so I told Beldon I'd go along and help recover his property. I left him bellering his grievances to the bald-headed old bartender and his Mexican boy helper, which was all that was left in the saloon.

Richards had changed his saddle onto a fresh horse, and as we rode off I looked at the horse which he'd rode in. It was a pinto and it seemed to me like I'd saw it somewheres but I couldn't remember. It was so sweaty and dusty it was mighty near disguised.

We headed south along the dusty trail, nine or ten of us, Richards leading, and was soon out of sight of Piute. Them fellers was riding like Mexico was right over the next rise, but the miles went past, and I decided they was just reckless, damn fools. I kept trying to remember where I'd seen that pinto of Richards', and all of a sudden I remembered.

The trail dipped ahead of us down into a tangle of cliffs and canyons, and Richards had drawed ahead of the rest of us. He turned to motion us to hurry, and as he turned, the sun flashed from the silver trappings on his saddle and bridle, and, like a shot, I remembered – I remembered where I'd seen them trappings, and where I'd seen that pinto. It was the horse I'd saw tied near them big rocks away to the east of Piute.

I involuntarily sat brother Bill's horse back on his haunches. The rest of the gang swept on without noticing, but I sat there and thunk. If Richards was with that gang *east*, how could he be with the bunch driving cattle acrost the border away to the *south* of Piute? He come up the south trail into Piute, but what was to prevent him from cutting through the hills and hitting that trail just below the town? Richards had lied to Beldon; and Beldon had said that if a man wasn't for him, he was for McBride.

I reined up onto a knob, and stared off eastward, and pretty soon I seen what I expected to see – a fog of rolling dust, sweeping from southeast to northwest – toward Piute. I knowed what was raising that dust: men on horses, riding hard.

I looked south for Donnelly and his men. They was just passing out of sight in a big notch with sheer walls on each side. I yelled but they didn't hear me. Richards had pulled ahead of them by a hundred yards, and was already through the notch and out of sight. They all thundered into the notch and passed out of sight. And then it sounded like all the guns in southern Arizona let go at once. I wheeled and rode for Piute as hard as brother Bill's horse could leg it.

The dust on the horizon disappeared behind a big boulder that jutted right up into the sky. Then, after a while, ahead of me, I heard a sudden crackle of gunfire, and what sounded like a woman screaming, and then everything was still again.

Ahead of me the trail made the bend that would bring me in sight of Piute. I left the trail and took to the thickets. Brother Bill's horse was snorting and trembling, nigh done in. The town was awful quiet – not a soul in sight, and all the doors closed. I circled the flat, tied Bill's horse in a thicket back of the saloon, and stole toward the back door, with my guns in my hands.

They wasn't no horses tied at the hitching rack. Everything was awful quiet except for the flies buzzing around the blood puddles on the floor. The old bartender was laying across the bar with a gun still in his hand. He'd stopped plenty lead. His Mexican boy was slumped down near the door with his head split open – looked like he'd been hit with an ax. A stranger I'd never saw was stretched out in the dust before the porch, with a bullet hole in his skull. He was a tall, dark, hard-looking cuss. A gun with one empty chamber was laying nigh his right hand.

I believed they'd captured Navajo Beldon alive. His carcass wasn't nowhere to be seen, and then the tables and chairs was all busted, just like I figgered they'd be after a gang of men had hog tied Beldon. That would be a job that'd wreck any saloon. They was empty cartridges and a broke knife on the floor, and buttons tore offa fellers' shirts, and a smashed hat, and a notebook, like things gets scattered during a free for all.

I picked up the notebook and on the top of the first page was wrote,

"Swag McBride owes me $100 for that there job over to Braxton's ranch."
I stuck it in my pocket but I didn't need no evidence to know who'd raided
Piute.

I looked out cautious into the town. Nobody in sight and all doors and
winders closed. Then come a sudden rumble of horses' hoofs and I jumped
back out of the doorway and looked through a winder. Seven horsemen
swept into the village out of a trail that wound up through the thickets
back of the town; but they didn't stop.

They cantered on down the south trail, with rifles in their hands. They
didn't look toward the saloon, and nobody stuck their head out of a house
to tell 'em about me, though somebody must of seen me sneak into town.
Evidently the citizens was playing strict neutral, which is wise when two
gangs is slaughtering each other – if you can do it.

As soon as the riders was out of town I run back through the saloon and
hustled up the hillside, paralleling the trail they'd come down. Who says
all this wasn't none of my business? Beldon had hired me and I'd been a
pretty excuse for a man if I'd left him in the lurch.

I hadn't gone far when I heard men talking – leastways, I heard one
man talking. It was Beldon and he was bellering like a bull.

A minute later I come onto a log cabin, plumb surrounded with trees.
Five horses was tied outside. The bellering was coming from inside the
cabin, and I could hear somebody else talking in a kinda sneery, gloating
voice. I snuck up to the rear winder and peered in, well aware that I was
risking my life. But the winder was boarded up and I peeked through a
crack.

Plenty of light come in through the cracks, though, and I seen Beldon,
with blood oozing from a cut in his scalp, setting in a busted chair by a
dusty old table, and looking like a trapped grizzly. Four other men was
standing acrost the table from him, betwixt him and the door, with their
guns leveled at him. One of them was awful tall, and rangy and quick in
his motions, like a catamount. He combed his long drooping mustache
with one gun muzzle whilst he poked the other'n into Beldon's ear and
screwed it around till Navajo cussed something terrible.

"Huh!" said this gent. "Boss of Piute! Hah! A fine boss you be. First and
biggest mistake you made was trustin' Richards. He was plumb delighted

to sell you out. You thought he was with your men on Eagle River, didn't you? Well, he was with me in the hills east of here all mornin', whilst we laid our plans to get you.

"He sneaked away from your bunch on Eagle River last night. He brung you that lie about them cattle bein' stole just so I could get your men out of the way. I knowed you'd send every man you had. You won't ever see 'em no more. Richards will lead 'em into a trap in Devil's Gorge where my men done laid an ambush for 'em. Probably they're sizzlin' in hell by this time. Them seven fellers I just sent down the trail will join the rest of my men at Devil's Gorge, and they'll clean out your outfit on Eagle River. I'm makin' a clean sweep, Beldon."

"I'll get you yet, McBride," promised Beldon thickly, gnashing his teeth under his heavy mustache.

McBride combed his mustache very superior. I was wondering why they'd taken Beldon alive. He wasn't even tied up. I seen his fingers clinch and quiver on the table. I knowed he was liable to make a break for it any minute and get shot down, and I was in a stew. I could start shooting through the winder, of course, and snag most of 'em, but one of 'em was bound to get Beldon sure.

I knowed very well that at the first alarm they'd perforate him. I wisht I had a shotgun, because then I mighta got 'em all with one blast – probably including Beldon. But all I had was a couple of .45s and a clear conscience. If I could only let Beldon know that I was on hand, maybe he might get foxy and do something smart to help hisself, instead of busting loose and getting killed like I knowed he was going to do any minute. The veins in his neck swelled and his face got purple and his whiskers bristled.

All at once McBride said, "I'll let you go, alive, if you'll tell me where you got your money hid. I know you got several thousand bucks."

So that was why they taken him alive. I mighta knowed it. But the mention of money reminded me of something and that put a idee into my head. I pulled out the notebook I found and tore out the first page and begun work with a pencil stub I had in my pocket. I didn't write nothing. What I wanted to do was to slip Beldon a message he could understand, but that wouldn't mean nothing to McBride, in case he seen it.

I remembered that talk about a Jeopard, when I first met Beldon, so

I drawed a picture of a animal like a panther. But I couldn't remember whether that feller from Santa Fe said a Jeopard had spots or stripes. Seemed like he said stripes, so I put a big un' down the critter's back. Beldon would know that pitcher meant that Buckner Jeopardy Grimes was lurking near, ready to help him the first chance I got, and, knowing that, he wouldn't do nothing reckless.

Whilst I was doing this Beldon was thinking over what McBride had just said to him. He didn't crave a lead bath no more'n the average man, and he was one of these here trusting critters which believes everybody keeps their word. It's hard to credit, I know, but it looked like he actually believed McBride would keep his'n, and let him go if he told where he hid his dough.

McBride didn't fool me none. I knowed very well the instant he told 'em, Beldon would get riddled. I knowed McBride itched to kill him. I seen it in the twist of his thin lips, and the nervous twitch of his hand as he pulled at his mustache. I read the killer's hunger in his yeller eyes which blazed like a cat's. But Navajo didn't seem to recognize them signs. He was awful slow thinking in some ways.

McBride was pulling his mustache and just getting ready to say something, when I took a pebble and throwed it over the shack so it hit the stoop and made a racket. Instantly they all wheeled and covered the door, and I throwed my wadded-up paper through the crack in the winder boards, so it landed on the table right in front of Beldon. *But he never seen it.*

He'd rose halfway up like he was going to make his break, but quick as a flash McBride wheeled and covered him again, with his lip drawed back so his teeth showed like a wolf's fang, and his eyes was slits of fire. If it hadn't been for that dough he wanted, he'd have shot Beldon down right then. I seen his finger quiver on his trigger, and I had him lined over my sights.

But he didn't shoot. He snapped, "You fools, keep him covered! I'll see to this!"

The other three turned their guns on Beldon and he sunk back in his chair with a gusty sigh. They was a hard layout – one short, one tall, one with a scarred face. McBride stepped quick to the door and jerked it open and poked his gun out.

"Nothin' out here," he snorted. "Must have been a woodpecker."

I was sweating and shaking like a leaf in my nervousness, waiting for Beldon to see that wad of paper laying right in front of him, but he never noticed it. He hadn't seen it fall, and a wad of paper didn't mean nothing to him. He couldn't think of but one thing at a time. He had nerve and men liked him; that's the only reason he ever got to be a chief.

McBride turned around and stalked back across the cabin.

"Well," he said, "are you goin' to tell me where the dough is?"

"I reckon I gotta," mumbled Beldon heavily, and I cussed bitterly under my breath. Beldon was a goner. All I could do was start shooting and get as many of 'em as I could. But they was sure to drill him. Then McBride seen that wadded-up paper. He wasn't like Beldon; he was observant and keen-witted. He remembered that paper hadn't been there a few minutes before. He grabbed it.

"What's this?" he demanded, and my heart sunk clean to my boot tops. He wouldn't know what it meant, but it was gone out of Beldon's reach for good.

McBride started smoothing it out.

"Why," says he, "it's got my name on it, in your handwritin', Joe."

"Lemme see," said the tall feller, getting up and reached toward it. But McBride had straightened the paper all the way out, and all at once his face went livid. For a second you could of heard a pin drop. McBride stood like a froze statue, only his eyes alive and them points of hell fire, whilst the other hombres gaped at him.

Then he give a shriek like a catamount, and throwed that piece of paper into Joe's face, and his gun jumped and spurted red. Joe flopped to the floor, kicking and twitching. The other two fellers was white and wild-looking, but the short one says, kind of choking, "By Heaven, McBride, you can't do that to my pal!"

His gun jerked upward, but McBride's spoke first. Shorty's gun exploded into the floor and he slumped down on top of Joe. It was at that instant I kicked a board off the winder and shot "Scarface" through the ear. McBride howled in amazement and our guns crashed simultaneous. Or rather, I reckon mine was the split fraction of a second the first, because his lead fanned my ear and mine knocked him down dead on the floor.

I then climbed through the winder into the cabin where the blue smoke was drifting in clouds and the dead men was laying still on the floor. If the fight had been a tornado hitting the shack it couldn't have been no briefer nor done no more damage. Beldon had had presence of mind enough to fall down behind the table when the fireworks started, and he now rose and glared at me like he thought I was a ghost.

"What the hell!" he inquired lucidly.

"We ain't got no time to waste," I told him. "We got to take to the woods. Them seven men McBride sent south ain't out of hearin'. They'll hear the shots and be back. They'll know it wouldn't take all them shots to cook your goose, and they'll come back and investigate."

He lurched up, and I seen he was lame in one leg.

"I got it sprained in the fight," he grunted. "They was in Piute and stormin' my saloon before I knowed what was happenin'. Help me back to the saloon. My dough's hid under the bar. If all my men's been wiped out, we got to travel, and I got to get my dough. They's horses in a corral not far from the saloon."

"All right," I said, picking up the wad of paper I'd throwed through the winder, but not stopping to discuss it. "Let's go," I said, and we went.

If anybody thinks it's a cinch to help a man as big as Navajo Beldon down a mountain trail with a sprained ankle, he's loco as hell. He had to kind of hop on one leg and I had to act as his other leg, and before we was halfway down I felt like throwing him the rest of the way down and washing my hands of the whole business. Of course, I didn't, though.

Piute was just as quiet and empty as before – heads bobbing a little way out of doors to gawp at us, then jerking back quick, and everything still and breathless under the hot sun.

Beldon cussed at the sight of the dead men in the bar, and he sounded sick.

"I feel like a skunk," he said, "runnin' out like this and leavin' Piute to the mercies of them devils which follered McBride. But what else can I do? I – "

"Look out!" I yelped, jumping back out of the doorway and blazing away with my six-gun, as there come a rattle of hoofs up the south trail and them seven devils of McBride's come storming back into town. They'd already seen me, before I fired, and they howled like wolves and come at a dead run.

At the crack of my six-shooter one of 'em went out of his saddle and laid still, and they swung aside and raced behind a old dobe house right across from the saloon.

Beldon was cussing and hitching hisself to one of the winders with a rifle he'd brung from the cabin, and I took the other winder. The old dobe they'd took cover behind didn't have no roof and the wall was falling down, but it made a prime fort, and in about a second lead was smacking into the saloon walls, and ripping through the winders and busting bottles behind the bar, and when Beldon seen his licker wasted that way he hollered like a bull with its tail caught in the corral gate.

They'd punched loop holes in the dobe. All we could see was rifle muzzles and the tops of their hats now and then. We was shooting back, of course, but from the vigor of their profanity I knowed we wasn't doing nothing but knocking dust into their faces.

"They've got us," said Beldon despairingly. "They'll hold us here till the rest of them devils comes up. Then they'll rush us from three or four sides at once and finish us."

"We could sneak out the back way," I said, "but we'd have to go on foot, and with your ankle we couldn't get nowheres."

"You go," he said, sighting along his rifle barrel and throwing another slug into the dobe. "I'm done. I couldn't get away on this lame leg. I'll hold 'em whilst you sneak off."

This being too ridiculous to answer, I maintained a dignerfied silence and said nothing outside of requesting him not to be a fool.

A minute later he give a groan like a buffler bull with the bellyache.

"We're sunk now!" says he. "Here come the rest of them!"

And sure enough I heard the drum of more hoofs up the south trail, and the firing acrost the way lulled, as the fellers listened. Then they give a yell of extreme pleasure, and started firing again with wild hilarity.

"I ain't lived the kind of life I ought to have," mourned Beldon. "My days has been full of vanity and sin. The fruits of the flesh is sweet to the tongue, Buckner, but they play hell with the belly. I wish I'd given more attention to spiritual things, and less to gypin' my feller-man – Are you listenin'?"

"Shut up!" I said fretfully. "They is a feller keeps stickin' his head up behind that dobe, and the next time he does it I aim to ventilate his cranium, if you don't spoil my aim with your gab."

"You ought to be placin' your mind on higher things at a time like this," he reproved. "We're hoverin' on the brink of Eternity, and it's a time when you should be repentin' your sinful ways, like me, and shakin' the dust of the flesh off your feet – Hell fire and damnation!" he roared suddenly, heaving up from behind the winder sill. "That ain't McBride's men! That's Donnelly!"

The fellers behind the dobe found that out just then, but it didn't do 'em no good. Donnelly and six of the men which had rode out with him come swinging in behind 'em, and they was ten more men with him I hadn't never saw before. The six men behind the dobe run for their horses, but they didn't have a chance. They'd been so sure it was their pals they didn't pay much attention, and Donnelly and his boys was right behind 'em before they realized their mistake.

Of course, we couldn't see what was happening behind the dobe. We just saw Donnelly and his hombres sweep around it, and then heard the guns roaring and men yelling. But by the time I'd run acrost the street and rounded the corner of the dobe, the McBride gang was a thing of the past, and three of Donnelly's men was down with more or less lead in 'em.

"Carry 'em over to the saloon, boys," said Donnelly, who had a broke arm in a blood-soaked sleeve hisself. We done so, whilst Navajo, who had got as far as the porch on his game leg, bellered and waved his smoking rifle like a scepter.

"Lay 'em on the floor and pour licker down 'em," said Beldon. "What the hell happened?"

"Richards led us into a trap," grunted Donnelly, taking a deep swig hisself. "They got Bill and Tom and Dick, but I plugged Richards as he took to the brush. They'd have snagged us all though, if it hadn't been for these boys. They was with the outfit on Eagle River, and when Richards rode off last night they got suspicious and trailed him. They was just south of Devil's Gorge where the ambush was laid, when they heard the shootin', and they come up in time to give us a hand."

"And if it hadn't been for Grimes, here," grunted Beldon, "McBride would have been boss of Piute right now. What you lookin' at?"

"This here paper," I said. "I'm tryin' to figger out why a pitcher of a jeopard would start McBride to killin' his own men."

"Lemme see," says he, and he took it and looked at it, and said, "Why, hell, no wonder! It's got McBride's name at the top, over that pitcher. He thought that feller Joe had drawed it to insult him."

"But the pitcher of a jeopard – " I protested.

"You might have meant it for a jeopard," he said, "but it looks a darn sight more like a striped skunk to me, and I reckon that's what McBride took it for. I told you he went crazy when the subject of skunks was brung up. Never mind that; a hombre as quick with a gun as you are don't need no other accomplishments; how about a steady job with me?"

"What for?" I said. "With the McBride gang cleaned out I don't see what they is for an able-bodied man in these parts. Besides, I see art ain't appreshiated here. I'm goin' on to Californy, like Pap told me to."

SOURCE ACKNOWLEDGMENTS

"Mountain Man" appeared in *Action Stories*, March April 1934.

"Meet Cap'n Kidd" is from *A Gent from Bear Creek* (Grant 1965).

"Guns of the Mountains" appeared in *Action Stories*, May June 1934.

"The Peaceful Pilgrim" is from *Mayhem on Bear Creek* (Grant, 1979).

"War on Bear Creek" appeared in *Action Stories*, April 1935.

"The Haunted Mountain" appeared in *Action Stories*, February 1935.

"The Feud Buster" appeared in *Action Stories*, June 1935.

"The Riot at Cougar Paw" appeared in *Action Stories*, October 1935.

"Pistol Politics" appeared in *Action Stories*, April 1936.

" 'No Cowherders Wanted'" is from *Mayhem on Bear Creek* (Grant, 1979).

"The Conquerin' Hero of the Humbolts" appeared in *Action Stories*,
    October 1936.

"A Gent from the Pecos" appeared in *Argosy*, October 3, 1936.

"Gents on the Lynch" appeared in *Argosy*, October 17, 1936.

"The Riot at Bucksnort" appeared in *Argosy*, October 31, 1936.

"Knife River Prodigal" appeared in *Cowboy Stories*, July 1937.

"A Man-Eating Jeopard" appeared in *Cowboy Stories*, June 1936.

IN THE WORKS OF ROBERT E. HOWARD SERIES